Tourists to the Rebellion

Also by Nancy Davies

The People Decide: Oaxaca's Popular Assembly

Messages in a Small Town

Tourists to the Rebellion

A NOVEL

Nancy Davies

Published by Nouveau Proletariat Press
nouveauproletariat.com

ISBN-13: 978-0692824542

Prologue

January 1, 1994

Frank Ruthven, known to his buddies back home in Ohio as Frank the Fugitive, opened his eyes at the crackling of gunfire, and immediately closed them again. For a moment he lay quietly, his head pillowed on his backpack and his feet in ratty gray socks pressed against the back of the van's passenger seat. He knew he wasn't in training camp, nor in base in Saudi Arabia. He knew it wasn't 1992 all over again.

He wiped his face with his palm. A light film of oil and sweat came away on his hand, and he wiped it on the thigh of his jeans.

"Well, my fuckin' misfortune," he mumbled. Here he was fleeing the memory of war, fleeing in his battered Plymouth southward, a drunk from the U.S of A., racing south through Mexico, down highway I-99, east toward Guatemala. He planned to drive to Central America, South America, to the South Pole if the van held up and the penguins didn't get him.

Nothing ever worked out like you wanted.

So who the fuck was shooting? On January 1, 1994, in a piss-poor area of snakes and Indians, just like in the movies, he damn well knew small arms fire when he heard it.

Cautiously he twisted himself halfway to sitting, and hoping nobody saw his pale face inside the van, peered through the window dust at the main street of Avenida Central in the town of Ocosingo, in Chiapas, Mexico. The concrete painted houses uniformly sat blind behind walls. Far down to his right he could make out the arches of the municipal mercado. The street, semi-paved and rutted, looked as abandoned as any ghost town, in both directions. Happy fuckin' New Year.

Last night he had driven in by darkness, the one lane road rough beneath the tires, making the empty beer bottles clink against each other behind him. His headlights picked out nothing but a faded white line between his van and a ditch. Vague shadows of fields and fencing stretched beside the road on both sides. As he wheeled into the town he rightly guessed nothing was open, and unless he wanted to wake the keeper of the one hotel his guide book mentioned, he'd best sleep in the van, as he often did. At least he could defend his gear against thieves.

The firing grew intermittent, slower, stopped, and then abruptly grew rapid again. As he peered, a group of wiry figures in a miscellaneous mixture of army fatigues, cotton shirts, barefaced or with red bandannas tied around their faces, raced across the cement patio in front of the municipal building, dodging through its archways and columns. They ran with old Russian M-1s. Some other rifles were returning fire, and these must be inside, or coming from the side where more men were streaking across the street. One figure masked with a black wool hood pulled over his head suddenly leaped into the air with his arms outstretched as if to embrace the scene, and while Frank processed the crack of gunfire the figure fell heavily. Like a sack of concrete, he hit the dirt road and lay motionless on his back, the black mask turned up to the dawn. The topknot on his homemade balaclava looked like a toy, like a doll. The man lay inert.

Frank's mouth tasted like bad tequila, bile, unbrushed taco teeth. He stared at the fallen form, and then realized that others were still running, shooting, falling. Falling like dead.

He pushed open the van door and swung out his bootless feet, retracted them and jammed on his boots, furiously working the gritty laces. Out. Out of the van in a crouch he ran toward the guy who had fallen first, and dragged the body back to the lee of the van. Back out around to get the next one.

Blowing out his breath to calm down, Frank peeled off the woolen knitted mask from the face of the first guy. A kid. A thin tentative moustache lined the upper lip. Maybe like himself going into the Gulf, this was a kid who'd rather do other things. Too late now. Blood trickled from the kid's khaki shirt, and from his mouth. Or maybe not. His captured grimace was undecipherable, maybe eagerness, maybe terror. Anyways, dead.

Frank stared around from the fender, across to the action. Apparently the masked guys were taking the municipal building, or maybe they weren't. Blue uniformed police were shooting now from the windows, and one squat military vehicle rolled into view from the far side, churning the dust past the market building. Frank glanced at the second body, and this one was breathing. The bloodied shirt rose and fell. This one wore a red bandanna over his mouth and nose, and Frank pulled it down to make breathing easier. Thin guy, also young, black indio hair and brown skin. Both of the attackers had the Mayan look of the region, with cheek bones like golf balls tucked beneath their almost fleshless skin. The guy whispered something to Frank in a language Frank didn't even recognize, let alone understand in the half-assed way he understood Spanish. What the fuck was he supposed to do now?

The water in the van. He inched his way around toward the double back hatch. Locked of course, Frank never slept, even if he was stoned out of his mind, without locking. The driver's door, then. Carefully, bent at the waist, he trotted forward along the exposed side, wrenched open the door and dove head first into the van as an automatic weapon crackled.

They weren't aiming at him. He dragged out a liter bottle of water and ran back to the wounded guy. The man made no noise. His dark eyes hid behind their eyelids. Frank lifted the guy's head and trickled water over his mouth. The tongue came out and licked it. The guy nodded without opening his eyes. Frank held him and gave him water.

So Frank the Fugitive Ruthven, as patriotic as any guy you know, as loyal to his government as any other guy who bitches and moans about Washington, quit running and paused to help the Zapatista rebels when they declared war on their government, The United States of Mexico. Goddamn, but the Mexican government was an ally of the USA if not primo Little Brother. Unknowingly, Frank was abetting the wrong side of the US government-neoliberal collaboration.

At the end of the day the killed and wounded were taken from the lee of Frank's van by other hooded figures who nodded gravely in his direction and said nothing. Frank examined the visible aspects— jeans, or shabby pants, the shabbiest wearing huaraches and the guys with jeans wearing boots. All small, with the slender hips and short legs Frank identified as markers of the indigenous people. One guy his own height, maybe five nine or so. Silent. But their eyes signaled something. Frank accepted it as thanks. No problem, he responded, in his rude Spanish, no preocuparte.

With the wounded gone to the care of their own people, Frank looked around for a bar. New Year's Day. Everything was shut tight, the street deserted. He had both the easy gait of a white American and the cautious side to side head-swing of a trained soldier. No weapon, empty hands. The one paved street gleamed with straggly ornaments and dangling lights in anticipation of January's Día de Los Reyes, the market stalls empty but deployed as if waiting for the next surge of fiesta. The unpaved perpendicular streets leading away stood empty and shuttered.

He could see that the masked attackers, some wearing soft peaked field caps, some barefaced, held the upper windows of the few buildings with two stories, and a roof here and there where they had a clear shot to the municipal building. Probably the municipal police, and maybe Chiapas state police, were waiting for the arrival of federales to rescue them or tell them what to do. Frank needed a drink, bad. He walked the length of Calle Central, scarcely three blocks long, passed the tile-roofed hotel and retraced his steps. Finally he identified a cantina, ducked under the tiled eaves and recklessly banged on the turquoise painted wood double door. After a few silent minutes he banged again, and the door cracked in the middle. An older man with a tired gut peered out, and maybe took stock of Frank's baseball cap, his blunt features and stocky body, the black tee-shirt sticky and stained.

He gestured with his head, opening wider the door, and Frank stepped in. The cantina was a cement room with a bar counter. No stools, the chairs were chrome with plastic in various degrees of gutted green disintegration, the semi-crippled tables were pine, disfigured with scars. Like the man's brown-skinned face. The bar keeper stepped behind the bar. Behind him an open square in the cement wall revealed the kitchen area and a woman with dull hair, pulled in a braid, who quietly stayed in the recessed area.

Frank sat alone at an empty table. They were all empty, except for one old man with a full gray moustache who leaned silently on a table in a far corner.

In the hot climate near the Guatemala border the sun had fallen with a finality that left him chilled in the winter night. He threw down one glass, and then another. His jacket was back in the van, and he didn't feel like going after it. Since his own war from the skies he could not see his way to solve anything by murdering people. Follow orders, my country 'tis of thee. By the third drink he began to feel ok. He'd been more or less trained as a medic, except it was only for in the air where nobody got shot. The wounded lived on the ground, or fled on the ground along the roads, like a trail of ants. By the time his ground duty came it was more a mop up operation, moving ruined trucks through the dust and shoving abandoned tanks off the pitted roads. A few splattered by land mines. Not much medicine to do there.

In Ocosingo on the ground, this war was so low tech you had to wonder if the guns were real or carved wooden toys. The ground itself was so low tech fucking useless you could hardly see what there was to fight for—cement houses painted in parrot colors. He didn't worry about vehicles and tanks rolling into the one paved street, Avenida Central, from the so-called highway he himself had traveled just yesterday. The countryside was blanched, scarred by erosion, empty of people. The few times he'd driven through a settlement he'd glimpsed barefoot women in the shadows of windowless huts or cinderblock shells. Children. Poverty. He passed the big spreads, with horses and cattle. So that was where the men worked, and the women and children suffered alone working their home gardens as best they could.

He had helped out when he could today, automatically, reverting to his training. Retrieving the wounded, giving water. He helped the guys in masks, but that was maybe an accident. If he'd been on the other side of the street maybe he'd a helped the military police. Military guys stuck together, right?

The bar owner caught his eye and Frank asked, "Qué pasa?" The barman shrugged. Who the hell knows. But finally the barman spoke, "Rebelión. Los Zapatistas."

"What do they want?" Frank asked.

"Dignidad," the man with the gray moustache responded laconically, for the silent barkeep. "Dignity. They are so poor, they choose to live with dignity or die with dignity."

Frank didn't worry about driving drunk when he drove the van down the same street to the only hotel in town. The quiet was intense, made more quiet by the punctuation of a single shot. The street lay empty under the stars, its cement houses locked behind their walls and metal doors. The rebellion waited on the next morning's light, or news or commands from elsewhere.

He left the van on the street, no choice. He locked it carefully, sure that locking was futile, wondering if he'd come out in the morning and find only scraps of metal. He knocked at the hotel door, and repeated the knock. The wary outward glance was repeated, and the accepting recognition of a white face. Frank could hear them dragging away some sort of barricade inside, and the door opened into the patio that fronted the hotel. The building was old, small—maybe a dozen rooms up and down, Frank guessed. He recognized the colonial architecture, the balconies and fountain, real Mexican. Following the man who opened the outer door he made his way into the hotel reception, an area that consisted of a desk with key boxes on the wall behind it. None of the keys were missing, yet nobody was here. No women were visible. But the place looked clean and maintained, the plants had recently been watered. He was vaguely sorry about how bad he stunk, of sweat, fear, yesterday's beer and tonight's mescal.

"Is there any food?" He asked the man who took him through the interior patio to a room. The room held a bed, a heavy wooden wardrobe. Overhead, a ceiling fan.

The man shook his head. Frank nodded. He was half starved but worse tired. Is there hot water? In the morning, the man replied. In the morning you will have hot water. It's been a difficult day, he shrugged. His face was brown also, and broad like the indigenous Mayans'. Frank realized that virtually everyone here was part, if not all, Mayan.

The bad guy rebels must be pretty damn desperate to declare war on their federal government—these few small men, and, as he had figured out during the long day, women too, running and shooting alongside. And the paper they had posted on the wall of the municipal building: Ejército Zapatista Liberación Nacional. Named in honor of Mexico's mythic revolutionary, Emiliano Zapata. The EZLN, a national liberation army of a few rag-tag, badly armed people with no hope beyond that of forcing the public's attention.

Attention must be paid. That was a line from something or other. With a small heartfelt groan Frank lowered his body onto the bed, and rolled the blanket from the side up over himself. He hated to dirty the sheets.

The grievances of the indigenous people of Chiapas were explained to Frank the next day, by a fellow named José, who seemed to be in charge of maintaining the Zapatista supply line.

Frank had finally showered, shaved, brushed his teeth, brushed his soft palate, dressed in a clean tee-shirt. He bundled his dirty laundry, guessing it could be taken care of inside the hotel for a few pesos. The second day of war against the government of Mexico did not prevent Frank from eating a breakfast of eggs and tortillas, refried beans and rice. He took his time, drank his coffee, picked his teeth. Inside the hotel dining room he was the only white face, the only tourist. He checked to be sure his passport and money were zipped securely into his money belt beneath his shirt, and he kept his head down. Across the room, a few men whom he spotted as government officials of one sort or another drank hot chocolate from bowls and dunked sweet bread. One wore a military uniform, a captain with a deformed ear, Frank could see. Another was certainly the mayor, another maybe a Ladino, more European than Mayan in appearance, with well-pressed trousers over fancy leather boots, like a Texas rancher wearing a clean ironed shirt. A boss.

He couldn't make out what they were talking about. But it didn't take a brain surgeon to know it was the attack, and what to do and whose orders to wait for. He put down a twenty peso note and quietly stood.

Outside, he glanced at his van, still safely locked. He sauntered back toward the zócalo. Silence made him more uneasy than the shooting. Take your time, he advised his anxious gut.

Sun was warming the square, yet nobody was around. The open market stalls sat empty; many corrugated metal doors remained down on the sidewalk and padlocked. Frank sat on a bench, and immediately the other man, José, sat next to him.

"This is not such a good place to be, amigo." He was calm and pleasant. Frank sat. He placed his arms outstretched along the bench back, and swung his boot up and down slowly.

"So explain to me."

"In a country once our own, oppression and racism against us at all levels. Add to that, on January One comes NAFTA, selling cheap American corn to compete with ours. There is much hunger here."

"So they start a war against the Mexican government? No way, man, that's dumb! How can they hope to gain anything by war?"

José shrugged. "My job is to bring in the supplies of food, water, ammunition. One day more perhaps for the fighting. To make an impression with the bullets. Also to use the time for the propaganda. When the federales show up, we leave."

But the Mexican army showed up that morning. While the sun wore its way through the sky, Frank, outside the official lines and once again feeling compelled to do something, toted bodies. This time, at José's instruction, he struggled over several cobbled streets to the makeshift field hospital in the back of a truck. His short stature left the wounded men dangling limbs over his chest and ass. Strong enough still, despite two years of booze. Frank would have used his own van for the wounded but there was no way without calling down artillery. The gunfire blasted his ears.

He ended up in the cantina again at nightfall, shutting the door against the drone of military helicopters. He could get in his van and head out to the countryside. Or maybe drive straight into a battle area—who knew what was happening beyond the town. His nerves were beginning to fray at not getting killed, and he wondered how the young Zapatista soldiers could wait. On one or two walls, signs and slogans had appeared as José predicted. DIGNIDAD. Dignity. Free the Tzeltal Eight.

So these people were Tzeltales? Frank wondered if the forested countryside belonged to them, and that was why they were locked up in some jail. They objected to trespassers and got arrested. Again Frank found a lame wooden chair in the cantina. He placed his back to the peeling cement wall and waited. The old man came in. Sitting alone, Frank swallowed beer and briefly wondered again if he was illegal. Aiding a rebellion in a foreign country. Was there a law? But what the fuck, there was no information, the wounded can't be left without assistance, that's the first law. He grunted to himself and stretched his tired back. He was done, he had done his good deeds.

On the third morning, Frank went out from the hotel carefully, looking up and down the street before he stepped toward his van with every intention of leaving Ocosingo. Too late. He could see tanks lodged at the end of Central Norte, and feel more than hear artillery fire. A motorized vehicle lumbered past, and Frank, exposed and vulnerable, leaped into a doorway. After the armored car went by, he jogged perpendicular to Calle Central, and then cut parallel again. He was on a dirt street lined with the usual cinderblock and adobe houses, stuccoed and painted. The sidewalk was elevated above possible tropical downpours, with steps up to the worn stone paving. He leaped down into the roadbed and sped across. A block from the zócalo he came up on another Zapatista "headquarters"—a truck with several masked and armed people waiting near it. One of them was José.

"We leave now."

"How the fuck do you get out? They'll get blasted from every side!" He meant the ones left in the zócalo.

"No, only two sides. We will cover them." He shook Frank's hand, and disappeared. One of the others waiting was a woman, her dark hair shoved up under her military cap and her face covered with the by-now unmistakable red bandanna. Only her eyes betrayed her sex. An old man, the man from the cantina, strolled past. The woman watched the straight-backed disappearing form.

"That's a good man, you know?"

Frank shook his head. No way. He couldn't see it. War on their own government. Traitors.

"We have nothing to lose, absolutely nothing." The woman soldier looked at Frank. "What does a rich American know?" Frank was silent, his mouth pulled into a grimace. And then she went on, "No decent roof over our heads, no land, no work, no food, no education for our children." Frank hardly listened to her soft words, whispered almost as a mother whispers, hush hush to a child. She didn't give him no credit, he'd helped, hadn't he? He heard gunfire, not this voice next to him. Then a short hard whistle. The young woman hefted her gun under her arm and began to run toward the zócalo. Frank willy-nilly jogged beside her. Racing toward them were the masked Zapatistas, well in front of Mexican soldiers in full gear and uniforms. The fleeing men flapped their arms and black covered heads like scarecrows. While Frank crouched and ran forward, the woman beside him began to fire behind the Zapatistas at the military. One Zapatista fell in front of him, and without a moment's thought he bent and hoisted the wounded man onto his shoulder and turned back toward the truck. He hoped to hell they had more than just this one truck, one truck! Oh, man!

He heaved the wounded rebel onto the back of the vehicle and himself up next to him. The young woman soldier appeared, and two others. The truck was already moving. Frank grabbed a hand and hauled. The three flopped beside him as the truck gained speed. On the floor, leaflets were piled up and tied with fibers. Frank cut loose a bunch and spread them for a mat. The wounded man was stretched out, moaning but not fatally hurt. Beneath him the leaflets absorbed the blood from his leg as Frank used his knife to cut away the pants. A fair-sized hole, but right through both sides.

The woman handed him a roll of bandage. Frank had nothing to disinfect the wound, nothing to give the man.

"Have you doctors?" He could read the leaflet where it was turning wet. "We say enough is enough!" The seeping blood covered the rest.

"Yes," the woman answered. "There are a few. They wait for us there."

Frank holed up for a week in a wood slat and mud house with dirt floors. Eight to ten people slept together in one room on three beds.

He practiced his minimal Spanish when he could, but most of the people spoke some Indian language. Nobody ventured out of the tiny settlement. The only water was from a nearby stream, and it was used for cooking, cleaning and drinking, and, he feared, the draining of their own waste. Frank, sponging off his sweaty torso in the same water, figured if he didn't leave he'd soon be sick, and besides, this was not the kind of fugitive life he could stomach. Not this rat-hole calm. Not children coughing, not slow starvation. Not this kind of existence among people who had nothing. Nothing but their determination to endure. Not enough. He had an American passport and God bless America.

With his clothes filthy and his feet sore from wearing the same socks for ten days, Frank struck out for Ocosingo, hitching rides on ramshackle trucks and finally flagging down a bus. It let him out opposite the cemetery, as if that were the logical place. Frank was not so sure; he was in Ocosingo in search of his Plymouth and his gear, not details of the dead left in his recent tiny war.

The common grave of eleven people had just been uncovered near the municipal cemetery. It was in plain view of anyone who entered, next to a rough hole in the adobe cemetery wall.

The men who excavated the grave reported to the onlookers that they had dug it "at the request of the soldiers of the Mexican Army." The soldiers came on January 3 in the morning and said they needed volunteers.

"They said they were going to make a grave to bury some dead. Eight of the dead were in the public health clinic refrigerator, others were outside the cemetery, and one they brought with them. The dead who were carried to the grave looked like civilians. Some of our companions said they were Zapatistas, but who knows. Two had received bullets in the head. The soldiers said they would watch while we buried the dead. We made a hole in the cemetery wall so we wouldn't have to cross the line of fire, and brought the dead through that. But the shooting was so fierce we didn't finish filling in the grave. The same morning two others were buried, a man and a woman, both shot." He pointed again to his head with his finger.

Deposited at the entry to the cemetery, Frank halted there, listening. His feet froze to the chewed up ground, his boots catching the clods. He figured this mass grave had been dug as he was running alongside the Zapatistas. The cemetery was called hereabouts in Mexico a panteón, filled with tiny chapels and altars for praying and interring the bones of generations of each family. Flowers and photos adorned most graves, urns and pots held dead flowers, plastic flowers, living flowers. A legend engraved in the stone archway of the entrance read, know that you are mortal, bow you head, wordly pride ends here. After a while he moved inside and stood out of the way as the men dug. He knew all about being mortal. And pride, and losing pride, and wanting pride. Not him now. Even out in the country he managed to find a guy with a jug of home-made rot-gut mescal.

A line of people passed through to look at the disinterred as they were lifted free of the thick dirt, to claim their dead if they could. Frank's legs felt frozen, his arms like cement. He couldn't understand himself why he was here, how he had got back to this exact spot; he fought for his country and survived, two years ago. It wasn't his fault if guys died. Around him in the panteón the slow file was quiet. Nobody spoke. Everyone knew what had happened.

At his side an old man appeared and after a moment spoke to Frank. "My name is Tomás." Frank recognized the bushy gray moustache. "Frank," he replied, extending his hand. The old man nodded. "It's going fast, this war," the old man continued, linking his freed hand into Frank's arm, apparently unconcerned with the stench and filth Frank wore. Tomás, several inches shorter than this gringo, firmly led him away from the panteón.

"A Committee for Human Rights has been formed by the Dominican priests in sympathy with the struggle. Those of us who can, aid and assist. Look at this." They had left behind the flowers and chapels of the cemetery and reached the church courtyard. They passed through into the open gallery of stone pillars, into the rear garden. Tomás handed Frank a bulky layer of newspapers. The first recorded events during the Zapatista occupation of the municipalities, where the EZLN struck and retreated: San Cristóbal de Las Casas, Las Margaritas, Altamirno, and Ocosingo. The estimated number of dead from 145 to 1000. Frank realized the size of the rebellion far exceeded his imagination. The nation was involved. Unbelievably, many supported the rebels.

"President Salinas set up the new Commission for Peace and Reconciliation in Chiapas," Tomás informed Frank when he looked up from the papers. "Yesterday he announced his decision to order a cease-fire in Chiapas. He named the unilateral cease-fire the first step toward saving lives and finding reconciliation. Also, he added that if the armed groups continue to act aggressively the Mexican army will be obliged to defend itself and the civilian population."

"What's that mean? The Mexican army defend itself against the rebels? Those poor bastards have nothing to throw against a national force. I don't get it. They must have something! Will they negotiate? For a settlement?"

Tomás shook his head. Yes or no? Frank wasn't sure. They sat in the church courtyard shielded from the sun. In the center a small garden was planted with one grand agave, and several smaller cactuses Frank couldn't identify. The effect was neat, and somehow controlled, almost self-contained, like the men themselves who began to appear, seating themselves under the stone gallery of the old building. Frank turned his head. Suddenly he found himself at a meeting, among Mexicans who had declared war on their own government, sitting on a stone bench reading the newspapers and drinking not mescal but coffee. Apparently welcome.

He was known by some grapevine as the American who aided the Zapatistas, as he was to discover later. On January 10, while Frank was still out in the countryside, they formed a committee. The Committee needed staff to accomplish any Human Rights work. And maybe to do other work, nobody yet seemed to know what. Volunteers, they would need whoever could volunteer.

While the speakers laid out the situation, Frank took off his cap and ran his hand over his shaggy neck-length hair, and down his face. Sometimes he wondered who he was, and sometimes he thought he could learn by touch; like a blind person might become familiar with him, he stroked his own face, his own flesh. He wanted to know whose flesh this was, alive and unharmed.

Tomás next to him looked carefully at the tanned square face and thin vulnerable mouth. Vulnerable, yes, this American, with his long eyelashes and bewildered eyes. Freshly returned from the campo, where life knew death as a family acquaintance.

Frank repeated, "Does this announcement mean peace?"

And the old man Tomás said, "No, hombre. It means a long slow genocide."

Carefully, Frank replaced his coffee cup on the plastic tabletop. He swallowed something rising in his throat and stared at the man. Genocide was a word he knew. "The Mexican army is going to kill the Indians?"

"Not them, they hire local men to do the actual shooting." Tomás added, "We are familiar with this. The military coordinates, the hired men shoot. It is very simple, really."

"Oh," Frank said. An image rose up in his mind of the captain with a twisted ear. "There's this guy I saw," he began. He paused. He had nowhere to go with that.

"You will be needed," Tomás said. "Everyone willing is needed."

I suppose you wonder how I know all this. Well, reader, I'm the omniscient narrator. I follow the internet. And a great deal of Frank's story he told me himself, during those weary months of chemotherapy in Houston, and then while he waited to die. It's no part of the Zapatista story that cancer of the pancreas ended Frank's efforts to make restitution for whatever he had done, or thought he did, or mourned that he didn't do, in the first Gulf War where his government placed him in contact with weapons made with depleted uranium. Nor does it relate to the Zapatistas if Frank felt some hint of bad times ahead when he declined to accept the permanent love offered to him, committing himself instead to journeying endlessly across the landscape, a pilgrim if you will—and as you shall learn, not the only one.

Or maybe it is all related. As omniscient author, I'm allowed to wonder about those links. It occurs to me now that this is a story of several endless journeys, as well as a story of government treachery, and the story of every people's struggle for dignity. All those links. I'm also allowed to report on the Zapatista National Liberation Army (EZLN) from the advantage of hindsight, as Mexico observes the 10th anniversary of its emergence into public view.

By the summer of 1996, two and a half years after the start of the Zapatista armed uprising, Subcomandante Marcos, speaking on behalf of the EZLN in a public relations coup unrivalled by many heads of state, attracted to the Lacandon selva four thousand non-Mexicans, young and old, from forty-two different countries. Some came to Chiapas like Frank, blown in by private demons, but others came purposefully, deliberately aiming for this young war. The foreigners came clad not in ski masks but in what might have been hippie clothing retrieved from a quarter-century's storage in attic trunks. In the magic of idealism, they converged by plane, bus and caravan on southern Mexico's border state, to respond to Marcos' invitation to meet.

Among them arrived the widow of French President Mitterand, half a dozen world-class writers and intellectuals, a caravan from Pastors For Peace, assorted religious nuts, and more non-governmental do-gooders. Invitations went out to Garcia Marquez and Oliver Stone. An office was opened in the city of San Cristóbal de Las Casas to register attendees to the upcoming discussion grandly called Encuentro Inter-Continental por la Humanidad y Contra el Neoliberalismo: an intercontinental meeting on behalf of humanity and against the policies of neoliberalism.

Why did they come? Why were four thousand foreigners present? I mean, the ones who came on purpose—no-one articulated for me any such reasons as I have attributed to the characters in these pages. Therefore the reader might choose to suppose most went for idealism or political motives. Certainly they discussed endlessly what many yearned for: an alternative political system, an alternative cultural system. Although I have tried mightily over the course of several years to articulate what I observed at this moment in history, I never heard anyone clearly present the vision of a newer and better system for the western world better than the Zapatistas themselves. Everything for everyone. For ourselves, nothing. It was too new then, only after twenty years of endless struggle have we begun to understand. Even the so-called leaders of the various American organizations said only "this is going on" and "this is unjust" and "this harms people." They never articulated why they were, or are, impelled to support the Zapatista vision until it's meaning became clear through the exercise of autonomy and the committees for good government. At the time of the uprising, it was blind faith and hope.

In the face of the power structure that oppresses them, the EZLN twenty years on still demands protection for local agriculture and their communal life-style, threatened by timber cutting, hydro electric development, oil exploration, land expropriation, biological theft and ecological destruction. Random murders and mass killings are supported by the federal government (theirs and ours) under neoliberalism. That's a word you and I know from reading the newspapers these last two decades. At the time of Frank's first contact, he didn't know it, and hardly anyone else did either. At the outset of their rebellion, the day NAFTA took effect, the Zapatistas simultaneously called for deep structural reforms to the Mexican political system to allow communities to exercise local control, especially over management of their resources. Localism, not globalism.

And so from all parts of the world people came, to unknown places like Oventic, La Realidad, La Garrucha, Roberto Barrios: minuscule villages of adobe or thatch houses, homes made of wooden slats and inhabited by chickens and snakes, mud streets, impoverished people taking on the huge tasks of unraveling political issues, economic injustices, cultural destruction, social issues, indigenous issues, human rights and women's issues. Handcrafted Marcos and Ramona dolls, woven bracelets, Chiclets peddled by small boys at all hours of the day and night on the local streets. At the meetings, the discussions were prolonged and intense.

Meanwhile in international awareness it slowly became evident that the Mexican Partido Revolucionario Institucional, the PRI, the world's longest-dominant political governing party, was in deep trouble along with the Mexican economy, as the friendly neoliberals from the north demanded more and more access.

There are thirty-one Mexican states. Most Americans like Frank knew next to nothing about Mexican politics, or Mexican life conditions. Many observers believe that when the Zapatistas fired their "shot heard round the world" they outlined the dimensions of the coming struggle to confront neoliberalism. It certainly was their action that propelled Mexican Civil Society toward the Mexican electoral Revolution of 2000. That is, the PRI was thrown out of power, a wonderful political cataclysm, but a neoliberal party replaced the "dinosaurs". Another decade and the PRI returned, nothing changed.

The state of Chiapas remained under military occupation until January of 2004, and the government military, supplemented by freelancers financed by wealthy landowners and foreign corporations, still maintains relentless pressure against the Indian communities.

So this is a story of people who came as tourists, and like Frank, didn't know a hell of a lot when they arrived. Some stayed over several years, from the January 1, 1994 uprising through the inauguration of Vicente Fox of the PAN, as president on December 1, 2000, to the appearance of Zapatista commanders in the Congress of Mexico; and maybe some, picking up on the political implications of refusing to support the rich in power—because that's really what it's all about—stayed forever. Now the story relates to a new sociocultural way of being, as the Zapatistas create their networks for good government in their besieged territory, and other campesino Indians in Latin America defend their right to object to foreign decisions for mining, land and water use on their territory. They demand local control, they demand the right to be heard. Their protests make them zapatistas.

Documentation is widely available for major events, although all characters, including myself, are fictional. San Gregorio and Cuates de Santa Ana are fictional towns.

Part One: 1996

1

Martin Immanent

Within two years, news of the Zapatista rebellion was available on the internet, with letters and comments by Marcos, charismatic, charming, well-educated and urbane, on horseback in the remote jungle. Around the world political activists rushed to aid the rebellion of the indigenous people of Chiapas. In mid-Iowa, in the United States of America, Martin was jiggling up and down on his bony ass on the floor of the Golden Dome.

On either side of him in the recessed light from high on the curved walls, he could sense, feel palpably along his nerve endings, within his infinite dendrites, his very ganglia and corpuscles, the heavy physicality of certain bodies in this all-male exercise. Others like himself were sweating, grunting, heaving little exclamations of pleasure as they tried to levitate.

Martin wasn't having much luck, and he supposed nobody else was either, but since everyone kept their eyes closed, maybe he was wrong—maybe one of those physical beings positioned nearby with pale folded legs hidden in sweats, body odors faint in Martin's nostrils, digestive business leaking sounds of moisture and gurgling, maybe one of them was actually rising off the mat upon which everyone hunkered in the lotus position, and was levitating, hovering in the air six or eight inches above the rest, above Martin.

Martin hoped not. Martin, although he doubted he could levitate, on the other hand knew with quiet certainty that if anybody could do it, it would be himself. His soul often transcended the here and now, unless it was one of those days when Martin, with eyes wide open, was experiencing his immanence like thirst on a hot day.

Why was there such a contradiction?

Wasn't sex, for example, like in his father's barn with his cousin Rosanne, transcendent and immanent at the same time? A kind of Baptism?

Seeing the light, he thought. This literal experience excluded intellectual or political categories. It was purely seeing light, the brilliance of something glowing behind his eyelids, just like it said in his parents' Bible, just like others had reported. An angel nearby, and a brilliant white light. He had that. He had that almost every day. It was only immanence that kept him from floating into the air above the thick cotton mat he rocked and bounced on, dutifully keeping to the clockwise movement of the men circling in the lotus position with their eyes closed, legless under the Golden Dome.

Outside, he knew, the air would be a cold blast, hitting his lungs with Iowa wind. The dome had been built in the middle of a flat plain, a dome like a tea cozy, unlike any construction at home in Georgia. It was the levitation area, separate from the cottages in which the men and women lived their secluded lives. He had become accustomed, crossing the campus to the dome, to scan the sky with its several daily rainbows hovering as if Holy Master had caught them in his hand and brought them to his disciples. It sufficed; they never read the newspapers or watched television, which in any case carried no news of remote southern Mexico. You had to be on-line and in the know.

Twenty minutes more. HM had sent him to the dome for his last practice before launch. Well, strictly speaking, before his next motorized flight. Holy Master had sent Martin on duty before, to Somalia, to Ireland, to Yugoslavia. Martin always flew by commercial airline since at this time he had no extra-terrestrial abilities. But Holy Master thought highly of Martin nonetheless, to send him on these missions. Although he had to use one of HM's many frequent flyer miles, Martin was posted to far-off trouble spots to send into the ambience his transcendent vibrations of Peace. Who knew how much worse these conflicts might have been without earthbound Martin there on the rim, gloriously transcending, readying his levitation skills, and sending beneficent thoughts of peace coasting along the ether toward angry men. Put down your weapons, Martin's thoughts coaxed. Shake hands with your brother. He sent message after message as HM dictated them: Honor the dignity of others. Embrace democracy. Guard the environment for birds and lizards.

Locally, it didn't suffice that right here next to Palmerville all these disciples generated good vibes. Martin knew that others less well qualified than himself took on the local responsibility of discouraging the Palmerville teenagers from screwing without condoms on top of the comfortable graves in the cemetery, and/or driving drunk. Outside events in the global village didn't reach them any more than did the meditators. Many spring evenings Martin strolled past the cemetery along the dirt road, and listened to high cries of sex and the low growl of engines. Once in a while he came upon an empty beer can or plastic six-pack container lying in the grass. He fended off the desire to be invited in by a beckoning hand. A fair Iowa girl with a blunt nose and freckles who would help him shed his robe...

He was familiar with feeling the alien outsider; it fit him like a private mantra. It endured from his sorrowful past even before Robert John's death ten years ago. Martin sometimes wished he could do more in a tangible way, somehow be included in the life of the town. The Hindu community on the corn and hog plain was a lonely outpost.

Martin didn't believe he needed to make amends, exactly—after all, he'd never actually done anything bad to Robert John or to anybody else. However, he never told HM about that part of his former life. Even as a kid he'd known his thoughts were powerful.

Now Martin chose to bring peace, to sooth rebellions. He could beam out thoughts cleaner and more rapidly than most. So Martin was almost always sent by HM, even when HM deemed it necessary to send along a hundred others also, to achieve optimum effect. Tonight he'd be off to Mexico, to an area he'd never heard of, Chiapas, a southern state where the indigenous peoples had rebelled two years before. A war was going on. HM, as if His Majesty (as Martin sometimes secretly called Holy Master Ragadam Baram) knew everything happening everywhere on earth, at all points of the globe, at all times, day and night. He knew that the Zapatistas called for everyone to come who could rally to the call for justice. Probably HM kept his access to the internet connected, probably HM read The London Times on the web and CNN, and knew all the Zapatista net sites.

Internet was important. Soon all the Teachers following HM would have their own modem equipped laptops to take with them wherever they were sent, but thus far HM hadn't offered one to Martin. Maybe this time? Maybe at this very moment HM was packing one of the slender black nylon briefcases, and barefoot despite the thin snow cover, shrouded in a white silk robe, stood in the doorway of his quarters waiting for Martin to pass on his return from the Golden Dome. He would stretch forth his arms, and with a rose in one hand and the black nylon briefcase in the other, utter the benediction Martin required to make his Mexico mission a success.

Determined, Martin tensed his buttocks and abs, and heaved himself three inches forward. Ten more minutes. If he had to go without a laptop, at least he knew he would be in touch with HM by telepathy, and fulfill his duty faithfully, to the best of his ability.

He had done it before, and although the results weren't always definitive, every place he went the American newspapers and television reported a pacification, if not outright exhaustion of the warring parties. Starvation ended, leaders were inaugurated, and seeds of peace flourished in small ways. If only the public knew how World War III was deflected daily! Martin could be proud of his work. Holy Master often told him so, in their quiet moments together when Martin was invited to share HM's frugal yogurt and cucumber lunch.

Martin was proud of his work. He heaved himself and was rewarded by feeling his butt leave the mat. I'm getting the hang of it, he said to himself.

Resting, he imagined a small dark population. Declaring war on the government of Mexico with an army of 70,000 troops inside a state the size of Connecticut, and millions of dollars worth of military equipment. He better check before he left. He wasn't sure—which side was supposed to receive his rainbow of peace? Well, both of course, he answered himself. HM didn't take political positions. Martin, in all his trips as a broadcaster of peace vibrations, never identified who were the bad guys.

2

Billy Signs Up

Billy Boyd Grennich stood in his sexy navy blue briefs in the narrow space between his dorm bed and maple desk to read his own emancipation proclamation:

ACTION ALERT!

"CAMPAIGN FOR DEMOCRACY THROUGH PEACE NOT WAR"

Wow. Goosebumps popped out on Billy's skinny legs, making their pale reddish fur stand erect. In the mirror above the dresser he glimpsed himself. He looked like a popsicle which had gathered lint. So what. Everyone made fun of him anyway and ignored him and took for granted that he still remained a virgin, although this was absolutely not true.

Conditions in Mexico were increasingly dangerous. The Mexican government was going nuts trying to control social unrest without giving rights to the indigenous people. In at least 16 states and Mexico City, the Mexican army was out in force. In Chiapas, Mexican aerial commando units were ready for lightning strikes in the highlands, the northern part of the state, and the jungle. Approximately 4,000 parachutists waited, prepared to attack, hunt down and kill the Zapatista leadership.

Billy received news on the internet from the EZLN site, and now here he had it in print. A call for action, addressed to him personally. The growing militarization was one of the best kept secrets of American policy towards Mexico. He could be the one to tell all, how US political and corporate interests supported military aid to Mexico, hell-bent on forcing the Zapatistas to surrender by starving and slowly assassinating their base. Convoys and helicopters, along with paramilitaries who assassinated on orders, terrorized the Chiapas countryside.

"The Zapatistas," he read "must be supported in order to avoid a blood bath! Increased national and international pressure and presence is critical! Act now and provide vital support to the Mexican people as they struggle to build a political system based on liberty, democracy and justice!"

Billy raised the fresh internet printout and pressed it against his face with both hands. He inhaled the scent of the ink and imagined the paper was his Darth Vader Halloween helmet.

All he had to do was make a proposal to the Friends of Guatemala Student Committee. To pay his airfare down to Mexico to investigate. He doubted many classmates were up to date on the Zapatista rebellion, if they knew about it at all.

His mind raced over his fellow students in the Friends of Mexico group. No use; they had already committed to spending their annual $2000 research stipend on investigating some holiday in LA, Cinco de Mayo or whatever.

Billy chose the Guatemala committee because all the Poli Sci majors had to participate on a committee, and he thought maybe

Guatemala would be easier to deal with than the other open slot, on Friends of Africa where the students hated him. They all towered over him, even the girls, who snapped their gum and referred to him behind his back as The Skinny White Trash.

Which he was, but it wasn't his fault, was it? If his mother remarried that Grennich and insisted he add Grennich to his own father's name of Boyd. Boyd was not white trash. Boyd was a convict, specifically Mr. William Christopher Boyd Senior was in jail in England for trying to smuggle gun money from Austin Texas to Northern Ireland, and Billy was supposed to remember him but didn't.

Billy hardly ever did what he was supposed to do. Remembering his father was based mostly on a photograph of a man with lumpy skin and a stiff white haircut that sprang from his head in several directions. Billy was ten before he realized that a snapshot in black and white wouldn't reveal the true color of his father's hair. He asked his mother, but she claimed she didn't remember. Her hair was an ordinary brown, and so Billy surmised his own carrot top came from the paternal side of the family. What else came with it, he didn't know. He was no angry rebel. He wasn't in jail, and didn't plan to get there.

The Friends of Ireland committee was out of the question from Day One. None of those guys descended from fathers who got caught. Their fathers were the ones who fled to the United States, got rich and had brains enough to never go back. Somehow those ancestral grievances had petered out, and left this generation with shamrocks on Saint Patrick's Day and framed pictures of John F. Kennedy. They hated him because his father didn't know when to quit. They assumed he carried a hidden burning desire to throw out the Brits and free Northern Ireland, like Liam whatsizname in the movie. Billy Boyd Grennich didn't enjoy movies where the hero was likely to get hurt. In his Mexico plan he was a tourist, a Witness, like the paper said, "a presence."

The Guatemala kids hated him too, but it was a real small committee, and the only idea that didn't scare the shit out of them was to fund hurricane recovery. Many of their families arrived in the US without documentation. Relief wasn't research, and Professor Barrios rejected it. So the committee was at a loss, and Billy would leap in with this proposition to investigate a rebellion not far from the Guatemala border, and furthermore, he could go because he had a passport. This unused document from his high school days was stored at his mother's home in Austin, waiting for the future school vacation when they would travel to Britain to visit his father in prison. A day not likely to ever arrive, it seemed, as each season his mother referred more vaguely to the journey, and lately not at all. Billy's father never wrote, not to his ex-wife now remarried, or to his abandoned son.

From Billy's perspective as an earnest Political Science major, he used his study time well, reading a certain number of spy novels by John LeCarré, and his favorite, Graham Greene. So he understood that his father kept him out of the loop. Nobody from Scotland Yard or Interpol or the CIA had him in their sight, and for sure nobody from the Guatemala committee would care where he went.

The clincher was the people of Chiapas were Guatemalan Mayans in origin; Chiapas once belonged to Guatemala like Texas belonged to Mexico.

He could pull it off.

A fantastic excuse to get out of here. He didn't belong and he wasn't learning anything, except how to ignore being skinny white trash. Unlike his incarcerated father, Billy knew when to quit.

He pressed his quitting paper again to both his cheeks, and breathed deeply. The inhaled paper indented against his nose, and grew damp over his mouth. A faint ink smudge transferred to his upper lip. He folded the news item like a love letter and slipped it into his notebook.

First step: get his passport and malaria pills. He'd have to go home and visit his Ma and Jim Grennich, his stepfather for fourteen years. Jim wasn't a bad guy; the pejorative "trash" wasn't fair, Billy knew. It popped into Billy's mind in reference to himself, and he resentfully extended it to Jim who actually earned a decent living as a plumber, and kept Billy and his mother fed and housed. His mother simply tired of fun and adventure as organized by William Boyd, Sr. Billy would tell them he was going to do an assignment required for his sophomore finals, the absolute truth. Jim would encourage his mother to behave as if Billy had the right to grow up. Billy silently gave Jim credit for that, although it hadn't yet come to pass.

Fortunately, neither his mother nor step-father were aware of the Zapatista rebellion. Unlike the ruin of Northern Ireland, 1994 and NAFTA passed without their notice.

Billy didn't bother to clarify for himself that on January 1, 1994 he himself was in his senior year in high school, ignorant of the world, and desperate then as now as to how to survive among classmates who didn't give him no respect.

Now, he finally found a solution. Leave. Mexico awaited. Once more he took the sheet of paper and read:

Communiqué of the Clandestine Revolutionary Indigenous Committee—General Command of the Zapatista Army of National Liberation.

Mexico, 19 September 1996.
To the people of Mexico:
To the people and governments of the world:

Brothers:
Today, September 19, 1996, it has been 11 years since the emer-

gence of a new political and social force, which is the result of the government's inability to confront the problems of the earthquake which shook the capital.

While the government vacillated between false declarations and the theft of humanitarian aid, civil society organized itself by itself to revive and reconstruct a city which quickly, amidst all the pain, reminded itself that it is nothing without its inhabitants.

Thousands of residents mobilized themselves with nothing more than feelings of collectivity, feelings which had supposedly been buried by the earthquake of neoliberal modernity. Amidst the debris, destruction and death, these Mexicans rescued self-criticism and dignity...

The anonymous heroism without a face which illuminated September 1985 was the response to the men in gray in power who plotted the sale of dignity and the forgetting of history.

Being the first spontaneous response to this catastrophe, this force which emerged 11 years ago followed its own path, and, in many cases, made itself a civic organization. This self-revelation of September 1985 was sufficient and it was necessary to care for and cultivate this strength and organize it.

This civil force which has existed for 11 years organized itself and became, little by little, an example that one can participate without aspiring to public office, that one can be organized politically without this meaning that one is part of a political party. That one can keep an eye on the government and can pressure it so that it will "lead by obeying", that one can be efficient and discrete, giving of oneself and not self-interested, and can be noble and honest. This is how organizations were born, and many exist which serve people in the city, and of those who comprise them, they only receive the satisfaction of having done their duty and of the national and international recognition of their work...

All the while, those who are in power trample each other, administer violence and death, militarizing Mexican life through a takeover of the state which, although it is slow, is no less authoritarian.

All the while, those who are in power make themselves deaf, distribute monologues in useless negotiating tables and give weight, as the only important issues, to pride and arrogance.

All the while, those who hide behind power, expropriate the liberty of dissidents and of those who don't conform, give the gift of impunity to the real criminals, those who yesterday and today make up the government.

Billy muttered, "Yeah, yeah, yeah."

Two national projects, two countries, two Mexicos which confront each other...

He lifted his head. He had no memories of words like this, but it sounded familiar. How could this be?

Sovereignty is squandered. The powerful of Mexico, the Mexico which is in agony.

On the other hand, the nation of community organizations, the country of civil society, the Mexico of Mexicans. The national plan which carries the banner of democracy, liberty and justice. The national plan which means its reconstruction, justice and life, peace everywhere and for everyone. Dialogue as a way which makes its own way and from which springs forth hope, with reason and heart as its driving forces. Sovereignty expropriated, but now by the Mexican people. The Mexico of civil society, the Mexico that lives again.

Two countries which struggle amongst themselves to find a place in the future.

One, that of the powerful, using force.

The other one, that of society, using reason and feeling.

One, that of the powerful, for war.

The other one, that of society, for peace.

We, the Zapatistas were criticized yesterday for wanting to dialogue with civil society, for addressing her in our initiatives. Today, we are criticized because instead of seeking the support of political organizations, those armed and unarmed, we reiterate instead our belief in civil society. They tell us that it is a bad bet, they tell us that we will lose and they sentence us to defeat. They tell us that one doesn't speak to or listen to civil society, but rather one commands it...

Civil society, this discomforting concept and the disturbing reality. The forgotten of always, except at election time. The disposable ones, except at the time when it is required that they fulfill their obligations. The excluded, except at tax time. The ones held in disregard, except at the hour of death.

Civil society and its proposal for the nation, now not only an intuition, but a possibility, confronting the powerful and their destruction.

While the powerful militarize their plan of hopelessness which is already civil war on Mexican soil, civil society insists on holding back war and turning back the militarization of the nation.

While power gives a monologue, civil society demands a national dialogue which is effective and inclusive.

While power imprisons its opponents and leaves criminals free, civil society questions the lack of accountability of the powerful and the imprisonment of political prisoners.

While power brutally imposes a murderous economic model, civil society demonstrates in favor of a new political economy.

While power destroys, civil society constructs. While the powerful wage war, civil society looks for peace.

While the powerful belittle the process of mediation, laugh at legislators, attack honest intellectual leadership, civil society works to create a commission for mediation and accords for all of the nation.

While the powerful kill, civil society lives.

The political parties and political organizations, both the armed and unarmed, legal and illegal, open or secret, regional or national, have to choose, sooner or later, between these two national plans.

The EZLN has already chosen.

Long live the Mexican homeland, the new one.

No more a homeland of ostentatious and useless military parades which scare no one. No more homeland full of gray speeches from gray bureaucrats. No more of the homeland for any old sale in the neoliberal marketplace. No more of the dead homeland found in books and museums.

May power and its war always die.

May the men and women of civil society always live.

Democracy!

Liberty!

Justice!

From the mountains of the Mexican Southeast
By the Clandestine Revolutionary Indigenous Committee- General Command of the EZLN

He could do that, that civil society stuff. Billy laughed, a high sound in his throat that emerged somewhere between amazement and exultation.

3

Frank Gets Involved

Frank undertook the task he felt best suited for—supplies runner. It didn't require too much analysis and he didn't need to define his comings and goings in terms of fighting the government of Mexico, nor the government of the United States whose helicopters clacked overhead in the war zone.

All he had to do was stay out of view and drive. The many paramilitary groups lived scattered, usually invisible until called in. They might be ordered by the military to shoot him, but they had catch him first. He stayed mobile; if he used any base, it was a house in the town of San Gregorio run by Estación Norte.

Among the villagers in the outlying campo, there was word of a new colonel, whom they referred to Tornilloreja, "Screw-ear." This man performs the task of recruiting and directing the paramilitaries, men who kill for money or the promise of land, they told him. Be careful.

Frank and Tomás drove to San Cristóbal de Las Casas so that

Tomás could participate in the citizen meetings. It was Tomás who told Frank about the murder nearly three years ago of José's wife and child. While José was not far away, his family was cut down, not with bullets but with machetes. They even killed the animals: the goats, the chickens. Their yard, when José returned from the meeting, swarmed with flies. After carrying his wife and child inside to wash their bodies, he washed his shoes.

Tomás related this story to Frank at a café where they were eating a late-afternoon comida of soup, rice and a chicken leg. Frank put down his fork. That was why José had been in Ocosingo on the first day. A man of dignidad. Frank hadn't known the wife, but these were quiet gentle people. Not rising in rebellion until pushed to the wall. Tomás did not say what meeting José had been at, but Frank could put together two and two.

Tomás continued to eat as he related the story, moving the beans on his plate with his rolled tortilla, picking up the chicken with his fingers to suck off the last scraps. The old grief slept far behind, raw new grief woke them daily. "And on the other side, hijo, in the Federal garrisons the number of desertions within government troops has increased. This comes as always whenever the federal army prepares an offensive action."

But it was small comfort. The rumors of an imminent action against the Zapatistas were uncontrollable. And now learning about the slaughter of José's family, even before the first shot was fired. Frank hoped he wouldn't upchuck his meal.

"How can you do this," he whispered to Tomás.

"We are rebel citizens who have taken up arms because we have no democratic spaces for peaceful political participation." Tomás spoke formally, but then, he often did. The language rolled in a formal Latinate series of multi-syllable words. In Frank's ear the words often flowed like a river justified by its own current. But he felt sickened.

The slaughter of José's family had been more than a warning, Frank saw the black hangman in the deck.

The dulce, a peach in sweet honey, arrived at the table. Frank looked out the window at the passing foreigners who also had come for meetings here in the city and out in the countryside. Nowadays, meetings were commonplace; but these were not meetings of secret conspirators. They were wide open. Elated youngsters, exalted men and women, faces burned and grinning. The city filled with foreigners. A network of small people who expected to weave the fabric of grand events—peacefully. It wasn't the Zapatistas who were shooting now. They had made their point once, and then opted for negotiations, the final San Andrés Accords were signed by the government's representatives. Then nothing happened. The agreements for "Indigenous Rights and Culture" sat like desiccated paper.

Each time Frank entered a community he heard the angry talk. On the plank tables, seated on the rough plank benches, each small dark man placed before the group his thoughts. The government treated them as subjects to be given alms, but not as political actors. They were captured and confessions were extracted by torture; they were imprisoned as criminals and terrorists. The growing number of air-transported troops entering Chiapas specialized in fighting in jungle terrain. Air and land patrols increased their duration and frequency. Land columns incorporated tanks and heavy weaponry in dark convoys, moving like strange prehistoric animals. Two years of the mano duro, the hard hand.

Chewing quietly, Tomás watched Frank struggle. The man's pale brown hair was newly clipped, revealing his wide white forehead. But Frank's arms, with their well-defined muscles, were brown, almost the color of Tomás' body.

Frank had never been a high-fiver, never a rebel. A quiet, introverted kid, he once thought maybe if he could, he would go to college, maybe become a doctor. At this moment bewilderment plucked his thin lips into a twitch. Two years of driving from community to community became two years of silent observation for Frank. He learned. He knew.

"Now begins a permanent campaign of persecution and harassment against foreigners. Men and women from all over the world come to help indigenous communities to live, while the government seeks their death." Tomás pushed aside his plate and spooned the peach. He spoke quietly, turning his head away from the view of other diners. "These foreigners are accused of collaborating with the EZLN. The government ignores the fact that they do not come to help the EZLN but the indigenous communities, you know? Like yourself. The government seeks the elimination of embarrassing witnesses of the genocidal war it carries out. Are you going to finish your food? If not, please give it to me. I don't eat in restaurants very often!"

Frank looked at Tomás, thin enough for sure. He pushed his plate, and his own small dulce toward Tomás. "Here." He watched Tomás, who bent his head over the food again. His motions were neat, almost dainty, Frank thought. So. Negotiations with this government were a joke, for sure. They would never be honored. The Zapatista communities wanted respect and dignity, the peace of life, not the peace of surrender and death. Negotiations were a stalling tactic, just another way to fuck them over.

Frank felt trapped like a tree in a firestorm; the war was enclosing.

Tomás, reading his expression, spoke between mouthfuls. "The support which we seek and need, is this." He waved his hand at the passing people, Mexicans and foreigners. "National and international civil society. Their mobilization." Among the foreign passers-by Frank saw a carrot-topped boy, just a kid. A woman with blond hair, men with crew-cuts. An unimpressive group. The Mexicans somehow looked more substantial, maybe because of their dark hair and eyes.

"From our side, we have enough of weapons and soldiers because no matter what comes to pass we cannot have enough. We have our communities organized. What we desire is that all Mexican people, without political party and organization, make agreements about what they want and do not want, and become organized in order to achieve it. Not to take power," Tomás added to quell Frank's alarmed glance. "No, but to exercise it. I know you will say this is utopian and unorthodox, but this is the way of the Zapatistas. Too bad."

Tomás swallowed and wiped his moustache. "We are different. And the difference is, the government struggles for power. We struggle for democracy." He grinned. "We did declare war on the Federal Army, a challenge they will never forgive! But Frank, truly the difference is in the political proposals. We have carved out a new and radical path. Autonomy."

"Ok," Frank said wearily, to put an end to the conversation. He could not get his head around fighting your own government. Nor could he accept the slaughter without fighting back. Autonomy was a fantastic dream. He wanted a drink. The newspapers, for Chrissake, said sixty thousand troops were in the state. And that count didn't include the paramilitary.

"There's gasoline in the tank, but not enough. Don't trust the gas gauge. Where are you going?"

Tomás often traveled while Frank went on deliveries, disappearing on mysterious errands about which Frank knew nothing. "You don't want to know, hijo," Tomás assured him. Frank guessed that in case of capture he should have nothing to divulge, no matter what the torture. The dozens of Human Rights committees which sprang up during the two and half years that Frank had been carrying supplies and working with Tomás didn't save anybody. They protested to the United Nations after a body was found in a pool of blood.

"Fat chance, this rebellion, Tomás!"

"We make a beginning," Tomás replied. He wasn't insulted, but he wasn't happy. Impunity had become the press's watchword, impunidad. The paramilitaries stole vehicles and used them for transport. Pickups bumping along the primitive back-roads signaled trouble for the communities. They were never traced.

The two men finished eating. Frank rarely drank these days, for which Tomás thanked the Virgin and all the saints. He watched Frank's fingers start to drum on the table and prayed again. A rare affection had developed between the two men a generation apart, a culture apart. Frank had fought one war and thought he was finished. But was struggle ever finished? In his heart Tomás yearned for Frank's innocence. Education takes time.

Estación Norte assumed the task of welcoming new Witnesses—foreigners coming to Chiapas, not all of them sane, Tomás believed. But still, if they were foreigners, that was exactly what was required. If an American or Frenchman got shot, the Mexican government would look bad and perhaps the international corporations would withdraw their investments. Good for us, bad for the government.

"Sit beside a foreigner if possible," he joked. "As I sit next to you, Frank!"

Frank tried to relax. He could go just so far, it was ok. He kept to his side of the line—to save, not kill. Preventive medicine, he jokingly called it to himself. The Zapatistas themselves called for civil change, not violence. Tomás didn't judge him, or the lunatic foreigners. He looked fondly at the old man, whose moustache now held a few more crumbs from God knows where. He reached over with his paper napkin and brushed Tomás' face, an unheard of liberty to take with a fine older man. Tomás submitted. "Hijo, if they shoot me, I present heaven with a clean face. Meanwhile I must make preparations. Give me the keys to the van."

He stood up and tossed a folded xeroxed paper and a fifty peso bill onto the table. The money had been devalued and Frank wasn't clear on the change, but Tomás had it down pat. "Take care of yourself, m'ijo." He strode out the door and vanished.

Next week Frank would drive the van up to Monterrey, a damn long trip. The van needed new tires, and a fresh paint job. It had been seen too many times.

Zapatista Army of National Liberation
Mexico, September 1 of 1996

To: Mister Ernesto Zedillo Ponce de Leon

Mister Zedillo:

I have just finished listening to your second State of the Union address. We waited, uselessly, for some sign of your serious disposition to achieve peace. In fact, your speech was even further from what you declared on television on the 30th of August, 1996, and very close to the speech you made on February 5th of 1995, which preceded your betrayal of that year. Perhaps those advisors who approved the military solution of 1995 have returned to your side. Perhaps they never left. In any case, what they advised you to do in those days, and what they now repeat to you, does not consider the progress of this country, but its complete decomposition. Will you listen to them again?

We do not want power nor your position. What is more we do not care if you sit there, the PRI, the PAN, the PRD or the PT or the ERP-PRDP. We will nevertheless struggle for democracy, liberty and justice.

The delegation which you have sent to represent you at the dialogue of San Andres has treated our indigenous leaders with racism, discrimination and arrogance, it has done everything possible to impede the dialogue and to avoid any real solutions, it has not made any serious proposals to make agreements, and those which have been made have not been carried out. Its delegation has managed to achieve a new failure which is very likely definite at San Andres. Our people cannot continue in this dialogue which has been imposed by your messengers. We are willing to seek peace, but not the peace your delegation seeks. Our peace is another peace; one of which we and our children may be proud.

If you were unaware of this and if you really want a just and dignified solution, as we do, then do something. If you already knew this and in fact this was your strategy in order to wait for the opportune moment for the military solution, well, too bad. It seems you have achieved the terror your were seeking, and surely, you believe that you have in your favor the national and international opinion necessary to attack the Zapatistas. If this is so, then we will see one another in hell.

Vale. Health and a good trip to Bolivia. They say there are still people who believe Ché was killed there.

Subcomandante Insurgente Marcos.

P.S. If we are neither delinquents nor terrorists, then why are the alleged Zapatistas sentenced as though they were delinquents?

4

Emily Reports

The reason she got the job was that no-one else wanted to go. Most of the members of Mutual Community, a small not-for-profit, were middle-class and upper, Classical Anarchist devotees of Kropotkin; in their non-political lives professors, yoga teachers, researchers, dentists, and poets. Political trips had to be hired out; the members were busy in the US supporting their families

Emily, who had no political viewpoint of her own, faked it. She offered to go down to Mexico to write a feature article on the rebellion, per word, per photo. Her new employer knew the Zapatista rebellion was big, BIG, because it was the epitome of local organizing and local home rule, a war on the federal government that, without consulting the people, had signed Mexico onto NAFTA. Furthermore, the putative Zapatista leader Marcos had come around from a Marxist position—a feather for communitarian anarchists. As the news reports on actions came in from the hard-pressed indigenous communities, Mutual Community members shot their own e-mails back and forth. Suddenly they were seeing the real thing, real autonomous self-government!—or they would be, if they were in Chiapas.

So Emily was hired and dispatched to Chiapas to report on the progress of the rebellion. It was her first real paying job, no small thing for a woman of forty.

Danger, at this peaceful moment in the neighboring state of Oaxaca, seemed remote. How dangerous could it be, staying in a hotel with a private bath and hot running water?

In the internet café Emily pulled off her bush hat and ran her hand over her cropped hair. It was cool, still feeling like freedom after two months, and she didn't regret the ragged look which resulted from pulling hair away from her head and chopping new growth with manicure scissors. She had performed the operation twice, standing alone outdoors. Her blond hairs fell to the ground and moved slightly in the breeze. Maybe birds would use them for their nests. That pleased her, that small contribution. For herself, the idea was to have no bother—not from her hairdo and not from men.

She wondered if she even looked a little dyke. Without a mirror, she smiled at herself. She carried the ineffable self-satisfaction of a pretty blond blue-eyed woman. Beauty was her birthright.

But not now, she scolded herself. She pulled her elbows in close to her body, leaving the coffee to cool. Now was a time to flee. Men were a drag. At least, David was a drag. She didn't like being dragged on, and she had gotten out. Not in a kindly way. Men weren't kindly, in her experience. Nor reliable. Nor calm. Nor steady. Nor brave. Well, she could go on forever complaining. Instead, she left him. Wisely so, her friends told her. Urgently, her thrice-married mother told her, it's not a good situation for you. You should get out. Do something on your own.

The computer was set up on a tiny internet desk, one of four lined up in the café window overlooking the courtyard. The location was bad for light, it jumped on and off the screen as the sun passed. She stared at her text. She was no writer. Nor do-gooder, nor wife, nor divorcee, nor orphan nor fish nor fowl. She was tired, is what she was.

This escape was a brazen gesture. She was away from David's determination to make piles of money, and away from her mother's exhortations. She was away from the quizzical gaze of friends asking her if she was okay, as if a divorce were unusual or difficult. It was done every day, wasn't it.

She settled herself on the hard wood chair and faced the screen.

David supported NAFTA, free trade, oil drilling in the Mexican bio-reserves, anything that pushed stocks upward. I'm not opposed to NAFTA, Emily thought remorsefully as her fingers began to push out text. She didn't know what NAFTA actually involved, and had to pretend. On this trip she was a fake. She was a tourist to a rebellion. A half-assed fraud pretending to work for a half-assed organization of half-assed left-wing anarchists pretending to implement half-assed calls for political action on behalf of half-assed causes.

She typed:

THE MUTUAL COMMUNITY NEWSLETTER
MEXICO IN TURMOIL: Summer of 1996
By Emily Halliday

Two and a half years after the Zapatista armed uprising, Subcomandante Marcos and the EZLN invited to the Lacandon selva those willing to rally to his call for justice. Thousands answered. They came to the southern state of Chiapas, bordering on Guatemala, by plane, bus and by peace caravan.

Your reporter met up with them in this small city of San Cristóbal de Las Casas, founded by the Spanish conquistadores. The FZLN opened an office in the city to register attendees. With a press credential I was able to attend the Encuentro Inter-Continental por la Humanidad y Contra el Neoliberalismo: an Intercontinental Meeting on behalf of Humanity and Against Neoliberalism.

My assignment as your Mutual Community reporter and representative was to connect with the grassroots activism and rebellion in Chiapas, and distribute the contribution the generous donors like yourself entrusted to the Mutual Community Mexican Project. Our contribution was withdrawn in cash from the local ATM using the Mutual Community bank card, to avoid questions. I carried a packet of pesos, neatly folded into a plastic pouch and taped to my midriff beneath my shirt. The precaution may have been unnecessary, since I saw no theft, and I doubt the idealism of the occasion would have allowed any in the poverty-stricken communities.

It's the rainy season here in southern Mexico. Thousands of Mexicans arrived in the soaked, tiny and impoverished indigenous settlements in the Lacandon jungle. The Aguascalientes, as all such Zapatista meetings are now called, were staged in Oventic, La Realidad, La Garrucha, and Roberto Darrios. These are tiny villages whose occupants accepted the task of hosting conferences to discuss solutions to political and economic injustice, cultural and environmental destruction, and social issues such as indigenous and women's rights. The villagers built wooden shacks with tin roofs to house and feed their guests. Food and potable water were brought in by the outsiders. Individuals like myself carried bags of rice and cornmeal.

I was able to travel by van in a caravan to La Garrrucha, where I met with town leaders and quietly delivered our much-needed gift. You can be sure it was appreciated, and I was asked to forward hearty thanks to all of you. The spirit of joy and determined hope prevailed despite mud, fleas, scarce drinking water, and desperately inadequate latrines. It is an honor to have participated, if only as a delivery agent and reporter. The results of the discussions are being published by the EZLN, and will appear in the next newsletter.

Back in the small city of San Cristóbal de Las Casas, foreigners fill the streets, buying bright embroidered placemats, Marcos and Ramona dolls, woven bracelets, and getting their boots polished by boys who roam abroad at all hours. The people are very poor, and the Mexican PRI (Partido Revolucionario Institucional), the world's longest-ruling political governing party, is in deep trouble, along with the Mexican economy. The news my fellow reporters are sending, even now as I write, is highly critical of the governor of Chiapas and of Mexican President Zedillo as well.

The state of Chiapas is buried in federal military barracks and circled with blockades. The soldiers and police harass foreigners and expel foreign Encuentro participants. I left voluntarily, I hope to return soon.

She paused. This was her first paid assignment, and dimly she suspected that skill-wise, she was still back in college writing for freshman comp. Irritably she tapped the plastic side of the keyboard in front of the rented computer. She wasn't sure what tack she was sailing on, and the article was too wordy, scattered. Minutes ago she sat herself down to do some words for dollars; now she doubted. She doubted the minuscule Mutual Community would print a lengthy piece in the six-page portfolio that passed for a newsletter, mailed to 3,000 anarchists who oppose top-down government.

Bird cries floated through the open window from the patio. Momentarily she enjoyed an unusual awareness of nature. She pressed her back against the wooden ladder of the chair. Lucky if she didn't get splinters in her ass.

That's not fair, Emily's mind returned to the rebellion. A war isn't trivial. It's more than opposing a corrupt government. Desperate campesinos armed with wooden sticks and a few rifles, against the Mexican Government—that was downright personal.

To leave Chiapas I traveled to the airport with a private family who had been recruited by our own Mutual Community to provide not just a ride but protection. Sure enough, we were stopped at three military blockades. While I sat silently in the back seat between a pregnant mother and a nervous teenager, the middle-aged driver identified himself as a Chiapas resident going with his family to Mexico City for vacation. We were not detained. At the airport the "family" immediately vanished, leaving me in the tiny airport to resume my disguise as an American tourist. I had put my notes into my backpack, along with camera and film, to be as inconspicuous as possible. Military officers were eyeballing everyone's passports and making mysterious notes on official pads. I was glad when I was aboard the tiny plane and on my way. I hope to return to Chiapas to learn more soon.

Emily did look like an American tourist. She was still wearing her obviously American expensive leather boots, and remembering mud and lizards, dog shit and garbage, she wasn't planning to give them up. The bush-hat with an Australian style brim and chin-strap, usually clinging to the nape of her neck, was resting where she tossed it on top of her backpack on the floor. Both items had been purchased in a last minute frenzy from a travel outfit on Newbury Street, at outrageous prices. They were her mother's going away gift, as if she were heading off to college all over again, instead of to a remote third world corner in a foreign country.

She logged onto MCMC.net and sent off her article with the digital camera's photos attached. She paid the ten pesos fee, took her disk, and returned along the high sidewalks to her hotel.

Oaxaca wasn't so bad. It was shabby and showed signs of decay and rebuilding, an ongoing life-cycle of adobe and cement, a certain enduring vitality. Along the street the iron gates hid mysterious patios and interior lives she could only guess at.

Arrived in her room behind the flower-filled patio of Hotel Los Pajaritos, Emily could hear the fountain, running like a quiet commentary on the rain. She heard the laughter of other guests ducking under eaves, the opening and closing of doors in a room next to hers.

She had another week to investigate Oaxaca's communities where the old traditions still survived legally in autonomous communities. She could gather enough to satisfy Mr. Mutual Community, Terry Kingpin. Then she could deliver another wad of her earned pesos to buy her flight back to Boston. To confront David and the divorce lawyers. All she wanted was out, no alimony or settlement. Just out. She closed her eyes and then opened them. No use wallowing. It was time to stretch her legs. She pulled on her hat and left her backpack.

Hardly thinking, she walked a few blocks along the dried streets. Oaxaca was arid, puddles didn't linger. With no destination in mind she arrived at the vast abastos, a market area which sold food and shoes and mattresses and more herbs than she could name. She skirted it, and saw adjacent to it the second-class bus terminal. She crossed against the traffic, dodging the stream of rickety buses, and entered the concrete patio. Inside the open doors loomed a shabby room lined with ticket sellers behind wooden counters. What strange destinations, names she never heard of, and couldn't pronounce. Strange places toward the east, toward the south, toward Chiapas. She walked the long hollow building, reading off destinations. At each gate people sat waiting, carrying bundles and boxes tied in twine. They were brown skinned, normal looking, dressed in the cheap washed clothing so common in the poorer areas. They were all going. Where? To start life fresh, like a newborn motherless child? To meet with their families? To return home? Ah, but she had no home. Home is where you hang your head. She wasn't going to do any more head hanging. Been there, done that. No more. Ya basta, to feeling inadequate.

Emily, clearly American with her pale skin, jeans and cropped head, strolled down the long cement walkway, past ticket area after ticket area, ramshackle booths with hand-painted signs. Beyond the glass doors she could glimpse the huge station yard filled with shabby vehicles that looked dented and cast-off, like school buses from a decade ago. Men were shoving bags and boxes into the belly of a bus. At another, they carried their bundles on board, lifting the containers above their heads like refugees wading a river. Women carried children, bundles, suitcases, boxes, plastic shopping bags tied with rope. Emily wanted to take her seat in the ripped dusty interior. She wanted to belong to the crowd, assimilated into a long journey, discovering unknown territory dangerous and brilliant with sun and flowers.

Somehow a decision took hold of her, reached out like a magic hand in a magic country seething with change. She could take it. She could negotiate later on, from the middle of her trip, for income from Mutual Community or from her mother. She didn't care which. Maybe she could freelance her articles or photos. It wasn't important which. The journey was important.

In her traveling mind she fantasized how she would drink orange Fanta and smile at the women, eat fruit from a bag, carry with her tortillas and peanuts and bananas, buy slices of mango through the bus window. Her backpack was still at the hotel. A ticket, a few phone calls, clean underwear. Standing in the station she was already long gone.

Two days later Emily checked into a small hotel in San Cristóbal in Chiapas. It tumbled through her mind that she was behaving strangely, or at least strange for her. She wasn't timid by nature, yet her whole life had been circumscribed by accepted actions—she went to school, did well, went to the university, did well but not terrific, took a year of graduate school and decided she'd rather get married. So then she and David went to Europe to the acceptable cities of London and Paris where they toured the museums and galleries, and then somehow she was thirty years old. No children. No children, David said, they cramp your style. It wasn't too big a sacrifice for her. The idea of committing her time to motherhood didn't appeal to her—never to go anywhere without leaving a number with the nanny, or taking along the screeching baby.

Mexico was a revelation that way. The women carried their babies and toddlers in cloth slings. She never heard a baby cry or a toddler fuss. Maybe the warmth of their mother's bodies kept them happy. Or maybe the warm milk on demand, anywhere any time. Emily gazed at those long brown nipples, and the infants hung like marsupials, sucking while at the same time they looked about at the world with their black eyes. Brown skinned children. Where were the brown skinned children in Boston? Some other neighborhood, she supposed. She never saw them.

Moreover the news articles about the rebels hinted at some—what would she call it, some world view? Some sense of desperation which said not only ya basta, this is as far as we go, but hinted also at some different way to look at the world. By this time, two and a half years into the rebellion, Marcos was always up a tree, for one thing. But that seemed right. Emily read and saved the communiqués:

Zapatista Army of National Liberation Mexico,
August 30, 1996
To: National and International Civil Society From: Sup Marcos

Madam:
I do not know if your remember us. We met in January of 1994. Since then we and you have tried to find one another, to speak with one another, and to listen to one another. It has not been easy,

surely. Many times instead of finding one another we lost one another. But... do you remember how on that January 12th you became fierce and imposed that cease-fire which now the government claims as "evidence of its political maturity?" Do you remember the dialogues in the Cathedral in San Cristóbal? The security cordons you formed. Yes! and the caravans. Then the delirium of that August 8th of the CND in the Guadalupe Tepeyac now occupied by the military. And later, in spite of the "mistakes of December" and the press campaign, you once again shook out everything in February of 1995 and sat the government down to a dialogue. Remember the consultation? Remember our response? Remember how we invited you later to sit at San Andres in the first table, the National Indigenous Forum and the rainbows painted on the floor? Even more recently, remember the American Continental Encounter, the second table, the special forum, and even more recently, the intergalactic encounter? Remember now? We are the Zapatistas. Has there been anything which we have promised you which we have not fulfilled?

...It is clear now that the difference between the Zapatistas and other political organizations is not the weapons or the ski-masks. What makes us different is our political proposal. Political organizations whether they be parties of the right, the center, the left or popular or revolutionary, seek power. Some through electoral means, others through lies and fraud, others through the armed struggle. One and another declare themselves to be our leadership and they invite us to follow them and support them in their hold on power, so they may renew or take it. One and another promise they will resolve our future to our satisfaction.

...We do not want others, more or less of the right, center or left to decide for us. We want to participate directly in the decisions which concern us, to control those who govern us, without regard to their political affiliation, and oblige them to "rule by obeying." We do not struggle to take power—we struggle for democracy, liberty, and justice. Our political proposal is the most radical in Mexico (perhaps in the world, but it is still too soon to say). It is so radical that all the traditional political spectrum (right, center left and those of one or the other extreme) criticize us and walk away from our delirium.

It is not our arms which make us radical; it is the new political practice which we propose and in which we are immersed with thousands of men and women in Mexico and the world: the construction of a political practice which does not seek the taking of power but the organization of society. Intellectual and political leadership, of all sizes, of the ultra right, of the right, the center, of the left and the ultra left, national and international criticize our proposal. We are so radical that we do not fit in the parameters of "modern political science." We are not bragging madam: we are pointing out the facts. Is there anything more radical than to propose to change the world? You know this because you share this dream with us, and because, though the truth be repeated, we dream it together.

Now they want to trap us in an alley that has no exit with dignity. They want us to accept the humiliation of the racists who disguise themselves as government delegates. They want us to accept alms and to continue as beggars. They want us to make a mockery of the dialogue and a pantomime of peace. They want us to accept the role of "good" against "bad." They want us to sell out. They want us to surrender. Who are they? They, madam, are the same ones who seek to deceive you daily and now promise terror and order in order to give tranquility to their financial markets.

Madam, do we not have reason to feel alone today? All those forces, political and social, the personalities and leaders, who accepted our invitation to construct together and in peace a new country, now walk without us and in other directions. Have we stopped being useful? So be it. At any rate we have the satisfaction of opening new spaces of discussion and thought in Mexico and in the world. It is not a small thing to achieve at the national and international level. And it has been made possible because of you, madam. Now our time runs out, but so be it.

However, you must continue. Do not believe those who offer conformity and fear. And do not forget, madam. Above all, do not forget.

It seems that now I remember that I owe you three definitions (or was it four). Errant knighthood sends me to pay the debts I owe, especially when the line of credit is low. So here they are:

Federales: The government has soldiers. The indigenous people have soldiers. The soldiers of the government have dark skin. The soldiers of the indigenous rebels have dark skin. They appear to be the same, the government soldiers and the armed indigenous. But the government soldiers fire towards the bottom, where our people are. The indigenous soldiers fire up above. Not to kill governments, they say. But to awaken history, they yell.

Jodidos: The most powerful of the powerful practice a strange democracy, the democracy of contempt. For them there are no Indians or mestizos, whites or browns. For the powerful, the others have only one name, the Jodidos [the screwed].

One: One is not always one. One is, sometimes, three: one is the one who left, one is the one who could be. One is, other times, what others want you to be. Today, one is none of these. In the tomorrow we dream, one will be one.

Done, then.

Forgive then, kind madam, if the letter contains some of those vulgarities which provoke despair in my literary critics (of which there are good ones) and in good revolutionaries. Seems that Olivio found a hole in his football and he insisted upon replacing it with that moon which travels up above without anyone caressing it. So I climbed to the ceiba, helped by the smoke of the pipe, and there above, trying to figure out how to reach it, it occurred to me that perhaps elsewhere someone else contemplated this full moon and then I understood that the moon, like tomorrow, belongs to no one and yet to everyone. This is what I yelled at Olivio, making signs from above. But it was useless because as I was climbing the ceiba, Olivio made off with some candies I had and ran off with the same ability as Carlos Salinas de Gortari. I tell you. I have always thought that child has the making of a president of the Republic, or at least of the brother of a President.

What was I saying? Oh yes! Olivio left and I remained stuck up here, smoking and waiting, dreaming that the other cloud up above, up higher, lie down with me in order to alleviate this desire and asphyxiation...

Then, madam, I will bother you no more. I only wanted to say what I have said before and remind you that we are here, that we are still the same, and that, I repeat, we are behind you.

Vale. Health and please know that in order to dance and make love only two are necessary and a little tune. The rest, believe me, is unnecessary decoration. By the way, will you give me this dance?

From the heights of some ceiba tree in the mountains of the Mexican southeast.

The Sup refusing to acknowledge that he doesn't know how to climb down.

(Translated by; Cecilia Rodriguez National Center for Democracy, Liberty and Justice.)

Just so. Emily didn't know how to climb down either. But who was this Marcos? He wrote to civil society, to her, and she understood. In her thirties Emily had been bored and took up writing short articles for nonprofit newsletters and occasionally the Boston Globe. David never said anything flattering. Really, why should he? She wasn't that good. She remembered from English classes that you're supposed to make an outline, but she was a little lazy and never did. She wrote as it came to her, which was, like her thoughts, superficial and scattered. If she wrote "tree" it meant tree. Of course she didn't admit that to herself. David informed her.

Then she bought an expensive camera and began to use it. That was a better medium for her, she had an eye for what made a photo, details and small facts framed by her lens. But by now David had nothing good to say on principle because he was busy getting rich, and the small jobs she got weren't pocket money for a woman who wanted hairstyling on Newbury Street and clothes from Neiman Marcus. She couldn't even lunch out on that income.

And then she was forty. She took a newborn kitten from a neighbor, and on second thought took a sibling so the first would have company. They were slender black animals like miniature panthers and pleasant to watch. She petted them and fed them and took photos and soon decided that animals were not her highest interest. The cats—by then they were cats—sharpened their claws on the upholstery in the living room. But she had decided on a divorce, so the upholstery didn't matter.

She'd been married eighteen years. And what she had to show for it was frayed upholstery and low self-esteem. A rich husband whom she hoped would get his ass kicked when the market collapsed. Threatened vanity that left a flat taste in her mouth. A lousy, not to say non-existent, sex life. Time to get gone.

And now she was gone, wasn't she? The translated open letter by Marcos sat on a table before her. It was addressed to her. She took out her pen.

San Gregorio, Chiapas, Mexico
c/o Estación Norte

July 10, 1996
Joseph Atwood, Esq.

Attorney at Law
73 Brockwood Plaza Suite 3
Boston, MA 02108

Dear Joe:

I will be touring and perhaps out of touch for a few weeks. Some of the time I'll be gathering info for Mutual Community, but I admit to also enrolling in the Witness Brigade, from which I hope to return safely! This is just to let you know I'll be somewhere in Chiapas.

The Mexican government has ruled that foreigners are not permitted to aid the local people in the rebellion or anything political. Look at them, yes; help them, no. Interesting attitude. I guess foreigners "help" by publicizing Human Rights violations, which are frequent, especially in Chiapas, although a couple of Human Rights lawyers were also murdered this month. Also "help" is something like building a school or giving medical care.

I think it might be a good idea to give you Power of Attorney, for my bank account or whatever, while I'm away. Better you than my mother, if you can swing it, Joe, e-mail me how we do it, because we've been friends a long time and I know with you everything will be confidential and really there's no point in worrying Mother.

The PRI, (ruling party here) has the peasants by the balls, to put it crudely. Go along or get no government money—no roads, no schools. So the Zapatistas basically said, Take your money and shove it. So there's a rebellion going on. That's my thumb-nail explanation!

I will be safe enough, but just in case, I put your name into my passport replacing David's. Hope you don't mind! If I get killed, my mother would rather hear it from you, I'm sure!

Affectionately,

Emily Halliday

PS. I'll bring you a Marcos tee-shirt when I return, you'll love it.

She smoothed her backpack as if the bulging pockets were flaws in her new life. Then she located her small wash-bag for toothbrush and face cream, took it out and re-stuffed it into the top pocket to create another bulge. Now she liked the effect. Things were irregular; things were protruding. Like new nerve endings, like new brain bumps. She was meeting the van in an hour.

5

Constance and Harry Land in Chiapas

The flight emptied its passengers. Constance held onto the guardrail and made her way down the metal stairs onto the tarmac. Harry held her elbow as—blinded by the intense sun—they crossed toward the terminal, following dark shapes silhouetted ahead of them.

Inside the building they halted for a moment, standing quietly until their eyes identified the baggage claim, the ticket counters; identified the soldiers standing about in their khaki fatigues, pants tucked into boots, faces impassive, automatic weapons in hand.

"It's like this," Harry told her. "Wartime."

Constance remained silent. Her carry-on backpack slung over her shoulder immobilized her like a paperweight on a desktop. They had only one modest bag each to claim, having flown down with a minimum of clothing, knowing anything needed could be bought cheaply except for things that couldn't be found at all. She herself was clad rather ruggedly for a gray-haired woman, in hiking boots, jeans and tee-shirt. She was modestly proud that she was slender, and if her bosom had shrunk over time, at least she didn't attract unwanted attention. She was dressed for travel; she looked like a self-assured aging American, which she was, and she didn't pretend otherwise. Gray hair and minimum makeup, jeans and boots; here she stood.

She shifted her knapsack on her shoulders and wondered if she should be proud or afraid as the small black eyes of half a dozen young soldiers appraised the couple in their passage through passport check and baggage claim. They slung their bags out of the conveyor, and Harry took Connie's from her, although she protested briefly.

He liked to be courteous, as his mother had taught him long before opening a door for a woman became sexist. In fact, he was courteous by instinct. In this moment, as he surveyed the soldiers toting automatic weapons, he moved beyond courteous to protective. He had asked his wife if she wanted to go with him to Mexico without really explaining what it entailed. She read the news on the internet as he did, but life is not what one reads on a screen. He knew, having been in other third-world countries, and in other political trouble spots as well. Chiapas would not be exactly a vacation, nor just a job, although he would work. Something closer to a post-retirement adventure. Harry at sixty-five plus was in no mood to hang it up.

A fox-faced barefoot boy in ragged pants and shirt performed headstands in the middle of the halted traffic and was whirled from their sight. The van driver who met them at the airport had not lingered; he simply scoured the incoming passengers until he spotted them—a senior couple from America. After confirming, he grabbed Constance's bag and bullied them into the parking lot. The van was unmarked, a not too ancient vehicle, and Harry was glad both the driver, an older man with a full moustache, and the American-made van looked capable of getting them up to the city of San Cristóbal de Las Casas for their first stop en route to San Gregorio. An e-mail had come while they were still in Ann Arbor from a group called Estación Norte, informing Harry they would be met at the airport.

Harry didn't know the group or anybody in it. Their nonprofit mailings filled with news of the Zapatistas mysteriously began to arrive at their house. Why Estación Norte had been contacted to pick up the Skelbas at the airport he could guess; the request could have come only from the one source which expected them. He read their simple brochures: Estación supported the indigenous communities, recruited witnesses and peace observers, solicited funds for food and medicine. All a civilian NGO could do, they did. Picking them up at the airport was not tourist treatment. The brusque greeting and rapid departure were not tourist treatment either. No smiles and slapped shoulders. Their driver sat rigidly in front and insisted the two Americans sit in the back, looking and acting like visitors, Harry supposed. It was strictly against Mexican law to be politically involved in internal matters.

The slender Pan-American "highway" beyond the airport at Tuxtla Gutierrez ran past shacks of stucco, of wood, of naked adobe with thatch roofs, past barefoot women draped in plastic garbage bags against the sudden now torrential rain; barefoot women unprotected and stoic trudged along the wet road.

Constance, peering through the downpour, flexed her own back, now happily rid of the fifteen-pound knapsack. It was an old red bag, nylon and canvas, she toted on the cross-country hikes they used to take. Filled with self-admiration for their strength and durability they hiked in Nova Scotia, in Italy, and a few years ago in Wales. But not recently. The first twinges of arthritis in her knee appeared last year. These Indian women, who often looked six inches shorter than she, oblivious to the rain, toted bundled wood for home fires. Fifty pound loads they must be, held together with fiber rope, and tump lines across the forehead. She watched in awe.

The van climbed slowly toward the city along a narrow curved road. On each side, the mountains rose fiercely green, planted with corn on nearly vertical slopes. Those determined stalks, each one fit by hand into a rock-supported crevice, told Harry what he faced, bringing irrigation to mountainsides. Indigenous or poverty-stricken folks didn't own green flat fields. He peered upward through the water-streaked glass. Along the rim of the hillside at intervals of every few meters, tiny crèches stood. Each contained a cross and wilted wildflowers. A descanso, marking a death. Somebody who fell off his land, passed through Harry's mind. He sat quietly, letting the driver do his job. In truth, automobile accidents are more easily come by than subsistence, in a state like this. He took Connie's hand as they snaked ever higher, veering from one radical drop into space toward the next. She was staring fixedly ahead at the back of the seat.

"A little squeamish," she whispered. "I shouldn't have eaten those salted peanuts on the plane."

"It's the altitude. You'll hardly have time to get used to it. San Gregorio is in the Meseta Central. Lower by about three thousand feet. Just take it easy."

San Cristóbal snuggles into a dish nearly seven thousand feet high, a one-time lake-bed drained under the rule of the Spanish Conquistadores who ringed the city with churches on the high ground. To the American eyes of the Skelbas each city structure looked decayed, assaulted by earthquake, age, or arms. The cobblestone sidewalks, lined with walled houses of stucco and adobe, rose above the cobbled streets, leaving the van below the level where its doors could be opened. The gutters carried the brisk run-off from the rain away and down mysterious channels.

One of the dismaying contradictions of the city, Harry knew, is that no water storage facility existed, so that everyone purchased bottled water, or boiled faucet supplies where piped water was available, while the rain, as suddenly vanished as begun, drained away in minutes, just as the original lake did for the Spanish conquerors. On his first visit when he asked his San Cristóbal contact, Tonatín, why a reservoir system of purified water had not been engineered for the city at least, the Indian's shoulders went up and down. The government won't spend the money. There's no place to put a purification plant. There's no money to be made. Bottled water is a major business. But this is not our concern, Señor 'Arri. For us, it's water in the mountains. You come for help the mountain people, no?

They were passing a city street drying rapidly as they watched. Small brown people stepped around and over the remaining rivulets, passing into and out of a substantial stone church.

"Templo Carmen," the driver answered. "The place for the people's foro to discuss government reform."

"Oh, really?" Constance replied. "Here? Today?"

"All this week."

She wondered if Harry planned to come on this particular date. Irrigation? Agricultural improvements? Why had they been ferried here by Estación Norte's van, instead of simply taking the airport bus as other tourists did? Or a taxi? Constance had read the bulletins put out by Estación Norte. The organization tried to protect the Zapatistas from human rights violations, and shield the foreigners the government didn't want interfering or witnessing. The bulletins had been mailed to them, in fact. To their home in Ann Arbor. Delivered by their mail carrier like vacation brochures! Sad eyes and glorious mountains, Visit Beautiful Chiapas! Only of course they carried news of repression and military assassinations. She looked sharply at Harry. His shaved pink face remained expressionless. He brushed back his mop of curls with his right hand and stared straight ahead, avoiding her glance. To the driver he merely said, "Thank you."

They had arrived at their destination, another narrow cobbled street with anonymous stucco walls. Their Bed & Breakfast must be in a house dating from the days of the rich hacendados—the door in the long stuccoed wall was not metal but varnished gleaming wood. It would not be a Zapatista sympathizer living here taking in paying guests, more likely an old aristocrat gone to seed—people whose way of life had slipped from under their feet. Or dancing slippers. The information sent by the language school only read, "a lovely old Spanish Colonial Home," and the name of their hostess. It was better all around if they behaved like other tourists—it was sufficiently strange that they were here solo, without a tour group, what with the Zapatistas gathering in the city. But safely enrolled in a language school.

Pity the poor Mexican government, trying to be nice to the tourists while stomping on the activists who flooded Chiapas. Constance doubted that peace was on the agenda of the government, too much to lose. Constance, middle class and trained to be subservient to her man, voiced few questions and no complaints as the van entered the slow cobbled streets. She hid adventures inside her mind.

Harry, however, had years of practice being discreet, and wasn't worried about his ability to handle himself. As for Constance, he hadn't told her anything she might accidentally reveal about his task or his employers. Better to save that conversation for later.

Their driver rapped sharply with the wrought iron door knocker, and with their bags on the sidewalk, hastened back into the van and drove away. They stood waiting for the door to open.

6

Señora Gloria's in San Cristóbal

A slight black-thatched man in shorts ran down the center of the street, striding over the rough stones. He carried a hand-bell. It uttered a whanging sound, up and down, in disagreement with the runner's effortless even pace. None of his hair moved. Like an Olympic athlete, the runner raced onward, and clanged to signal the soon-to-arrive trash collection truck.

Trash and garbage magically appeared at curbside, in a variety of containers, exposing banana skins and mango peels and husks of corn. No shopkeeper or restaurateur or homeowner hurried to place at the curb a plastic bag with a neat wire twist. No trash bags. Constance, she of years of homemaking with plastic bags and plastic twists and plastic covers, watched while cans and buckets, fiber bags and cardboard boxes, were lifted and emptied.

That part of her life was over. She couldn't imagine her daughter Judith or even her son-in-law dealing with garbage. Garbage was no longer part of life in her America; it had vanished like slums as gentrification overwhelmed the city. A garbage disposal in every home.

She was strolling in San Cristóbal without Harry, a multicolored string bag over her shoulder, and her usual jeans softened by sandals that showed her small feet. Harry was off to discuss drainage and meters of pipe. He had told Constance rather briskly that he had to leave her at Señora Gloria's decayed house while he met with the leaders from Cuates de Santa Ana. They had come into San Cristóbal, Harry lied, as the place from where supplies could be ordered. A meeting to which his wife was not invited.

Quite all right, she had little interest in plumbing per se. This project involved all of Harry's skills—topographical and engineering and environmental. He wanted to use his training—well, fine. He wasn't too old to work, not at all. Harry's intermittent forays into confronting with hard facts government projects designed to make money for somebody's constituents had always left her with a slight tightening of her intestinal wall, as if to protect her innards against a blow. The tightness showed on her face, something observable happened to her facial lines from nose to chin, but then Harry wasn't all that observant. She said nothing on such occasions. Perhaps she felt some small guilt, that unlike herself, liberal Harry always thought in terms of forcing government reform, or at least municipal reforms. At least in the US.

Here it was the indigenous, and finally the Zapatistas' demands that he embraced. Offering some of his ability—why should that trouble her? Few, in Mexico at least, had his training. Ah, the difference was that Harry had given up on normal federal government bureaucracy. It simply couldn't be influenced by ordinary people without money. Probably nobody knew a top-notch American engineer was here to free-lance in Mexico, donating his services. The very method of Zapatista local self-government—that thrilled him. She smiled to herself as she realized Harry had privately embarked on a vast do-it-yourself project. Why not? Why wait for the government, especially in Mexico, to do anything? Anything they did do, they owned.

She thought only in terms of giving love. Of course love was never enough, not while people were brutalized and starving and excluded and et cetera. She knew all that. But somehow could not make the big picture part of her daily actions. She thought local. Curved tile covering the roofs. Pastel paints, looking more like postcards from Mexico than reality should look, covering the stucco-over-adobe walls with flat palettes of yellow, green and blue. In some streets the raw adobe, exposed from earthquake or age or perhaps never stuccoed, loomed rough as old sores. Bits of grass and twig, embedded in the baked bricks, stuck out like dead skin.

She strolled bemused through one street and then another, coming finally to conical thatched roofs, huts with dirt floors, horses, oxen, chicken in the yards. Women toting goods or babies on their backs, supporting the load with a rebozo tied around their shoulders. Graffiti spray-painted on the walls. PRI, PAN or EZLN. On all sides the slogans pleaded for peace: "FEDERAL TROOPS OUT, WE LOVE THE LAND", "WAR NO, NEGOTIATIONS YES."

The air burned dry on Connie's dry skin. The daily rain felt insufficient. It vanished almost instantly. She was thirsty again, all the time it seemed, as if her moisture evaporated faster than she could replace it, and she never needed to pee.

She turned back toward the center. It was wise to drink something, maybe have a bite of lunch. Her stomach wasn't yet ready for the heavy mid-afternoon meal, but something light might be nice. She wasn't afraid of eating at local places, and anyway, if you searched for a tourist level restaurant in San Cristóbal, you might search a long time.

She found a tiny café and sat at a sidewalk table inside its perimeter, under the overhang shade of the roof. The two oilcloth-covered tables nearby held no patrons. The owner, wearing a checkered apron tied with cords at her sides, took Connie's order for a refresco and a small lunch of beans and rice. Immediately children gathered like ants at a picnic table.

"Déme un peso," they whispered to her. "Tengo hambre." Give me a peso, I'm hungry.

She put into one small hand a warm tortilla from the basket at her table. The child smiled, the first smile Constance had seen among all these working children. Her heart lurched. The child folded the tortilla and tucked it out of sight inside her clothing. There was no way to guess who might eat it later on.

Resting her elbows on the clean oilcloth, Constance chewed slowly, wondering if there was something factual she could be learning about this strange city. She was a reader, an English major, a language teacher. She wasn't stupid, after all. Not that Harry ever implied. No. But she thought with her senses, her nerve-endings. She swallowed the last sweet drops from her bottle of soda and fished in her string bag for her coin purse. Finally she paid the check with a note too large. The owner sent another ragged child running down the street to locate someone with change while Constance waited, more or less patiently, trying to look interested in the brown-skinned scrawny children. But she was afraid of not understanding. It seemed to her that the minds of these kids were locked away from her, incomprehensible, as were the minds of most people she met. It troubled her, stretching her antennae in every direction, looking, listening, that still she scarcely understood. Secret lives swarmed around her, twisting like smoke. Yet clearly one kind word more to these children would lead her into an abyss of needs. She stood up to be ready to leave the moment the change came.

The child returned and the woman counted into Connie's dry,

outstretched palm, and re-counted, old pesos, new pesos, centavos. Finally Constance understood and turned to go. She peered from under the brim of her canvas hat to get her bearings on the street—they all looked somewhat alike, no shop windows, streets of stucco with metal or infrequent wood doors. Her sense of direction suffered, deprived of visual cues. She tried to remember from which direction she had come, and gazed hopefully into the sky for the sun. But she wasn't sure what time of day it was, or where the sun would be in this part of the world.

Then as she lowered her gaze from the perfect blue sky, she saw men turning the corner a block away. One was Harry, she was quite sure. Most of the Indians were small and dark; the few who were tall had about them the vertical look of flat boards. Unlike Harry, they had no asses. Tiny asses, short legs. Harry was built with longer legs, and ample buttocks. Not fat. Used muscle. These men stored nothing on their bones. They wore the stiff cream-colored hats Constance designated as cowboy-with-starch. Harry's baseball cap with its clown fringe of gray curls bobbed above them, and his rounded body was revealed in unmistakable American jeans.

She glimpsed briefly how he bent toward the smaller man at his side; perhaps the driver with the moustache who had brought them into the city? But then three others interrupted her line of view. As they turned out of sight, she hesitated, and then walked quickly away in the opposite direction. She would die rather than let Harry think she was keeping tabs on what he was doing.

And what was he doing? Constance absorbed the scene. San Cris was well-sprinkled with Americans, French, Italians, Germans—not all of them university age. Some were older, grimmer, shouldering their backpacks not as advertisements but as carriers. They seemed purposeful, moving toward a destination, while she was not. Harry? Sure. But what purpose—these others weren't here to engineer water.

Something called them to rush to a strange land to defend the rights of indigenous people. She pictured a floating blue globe with lines and pathways crisscrossing, traipsing feet of refugees and tramping feet of soldiers and struggling feet of laborers and feet in sneakers and boots rushing to aid. All over the world people rushed across oceans and continents to engage in battle far off. Who stayed home these days?

Worse, none of them appeared to be wandering, as she was. This was not a place for idle window shopping or dog walking or caring for children at the playground. Observing their determined pace, Constance imagined secret motives held like birds within cages.

She walked another block and turned back. Almost anybody could tell her in what direction the zócalo lay, or the cathedral. From there she could easily find her way back to the Señora's. She doubted anyone from that house was taking part in the forum to discuss the future of Mexico.

7

Merwin Meets Mexico

He walked through an outlying neighborhood Sunday at noon. Vendors of cheap clothing and sticky discarded soda bottles cluttered the streets. Families coming out of church looked hungry, anxious for comida. Each family sailed along like a self-contained boat, Papa, Mama and the children dressed for church. And the smallest girl, the little princess, black hair pulled high and tied with ribbon. She toddled past Merwin in her white satin ankle-length dress. The ruffled tiers bounced, wider side-to-side than front-to-back. Beneath the dress he could see tiny ankles encased in stockings, and shiny patent leather shoes. The child carried a little beaded purse.

The scene struck him with a strange force. El Paso on a Sunday morning in the barrio, where he had made his own first communion. His mother didn't especially believe; she thought generally the saints and the church and the priests had robbed them more than helped. Robbed them of the ability and will to protest, their freedom to deny poverty, to refuse the gifts of candles and flowers and incense. His mother carried on a dual life, Merwin realized. She had gone through the motions with each child, just in case. But the case was not that the church might provide heavenly salvation. No, the case was if her children failed to escape from the Chicano neighborhood. In that case they would need their birth credentials, because it was a tight community after all.

But he had so thoroughly escaped with his eastern education that now he immediately recognized the Spanish Royal Infanta portrayed by Goya come to life, complete to the last bit of fake lace. But no beribboned lap dog trotted alongside this Infanta. Only gaunt-ribbed gangs of unwanted dogs roamed the unpaved alleys.

Then where did he, an American, belong? Merwin had no doubt he was American. He knew his birth country's prejudice. Merwin's ancestors were Catholic for three hundred years before his grandmother made her way north on her own, in 1929. She accepted the "Americanization" programs of Protestant missionaries, learned to sew and cook and show up for work every day on time. But she never relinquished her private faith, a mix of inherited gods, heroes, saints, superstitions, and her privilege to believe or abstain from belief. She married a Mexican who had come like her to find work on the other side, and by the time her daughter was born the Mexican population in El Paso was more than 68,000. Merwin's mother completed eighth grade at the Protestant missionary school and went to work in a tortilla factory. Spanish in Segundo Barrio, Merwin's neighborhood, was spoken more than English.

His family never left the barrio, but by the time Merwin was born, the women—his mother, sisters and aunt—knew it was time to educate a boy. Catholic was just a part of living in the barrio. His father, Raúl Jimenez Flores agreed. They encouraged Merwin to read and speak English instead of Spanish, although his grandmother taught him the old language. Even in America at a time when racial incidents were common, for them "race" was not a lifelong mark based on physical birth features. "Race," as they had brought with them from Mexico, was a different construct altogether; it meant "Mexican," the true people of Mexico, la raza. Those indios in Mexico who did not intermarry or assimilate remained the subordinate class. But if they chose at any time to join "mainstream" Mexico by speaking Spanish and accepting the colonial heritage, neither skin color nor appearance threw up a major obstacle. The obstacle was acculturation.

From that, the Jiménez parents generalized, Merwin must be American, look and sound American, stride along the streets with the careless self-confidence of American boys, know how to play baseball and even to swim. And be educated. The brown skin would take on inconsequence.

But they also wanted him to have the option of moving between all worlds. What if his destiny was to marry a Chicana? Or live in Mexico or even Spain? His mother's dream for all five of her children was options, choices. She herself had never crossed to the South. Knowing the Chicana culture was not Mexican, knowing that she spoke a different kind of Spanish, Spanglish the kids called it, she was a little afraid she would not know how to act or speak in the Michoacán countryside from which her mother had emigrated. She dreamed of a trip to her mother's home, but neither she nor her husband really expected to go, despite cheap airfare and easy access with American passports.

Merwin, schooled in the old language and ways by his grandmother, would know how to speak and understand, and as he moved further from his family, to high school and university and graduate school in the East, she gave him nothing but praise. Of the others, two girls finished college also. You have choices, his mother told them, the family remains here for you, but you have choices. His father nodded. Merwin knew that the wonderful American freedom was nothing more than having choices open to you.

He shed his Texas accent in graduate school. The prejudices of the educated did not permit it. He owned no Texas oil wells, he carried the double handicap of appearing Mexican and having a Mexican surname. His given name of Merwin confused people, but then made them think perhaps he was some European mixture. His mother chose the name from a baby book. Second generation American! Why not?

In Mexico, Merwin understood, just as in the United States, many indios keep themselves intact by clinging to remnants of their destroyed cultures. But the price! They remain unassimilated, the others—the conquered. The losers.

In Mexico City, the biggest city in the world, Merwin saw the visible price paid for assimilation—alienation, loss of language and customs. But which was preferable? It came to choices again, didn't it. That people could choose without being punished, could remain in their indigenous culture without marginalization, could be accepted if they so chose, without discrimination—that was a goal! It could be simple—but nothing in society is simple. Being in Mexico City felt like riding a tornado. One is swept along like wind and debris. To stay on one's feet is a triumph.

Clearly the many indigenous people who had previously moved to Mexico in search of work also stayed on their feet, but as they hustled to their street stalls and called out to him to buy, Merwin could see they were often marginal. In some other neighborhood some were assimilated, some became established residents as Mexico DF grew. Spread over miles of land and water, they must be an active part of Civil Society, serving a double duty: first as citizens of Mexico, and second as carriers of the memory of what it meant to be a rural Indian.

Merwin had applied for a grant to do his postgraduate work in Mexico. Bilingual, PhD., Mexican surname—it was something of a cheat to put on the line for "race," Hispanic. He was but he wasn't, and he took advantage of the simple blank lines with their simple questions. Nobody asked him to explain his life story and he never volunteered it. Hardly any member of the Harvard Graduate Committee knew that Mexican women had been coming to work in the United States since the beginning of the century. They knew only that UNESCO's World Heritage Committee for Cultural Patrimony would be happy with a Harvard scholar in Mexico. And so it happened.

He arrived from Cambridge with distinct culture shock. Neither Boston nor El Paso prepared him for the size of Mexico City; three hours away from his largely rural home state, it was a massive volatile city where protesters were Mexican workers and rocks flew.

On his grant money he had booked into a cheap tourist hotel serving bland tourist/Mex food brought by waiters who clearly favored blondes. Not a warm tortilla came to the table; none were on the menu. The shower was hot, the soap and towels white, the carpet free of mildew. It was more American than Mexican.

In the morning, dressed casually in his usual chinos and sneakers, he left the hotel to find the real Mexico. That first day he counted six public demonstrations, four of them blocking streets to traffic, one in the Zócalo, another on a sidewalk in front of a closed printing shop spilling into the narrow street. Espacios de ingobernabilidad were carved out everywhere. Go for that in the US—if the cops didn't kill you, the taxi drivers would.

Booths of vendors located on the sidewalk in front of the church. Enormous black market bazaars sold used car parts and sex videos, stretching back a block deep into empty lots. Behind their makeshift display tables, the street vendors stashed their arms to prevent entry of the federal police. The streets themselves seemed to move, young guys with greased hair, gays and lesbians, middle class women with plastic shopping bags, students, prostitutes, evangelicals.

He loved it. This was options made fierce, because the choice was either make your way or starve. Mexico spoke to him of an energy he had not seen in his Mexican-American life in El Paso; and never in the polite streets around Harvard Square.

At the kiosk on the street near his hotel he picked up an American newspaper and read:

LA Immigrant Strikers Target Mexico's Tortilla King (Pacific News Service)

Merwin was amused and horrified. The story reported that a Mexican firm turned on its head the classic NAFTA symbol of the U.S. plant moving south in search of low wages by moving north, and it became the world's largest tortilla producer in the process. Then the fact: the company's delivery drivers routinely put in 60 to 80 hours a week. Paid piece rate with no overtime, they earned an average of $180 per week, sometimes as little as $108.

The story continued. The Tortilla King was the U.S. arm of a deep pocketed Mexican monopoly with extensive ties to that country's ruling elite, including the current Mexican president and his predecessor. At its largest and newest U.S. plant, 50 assembly lines and 1,200 workers worked to supply tortillas to the U.S. Army, as well as a number of fast food chains, including Pollo Loco, Taco Bell, Del Taco and Carl's Jr.

No small storefronts there, thought Merwin. The Los Angeles Manufacturing Action Project supported the strike. Merwin's parents were among the 25,000 workers nationwide producing the two and a half billion dollars worth of tortillas each year. Merwin thought of calling his father and didn't. They lived in El Paso, after all, and his father was a shop steward. If there was trouble, his father would know how to act. Locally. The big picture, of corruption and government payoffs, the elimination of small producers and the occasional murder—that was all beyond their sphere. The flight of President Carlos Salinas after Zedillo took office, aboard the jet belonging to this same Mexican corporate tortilla honcho, was outside their sphere. But maybe they would learn later—after all, unionization of undocumented as well as legal workers like themselves was becoming common—they might come to broaden their grasp.

Well, damn his righteousness, the implied criticism of his parents! Speaking of broadening! On the same page, he read about the Zapatista rebellion in the southernmost state of Chiapas. Real indios, of flesh and blood, belonging to one of the 56 authentic pueblos who live in Mexico, unnoticed by the national institutions, began an armed rebellion last year on January 1, to proclaim Ya Basta and their opposition to NAFTA. The UNESCO guidelines Merwin had received mentioned the Zapatistas only in a tourist warning, two lines to a rebellion.

This article reported that the government's tactics against the rebels were to reduce everything to local questions, and then publish abstract declarations. Merwin struggled briefly to get a grip on these two sides of NAFTA, two related presentations. But he was on a bench, among a throng of taxis and pedestrians, of police waving and children running.

Merwin shook his head. After eleven days of the Zapatista rebellion, he read, a cease-fire had been declared. Then the San Andrés Accords were negotiated between the Zapatistas and a committee appointed by Congress, to bring the rebellion to a peaceful conclusion. He understood that much, and the Mexican Government's policy: Negotiate first and deny afterward. Some education he had. He was better at stone structures than social structures, for sure. But here he sat! How could he appreciate the architecture without understanding who created it?

Anyway, there was no doubt that for the Zapatistas and the indigenous people it was fight or go under—the options did not favor their side. Create a new option, then. Perhaps a new option was already forged, was waiting, like the hidden cities—Merwin embarrassed himself. He had strange new idealistic hopes for these people. Some tourists saw them as backward, uneducated, primitive—lots of pejorative words. Others saw them as racial purists. Merwin didn't like the constraints—there must be something else, but what, he didn't know.

The next three days were days of acclimation, unlimbering his traditional Mexican Spanish so long unused, learning new phrases, the slang, the music that blasted out of every shop. He was reading the Mexican newspapers daily now. He looked about with increased awareness of urban clothes, hair and lifestyle of the small middle-class in Mexico. An UNAM professor invited him to stop by and speak to a group of students about the Cultural Patrimony project. Remnants of the colonial culture in expressions like the right people to refer to people of white or wealthy families popped up thoughtlessly in the students' questions. Nevertheless they knew of the uprising. They knew the family secret of impoverished indigenous southern Mexico; they were surprised that Merwin knew also.

Merwin himself was surprised; he only learned a week ago! But he didn't say so. He fidgeted in a non-academic urge to be elsewhere. Looking around at the thin ascetic professor and serious young people his mind drew away toward the magnificent cathedrals soon to be re-gilded. He saw himself suspended in mid-air, floating, as if one of the statues of heralding angels had broken loose and leaped into space on another errand.

For two days more he strode about the city, recklessly using up his rolls of film to catch not the architecture, but the people sitting in the Zócalo drinking bottles of Coca-Cola. He went to see the mythic images: the bigger than life murals in the National Palace painted by Diego Rivera. Hanging astonished over the balcony railing, he ignored the depths below and above his slender body, ignored tourists, walked around a uniformed palace guard in earnest conversation with his girlfriend. He gazed up, dwarfed by the history of the Spanish conquests, torture and enslavement of the indios, the development of the industrial base, the faces of Stalin and Lenin like a thumb in your eye, and the Mexican revolution. The original Zapatista, Emiliano Zapata, in his sombrero and bandoleer: huge, muscular, brown, bigger than life, looked straight at Merwin who stared back.

Outside, in front of the palace, in front of the government buildings, vendors had set up the usual booths with crafts and plastic gadgets, and a group of "indigenous" dancers on the paved square were performing in feathers and leg bells, undeterred by the mild rain. In one corner of the plaza a woman sat on a stone bench, facing the impervious walls of the palace. Between her legs, a man kneeled on the pavement, speaking words Merwin could not hear. The woman was weeping, wrapped in the privacy of a public space.

Expanding on new unnamed emotions, both public and private like the woman's, Merwin paced through the streets. This was not a roots thing: that was bullshit. But the city itself, so vast, so mixed in colors, called to him. He went into an abastos and gratefully bought juice and water, inhaling the odors and even the colors into his lungs. Street vendors on the corners offered him cheap manufactured clothing and hair decorations. The most recognizable costume was that of the little girls traipsing from first communion dressed in the wide ruffled satin dresses painted by Francisco Goya. Nevertheless, Merwin knew the ancient Mexican people still lived.

He traveled south by bus, through the valley. In the distance, the mountains seemed magical, full of mystery; light and shadow created strange designs on their sides. The hills displayed an architecture Merwin had seen only in Colorado, hiding and revealing green and blue and yellow facets and forms. It was awesome.

In the countryside south of Puebla, the military roadblocks began. He showed his American passport and his UNESCO research visa. South. East. He changed busses, he slept fitfully. He could have paused and gone to a hotel. But he did not. Beyond the capital of Oaxaca the soldiers, young and impassive, demanded to search his duffel bag and knapsack. He kept his camera around his neck buttoned beneath his shirt. He bought mandarinos through the bus window, and tossed the peels out as the bus climbed the choppy road. The tart juice filled his mouth. He slept again as the bus carried him into Chiapas.

CIVILIAN PEACE CAMPS

San Cristóbal de Las Casas
"FRAY BARTOLOME de Las CASAS" Human Rights Center

Coordination of Non-governmental Organizations for Peace (CONPAZ)

Contents:
INTRODUCTION
OBJECTIVES
GUIDELINES
    I. for Coordination
    II. for the volunteers in the Civilian Peace Camps
    III. for the observers
    IV. Basic norms of behavior in the camps and the
    Indigenous communities (for volunteers and observers)
RECOMMENDATIONS

INTRODUCTION
    Since February 9th, with the initiation of the military offensive and the breakdown of dialogue, thousands of indigenous people in the areas which include the municipalities of Ocosingo, Las Margaritas and Altamirano, escaped to the mountains seeking refuge from the threats they felt with the presence of the Federal Army.
    The displaced people as well as those who have stayed in their communities have suffered a great deterioration in their health, because those who fled only took with them what they could take quickly and those who stayed in their towns have suffered the theft and destruction of much of their belongings, including their food reserves.
    Because of their severe health problems, some of the people displaced have started to return to their communities despite the frail security they feel because of the presence of the Federal Army. Up to now, there have been reports among the displaced people of children and pregnant women who

have died because of starvation and disease.

Despite the orders from the Supreme Commander of the Armed Forces of the country to stop the advance of the military troops and to limit their role to supporting the security of the population, the military continues advancing throughout the region and spreading fear and mistrust in their way.

As a response, many Mexican and foreign men and women have felt the need to act to stop the situation from worsening and ending in genocide through starvation and disease. For this reason a permanent civilian presence in the region is necessary and important at this moment.

We consider the installation of Civilian Peace Camps which are well coordinated, which can help the population in danger, which monitor the situation in different parts of the region and which in their development and in their hope for a peace with justice and dignity are supportive of the communities' own process, to be urgent and important.

OBJECTIVES

1. To open a civilian space that helps maintain hope and dignity and that helps reconstruct the communities while respecting their own dynamic, according to their self-determination.

2. To observe, give testimony and distribute information about the human rights violations that are carried out against the population.

3. To maintain a continuous flow of supplies and support to the communities until their means to produce for self-consumption are normalized and reestablished.

GUIDELINES
For Coordination

There is a process of coordination in San Cristóbal del Las Casas, Chiapas, in which the National Commission of Mediation (CONAI), the Human Rights Center "Fray Bartolome de Las Casas" and the Coordination of Non-Governmental Organizations (CONPAZ) participate. The two latter organizations will be responsible for the coordination of operations.

In order to have a pertinent and efficient effort the Coordinating body will have the following functions:

1. Register and accredit proposed participants in the Civilian Peace Camps, following the established criteria.

2. Establish the places where the Civilian Peace Camps will be installed.

3. Coordinate the supply distribution to the communities.

4. Determine the number of participants in each camp.

5. Schedule the visits of observers to the communities according to needs.

6. Based on reports from the camps, it will distribute information bulletins, denunciations, and urgent actions as they are needed.

7. Name the person responsible for each camp.

8. Provide needed support to volunteers and observers.

II. for the Volunteers in the Civilian Peace Camps.

The Volunteers in the Civilian Peace Camps will comply with the following requirements:

1. They will register in the Coordinating office, where non-transferable identification will be provided to be carried or worn during their stay in the Civilian Peace Camps.

2. They need to remain at least ten days in the camps.

3. They need to be adults.

4. They will have written recommendation from an institution or organization.

5. They will be responsible for their own expenses, such as transportation, housing and food during their stay.

6. They will follow these guidelines.

7. If they are foreigners they will be fluent in Spanish.

8. At the end of their stay in the Civilian Peace Camps they will produce a written report of their activities and of the situation they confronted, to be turned in to the Coordinating office.

9. They will distribute all public information to all possible media within their reach.

III. for the Observers.

The observers are those who:

1. will register in the Coordinating office, where non-transferable identification will be provided to be carried or worn during their stay in the Civilian Peace Camps.

2. will visit the Civilian Peace Camps for a maximum of two days.

3. will subject themselves to the internal regulations of the Civilian Peace Camps and follow the instructions of the person responsible for the camp.

4. will also respect the life, customs, and decisions of the community or communities they will visit.

5. will distribute all public information to all possible media within their reach.

IV. Basic norms of behavior in the Camps and the Indigenous Communities. (for volunteers and observers)

1. To always respect the customs and daily life of the community.

2. Not to consume any kind of drugs or alcohol.

3. The person responsible for the Camp will deal with communications between the community(ies) and the observers and volunteers.

4. All the decisions in the Civilian Peace Camps will be taken as a group with the guidance and approval of the person responsible for said camp.

5. Not to respond or start any type of provocation.

6. Not to leave garbage in the Civilian Peace Camps and to try not to contaminate the environment.

7. Not to make promises of material help that could create false expectations in the people.

8. Any failure to comply with the regulations will be cause for expulsion from the Civilian Peace Camps and will be reported to the organization which provided the recommendation of the participant.

General Recommendations

1. Each volunteer and observer group will be responsible for taking all

that is needed for their stay (food, medicines, clothing, sleeping bags, etc.)

2. To take necessary equipment to document their experience (tape recorder, video or photographic camera, paper and pen, etc.)

3. If they are foreign observers, to have a translator in their group if possible.

4. For volunteers: to provide a service or knowledge to the community during their stay (health, education, agriculture, construction, etc.)

5. Documents: It is always necessary to have your documents.

Mexicans: Voters' card, professional identification, etc.

Foreigners: Passport and immigration documents.

For Everybody: Identification from the Coordination. To provide two pictures. One for the identification and another one for the records.

Recommendations of things volunteers should bring:
2-3 changes of clothes
sleeping bag, blankets, or hammock
flashlight and batteries
boots (for hiking)
insect repellent
personal hygiene items
food utensils (not disposible)
garbage bags
towel
can opener
toilet paper
hat/sun covering item
biodegradeable soap
raincoat, sweater
water purifier
water canteen

Do not bring political books or materials or anything that looks like a weapon.

Rights and obligations of foreigners and nationals from the Constitution:

Article 1: In the Mexican United States all individuals will enjoy the guarantees that this Constitution provides, which cannot be restricted or suspended except in cases that are established in it.

Article 11: All people have the right to enter the Republic, leave, or travel through its territory and to change residence, without need of a security letter, passport, safe-conduct, or other similar requirements. The exercise of this right is subordinate to the faculties of the judicial authority, in cases of criminal or civil responsibility, and to the administrative authority regarding the limitations imposed by the immigration laws, and public health of the Republic, or about pernicious foreigners residing in the country.

As you may have noticed, in Mexico, foreigners have the same rights as Mexicans, regardless of their immigration status

Article 33: Foreigners have right to the guarantees provided in chapter I, first title, of the present Constitution (basic rights); but the Executive of the Union will have exclusive faculties to force the removal from the national territory, immediately and without previous trial, of any foreigner whose stay is considered inconvenient.

The foreigners will not, in any way, get involved in the political affairs of the country.

If you came into the country as a tourist, your immigration status is non-immigrant and the activities that you can do will be for recreation, health, or artistic, cultural, or sports related reasons without remuneration or profit.

Recommendations

If the authorities cite some articles as argument to sanction you, demand the full quotation and that they show you the book they are referring to.

Do not offer information, only show your documentation when you are requested to do so.

Issued by National Commission for Democracy in Mexico

Coordination in the USA

The National Commission for Democracy in Mexico will provide general coordination of this Peace Campaign in the United States. Please look for further information on the subject titled "US Chiapas Peace Brigades/ Camps" in the net. The coordinators will provide additional information and contacts. The project coordinators will provide coordination, so that each brigade member will have the same information. At the same time they will facilitate the contacts so brigade members can know about each other's presence in Chiapas, increasing support they can give to each other. Some members of the brigade may be asked to assume coordinating positions particularly in San Gregorio, where new people may need to be welcomed and guided.

Individuals and committees are encouraged to participate and communicate any interests and questions to the project coordinators..

8

In the Mountain

José carefully navigated the mud and gravel hanging to the rim of the mountain. This trip was bad. It was still the rainy season, early March. If he had no foreigners to bring in he would have come on foot with a burro. Below, the fog roiled and billowed, occasionally eating a piece of the road. The presence of foreigners was a protection. Better not lose any!

In the crowded van Emily was squeezed in the front jump seat between two men, rather like a child in a child's car seat. In the back seat, and in the rear on top of the spare tires and backpacks, their group slept in exhaustion. The fog was silent except for muffled sounds of water cascading down the precipices.

"Are you afraid?"

"No," she replied softly, so as not to project her voice out into the fog. "I was born beside the ocean. I understand fog. But the odor is different. Here, the fog smells of leaves and trees, not of the sea." She lapsed into silence.

He could not take his eyes off the road to glance at her. He could smell her along with the fog. It was an American smell, that he knew, not like his own Ana Luz. His wife had somehow smelled of cooking smoke, and underneath her clothes, the odor of the river. He missed her and their son in a deep remote part of his being toward which he refused to venture. A woman with an infant. Who kills like that? He couldn't absorb it, even yet.

Emily darted a glance at José's profile. Had she lied about her fear? Held upright as much by the confinement of the truck as by her will, she was indeed very alert. One failure of the roadbed could tumble them off the heaving side of the mountain. Estación Norte couldn't choose the easiest, safest roads; they threaded through hundreds of military posts. The shooting war was replaced by the dirty war. Así es. Light was fading. José kept the van moving around the flooded ruts and gullies and through the rivulets at a steady six kilometers per hour.

Emily was thinking, an activity that distanced her gut fear. This man has been driving non-stop for twelve hours and still he's steady. He hasn't tried to hurry. He hasn't pushed the van or the mountain. There have been accommodations, like a person with a long night's sleep ahead finds the fit of her body in the bed.

Weeks ago she had intended to return from Mexico to Boston with material for a photojournalism piece, something more literary than what Mutual Community would want, a magazine piece. Arty. Photographs of sacred mountains wreathed in fog. Dark-eyed children. She'd been accused by David of being arty, and she had wanted that accusation to become a source of real income, maybe a lifestyle. Pay off. As late as her bus ride from Oaxaca to Chiapas she had been thinking the same way.

And then something happened. Or maybe better to say, something penetrated. It wasn't a lifestyle, to live in dire killer-poverty in a war zone. To hold onto whatever hopes the leaders encouraged: better to die than live like this forever. Emily's photojournalism became futile, almost laughable. As pointless as telling a child about the ideas of the ancient Greeks. She had explored for six weeks in Chiapas, spent two weeks in Oaxaca visiting remote villages of the Sierra Juarez mountains and then the city, and finally returned impetuously to Chiapas, to present herself as a Witness. She had nothing to say.

Or if she did, it was Something Else, as yet unarticulated. She couldn't photograph any single truth that would reveal this nation, poised between revolution and repression, as they were now in their pale truck poised between the declivity below and the mountain above.

It was a simple fact that both in the USA and in Mexico, retention of privilege by and for the privileged was top priority. Tomás told her the US was sending money and military to suppress the rebellion, and she felt stupid, the only one who didn't know, in that briefing for Witnesses. But not everyone understood that Chiapas was haunted by a shadow. Neoliberalism could have nothing to do with a feudal economy of manual labor, a slave and master leftover, preserved by wealthy landowners. Tomás explained—the landowners themselves didn't get it—regardless of the Zapatistas, they were doomed by agribusiness, by machines, by the ability of the USA to produce. They thought they were fighting the campesinos' demand for land, and the Zapatistas' demand that indigenous people be included. But they were striking the wrong villain. Those old hacendados didn't know which side they should be on. Wait until the bioengineers produce frost-resistant bananas.

That was the kind of article somebody really sharp could do. She turned her head to gaze at José again. He was hidden from her by the darkness of his skin, by the darkness of the early mountain twilight, by his quiet face. He knew no English, and her Spanish served only in a child-like way. She wondered what he, what the indigenous people thought they were doing. "The other way," Tomás called it. But inside José's mind, what's that all about?

She wished she'd been trained for that kind of comprehensive insightful research. Not for faces and fog. Damn David's superiority. He'd taken the intellectual highroad and left her to do the arty-feely crap. It was crap. The world did not need more sentiment. It needed more hard analysis.

She stretched her cramped legs, and flexed her toes inside the boots. Water was falling from the mountain, down onto the road. It seemed to come from nowhere, some mysterious throat. Ahead of them the road narrowed even more. José halted the truck. He opened the cab door next to the mountain and disappeared, until Emily saw him reappear in front of the vehicle, testing his steps and eyeing the width of the road.

He shook his head.

Back in the cab of the truck he switched off the ignition. In the silence, he looked at Emily and then at the man beside her and twisted to see the sleeping forms in the rear. The man spoke in Spanish.

"This is as far as we go?"

José nodded. "Así es." That's how it is.

Panic heaved up into Emily's throat. They were fucking nowhere, on the side of a crumbling road too narrow for even one vehicle to pass safely. And if the water took more road, then what?

"So!" She hoped her voice sounded strong and not like a bird cry. "We stay here? Or walk out?"

"I go to get help," José was pulling his huipil, along with a machete and a flashlight, out of the knapsack he kept at his left knee. "First I find the community and then we decide how to bring everyone in safely." He peered again at the occupants of the van. "You should try to sleep, Emily." He pronounced her name Ay-Mee-lee. It took a long time for him to say it, his face serene and smooth as always. He spoke kindly, seriously. "Nothing bad will occur if you stay in the truck. If any need to make water, don't go on that side, go on this, don't go past where one can place a hand on the metal."

She nodded. Before the translation was completed he left, a small figure hugging the firmness of the fast-fading side of the mountain, walking into darkness. And then he vanished.

She stared into the shadows, hoping for the wink of his flashlight, but there was nothing. Next to her the fellow who had translated remarked, "I like the rasping of the crickets, don't you?"

Emily tried to smile. This fellow was all right, she felt no bad waves coming off him. In their group they were mostly Americans, some toting video cameras, two college kids with fake ratty Rastafarian dreadlocks. Two German guys. The social worker and this guy. Merwin. All of them here to do—what? Good deeds? Not likely. Witness. Learn and spread the news. They were the Zapatistas' links with the world. She herself, a self-proclaimed reporter. Ha ha. But even if they knew she was the most minimal of reporters, with the most minimal of audiences, they were gracious and willing. Like this José. Risking his life, really, for the likes of them! The indigenous people must think there's a whole lot more at stake than just international goodwill.

We're not the only ones here either, Emily knew. Thousands of foreigners were flocking to this struggle.

"What are you doing here?" Her question was so abrupt that for a moment Merwin had no idea how to answer.

"I'm on a post-doc grant," he finally responded. That didn't answer what or why. "Researching the archeological ruins?"

Emily had decided he wasn't going to say anything else when he added, "I want to be of some use. At least, stay on the right side. Pretty noble, eh?" He snorted, apparently laughing at himself.

Emily didn't laugh. She wondered if she was the only one of this group who wasn't touring the high indigenous communities for a reason; she meant a reason not selfish. She was selfish. She wanted only to be somewhere not in the same city with David and her mother, doing something different from what anyone expected of her. She was the only person here for herself.

Merwin added, "I don't have much of a political analysis, if that's what you're thinking."

"Me neither."

"But, for people not to get beat up on? Or destroyed to benefit the rich?" His profile, also darker than hers, gave away nothing. His black hair was covered with a baseball cap, the collar of his windbreaker lifted around his jaw.

Emily stared out the windshield. While they spoke the glass was accumulating a curtain, a muslin fog. She was frightened. How could she think anything under these circumstances? "So you think the rebellion is really against NAFTA? I mean, really?"

"Really, no. I think it's for local autonomy. Democratic politics plus sustainable economy equals a decent life. You know, they call it dignidad? Living in a community of mutual support."

She turned her head and in the darkness stared in his direction. So that was real? She shook her head and peered forward again. They were enclosed. No visibility beyond the cab, and the night was getting darker. In a moment they would be sitting in total blackness, the kind that comes when there is no light, nor any hope of light.

"I have a flashlight in my pack," Emily said. She recalled changing the batteries, but not the bulb. She hoped to hell it worked, and that her bladder would hold out.

"Have you any idea how far José has to go?" Merwin reached forward and tried to wipe the glass with his fist. It was useless. The moisture was on the outside.

"No. Maybe we should try to sleep." Emily doubted sleep would come. But carefully she closed her eyes, as if by closing them she would make the morning light come. Twelve hours to wait.

9

Harry Behind the Foro

Harry looked up. Instinctively his fingers doubled over the palms of his hands. Glass shards jutted from the cement walls surrounding certain houses, their windows were barred, dogs paced relentlessly in the courtyards.

He followed Tomás in rapid and effortless gait up a flight of stone stairs connecting one street to another, parallel and higher up the hill, and suddenly they were in the midst of a crowd outside one of the many small churches of San Cristóbal. Across the street from where they emerged stood a bank, a government building, a hotel and three clothing shops. Against the yellow church wall, beneath the frieze painted bright orange and white, a TV screen showed a video of a Zapatista in the famous ski mask, reading a prepared statement. No more a Mexico without us. About thirty people bunched on the sidewalk listening. A man held his black-eyed son on his shoulders. The first TV films of the Challenger explosion could not have been more riveting. Or maybe a war-room briefing, focused and silent. Juice on a hot wire flowed among the watching men, threaded a flower displayed in memory of the slain Zapatistas, ran across a small stand peddling Marcos tee-shirts and tapes, flowed over FZLN posters glued to the church walls proclaiming No necesitamos pedir permiso para ser libres: We don't need to ask permission to be free. Harry could feel the electricity, palpable, irrefutable.

On the bank's side of the square, on the sidewalk keeping vigil beneath the portico, sat other street vendors wearing handsome village blouses, embroidered on brilliant white or red fabric. All women. Rough wool wrap-around skirts were bound to their waists with red sashes. Tiny children alongside their mothers worked at the beads and threads. They were silent, those who nursed at their mothers' long brown breasts, those working, those who only sat and stared. Never see kids so quiet in the USA.

But the back of Harry's neck told him, they are all staring. Or staring through their elbows and hands, watching through their shoulders or ribs. The sense of alertness wasn't altered by the approach of some older children pleading, "Cómprelo, cómprelo," in wheedling voices.

He doubted they knew any more Spanish than this. "Buy it, buy it," importuned two tiny girls. They each carried over their skinny wrists woven bracelets and belts. One held in her fist ballpoint pens encased in gaudy woven cases. They were dressed in the same wool wrap skirts as the Tzotzil women, sized down. Over the skirt each wore a similar bright red blouse, once bright but now soiled and ragged. On their feet, nothing. Another held up for Harry's inspection onions tied in a bunch with banana leaf fibers. Ahead of them, roasted corn blackened on a brazier; a mother and daughter sat side by side on the sidewalk. The few men peddlers occupied an opposite corner, indolently crying out hamacas, hamacas!

They were all indigenous. That was the defining category.

The women weren't here to sell, they were here to listen and watch their men, watch out for the police and the military, the crowds of men with stones and sticks and maybe guns, who might descend from nowhere and begin a slaughter.

He unconsciously moved closer to Tomás. "Is this where you're taking me?"

"No, this is just the entrance," Tomás replied. "Further is the place."

Harry followed his three companions. They turned the corner of the church, and after a few yards came to a portal where the old wooden door stood open. Tomás stepped through. There was a pause, some low voices.

Pásale, spoke another voice from within. Obediently, Harry stepped in.

He was in a cobbled church patio. Several men perched on cut-off tree-trunks, their elbows on their knees. A few folding chairs surrounded a white square plastic table, and another table of wood, around which sat several men. These were the small Indians Harry was accustomed to, hatted in starched white hats and covered with huipiles despite the relative warmth of the day. He could glimpse beneath their huipiles shabby gabardine trousers, thin legs and sandal-clad feet. One man wore jeans and work boots. The leader, Harry supposed. He wondered what they made of him, his own solid girth, his leather boots.

The first to speak was a tiny man. His starched hat gave his head an outsized importance and his huipil lent bulk to his seated form. Only his feet showed his true size, a child's feet in sandals. His skin was dark, almost mahogany, and his hands upon the table showed black-rimmed fingernails.

He began to speak in Tzotil, at a deliberate pace. The man in jeans followed each sentence with a translation into Spanish.

Oh Christ, Harry thought. His Spanish was coming along, but in these situations with no outside clues he got lost. Tomás at his side began to translate from the Spanish into awkward English. Some words Harry could get on his own: soldados, soldiers, agua, water, muertos, the dead.

He settled down, hoping his face appeared courteous and interested. These were not the men who would discuss water pipes. Those would come later. This was the introduction.

Momentarily his cheek creased with pride. Hey, get this. At past retirement age, they treated him with respect, and clearly with respect came the need to make sure he understood what he was in for. What he was about to do was illegal. That implied the community was in resistance—it was therefore a political act upon which he would embark. Aiding and abetting. It didn't take a speech to make him understand the omnipresent troops. He was a foreigner. Other men would be delegated the official purchasers and owners, as indeed they would be. He would spend weeks isolated in the mountain village, or risk traveling back and forth to a city where telephones and internet existed. And where his woman could live safely. No one could foresee. Nothing was certain.

Harry had done his homework pretty well, he thought. He was not uninformed about the rebellion and its consequences. The militarization. The only piece he hadn't done was to offer a good explanation to Constance. He hadn't told her Cuates was in resistance. As a matter of fact, he had no real verification—the army hadn't showed up yet. The residents simply existed, as people did, minding their own business. Anyway, Constance was a good sport. She'd be fine once they had their own apartment in San Gregorio.

She knew he would be building an irrigation and water transport system. They often talked as old married couples, in shorthand. He trusted her to understand what he wanted. After the forced retirement, the golden downsizing. He would have offered to work for nothing if people did that in Michigan. But they didn't. To keep on keepin' on, he silently yearned. As usual, she agreed. The rest of it was his business, right?

He tried to sit quietly on the small wooden chair. Around him the other men sat motionless. Once in a while one would sigh softly, or lean forward with his elbows on his knees to roll a cigarette. They looked like good men—hard-working men.

Harry judged men by their willingness to work. He had no patience with goofing off, or with pretentiousness. He himself worked his ass off when he needed to. His arms, revealed by the short sleeves of his denim shirt, were brown and firm, despite the aged skin and stained hands. What he couldn't get his head around was how hard these men, these women, worked for nothing. To stay alive. How they managed to scrape up cash for the project, he could only guess— relatives in the United States, jobs in the northern maquiladoras, jobs on the southern coastal plantations—God knows. A peso at a time. If anything roused Harry's righteous indignation it was the idea of a man laboring for three dollars a day—and then getting kicked as a reward. It infuriated him, and he had worked overseas on US government contracts for big corporations, and for Middle East governments. He saw it everywhere.

He gazed around the quiet shielded patio. The church walls were gray stone, worn smooth along the height of a man by hundreds of years of hands. The speaker was winding down, and Harry tried to listen more carefully. They would soon be past the recounting of the decision-making process and onto the decision itself: Build it ourselves. We need water and the government will never bring in pipes, just as they never brought in electricity and we had to bring it ourselves, cutting into the high cables. Never brought clinics or schools or roads.

Now the community had declared itself better off without this bad government that steals and kills.

We do it, we own it, Harry interpreted. Right on. It might be the first time in the history of Mexico that indigenous workers would own what they created. Community property. Community use. Harry was only an engineer, only one man. Long after he was gone, they would have water piped down to their homes and clinic and school.

He was not a praying man, so he inhaled deeply and breathed out. A taking-in of the oxygen they all shared. It was agreed.

Tomás was heading back to Ocosingo and Harry would be on his own from now on. The Indian man he was introduced to on his first visit, Tonatín, would be his contact with the men of Cuates de Santa Ana, his employers.

Outside in the courtyard Harry shook Tomás' hand, and then Mexican style, returned the embrace offered by the old man. Old man! Jesus they were the same age. Not ready to go under. Hey, nobody here was ready to go under, although Harry knew if they must they would do it with calmness and that same dignidad so often mentioned.

10

Sweet Day

On August fourth the returnees from the Encuentro and a couple of hundred Chiapanecos, other Mexicans, and civil organizers mounted a brief march and demonstration in the San Cristóbal zócalo. This very same weekend, Señora Gloria told them, was the Feast of the Sweets, an annual event staged under the portico of the Government Palace.

Harry left the house early, hoping to catch sight in town of his contact, Tonatín. Probably hopeless. Those guys didn't hang around. If there were business they appeared as readily as the rain. If not, they were invisible. Harry watched their eyes when they came, and when they went. They held a message, but Harry was never sure he got it right.

Dozens of women stood behind a line of tables loaded with platters, bowls and panels of crude paper. After a minute of focusing, the clutter emerged as sugared fruits, sweet breads and cookies in all shapes, candied fig and candied pineapple and candied mango. The fruit was dark, as if sugar had burned away bright colors.

The municipal band began to thump and tootle. Harry spotted eight plain-clothes men huddled with their walkie-talkies in the square. The rally began to move like segments of a caterpillar, with participants crowded elbow to elbow, in all manner of outfits, tee shirts and shirts, jeans and sneakers, backpacks and baseball caps, many of them soiled and faded. Harry planted his sneakers and back against the wall of the bank building. Young foreign enthusiasts leaped up and down, shouting slogans and raising their fists in a spontaneous dance. Here and there Harry thought one of the young fellows was ill, with feverish cheeks and flopping hair. God knows where they had been the past week—jungle insects and diarrhea flitted across his mind. He had worked under jungle conditions only once, in Africa, and wouldn't do it again.

In the tall windows above the portico, government thugs disappeared and reappeared, flanked by armed police. Harry tried to memorize faces, or even bodies, but he could see only the automatic weapons clearly. The thugs snapped photos of the demonstrators, while the women below handed over cookies and made change for the few tourists and returnees from the selva. The crowd of women standing behind their tables of sweets—who was left to buy? Or maybe it didn't matter if anyone bought, it was a display, a display that masked some deeper current flowing through the town. They were in the midst of an armed rebellion, no less. The women waved their hands and aprons over the tables of buzzing candies, demonstrating that life goes on, rituals continue, history is far away. In similar manner the band struggled with its music. Beating to death an animal, is what Harry thought, as the tuba and drums reiterated the rhythm. It was not music but a social equivalent of music.

The march snaked around the small zócalo and returned. The accordion thumped. The tourists, several of whom seemed to be

American college girls carrying knapsacks and showing wrists adorned with braided thingies, licked their fingers sticky with honeyed squash and sweet cakes. The marchers shouted. They sang Zapatista songs. They chanted the chorus, "We go, we go, we go, we go onward to advance the struggle ahead, because the people are crying and they need the strength of the Zapatistas."

The sun beat down. After a week of rains, this was a fine dry day. He was relieved that nobody in the crowd was armed. He looked around for Tonatín, but as expected, the man was nowhere in view. Tonatín was too smart to get photographed, and belatedly Harry wished he were too. He wondered if he could trust to Mexican ineptitude to lose the pictures or do nothing with them—hand them over to the CIA helping to repress the Zapatistas—he'd be on the US government shit list if they got that far.

He put those thoughts out his mind. He was here now.

Constance walked down the high narrow sidewalk in the direction of the sound.

She knew they were back from another civil encounter, a few hundred Chiapanecos, other Mexicans, the clearly visible European organizers, trying to bring into public discourse the problems all Mexico faced, and to suggest common solutions. Among them trailed youngsters, college kids, Americans in good leather or waterproof Gortex boots. The French with bare legs and heavy ankle socks. Italians. Germans. Or were they Swedes? She wasn't sure.

All of them carried backpacks; they always had those packs, half slack or bulging, as if at a moment's notice they'd be ready to leave for some more interesting or desperate revolution. They were on their way now to show their strength, to jump onto busses for the next demonstration. Well, kids.

The march circled the jammed zócalo, passing the portico with dozens of indigenous women still seated on the ground in front of the bank and tourist offices. They looked the same as ever, she thought, with their dangling brown breasts and dangling brown babies. Stoic women tending to their sales.

Constance walked behind the crowd. She wasn't marching, certainly not. If somebody was taking photos she wasn't involved, but gosh she was there, how could she be invisible?

Under the portico of the government palace as the crowd moved along the second side to the third side of the square, dozens of women stood behind a line of tables. These were city women, clearly, dressed in home-sewn dresses of the type Constance had learned to make in Home Economics classes half a century ago. They were non-indigenous, lighter-skinned mestizo women. Their black hair hung down loose or was pinned up with plastic combs.

In front of them their laden tables displayed an astonishing variety of sweets, braided breads and raised cookies, candied fruit almost invisible under the wasps and hornets hovering over everything. Some of the younger girls idly brushed them off. She never saw locals run screaming and waving their arms like Americans or Europeans. They presided calmly over the golden buzzing swarm.

Abruptly at a hidden signal the municipal band began to thump and blare. Fiesta music. Eight plainclothesmen huddled with their walkie-talkies in the center of the square.

Harry always teased her. Plainclothesmen! Now how could she possibly know that? Nevertheless she was sure. Who else in San Cristóbal would wear a suit? Not even an undertaker! Really there were no undertakers, families buried their own dead. No bankers. Who else? And with walkie-talkies?

The rally flowed around and past the tables of sweets. The young enthusiasts jumped up and down like popcorn, shouting slogans and raising their fists. The government thugs disappeared and Connie saw them reappear flanked by armed police, in the tall windows above the portico. They were taking snapshots of the demonstrators, while the women below handed over cookies and made change for the tourists and intermingled returnees from the selva, and the band manfully struggled with the music.

Constance looked at the foreigners, aware of herself as a foreigner also. But dressed in cotton slacks and a neat shirt. Her woven shoulder bag rested on her belly with one protective hand covering the clasp. Ordinary foreigners were no longer common here in San Cristóbal. It had been a tourist town; she doubted that since the uprising even the omnipresent French vacationers did much more than pass through the market. But here moved different foreigners, insisting on social change for the impoverished and repressed indigenous people. Clearly the government would take note. Take photographs. From above the crowd, with special lenses, as well as across the square. In 1996, Mexican ineptitude, Constance half believed, served the foreign visitors well. Although frequent road barriers and blockades were manned everywhere on the periphery of the city by uniformed troops, the soldier who took the name and passport number was writing in the rain—literally—with a pencil on a piece of paper soon to become sodden mush. Government computers were remote, if real at all. Constance dismissed the idea.

But this was not to imply that the soldiers were not intelligent, these brown-skinned young men, not far from their own indigenous roots. Maybe like grunts the world round, they did what they could in the way of subversion.

The marchers showed their disdain by shouting DOWN WITH THE PRI! SET THE ZAPATISTAS FREE!

The column snaked around the zócalo and returned. The accordion thumped. After a week of rains, this was the first dry day. She was aware of the sun beating down on her cotton hat. From under its brim she observed the youngsters licking their fingers sticky with candied squash and sweet cakes, gobbling like they were half starved from their trips.

Among them her eye settled on a young girl, a college girl, she was sure, but no, maybe a little older? Connie always enjoyed speculating, always providing anyone she saw with a life and history and a place they came from. That was because they were a mystery to her, others, with whom she shared no world. It was normal for her to feel isolated, like an alien on another plant. Constance never asked herself if she was peculiar, surely she was. She created stories to place herself and these others in the same familiar world.

Maybe this woman was divorced, or had an abusive drunken mother. Some angular look of pain. But maybe she'd been in the jungle. That would make anybody angular. But why had she gone? The girl had short blond hair chopped to follow the line of her skull. It was so uneven Connie was sure she did it herself, or maybe a friend. An un-American disregard for personal vanity. The sun beat down. The girl had no hat and her face showed the burn of fair skin, strawberry mottle on her cheekbones and nose. Dirty jeans. Clean tee-shirt. Bandana around her neck. That was the kids, the kids all looked like that, plus an expression of relief that said, Wow I'm still alive and I'm in a revolution.

As Constance gazed she realized the girl was not as young as she first had thought. She was forty if she was a day. The girl pulled out of her shoulder bag a tiny wet pad in a foil wrap. She opened the foil and pulled out the napkin, unfolded it. She washed her fingers. Constance knew those wash things, they were sold in the US to people who were raised where hygiene was paramount. As Constance watched, the woman crumpled the used wash pad and foil and stuffed them into her bag. She had a camera. She turned back into the crowd now bunched in front of the yellow wall of the church. A stage of sorts was set up and speakers shouted into hand-held megaphones. On one side a video played, its long black cables disappearing mysteriously round the corner. Showing—what?

Constance was too short to see over the heads of the crowd and instead found herself staring into the eyes of a little boy, maybe three years old, hung over the back of his father. The little boy stared back at her. His black eyes showed his surprise. Connie was suddenly very aware of her floppy canvass hat, her dried white skin. But her own eyes were dark also, and maybe that reassured the child. He finally turned his head away.

The young woman had vanished.

Emily took a few shots and put her camera back into its case. She leaned against the corner pillar. In front of the crowd watching the video she spotted Billy, but she was in no hurry to join him. Although he was useful. A male figure at her side when she didn't want to be a single woman. But just a kid. Grateful, she thought, for permission to put his arm around her protectively in public for show. She remembered the few times they'd been in crowds where shoving, while unintentional, was still unpleasant; her unwilling feet were forced into the mud; her back was poked by the person behind her. She imagined that while Billy protected her with his own lean height it was for show, that somewhere in his mind he was developing another program. Like all the men she had known, like that pinche David, he wanted to appear to be a male shielding a woman, his mujer. Yeah. She thought Billy was a nice kid, for all that. Give him another twenty pounds and another twenty years he'd be okay.

She was facing the crowd. From the corner of her eye she could see the hammock venders, and the group of men and women she identified as the leaders. The organizers. For the day, San Cristóbal was once more in Zapatista hands. Never mind the government boys monitoring the whole thing. Their firepower was only good out in the countryside where they didn't even do their own shooting; they hired campesino shooters. And they looked like they ate regular meals and took a few drinks every night. Emily rubbed her tongue against the roof of her mouth to scrape the bad taste. The candied figs were too much. They clashed with the bitter bile rising in her stomach.

Billy had turned and was craning to locate her. He was tall, and his fair skin made him a mark. His carrot hair was covered by the usual baseball cap. At the encuentro, hunched on the raw wooden benches in the sun, she had insisted he not make himself sick with sunburn. What a doofus. She was burned herself, but not like him. Out of her pocket she pulled her own bush hat, and tugged it down onto her head. Now he saw her, and was coming toward her.

From one side another man approached him and put a hand on Billy's arm. Emily couldn't hear what was said, but watched how Billy inclined and listened. Then he straightened up and she could see how his eyes wandered, as if something in the crowd would give him a clue about how to respond.

The man was also American, or could be Canadian, with flat brown hair, nearing thirty. He was somewhat chunky, not too tall. Fireplug with pale skin. He spoke earnestly to Billy, touching his arm to urge his point. Billy finally nodded. The man handed him a slip of paper and disappeared into the crowd.

"What's up?"

"I need to go buy stuff. Supplies. See you later, Emily." He turned away.

Emily stood dumbfounded for a moment, and then burst out laughing. Men couldn't be relied on.

11

To San Gregorio

Harry did something totally unforgivable. He rented an apartment for them without the prior approval of Constance.

He had disappeared for two weeks into the mountains, leaving Connie to fend for herself at Señora Gloria's. He felt sure she was okay, but he didn't like the pressure building against foreigners by the Mexican military. There would be less scrutiny in San Gregorio.

Perfectly safe, somewhat boring, that was Connie's report on her stay alone in San Cristóbal. The food was prepared by the servants whose repertoire was limited to the local tamales and greens. On the day that Señora Gloria's nephew brought them worms, deep fried to the satisfaction of the Señora's other guests, Constance abstained. Afterwards she was sorry; it's always good to try something new.

Señora Gloria's spacious home sat on an ordinary residential street near the center of the city. Street-lights illuminated the front, and across the street, a movie theater showed Mexican-made films on Saturday and Sunday. Señora Gloria's house, when Constance made her way along the elevated sidewalk, could be identified by its handsome wide wooden door.

The house remained from the grand colonial tradition, behind walls hiding it from outside view. Its many rooms circled a courtyard, with bathrooms for the master bedrooms. Luxuriously, their own bathroom possessed a leaking sink with a plug, and a toilet paper holder. In most places in San Cristóbal, whatever amenities existed had literally fallen away in the economic struggle. Sometimes hot water was available, heated on request by one of the two women who slept upstairs on the enclosed roof area with their children and chickens. The male servants came on a day basis.

For "family life", it was these people, the low-slung women and stoic men, the nurtured children, who made the heart of the house. Harry and Connie's home lost its heart when Judith went off to college. Or so Harry ruefully claimed, although Constance maintained that their shared study, with its small fireplace and bookshelves and two computers—his and hers—throbbed like a heart. More like a brain, Harry retorted. But he felt disoriented. He didn't expect to feel so bereft. One of his major jobs was fatherhood, and now he was doubly unemployed.

The warm heart of the Señora's home was the servants. Concepción of the long braids and black mole on her cheek corrected Connie's flawed Spanish with graceful kindness. Concepción was accustomed to students and foreigners; this after all was the "best" home in town accepting paying guests. Pasquala washed out laundry for five pesos, scrubbing jeans and chinos as well as underwear and socks, with cheerful brawn, despite her diminutive stature. The clothes vanished up onto the roof until they just as mysteriously reappeared in the bedroom, neatly folded and laid out on the bed.

Señora Gloria survived as respected widow of a local historian. Her paying guests often numbered ten at a time, most of them young

students from affluent families who could afford to send them beyond their small pueblos to prepare for university. San Cristóbal had
a preparatorio. Harry and his wife were old, therefore usually ignored
at the dinner table by chattering girls who only fell silent, lit up with
expectation, when Constance was offered worms. Señora Gloria tried
to treat her with kindness, carefully explaining the local culture

Concepción and Pasquala alternately cooked and waited table.
As they passed in and out, Señora Gloria assured Constance that the
indios were lazy and ruined her father's land. The dining room resembled a shabby ante-bellum movie, reminiscent of Scarlet O'Hara and
slaves. Constance knew the women worked twelve hours a day. But
then she realized that Concepción and Pasquala, and the boy who led
Señora Gloria's blind brother-in-law, must no longer consider themselves indios. They spoke Spanish and dressed in western clothing.
They were assimilated.

Evenings Señora Gloria sat in the dining room wrapping her
thinning fair hair in curling papers, as if alone. In San Cristóbal Señora Gloria was the white woman, an example of what Connie's own
mother half a century ago referred to as "decayed gentility", retain-
ing all the class prejudices and attitudes, little of the wealth. Señora
Gloria frequently claimed the area was infiltrated with communists,
although, Harry assured her, there was no country he could think of
with a surfeit of communists available for export.

"The indigenous people are lazy and won't work," she resumed
her usual conversation each evening with Constance. "But this rebellion business—there's no reason to be alarmed. The government
protects us." She sat on her couch with her neat ankles crossed below
her black straight skirt. Her fingers picked at the corners of the sofa
fabric. Constance wondered who "us" might be—herself, white? And
where had Señora Gloria been on January 1 of 1994?

Connie's room with its double bed, now half empty, looked out onto the street. At night she closed the wooden shutters, pulling inward toward herself a kind of darkness not experienced since World War II blackouts during her childhood. But the normal noise of the city, the parades and exploding rockets penetrated, and Constance woke from her deepest dreams at all hours. Two A.M. and five A.M. marked favorite times for celebrations. They might have been hours for attack, but how could she, lying in the deep blackness under the light wool blanket, know? She listened intently at each occurrence, hoping to recognize sounds of a band. When she heard music she could fall back to sleep. Often in her dreams the music appeared transformed, inside her high school picnics, celebrations of the end of the school year. In these Chiapas dreams her group of friends sat next to her again, and they exchanged superior comments about the boys in the band. The tuba player had bad acne. Constance was never intentionally hurtful, but she knew the boy realized they talked about him. He looked sullen and red-faced, but maybe blowing a tuba did that. In her dreams she wished she could apologize, or say something friendly, but the music faded in the dream as it faded on the street when the tiny band of the night celebrations marched away.

By day Constance felt abysmally constrained in a small city on her own with no car, and despite the bus service, no place to go. Harry had warned her not to be excessively visible, in other words, stay with the normal flow. So her daily walk took her past the internet café to check the news, and to the language school to give herself a few hours of extra study. She watched foreigners come and go—they all seemed to be tall thin white boys with backpacks. For Constance, her rule was to wear only one Mexican garment at a time—if it was an embroidered blouse, wear jeans. If it was cotton drawstring pants, wear a tee-shirt. She was splitting the cultural difference. The language school also gave English classes to Chiapanecos, and briefly she wondered if she would find students when they got to San Gregorio.

Harry, up in Cuates confirming in his mind the topography of natural flow and the area for ditching, knew that food and a bed would suffice him for now, but not for long. Constance was in many aspects a nest-builder, and he enjoyed that characteristic in her, in fact depended on his wife as he had depended on his daughter, to play the supporting cast. He wanted to go home now, wherever "home" might be—it was where Constance established it. Danger lurked in the air, out of sight, in the straight backs of the men who came and went, in the alert faces of women who ventured out into the fields.

Maybe because of that heightened awareness of his physical self, sex was suddenly on his mind, and American food or at least something without beans and corn, and clean laundry—by which he meant soft briefs. His river-washed cotton briefs, worn on so many prior assignments around the world, somehow felt stiff and he got jock-itch although he knew sun-drying nearly sterilized them. Maybe the problem was drying them on bushes—maybe something in the bushes. He wore them until finally, unable to complain, he began to pull on his jeans with no underwear, and although few of the village men he worked with owned underwear either, he didn't feel as liberated as he had expected. He felt alternately aroused for no reason, and floppy. He needed a home base.

On his trip back it seemed sensible to stop in San Gregorio and find them an apartment. The town was so modest there was no problem. He asked at the first restaurant. He was directed to the home of a woman whose name was Maria Carmen Pintero Luna de Ayela. But since hundreds of women were also named Maria Carmen, she was called Carmen. And the address? Two blocks and then turn left and then right and then cross the street. Harry was dubious, but the woman informing him reassured him, "The doors are painted green."

Harry found it. That was the first miracle, and he thought probably if Constance were here she would insist it was karma. Why argue.

"Yes, I have an apartment for you!" The woman who answered the doorbell asserted. Her eyes were very black, her skin flawless, of a sweet clay color familiar to Harry. Her family probably came from the mountains. Her upper jaw protruded slightly in an appealing smile, friendly and not too formal. Her face struck Harry with its beauty, something pure and perfect. This area was predominantly Mayan. He tried to gaze unobtrusively at the woman, to identify the metamorphosis. Thousands of years had passed into the woman's bone structure and copper cast of her skin. She wore the normal middle-class clothing of the assimilated, and although she clearly was working on the property, her blouse and skirt were business-like, and clean enough to cause Harry to back away. His own body odor could knock a woman down. She seemed not to take offense, however. She led him through the patio and unlocked the door.

The space inside was sparsely furnished with a double bed and a shelf in the bedroom, a table and kitchen chair in the room that would be Harry's office, a kitchen with two small aluminum pots and two more chairs at a rustic table. The living room contained a wood frame sofa and matching chairs from a more modern era, maybe 1950s American. Painted vegetable crates holding votive candles, and sombreros hung on nails, served to decorate walls.

Carmen named the price with just the hint of hesitation. "Several American tenants have rented," she ventured, declaring that she favored Americans. In this remote town? Harry assumed she lumped together any foreigners but didn't care. The question of the price, Harry knew, was because tourists quit coming when the rebellion got underway. Any casual glance could make out the bullet chips on the façade of San Gregorio's cathedral. The fighting here had been no more than a two-day stand-off, but the wounds remained. Of those who could or would afford an apartment, only the NGO workers lived here long-term, and Human Rights activists.

Normally undemanding, Harry asked if they could have screens put on the windows. He could imagine Connie's discomfort as she began to realize that flies and mosquitoes buzzed everywhere. Carmen agreed at once. Harry asked about a phone, and Carmen regretted there was no line, but perhaps it could be arranged. They agreed to meet the following day at the telephone office. Harry signed into a dilapidated old hotel and showered in the tile curtainless stall. At least he didn't stink any more.

The apartment, as Harry realized the next day, stood in the original colonial center, with two tourist boutiques bordering it on one side, and a rather shabby march of houses on the other. From these, the stucco had fallen away in ragged pieces, and their old adobe brick showed naked and frayed. The market was not too far for Constance to carry home groceries, and in the next block a couple sold slaughtered chickens. They would wake to the roosters.

Their street (Harry was already beginning to think of it as their street), perched at the top of the city, almost leaping off into a new set of suburban cement block bungalows climbing the hills, but retained, as if trapped by the ankle, within the old decaying center.

Back in San Cristóbal Harry sprang this news on Constance who looked at him as if he had decided to have a baby without consulting her. But she seriously wanted to go, to settle in, as she thought of it. "I forgive you. Reluctantly." She wrinkled her nose at him, and hugged him and frowned, all at the same time. "Let's go soon. It won't take me more than thirty seconds to say farewell to Señora Gloria!"

They owned little to pack. Harry went on his own to consult with the local Estación Norte, a shabby office in a shabby house behind secure gates. They should know the route the Skelbas would take, be appraised of their approximate whereabouts, their passport numbers in case of bad problems, would tell them the location of the Estación office in San Gregorio. But the workers didn't anticipate any serious problems, not for Americans old enough to be harmless. Harry, momentarily affronted, kept his mouth shut and took their advice. For this trip it was decided they should go by public bus.

The buses were disreputable and old, and foreigners traveling them in Chiapas were conspicuous only to their fellow passengers. On a scheduled second-class bus route few military blockades would stop them. The road ran northeast, with no tourist attractions. Harry cautioned Constance that if they were questioned she should sit quietly and give the soldier whatever documents he wanted to see. They agreed on their ultimate cover story: they were traveling to see for the first time a Mexican grandson. La familia was the trump card.

They set out at six in the morning. Their duffels were tied onto the roof, buried beneath other bags and boxes. Harry hoped the driver would not have to unload the whole mess for inspection for guns and drugs, but he doubted that would happen on a rural route passing minuscule villages; the undocumented Guatemalans who made it as far as San Cristóbal usually headed northwest.

Constance, resting her head against the shabby blue upholstery, reviewed their cover story, imagining a small brown black-eyed baby who would be her own flesh and blood, from a son-in-law married to Judith in Chiapas. That was so improbable she had to change her fantasy. Why not change Judith? Her imagination could accomplish whatever she required. She began to construct Judith as a champion of Human Rights, a lawyer, an important personage...

Then, as the bus rolled along in its own dust-bath, Constance understood they were illegals. Harry was an undocumented worker. She hoped it wasn't for the indigenous in rebellion. But. She nervously tucked her hand into her pack to make sure she knew the exact location of her passport.

In fact, the worst problem on the eight hour journey was lack of bathroom facilities. Constance climbed back into the bus and reported to Harry, "I have a new insight into why the women wear skirts and no underwear. For a minute there I was afraid I wouldn't be able to get back up." She showed him her hand, and without comment he kissed the soft flesh gently and then began to pick out of her palm the tiny cactus splinters.

Several weeks passed before Constance realized she had arrived as innocent as a mountain indio to San Gregorio. Despite the weeks in San Cristóbal, she was unprepared. She could write down what she saw, as perfectly as taking a photograph. But with no comprehension, no links to connect what she saw to the distant world from which she had traveled. Amazed, she wondered if she were undergoing some strange metamorphosis herself. She looked and looked. The colors, the strange womb-shaped fruits, the very houses with their painted plaster walls, seen by her many times before, confounded her with their difference. Metal doors in the long walls along the street left her dumbfounded. Surely she had seen metal before, in San Cristóbal. Garage doors, surely, at home in Ann Arbor. But now this was her home. The doors were high and narrow, with heavy locks that put her in mind of secret gardens shielded from view. Theirs was green.

On the street she stared in wonderment at market women selling elaborate embroidered shirts, at vendors of peeled grapefruits and diced watermelon. What an onslaught of sights and strangeness. Over the distant streets loomed mountains from which she felt the peoples must have just descended. They had come as she came, with their jaws agape and their eyes startled. Wonder and magic, as innocent as the soil covered over with fallen flowers. She was filled, no room for fear.

Harry, practical as ever, strode about in his baseball cap and short-sleeved denim shirt apparently looking at nothing. He had no romantic notions about mysterious peoples coming down off the mountains. They only came when they were starved into it, and often the men came for work, leaving their women alone to manage however they could. He said none of this to Constance, who on her part was kind enough not to effuse over the beauty. A deal.

He recovered underwear, and made love to Constance several times, with a honeymoon kind of greed he couldn't himself understand. Furnishing their strange rooms they were transformed into newlyweds. He was very good at destinations, Harry was. He thrust forward his gray head and his work boots on his broad feet. For an old gent he was square and strong, and he navigated well. He got about. Yet Constance was sure he never really saw, not the way Constance herself saw. He allowed her to select the few wall tapestries she felt they absolutely must have, the few dishes. He was analytical, but she understood the aesthetics of magic. That was the difference in their personalities, still intact despite forty-some years of marriage.

The first week they were curiously euphoric. Like two kids they scampered through the streets of San Gregorio. Or maybe scampered is incorrect, although Constance thought that word: scampered. More likely they plodded, two senior citizens carrying backpacks.

They made love gently but thoroughly. Harry gallantly helped her on and off the flood curbs, held her hand when taxis and buses threatened to run them down, and let her go first through each doorway. She thanked him and praised him with her glances. It was ideal, a honeymoon they deserved after the years of waiting until Judith settled down, ooh-ing on cue over the first grandchild, the second, and finally retiring.

Constance loved the Spanish word, jubilado. They were as jubilant as could be, although Harry illegally had accepted this project in the mountains and would not consider himself retired, as he frequently explained; he'd accepted a fresh responsibility. Constance woke up one morning with the realization that their dream time was ending. But surely the beauty would stay.

Harry scheduled his next trip up to the Sierra Corral Chen. Getting settled was prime priority, because without his workspace he couldn't, well, work. Connie understood his sense of urgency, and although she didn't say so, she shared it. His stacks of accumulating papers, spidery with red and black lines, began to drive her crazy. After only a week in their apartment, maps turned up on the bed when she needed to rest, on the chair when she wanted to sit, on the floor where she needed to pass.

From her own side, the urgency lay in her ignorance. Sure she had read about the Zapatista uprising. But what it meant, politically and socially, was another story. People's sense of community, their insistence on autonomy, free from the PRI caciques and condescending government agents—she needed to understand how Subcomandante Marcos exchanged his Socialist revolutionary ideas for leading by obeying; how the communities opted for self-reliance, rejecting government assistance. Struggling to absorb, she put away her pack and the American purse she brought with her from Ann Arbor. She bought a new shoulder bag at the craft market, a soft cloth from Guatemala, with bold orange and burnt umber birds flying on it. Constance hoped she was herself absorbed, less visible, but with her canvass hat and pale face adorned with startled eyes, that was not likely.

By day their gate was shut but left unlocked. Constance loved the patio's astonishing vines and generous flowers of brilliant red, yellow, orange and fuchsia. She began to sit outside to read more about the rebellion in the Mexican newspapers. By mid-afternoon warm sun lulled her from rest to sleep. She placed her legs on the plastic chair opposite her own and napped beneath brilliant trees and vines. Ann Arbor, headed into autumn, was almost unimaginable.

The landlady Carmen lived several streets away, but came daily to tend the plants and refill the water tank on the roof. For Connie's benefit she explained everything slowly, and then explained again. Her attitude, as she looked into Connie's face, conveyed the sense that Carmen was speaking to her woman-to-woman, and would say more if only the language barrier permitted. Sometimes Carmen's hands twitched as if they would gesticulate, but could not express the appropriate sentiments.

To Constance, who seemed to have softly bungled her way through life like a calf butting its mother's underside until the right place was discovered, Carmen appeared to be a real go-getter. For one thing, she dressed very professionally by Mexican standards. At their introduction, she appeared in a dress with a jacket and high heeled shoes. Her short black hair was cut close, and seemed vaguely curly, as if too much curl would be unprofessional, but too little would be fey. She spoke authoritatively to the clerk at the telephone office, then shepherded Constance through the next phase of paperwork and the cashier's line. When everything was completed she shook hands.

"So finally everything is arranged. It has been only two weeks, very good! I will come at five o'clock tomorrow to be sure all is okay."

"At five o'clock," Constance echoed like a dutiful child. She was realizing what a year meant. Carmen asked, "Is that agreeable? Are you sure?" Her face had almost rippled, as if an underground river ran beneath her skin. Constance smiled. She was sure, five o'clock was fine. She forgave Harry for finding the apartment without her. They were home.

That night both Constance and Harry became ill. At five in the morning, after a night of intense bowel cramps in the black silence of their room, Constance finally woke Harry. In a taxi they made their way to the San Gregorio private hospital, and Constance received a shot in the rump.

"You have an infection of the intestines," the woman doctor gazed into Constance's own dark eyes as if to help her understand the Spanish. Constance understood infección. Carrying three different prescription slips, they taxied back. Harry sallied out alone to find a pharmacy.

By the time Carmen arrived the next afternoon, Constance was up and about. But Harry, after the briefest greeting, lay down with an explosive headache, and then a low-grade fever which made him ill-tempered and critical. His gray hair, tousled with sweat, frowzed around his face. Odd hairs marred his unshaved chin, and his new Zapata moustache stubbornly held onto fragments of the wheat bread she'd searched for.

Constance gazed appalled. The honeymoon was over. How could she settle into a new apartment, make a home with this man? Where was the jaunty soul who fathered her child, comforted her when she was unemployed, encouraged her to retire promptly although he himself worked longer? This man? This wreck, this nasty-tempered square fellow with bad breath?

Ah, but then the following day he was fine.

The next Monday they were assigned a phone number, and given a square black instrument to put on the stool that served as table. But sadly, no phone line was attached. Telmex had promised, had taken their pesos, but lines were scarce. Perhaps the following week. They used the internet café.

Planning around the useless telephone, Constance set up their home. Carmen sent a fellow to screen and repair the windows that didn't work, and Harry stuck duct tape across the bottom of the metal doors to discourage the biodiversity of ants, roaches and lizards from entering. Constance shopped for a mirror.

She took down off their nails the decorations Carmen had so carefully installed to make them welcome—straw sombreros, the straw doohickies, the wooden crates (perhaps for bookshelves?), several quasi-rugs with fringes, a bright blue plate with the word mexico lettered in white. She tacked up her two chosen tapestries. She purchased straw lampshades for the naked bulbs that dangled on cords from the ceilings.

With no guilt she hired a woman to come and clean once a week. For six dollars the woman would cope with the mysteries of a tile floor and a mop-cloth on a stick, a kitchen with no hot water. The few scratched plastic plates Constance replaced with ceramic.

Harry, recovered and robust as he should be, set about scrubbing the cabinet under the sink. Squeezing oranges for juice became a body-building task for his upper torso and arm muscles. Washing the fruits and veggies required a disinfectant in the rinse water. Boiling water for drinking and cooking was a nightly task for whichever of them had enough energy. Anyone who ever associated the words "lazy" and poor" has clearly never tried living in a third world country.

Connie feared so much housework would use up Harry's willingness to help her settle in. He had time for nothing but domestic chores, running to the bakery for rolls, running to the mercado for yet more oranges. No wonder a steady small trickle of thin brown men knocked at the apartment door to see how his plans progressed. Clearly he can't work outside the home!

She began to recognize certain faces on their street, certain unsold gourds hanging in the open doorways of the empty tourist boutiques, the sounds of processions. Drinking chilled jamaica made from hibiscus flowers, they sat together outside in the sun-filled patio. Constance read and Harry drew his thin lines in red ink. Their stomachs adjusted. Harry craved real meals. She stewed a chicken in garlic, hoping the whole while it would be free of whatever chickens might not be free of.

Harry, moving among his maps and plans, considered the project. The men had come and he had given his list of necessary supplies and his assent to their requirements. It was time to get up there again. Reading newspapers in Spanish had become an essential accomplishment. He went to the Estación house to get information. There was a war going on.

12

Frank in Monterrey

Frank absorbed the military buildup in Chiapas without reading any statistics. He knew the size of the platoons, ranks of the commanders, the appearance of weapons from the US, Israel, and Russia in the hands of the White Guards. His rear view mirror filled with army convoys; his stops at various communities became an ongoing reminder of how Zapatista families hunkered down. Frank didn't want to know all this, but he learned, driving the roads in his own van or using Estación's to make himself less visible. By the autumn of 1996 he had learned dozens of dirt back roads and cross-country paths, to avoid the growing number of military and immigration stops.

His brief rests in Ocosingo with Tomás included the daughter and granddaughters of Tomás, who offered him a place to sleep in their house. The daughter Alvira was a calm young widow, the kids sweet. But it was Tomás who made Frank a family man, held in Mexico. His own parents disconnected sometime back there—not hostile, just beyond emotion. He wondered if they had used up their feelings for him while he was in the Gulf, used up their anxiety and care, waiting week after week to learn he was alive.

And now Tomás waited and worried. But Frank waited and worried also. Neither man spoke of the feeling. They embraced when they met and when they parted. That is the Mexican way. It was a relief for Frank to take a break, to finally drive north to Monterrey, a modern industrialized city with bars, movies and hookers in good supply. He needed to buy new tires for his van, and carry back south tires for Estación Norte's. His own van he brought into a shop to have the body repainted a dark green and the seats re-upholstered black. Brakes and transmission, everything was available in Monterrey if you waited. He had a week to get drunk.

When he wasn't drunk or in his hotel room with a lady of the evening, he was nagged with confusion about who he was and what was going on. Loads of Americans who arrived in the country, in Chiapas, just like him, supported the Zapatistas. But they were tourists to the rebellion. Hanging around doing Witness and playing soccer with the kids. Frank was different. He sensed that Tomás watched him like a newborn, that Tomás knew Frank's physical sturdiness only hid how frail he was emotionally.

Frank wasn't old enough to have enlisted in two wars, he was only twenty-six. He had developed almost a nervous tic of running his fingers over his face to feel the shape and size of it, the cracks and creases. He wondered if he looked aged or his hair was turning gray; if he should grow a moustache. When he picked up a woman he wondered if he should be back in Ohio dating girls who looked like television sit-com stars. When he delivered boxes of aspirin, which was pretty much what medical supplies amounted to, he wondered if he should be back in Ohio applying for medical school. When he ate in a restaurant or sat in the park, he wondered if those who noticed him immediately figured him for a Zapatista supporter. His time in the desert during the Gulf War appeared in his dreams. War. It was all war.

Tomás talked to him. There are wars and wars. The government quarrels, the government thirst for power or oil or position, that was not your war. You are a human being, not a toy for the government to play soldier. If you go to war it must be your own war.

"How can this rebellion be my own war, Tomás? This isn't my country."

"No, war is not for a country. That would be the old way. This war is for human dignity. For everybody." Frank nervously laughed. He laughed at Tomás's lofty words and phrases, delivered calmly and deliberately while Tomás shoveled his beans with a tortilla on his plate, eating as if nothing were more delicious or more important. Here and now. Nevertheless, Frank took comfort. He wondered when his own father ceased to be a moral or spiritual guide, if he ever had been a guide, even when Frank was in high school. High school in Akron, Ohio! No way would he have listened to his own father, in case his own father ever thought of something to say to Frank. No way. His father didn't have the financial ability to give his son what Frank wanted, and after a while they quit talking about Frank's wishes, and Frank quit listening to anything else.

He went his own way.

If he woke before afternoon he wandered through the streets looking at the northern Mexicans who were so different from the southern indigenous people—lighter of skin, better dressed. But not all of them. There was poverty here also. The tourists were different, passing through on their way to enjoy the beaches in Yucatan, and the ruins left by the Olmec, huge statues like those he'd seen in pictures of Easter Island. Travelers who liked ruins and beaches made him nervous. The women wore bright colored shoes, the men often shuffled like middle-aged old wrecks in Bermuda shorts. These resembled the kind of tourists his parents might be, if his parents had money to travel. Innocent as shit, with wrinkled knees.

Monterrey was industrialized. Ordinary people were cynical and fed up with government repression and corruption. Frank contacted the people Tomás named, and managed out of his respect and love for Tomás to show up sober. His van would be well equipped, not only with tires. They were bringing weapons, and a Japanese car radio. The shop offered a car CD player which Frank reluctantly declined, wary of loading the van with tempting noise-makers. On his own, Frank purchased a nice pair of binoculars. He even bought himself new boots and shirts. Monterrey held luxuries.

He had driven north while the NGO community in San Gregorio was on high alert. Abductions, death threats and a fire bombing at the Peace Office kept everyone on edge. Public Security Forces using helicopters with tear gas and armored tanks attacked an unsuspecting population in a small municipality twenty kilometers outside the town. Threats were made against Bishop Samuel Ruiz out in San Cristóbal. Frank needed a break.

"Go," Tomás instructed him. "We must have the vehicles in good repair."

For sure the Mexican government coached Chiapas State Security Forces, which in turn hired the paramilitary. Only publicity coming from Subcomandante Marcos via internet and the national liberal press prevented all-out war against the resisting civilian population. Instead, as Tomás predicted, another Latin American style dirty war was underway. The government boys never got hurt.

Beyond that, Frank wasn't too good on sorting out details of the tangled struggles for power at the local, state and national level. When he talked with Tomás, it was like Tomás tutored him on history and events, but Frank was a poor learner. All he absorbed was the warmth and steadiness of Tomás himself. When telephone lines were cut at the Estación Norte house, and death threats appeared one morning on their doorstep, Frank left it to the Human Rights workers to deal with. Do what I'm asked to do, is all I need to do, Frank calmed himself.

With an off-duty week in Monterrey, all he seriously needed to know was, why was he here in the first place, a foreigner helping rebels in Mexico. Tomás had assured him, foreigners are crazy. So what kind of loony was he, to stay in Mexico? He missed Tomás' slow voice and Latinate explanations, even if he didn't always understand what he heard. You wouldn't catch Tomás in Bermuda shorts, not now, not ever.

Frank went shopping again and this time he bought himself a high-powered rifle with a telescopic lens. Ammunition. He bought a Spanish English dictionary to share with Tomás, and as an afterthought, a good short-sleeved cotton shirt as a gift. On his drive back down to Chiapas, he carried boxes of blank computer disks in the back seat, as well as automatic weapons hidden under the rear van bed. Nervously, he stroked his face. He needed a shave. He wished he had a mirror, although god alone knew what was to be seen.

13

Martin Arrives

The caravan from Meditators for Peace stopped briefly in San Gregorio. It deposited another group of enthusiasts, along with their hopes for partaking in the wondrous hope. In the morning sunshine, news floated like gossip, gossip became news.

Four were leaving the caravan for the Peace Camps. The van waited in front of a diminutive café with oil-cloth covered tables. Green checkered. The sugar bowl on each was sticky looking; wasps buzzed on the tables and at the counter where sweet breads slowly gathered dust. Gear was hauled out of the back of the truck. Martin sat down to wait.

He had been riding in the vehicle for a week, and certainly he wasn't physically tired, but despite his best efforts to invoke the best thoughts, his gut hurt. During the last three days he endured a diarrhea of sorts, something that came and went in spasms, leaving him no time to plan around orderly bowel movements as he preferred to do.

Martin's life had been placed on a schedule by Holy Master Ragadam Baram, and even in intestinal functions, Martin did not care to deviate. But so it was.

Immediately, begging children surrounded him. And since he learned long ago that there is no greater sin against the Absolute than pretending a fellow human, especially a child, does not exist, he smiled.

"What's your name?"

"Rosalita."

"Where's your mother?"

"I don't have one."

"Where's your father?"

"I don't have one."

"Who do you live with?"

"Her."

Rosalita, perhaps seven years old, with heavy black hair and black eyes, turned her head to point at a girl of ten, and then resumed. "Buy me dinner. Buy me a coke," she said in Spanish. Like ringing a bell-rope, she tugged at Martin's short cotton sleeve which hovered at the level of her head. Martin, with his fledging Spanish, the words he had learned on the bus ride, said nothing. Rosalita's small hand fell to his forearm, and stroked the bare skin briefly.

The child turned away and relentlessly began working the group of Americans with their sweet smiles and white skins in various degrees of scarlet from the tropical sun.

The van made more than one unscheduled stop at tiny villages where women fashioned clay pots and figurines, or wove fabric. The driver was educating his gringo passengers, and also apparently taking a small sum of money at each village for his role as conveyer of guilt-ridden northerners.

The Meditators' tour leader, Jeremy Blanding, had no say in this—he was along to deliver his crew of disciples and make sure they stayed on the Program while on their journey. Incidentally, he was trying to provide them with Spanish. God alone knew how they would fare after he left them at their next pickup spot. But of course that wasn't his problem.

On their devious route along the pothole ridden back roads, they entered yard after yard noisy with barefoot children and nursing babies. Martin, who stood aside in his new Guatemalan cotton shirt, ran his hands over his balding scalp and then put on his hat. He was thinner, and his large nose had undergone several changes in color depending on the sun's angle. Dogs and chickens crowded in to look at them. The women placed tables out on their cement slab patios to display their products. The children carried small baskets of their own creations: a rabbit, a leopard, a dove. "Buy this," they pleaded.

The clay figurines were badly fired and poorly shaped, as if the children could fashion no better than they themselves were, badly made in God's image.

Martin sighed. That notion was a sin. After all, he had once attended kindergarten and made horrible inadequate figures from greasy clay the teacher handed out. Although he was homely, thin, and more or less unloved, Martin did not pursue the logical conclusion. He wasn't Baptist now, he was Hindu, safe from thoughts like that. He had in fact seen children like this in rural Georgia—rachitic and malnourished.

Martin renewed his mental serotonin. He had a trick of closing his eyes and bringing in the good mantra that set his amines in motion with tiny moments of silence no wider than a sliver.

Some of the wealthier—that is to say, not permanent dwellers with Holy Master like Martin (who was virtually a monk and hence poor), but two others of Jeremy's charges bought one or two small inept clay figures. The best of the artisans' work was displayed at makeshift tables by the side of the road, in case rich tourists happened by in private cars.

Martin believed the best of our work should be displayed at home. But since he left for the university he had no home, and anyway the home was Robert John's, even after his death. Martin believed home was where somebody loved you. Martin's task on earth was to provide a home for everyone.

"Give me a pen to write with," a child with a missing front tooth begged Martin. He searched in his pack and found only a disposable yellow mechanical pencil which sadly he handed over. He wondered who sent the child to ask for it. Someone literate, he hoped. Martin knew that disposable pencils are manufactured not to last, and after a week, when the lead vanished, would the new owner curse Martin for having donated American junk, trash, to avoid giving anything of value? Martin hoped not. He muttered his mantra under his breath, intently listening to his intestines.

We are rich in peace, rich in the Absolute, also just plain rich, in a country where oxen and horses and burros and the fields of corn are more glossy, more valuable, better nourished than the children. Martin hoped that their calming meditation, by halting the killing would make life better for these children. But he doubted. They required more than peace. Although politically Martin wasn't well informed about capitalism or the IMF, because Holy Master regarded them only as secondary manifestations of lack of love, Martin had been informed that women comprised nearly one-third of the rebel army. He deduced that for those women the Zapatista army was clearly a better option than staying in the village and begetting children who would die one after the other from inadequate nourishment, bad water, and diarrhea. His gut rumbled an ominous threat.

Martin gazed at his watch and ran his finger beneath its orange plastic wristband. He seemed to have a rash, or the color of the plastic had stained his skin. He yearned to go, so they could arrive someplace with a bathroom. Twenty minutes of benevolent gawking was too much. He was pleased that the driver, seeing Martin check his watch, gave the signal to depart.

The bus rolled across beautiful land, a paradise of wooded hills in the Sierra Madre de Chiapas highlands. Sheep grazed on the hillside while a woman in her brilliant blue costume sat on the grass weaving with a back-loom. From the bus window, the crops looked rich, the animals plentiful—a scene from a Disney film. Martin gazed a while and returned to the bus interior. Most of the passengers were asleep. To distract himself from the sounds his gassy intestines were making, he pulled out from his backpack his copy of the speeches Marcos made. Martin began to read:

> "...The crash of these two winds will be born, its time has arrived, it has stoked the fire of history. Now the wind from above rules, but here comes the wind from below, here comes the storm... that is how it will be... When the storm calms, when rain and fire again leave the country in peace, the world will no longer be the world but something better." (Subcomandante Marcos, August 1992.)

Thank God for the translations. His Spanish was almost usable. Finally they were carried into the Meseta Central.

> Only the wealthiest few support the PRI, the traditional Church, the system of landholding, and illiteracy for the indigenous population. These few do not favor an educated organized population. These few are the wind from above.

Neither the wind from above nor the wind from below included Martin. He belonged to no class. Despite Holy Master's assistance, he felt pretty much on his own. He gazed at the lovely countryside. He wondered where exactly the war was.

The bus entered what was clearly a city. Martin could tell because although no building was more than two stories high, the streets were cobbled, and sidewalk ran alongside. They rolled to a halt.

San Gregorio, this street vendors' cauldron, like all Mexico, was history-proud. Street names were important dates or people: 20th of November, 5th of May, General Utrillo. September 16 marks Independence Day, and on not just the day, but for the entire month of September, the town was displaying green, red and white flags everywhere.

The four released Meditators, led by Jeremy, gazed about as they worked their way toward the zócalo. In the square a sprinkle of observers stood nearby while a military band performed on trumpets and drums. A brief drill with rifles, present arms—a drill reminiscent far more of high school marching bands than any fighting military. The boys stood disciplined, holding their hands at such an angle to the body that Martin guessed it must induce wrist cramps. Their boots shone mirror sharp. On whose side? Most likely the government's. The indigenous rarely lived in the city, rarely were included in any civil activity. Although as far as Martin could tell, they were all the same people.

Flowers were carried to the makeshift wooden dais by three women in uniform white blouses and green skirts. All three wore white stockings and high heeled shoes. The mayor prepared to speak.

In the time required to cross from one side of the cobbled zócalo to the other, all onlookers turned their attention to the newcomers and stared. The four Meditators, peering as best they could from beneath their loads, smiled at nothing. A smile was always helpful, no matter what.

Jeremy led his patient group, stooped under all their gear and sleeping bags, out of view, crossing narrow streets until they arrived at a painted metal door in a wall. It opened onto a courtyard. Within was another van—more decrepit, dented. Maybe a bullet-hole in the side window? Martin hoped not. They climbed in and put their gear down on the torn plastic seats. Martin longed for a bathroom. People who said asshole and shit were making a political declaration. Like they belonged to the ordinary people. Martin was not among them.

Bathroom, he pleaded with their new driver. Sanitario? Baño?

The driver waved the American toward one side of the yard, and gratefully Martin jumped off, and then hastily returned to pull a roll of toilet paper out of his knapsack. His fellow Meditators were already settled in and half-asleep across the two seats of dust and dangerous springs allotted to each when he returned from the shed that served as a toilet. He hoped he would not pick up a skin infection like the one on his wrist. Toilet seats were apparently non-existent, and he guessed most people would prefer an open field. He always washed as well as he could from a small bottle of disinfectant alcohol carried along with his passport and pesos in his nylon waist pouch. In his present condition his anus felt raw and stung. Alcohol was a mistake in that area.

Despite his discomfort he stoically took his place in the vehicle. Sitting again. Physical discomfort could be dispelled with higher thoughts. He closed his eyes. He disappeared into the aura of Holy Master, who from far away was soothing Martin's ass.

14

Harry Accepts Money

In San Gregorio, housing offers naked light bulbs, a drain in a tile floor, cold water for a shower, roaches, mildew, rachitic furniture, no closets, a rare luxury of toilet tissue holders or towel racks. Glorious sunshine when it's not raining. Boil the water.

In their rented space, Constance stored boiled kitchen water in a covered container. They poured for cooking and drinking. Water also ran into the sink from the bathroom faucet, and from the shower. Plenty of water. The city was inundated several times a week, and the run-off clearly went somewhere beneath the city. And then was it this same water which reappeared untreated in the homes? Harry hesitated. There was no black water treatment plant in evidence, and yet! Dear God. But he had been told that his task was in the mountains, not here.

Could it be much worse? Clearly people in rebellion had it worse. Harry didn't want to think what desperation impelled these people to seek him out. He knew that back in Michigan he was well known, and the chair of the engineering department where he taught seminars to those destined for Saudi Arabia or Somalia was a Mexican. The chairman knew Harry was retired and none too happy about that. An e-mail arrived. No interview. No CV. Harry didn't categorize his situation as hired. He wasn't entirely sure that fit his labors.

He came, with brave Connie along for "senior adventures," as she called them. Cheerful and stalwart. Momentarily he thought in a pleasant way of Constance in bed. After all these years together sex was fine-tuned, and when there was no sex, he liked to feel her foot with his foot, maintaining contact until he slept. For their apartment, Constance marched out to purchase real cotton sheets and a brightly covered bedspread. She created a love nest, and they used it.

Daily the sun beat down. The rain dropped in torrents for ten minutes at a time, and then the sun reappeared. Harry was accumulating his plans and supply lists, and waiting for a contact. An unexpected fax came from friends in Ann Arbor to the Estación Norte house: "You probably already know this but...". The airport in Tuxtla Gutierrrez had been closed. Now the rumors flew among Witnesses coming and going at the volunteer house. The alarmists foresaw a military takeover. How did they have the chutzpa to claim they're repairing cement runways during the rainy season? The Zapatista communiqués asserted that a military build-up was underway in an area held by government forces. The Mexican government was getting a deal on new American helicopters and munitions.

The following day, Harry, telling Constance only that he was going to talk with the Cuates men about the irrigation project, walked two blocks east from the Estación Norte house and climbed into a rusted pick-up truck. Tonatín sat at the wheel. They drove for three hours along back roads until they arrived at a tiny settlement hidden among corn plants, twisted peach trees and banana plants. The truck sighed as if exhausted. They jumped out.

Along a hidden narrow footpath they hiked upward into a dense area of flowering bushes and grasses. Overhead the epiphytes dangled, with occasional bright orchids in flower. For Harry, the path was almost impossible to discern. A Tzotzil-speaking women in the usual wrap wool skirt courteously pointed out the way to Tonatín. They climbed.

"Dirt poor," Harry said to himself. His own family had been professionals, his mother a teacher and his father an engineer like himself. Even his war-shattered Uncle Tad had done okay, doing Morse code for Western Union. Harry had never been poor. Broke, not poor. He and Constance were broke when they married. He remembered with pleasure their first chess set, made together by hand out of shirt cardboard. No movies, no dinners out. They were "poor," waiting for his first month's pay to arrive. But shit. This was something else.

Nobody bothered to halt the men or speak to them. Dogs lay in the dirt as if too starved to get up.

They toiled upward for another hour. Harry paused to drink from his water bottle. Tonatín waited, unhurried as always. Finally they arrived at an outcropping, cut into the heavily overgrown hillside. A dozen women waited, sitting on the ground or along the one log that served as a bench. Among them played eight or so children, all with runny noses, some still nursing. One small boy of four or five idly teased a puppy. His trousers were open at the zipper-less fly and as he bent over Harry could see his small child's penis, exposed and vulnerable. The boy was barefoot, as were the women. In the hot sun the women had placed folded rebozos on their heads to create a little shade.

This was not Cuates de Santa Ana. It was an outlying pueblo, hosting their meeting. They didn't want him accessing their remote town just yet. Why not? It wasn't that much further to travel. He doubted he was taken here to see this place, the poverty. They were not ready to show him Cuates. Not yet. Perhaps, Harry thought, not where. For the first time he wondered if he was being followed, tracked, on some Mexican colonel's list of subversive foreigners.

The one man already present, very drunk, must be from this pueblo. The women openly laughed at his attempts to sit down with a liter of whiskey tucked into his trousers. Then a second man, sober and cheerful, entered the clearing. He sat and began to carve on a wooden doll. Several women were fashioning clothes to send to the market in San Gregorio. There were no other men.

Nursery-school sized wooden chairs on precarious legs were set out for Harry and Tonatín. The women indicated silently, with smiles, that Harry should sit. He folded his legs, hoping his stiff knees would not leave him sitting forever when the time came to get up and move. He was facing the expectant women, and it was only by their murmur past him that he knew the visiting men had finally arrived.

He turned his head. Half a dozen thin, brown, small, upright men, silent and unsmiling, approached. Four wore the starched campesino sombreros. Two wore American style baseball caps. All wore bedraggled and torn gabardine pants, some with very clean white shirts, some in tee-shirts. Harry, perched like an over-sized royal guest next to Tonatín, rose to his feet as his guide rose. He recognized the men he had met in San Cristóbal. So he had passed the first hurdle. He was in the presence of those entrusted to conduct the financial business.

Neatly stacked twenty-peso bills were placed in blocks on the table in front of Harry. Account books were opened. In the first fierce moments of business it was discovered that some could not perform manual arithmetic in the western style. Only one man spoke Spanish. He requested that Harry check their figures, but then, needing to be certain that Harry knew arithmetic, sent Tonatín to fetch a calculator from one of the sod and thatch houses. Thus ready for down-payment, the faces nodded at one another around the circle. They were lit with anticipation.

Each block of money was attributed by name to a man perhaps present, a roll-call of able-bodied leaders of tiny clusters of ten or twelve families each, which comprised the municipio of Cuates. Those men didn't descend from the mountain, not even to this place. Their designated representatives had hiked to this outpost. Harry wondered how many hours, and Tonatín whispered to him, four hours each way. The paths were rough and steep. But they hadn't wanted Tonatín to bring Harry closer for this transaction.

Harry understood. He was now in the pay of a Zapatista town. There was no contract, no paper. But the presence of these men, and the witnesses sitting here, made it official. So had he been innocent, or stupid? In some part of his mind he knew all along.

While the pay process continued, the host women went on working. They were embroidering handmade jackets; carding black, white or gray bags of wool; spinning yarn on small hand spindles. Some were sewing tiny doll clothes. Harry shed his sweater and stuffed it into his backpack. He had not wanted to accept this money, as it came so clearly from impoverished family heads, in small parcels. A business transaction. Otherwise, where was the dignity?

Now he realized another reason for not accepting payment. But it was too late. The packages of pesos piled one on top of the next as the men watched and calculated.

The women smiled as if this business were their own. The nursing women sat with their long breasts poking through the embroidered blouses. The toddlers helped themselves to refreshment. Even the boy who had been teasing the puppy bent to his mother's breast and sucked.

At the close of the accounting Harry faced the serious men. The giving over of their cash, especially to an unknown foreigner, made them somber. If they were also afraid, Harry could not detect it. God knows he was. He recited in his awkward Spanish, "I'm very pleased to be here. I will do good work for you. Every family will have water."

He turned to the host women. "Here is some fruit for the little children. Thank you for your hospitality." The uncomprehending men stood aside, still at attention, silent and curious. The leader translated into Tzotzil. The men applauded.

All the women wore the same traditional wrap skirt in a black and gray stripe, held by a red sash. From their clothing it was not possible for Harry to ascertain status or rank. Maybe there was none? Several women and little girls wore the ten-peso plastic shoes made in Mexico. One little boy owned worn rubber boots, discarded long since. His naked feet were already gray above the heavy callused soles. Harry decided that oldest must be highest in authority. He handed the sack of fruit to an ancient woman seated on a log.

Hoping he guessed the etiquette correctly, Harry shook hands with the men, each in turn. He thanked them, and they thanked him, in Spanish if they could, if not, in their incomprehensible language. The old woman was already wielding a machete on Harry's yellow apples. They made a paltry gift. Tonatín had consumed the ears of roasted corn and the bag of bananas during the long drive to the settlement.

On the journey back to San Gregorio Harry turned to Tonatín. "This part of the project," he indicated the bulky package of pesos in his backpack, "is the least of the expenses. They know that, right?"

"The least in cash," Tonatín used the Spanish word, efectivo. It was apt. "But the most in trust."

For a moment Harry was afraid tears of terror would spring from his eyes. Trust was the most dangerous gift. He thought of Constance, and how much information he should entrust to her. He thought of possibile arrest and deportation, and hoped if it came to that, nothing worse would happen. He thought of the people at Estación Norte and who among them as foreigners ran the same risks he did, and who among them, as Mexicans, ran worse.

He swallowed hard. He had worked on many huge American projects. And said nothing, not to himself, nor to Constance, nor to his employers. Acquiescence marked his political life. He was a liberal, sure. But a silent majority liberal.

And now, what right did he have to be afraid? He was sixty-seven, and retired from that world of build-and-own enterprise capitalism. What did he have to lose?

What he had to gain felt less certain in his mind than it had. Something more than adventure. His own permanent structure—well, he wasn't Pharaoh building pyramids. Some social structure, he was supporting some new social organizing principle in Chiapas. Whoa, he cautioned himself. Take it slow and easy. It's only water pipes.

The trip back down went faster than the trip up. Harry gazed out the window as the truck bounced around curves and dodged its own dust. The countryside was beautiful. They passed small adobe houses on the outskirts of tiny towns. Dirt roads led off from paved road into the interior of villages, which Harry could almost finger like tiny pieces of a jigsaw puzzle.

Constance had told him of the fantasy she built around their agreed-to fiction of Judith in Mexico with a baby they came to visit. The image stayed with Harry. They might yet be called on to use it. Moreover, if you made up a story like that, was it in some sense true, because you created it, like a dam you created a blueprint or a map for?

It wasn't Harry's custom to speculate. He was a realist, working in scientific chemical and physical properties. Molecular tensile strength was more familiar to him than abstractions like oppression and justice and dignity. Those were just words, used by rhetoricians to justify doing what they longed for, in concrete. Like construct a piped water system. There was the abstract, and there was the manifest.

Ruefully smiling to himself he looked over at Tonatín whose eyes darted from the road ahead to the rear view mirror, without alighting on Harry. Harry used the moment to look at his guide without embarrassment.

"Do you have a family, Tonatín?"

"Cómo no? Everyone in Mexico has a family."

"I mean, a wife and children," Harry clarified.

"Ah," Tonatín responded. "I have two grandchildren already."

Harry's shock was only momentary. In this part of the world, to have a child at eighteen for Tonatín, or sixteen even, perhaps his daughter—he looked more carefully at the man beside him. Perhaps he was in his forties. Harry thought of everyone under sixty as vastly younger than himself, and he made a mental correction. Tonatín was not a kid.

"I have two grandchildren also," Harry said. But he could think of nothing more to add. They drove in silence.

The newsboy stationed in the center of San Gregorio knew the roads were blocked. He didn't know the Tuxtla airport was closed. His newspaper, the only paper that came to San Gregorio, didn't mention it.

Across from the news stand a family of Tzotziles sat on the curb. The man held a plastic disposable razor and a small hand mirror. Seated with his feet in the road he shaved himself in the gathering twilight while his wife and two children waited. Harry looked, and then looked away. Perhaps he had seen this man before. But perhaps not.

By the time he reoriented himself in the faded light, the truck had already vanished around the corner of the zócalo, leaving only the odor of its exhaust, and the patient family still visible in the background while he headed home.

15

Constance Meets Merwin

On her first social foray out of the apartment Constance attended a memorial service honoring the deceased bishop who was pushed aside by the Church in response to his defense of the Zapatistas.

Constance and Harry practiced no religion. Harry referred to himself as a "secular humanist," and Constance called herself "a religious atheist." Both retained the quiet knowledge that remote European ancestors, of who knows what name or persuasion, expelled or fled, safe in the United States, shed their past rituals without a backward glance. Constance and Harry never quarreled over which church Judith would be taken to—the clear answer was none. Harry never acknowledged that organized religion could do any good. He scorned Connie's strange mixture of beliefs, her claim that she saw walking on water the golden God in whom she did not believe. Sightseeing, when Constance almost involuntarily inhaled in sharp appreciation of the dim light, the coolness surrounding dozens of statues, he pretended with no comment that she was only observing cathedral architecture. Harry would growl at the waste of money and oppression of indigenous people who labored under the domination of the Spaniards.

Grudgingly he admitted Liberation priests in Central America and Mexico accomplished good deeds in the sixties and seventies, before Harry himself surfaced from his nine-year stint with Bechtel and back-pedaled toward independent assignments, short term contracts and part-time university teaching.

"I can't do this anymore," he confessed to Constance in their apartment in Ann Arbor. His head hung over his knees while he talked, sitting on the footstool in front of the upholstered chair. Connie held Judith on her lap, bouncing her in the Ride-A-Cock Horse, her jeans inching up her shin. While Judith giggled and Connie jiggled her leg up and down, Harry asked her if she would mind if he quit.

"I want out."

"What would that mean, exactly?" Judith giggled and screeched as the leg-horse lightly tossed.

"Less money, right now, anyway."

They had talked about a house of their own. The garden-apartments they lived in were occupied by a dozen couples just like themselves, who furnished their living rooms with bookcases made of planks and bricks. They slowly saved toward a down payment. "Not forever. But maybe never rich."

In those days, Constance recalled, she wasn't isolated, because women, mostly middle class like herself, stayed home with the kids and suffered together their boredom and anxieties. They repeated their husbands' belief in big liberal government, applauded social programs for the black and poor, drank a lot of coffee. She would be glad for an excuse to work, to use her university teaching degree. Judith was nursery school age, and it would do them both good to get out.

Released, Harry fled the blatant military-industrial complex, sickened by it, yet without articulating his opposition. He certainly held no religious qualms. His sense of righteousness came from somewhere else, some empathy for people he saw laboring to survive. Standing outside a cathedral or any other old structure, his engineer's interest could be engaged—indeed many of the buildings were impressive feats, with their high clerestory windows and tiled domes. Their purpose somehow demeaned the lives of the very builders who inhaled stone dust and grunted as they heaved granite into place. There was no reconciling ambivalence—neither his nor hers. One lived with it.

In this stand-off, Constance didn't feel obliged to share with Harry her interest in seeing the old cathedral in San Gregorio, declared a Cultural Patrimony by UNESCO. A plan had been announced, to restore it in honor of the bishop, and add a small museum. The daily news was dreadful—that unabated misery added to her reluctance to say anything to Harry. The government surely enjoyed support of the established church—the church hierarchy was supported by wealthy colonial descendants.

Constance entered through banks of lit candles, and settled on a pew in the rear of the nave. Children and dogs moved through the sacred space, after four hundred years as casually taken for granted as the solid floor. It seemed to Constance that weariness brought people here more than reverence. Weariness, and a hope as remote as winning the national lottery. The so-called middle-class mestizos clustered up in front, mostly women, with a few very ancient gentlemen among them. They must be the professionals, Connie thought, the ones who supported the rebellion with human rights work, or teaching Spanish to the indigenous who spoke none. The remainder of the congregation looked poor, women with delantals covering their dresses, rundown shoes and vein-wrenched legs. Among them a few old men in shabby gabardine trousers crossed themselves and muttered.

The service proceeded with deliberation, not a mass, she could tell, but some kind of homage to the bishop's work.

Sitting alone in the worn wooden pew, half listening to the incomprehensible service, she stood and sat along with the others. The rhythm pleased her; she let her mind drift. She wondered if she should be doing something useful with her education and experience, like Harry was. But he had wants—he wanted to be necessary, for one thing. And she? What wants did she have? Like Harry, she wanted the Mexican government to honor the peace accords. It seemed pretty unlikely. And meaningful as these Accords were to the indigenous population, to her they were so abstract, dealing both with simple rights and privileges she'd enjoyed from birth, and complex land-holding restrictions. So, for herself, what? She wanted to participate in Life with a capital L, but never knew how. She hardly spoke the local language, and the culture tripped her with strange food and customs. She put the question in the back of her mind to wait.

When she exited after the service, a young Mexican man lingering on the front steps smiled at her, so that meant he knew English, didn't it. She gratefully smiled back, and said hello. They stood and chatted, both of them gazing upward at the exterior facade damaged by earthquakes, bullets, and old age.

"What do the bells mean? We're overwhelmed!"

"Bells at 5:00 AM, 6:00 AM, and 7:00 AM mean it's time for morning mass." His mouth twitched as he launched on, "Bells at nine indicate the water truck is coming; bells at 9:30 indicate the trash truck is approaching and you must run out to the corner with your used toilet tissue and orange rinds, all neatly bagged. The gas truck sound is a low horn, also at 9:30, working uphill behind the water camión, but probably you need to buy gas only every four weeks."

The young man grinned, a gentle pleasure with his own wit and patter. Constance laughed. Courteous and friendly men scarcely thirty were common enough in Mexico, but rare in her life. "How does buying the gas work?"

"Oh," he explained, "the stove won't light when you click the sparker, so you know the gas is gone. Open and close the tanks appropriately. My guess is you have two twenties, most people do. Do you remember using wooden matches on cooking stoves? My mother does. And washing dishes in cold water?"

He was American, not Mexican. Both. "Tell me your name so I'll know who's teasing me," Constance replied. She felt her spirits soar. Here was someone she could speak to. "Actually, I do recall lighting the gas oven. Almost lost my eyebrows one Thanksgiving."

His name was Merwin Jiménez. She told him a new water cistern sat installed on their roof.

"Don't drink it without boiling," he warned. "The cistern, that's filled by city water during the rainy season, which is almost over, and you can shower and flush until the spring crisis, when it's gone. After that, quién sabe. The potable water sold off the trucks in fifty liter jugs is considered suspect by some, but it's probably ok. I guess."

Constance did not share with her youthful informant the fact that her thoughts about water centered around flushing the toilet. Harry knew all this.

"You're a treasure," she assured him. It was a pleasure to hear English.

All in all, their living quarters were as trashy as the rest of Chiapas seemed to be. But everything sparkled with sun and brilliant flowers. Maria Carmen had placed potted plants around their patio; a climbing bougainvillea was nearly florescent with fuchsia and red. Carmen spent endless hours on the plants, coming and going in a way which was somewhat intrusive but also reassuring. Constance deduced Carmen had no children. She did have a husband however, to whom she never alluded. Geraniums in heavy clay pots deeper than the color of Carmen's skin appeared one day to line the wall, then a rose bush, a gardenia bush, and only yesterday a ficus tree, which amazed Constance, who previously thought ficus were houseplants. In fact, all northern houseplants flourished outdoors, cheerfully inviting bees and hummingbirds.

The Sierra Mountains visible at the end of their street wore an ermine ruff of cloud. She pointed up-hill toward their street and invited Merwin to come for coffee. The cathedral was nearby, and he could stop in either coming or going to his work. Constance would be grateful if he did—she was spending more time alone than was good for her. San Gregorio's main cathedral once had an intricate tree of life painted on the domed ceiling, now sadly chipped. The exorbitant altar, saints staring down—it was fantastic, dripping gold, while everywhere beggars on the streets—blind, old, hideous in some degree—pleaded for pesos.

Constance looked at Merwin to gauge how he reacted to Harry's critique. Harry sat opposite Merwin in one of the newly purchased plastic chairs. Both men were bareheaded, the one gray and curly, the other black and straight. They were taking their coffee in the patio, like old friends. Constance wondered if she could start giving English lessons, if anybody wanted them, or how much she could charge. Her pleasure in Merwin's impromptu visit confirmed her need for human contact not Harry.

"There are street children peddling Chiclets and letter- openers," she seemed to apologize to Merwin for Harry's anger. "On the zócalo? You've seen the encampment of women and children? They've lived on the sidewalk for two years. This morning I saw some women washing little kids, naked in buckets of cold water. Their laundry hangs on the park railings to dry. They stay here to protest their men in jail, accused of belonging to the Zapatistas. The men confess after being tortured, and they're held indefinitely."

Constance sighed and fell silent. In former times she might have felt like a stooge for Harry, explaining his condemnation of the rich status quo church. Now she was not so sure. She found more often that she agreed.

"The military is out there," Merwin assented in a noncommittal way. His hands holding his cup were nearly the same color as its contents, a lightly creamed coffee. "Doing the dirty work for landowners. Human Rights abuse every place you look."

"The USA is never out of the picture," Harry added. He was freshly shaven but his new Zapata moustache was probably permanent. "It reminds me every day of School of the Americas, seeing these fat cats parading." Across the patio table Harry met Merwin's eyes. Merwin nodded in recognition of shared information. Merwin knew about disappearances in Latin America.

They drank coffee flavored with cinnamon, as Constance, ever on housewifely alert, already learned to make. The daily market gleamed like a fiesta, with small stalls for food and chicken, blouses, rebozos, wooden salad bowls. Mariachis singing their silver studs off. Constance knew now which stalls sold better tomatoes and which cheeses she better avoid. She bought local Chiapas coffee, poured into plastic bags.

"But how long will you be here?" Constance asked Merwin, refilling his cup. He had that pared look of someone who had gone, had witnessed life in the communities in rebellion. An unmistakable look, of haunted weariness around his dark eyes and still-young mouth. All the Witnesses saw beauty and desperate poverty. All reported the same fear and admiration. Connie wondered if any of them came back enthusiastic and awed, recognizing a great socio-political movement. They didn't speak of it. Just the emotion. Doom. Or for some, a desperate mad hope.

"I want to get up into the mountains for my research. I work for UNESCO, formally, I mean, they pay me." His journey to the Zapatista communities notwithstanding, he was here to investigate stone ruins, not living people. He better put his mind on it. Fragmenting. Selected attention. Intellectual discrimination, between art and life. Do his work before his grant ran out and he was left stranded.

Constance was impressed.

"Maybe we can hook up, for the traveling," Harry offered. "It would be nice to have another person along." He meant, another American. Merwin was probably legitimate, a guy with a good Mexican visa. Harry was experiencing the same need as Constance, to have another person to talk with, in English especially. The usual Peace Witnesses drifted in and out of Estación Norte, along with Meditators who struck him as cult nuts. Tourists to the rebellion!

Harry never mentioned this need to Constance. Nor she to him. It would have seemed whiny, each of them thought, since they set off for Chiapas together on their adventure.

That night they heard the rat-a-tat of small arms fire. Constance bolted upright in bed, pulling the blanket up over her breasts as if that offered protection.

"Just like San Cristóbal, isn't it?" Harry pulled her down next to him. "Fireworks again. A party every night." He stroked her thigh. So that was that, and with no further need for conversation each rolled over to sleep.

Rockets banged almost nightly, celebrating whichever saint's day it might be. They lived only a block from a local church, and the cathedral was hardly further. How did she forget? Something in her dream-world dreaded Harry's next trip. Of course she knew the fireworks. Every dawn brought out a raggedy marching band on their way to some damn celebration.

In fact, the morning was Independence Day. Harry and Constance strolled down to watch the parade. It seriously resembled small town Independence Day parades in the US, minus only the American Veterans of Foreign Wars.

"No old soldiers in San Gregorio," Harry said, and Constance finished, "They went somewhere else to die."

"Probably never lived to be old."

After the parade, horse shit littered the street, and Connie thought about resemblance and difference. Horse shit was part of her memory bank, not just parades but horse drawn wagons which were still used in her earliest childhood. Similes and metaphors recycled in her waking moments as well as in her dreams. In assimilating so many new experiences, getting them onto the right tapes, as she described it to herself, she relived scenes of her childhood. It would be nice if that were actually true, if she could resume her adolescence right now, inhabit her youthful torso and grow up all over again. Her mind wandered to her first boyfriend who had slipped his hand under the elastic of her panties, then to herself as a co-ed. Harry was already in the army, for the Korean War. They met at the university after his service, and he seemed infinitely more knowledgeable than younger fellows who hadn't been soldiers, although he never left the United States. But he knew things.

Her mind played tricks on her. It's like being caught in a time warp. What do you suppose happened to that boy, Duncan? But here, this is real, these people are poor, and poor is real.

She pushed her hand through her hair, carefully replacing the canvas hat on the top of her head so as to avoid giving herself a bad case of hat hair, as Judith called it. Harry held her other hand. It was strange to be old.

Really, it was strange to be old and watching a parade. Harry, at her side, saw very little of the parade. Although they stood together, he was looking out for men with cameras taking shots of the spectators. There were one or two—from the local newspaper, he hoped.

The crowd was thin along the parade route, mainly parents carrying kids. The luxury of owning baby carriages didn't exist, but oddly it was often the men, in this macho country, who carried even tiny infants. They moved toward the zócalo. Behind the area where seats were set up for the band concert, booths of food served people two or three deep. Heat off the comals grilling hot cakes and tortillas permeated the air.

Harry felt suffocated.

He was glad Constance didn't object to heading back toward their apartment. He didn't like the military vehicles stationed in the streets, nor troops with their rifles. The big guys in full uniform with their formal caps and stripes. He hadn't liked it when he was a kid in the army and less now, when he stood on the side of the enemy. If one of those colonels—shit that one has a deformed ear, that one's fat—if one of those guys gave the order to shoot, probably the troops would do it. As eighteen year old Private Skelba, he would have done it himself. We don't have judgment or the big picture at that age.

Constance, trailing at his side, wondered if any of these people would want to learn English.

16

September 25

San Gregorio
September 25, 1996
Dear Sally,

Well so far so good! She laughed at herself. Writing to Judith normally brought out the mother in her, but writing to Sally in Philadelphia was very much open-ended. They'd been friends for forty years, since college in fact, and stayed in touch from wherever they happened to be, with whatever husband or lover. Whatever.

Women friends were best, of course. Although over the years their letters gave way to discussions of calcium and Fosamax tablets. And now she wanted to talk about her life and the changes she felt, but really couldn't articulate. Least of all to Harry, maybe not to Sally either.

Independence Day week was interesting. The indigenous groups held

their own festival concurrently, so that on one side of the zócalo the mili-
tary band bur-burped, and on the other, Indians in costume danced to
taped music. Politicians were speechifying, naturally, so I went for the
dancers. The "professional" dancers wear elaborate full long skirts with
starched white petticoats, embroidered bodices, flowers in their hair, and
high heeled shoes. They did a German-inspired polka. They also performed
a simpler dance of planting seeds, so it looked like a combination of hun-
dreds of years of different traditions. Not "pure" by any stretch. The em-
broidery is actually a craft brought from China! I think the living indig-
enous people simply insist they be included as part of Mexico, and rightly
so. Too many outsiders think they can "save" a culture—cultures change.

People change, too. It might seem amazing that after forty years of
not changing she was changing. Or had she changed all along and not
noticed?

The Tzeltals, another group here, celebrated every night. I sat at a
long table in the square, in front of a woman who cooks and serves her
food. I didn't ask for the recipe! Families, men alone, passers-by, even a
few tourists - we placed ourselves in the row of wooden chairs like kids
at grandma's table. I ate empanadas, chili relleno, papas; skipped the fish
because their teeth look too much like dentures on a small fried face.

Dentures could only remind her of aging, although both she and Sally kept their teeth minus one or two. A small permanent bridge could
happen to anybody, right? It didn't mean you were decrepit. Here in
Chiapas missing teeth were replaced with gold if you were lucky, not
replaced if you were poor. She saw toothless women who were far too
young.

Harry was gone. She didn't exactly forget his absence but she
wasn't totally distressed by it. She put out a sign for MAESTRA DE

INGLÉS and although nobody yet rang the doorbell, she remained hopeful.

> *The ancient people in Mesoamerica cultivated corn. Chocolate was here, and how could we be happy without chocolate! Naturally the Europeans grabbed onto it, and coffee, too. This agriculture may have been as early as 4,000 BCE, I read. I find it amazing that a tourist of reasonable intelligence can ask where did the Mayans go—hey, they're right here! I want to leap up and shout Open your eyes, for heaven's sake!*
>
> *Indigenous peoples have not given up their own communal life style, nor their traditions nor their local languages, no matter what additional shows get staged. Meanwhile intellectuals and students come to study anthropology and sociology; they study herbal forest medicines of native practitioners; they study political systems and burying grounds and systems of astronomy; they study languages and linguistics. I guess it's ok—sometimes I think it's depressing, what with the rebellion going on at the same time.*

Open your eyes, indeed. Constance looked and looked, and now she came to the conclusion she better stop looking and start thinking. What did it mean, after all? Today was Sunday. The phone line they had been promised weeks ago was fading from Constance's expectations, she wanted to talk to Harry about a cell phone. Constance couldn't call Judith and Judith couldn't call her.

> *We're surrounded by a feeling of community, which while superficial, is pleasant. I think (I know how cynical you are) it's only partly based on the Chiapanecos wanting our tourist money. Everyone asks our names, where we live, how long we're here for, and calls us amigos. Each woman who speaks to me somehow attaches, touching my shoulder, taking my hands, leading me around the corners and across the street. A little person*

in a homemade dress (shades of my Singer childhood!), showed me the best place to stand to watch the parade, pushed me in front of Harry, touched me carefully many times, smiled showing her many kinds of metal teeth, inquired about my life and my children. And then she left! Another day, I sat on a park bench and another woman came near me and looked me over carefully. This one was old and completely without teeth. She sat next to me and touched me and took my hands, and then she asked if I like the band music, how long I am staying in San Gregorio, and so it goes; I am becoming accustomed to this kind of comfort in a strange land.

So I must be approachable, or at least something in my face says so. People here mostly remain impassive in front of gringos, there's a sense of stoicism. Eternal patience, rather. Five hundred years could teach you that!

Carmen, for example. Surely Carmen was probably assimilated pure Indian, or at least mestizo. Carmen came every day, Constance could hardly avoid seeing her. Her reason ostensibly was pumping water into the cistern, but there was more to it than that, Connie was sure. Approaching? Getting close? How could she? They had so many barriers. Constance was alone a great deal, with Harry gone so frequently. Perhaps Carmen was too—the husband was not in evidence.

Connie slept besieged by dreams, and often in her dream she spoke Spanish, and when awake, she wasn't entirely sure which language would pop out of her mouth—more than once she'd delivered an important monologue to Carmen only to realize Carmen couldn't understand a word.

A man named Ernesto introduced himself to us while we were buying extension cord. Ernesto insisted we visit his little "restaurant", a tiny room with plastic tables and chairs, open onto the street as such places are, with a few ants on the floor to attack our toes. He specializes in food (only tortas, so far as we could tell), Guadalajara style. The next day when we actually walked into his little place his expression was one of happy wonderment. Sort of like a child who unexpectedly manages to tie his shoe. He made us sandwiches which are indescribable – some mix of meat and salsa. Ernesto showed me how to eat the torta with my hands, how to hold the bread and dribble the salsa onto it. He made Harry a glass of Guadalajara juice: cornmeal, salt, sugar and lime. Harry was polite. Ernesto even had ice cubes, which my valiant Harry allowed to melt in his glass. I tasted. Ernesto peered into our faces to see our appreciation. We pretended as best we could. When we arrived back at our apartment we looked at one another, and remembering how ill we had been from past food episodes, crossed our fingers! But we were just fine. Harry bought a radio, so we could listen to music and news.

Only the news was too rapid to catch, her Spanish sufficed now for the street and market, but that was as far as she had progressed. She struggled with the newspaper, determined not to be unaware of what was happening in Mexican national news.

I have fallen down the rabbit-hole, Constance did not write. Only, in this strange place instead of growing smaller she had grown older. Looking in the mirror she was surprised again and again. She covered her mouth to see if her eyes would by themselves give away her age; the falling lids and corner white rays of sun lines where she didn't tan. White hairs were evident in her moustache and chin beard, which she plucked, it seemed, more than ever.

She put down her pen and walked to the patio door. She stepped out and again sensed, through the looking glass. Atop the distant mountain the satellite relay station flashed its lightening. Although she was not in touch, she still stood on the earth, with computers available at internet cafes and rain pattering on the tile roof. She was enormously grateful to have the mountain in view when she needed it, with its pulsing red eye at night and its serene blue and beige skin by day. She had become a senior citizen, or as they called it here, a person of *tercer edad*, the third age. But internally, something totally different was taking place. She lived in a different world no matter how she put it to herself, and why not. She knew perfectly well the dual reality—the affluent academic life in Ann Arbor, the tiny town of poor San Gregorio, where she jumped to her feet and looked around. The red beacon on the mountains, signaling and signaling.

She returned to her letter. She really wanted to ask Sally if Sally felt as she did, lost inside her own body, still sensual, her mind still childlike with why and why and why. Or perhaps it was that the new environment placed her alone, in a new position. Learning like a child. How could she grow within this diminishing body? She picked up the pen. But she felt defeated. After all, it was too difficult to express. She concluded the letter.

> *Be well, my dear.*
> *Much affection,*
> *Constance*

> *P.S. Lovemaking with Harry has become messy – I discovered lubricating jelly in my hair the next morning and knew it was because Harry hadn't wiped his fingers after applying it.*

That should do it! She understood perfectly well she was boasting to Sally that she was still sexually active. Not that old! Of course she was responding to a challenge Sally never uttered. The challenge existed only in her own head. Her letter said nothing important—no war news, no politics—anyway, if she was really through the looking glass (and she couldn't tell), the letter didn't lie. Sally was used to reading her outsider tourist reports of various scenes. After all these years Sally didn't expect any big revelations.

17

Aida and Constance Meet

Aida wasn't pretty. Her features were as blunted as those of worn stone saints adorning the exterior of the cathedral. Her nose was snubbed, her rounded cheeks seemed more rounded than her chin—as if time and rain smudged her, although in fact she wasn't yet thirty. But single.

Partly, her appearance could be attributed to the fact that her mother was Chinese and her father a Mexican, undocumented in the US for five decades until his death two years ago. Aida's body, accustomed to good food and the hills of San Francisco, was bulky, although one wouldn't say fat. Some men enjoyed the embrace of her legs like pillars, and the wide comfort of resting on her hips. Sturdy, she described herself, and never gave it a moment's worry.

Near her mother, her friends, and her transient lovers, Aida preferred life in San Francisco where many people, because of her skin color of pale manila, took her for Chinese.

In Mexico they took her for mestizo or indigenous—they of course were American tourists who didn't know any better. Not the local Chiapanecos, where she was studying.

She had graduated from Berkley, and earned her Master's in social work. That won her a job working for California's Human Services Department, in a position she despised. As a government social worker, the only acceptable advice was "Get a job." She began thinking seriously about a doctorate and enrolled again at Berkley, this time in the Women's Studies program. She genuinely liked women, a rare attribute having little to do with the Feminist Movement, although she believed her mother had been unfairly held back by her Chinese American family and then by her macho Mexican husband.

The Mexican relationships between men and women—now that was a subject for a dissertation. But maybe a cultural comparison of lives of women in less developed countries would do as well? She needed some preliminary investigation before selecting a thesis.

In the tiny university branch of UNAM in San Gregorio, Chiapas, there were only two courses: first "Law", the euphemism for corporate international business-management, although as far as Aida could see no international business existed except for purchasing air conditioners made in Taiwan, which by some manipulation of the state budget were installed in the municipal palace. The other course was "Anthropology", which meant displaying Mayan ruins for tourists.

She studied neither. Aida lived next door, based in the Rosario Castellanos Casa de Mujeres. Between interviews with the women who came for assistance, she wandered next door to observe university classes. Unlike the Casa workers, the academic instructors were mestizos with middle-class backgrounds, bitter over devaluation of the peso. Not aware of their own class privilege.

Aida chatted with them amiably. Cantonese was Aida's first

language, Spanish her second language, both spoken by age two, and English was her third—by age thirty months. Already using her dark eyes to assess the world, she began communications with her fellow humans fully equipped to handle any challenge.

Or so she thought, until she unexpectedly found herself in a war zone. The Zapatista uprising, reported briefly in January of 1994, rapidly faded from the mainstream news. Aida lived more in the Asian than the Mexican community. Oh sure she knew, in some remote corner of her mind, especially when her Mexican cousins forwarded to her the speeches of Marcos which came across the border by e-mail faster than wetbacks in person. But to know and to know were two different propositions. She flew to Mexico DF to find a location for research, and from there the female Human Rights lawyers in that city advised her to go see what was happening with women in Chiapas. They didn't amply prepare her.

Aida, to avail herself of informal talks with local people, was a regular at the new Alvaro's Internet Café, a pleasant place which apparently sprang up overnight after the rebellion, or maybe since the influx of foreigners. Whenever a sufficient number of people showed up, for breakfast or comida or coffee, a spontaneous conversation raced from table to table behind the backs of those ferociously typing at the window row of computers. These conversations centered on gossip, usually about military buildup and the politics of intimidation. Aida would enter with her magazines or newspaper articles about the Zapatistas, put them down on her table, and soon discover someone had walked off with her reading.

For most university students or teachers, it was merely news, something far away from the city, although God knows it seemed imminent to Aida. Maybe they just wouldn't discuss it. Aida heard that some workers at Estación Norte and the Human Rights offices were threatened with murder, mutilation and torture. San Gregorians were afraid to talk in public, no matter what their opinions. But in private conversation, what a wide range of the culture they revealed!

Sitting opposite the well-groomed female Mexican instructors, she observed their store-bought fashions. Nevertheless almost all wore their hair in the old style, long and ready to be flung about. Flinging hair was a sex thing, for sure. In her cotton long skirt and baggy blouse, Aida tried to look sexless and Mexican at the same time. She didn't try to take notes, she relied on her good memory. She was a good listener. Over a cup of hot frothy chocolate she heard about the prevailing mores, and the pretense of virginity at marriage.

Certainly everywhere she walked fierce necking was out in the open. She was embarrassed by the blatant groping, on benches, on walls, in parks. She was absolutely embarrassed to find herself at a church fair where in the front courtyard a bump-and-grind chorus of skimpily clad young women showed their crotches. In the watching semi-circle, men stood on the cobbles looking upward to the stage, the best possible angle. Their wives stood further back, observed, and said nothing. Machismo at its worst, and the women apparently didn't object. Get pregnant, get married, was the common experience. Every wedding included white gowns, flowers, fireworks and a band, a meal afterward with a lot of mescal, and she wondered who paid the bill.

Aida chatted with one young university student who assured Aida that she planned on a wedding exactly like that. Aida figured she'd never marry herself, so therefore she wasn't qualified to criticize. But still, these Chiapanecas were so conformist—a designation which in her book expressed contempt.

On the other hand, when she interviewed older women, at church festivals or sunning in the park in late November warmth, what she heard was a certain amount of self-congratulation. Worth had been established by producing many children. When the older women chatted, Aida overheard, "How many grandsons do you have? Only three? Too bad, I have five!" She began to compare lives of middle-class women and wondered if poor women were more interesting.

Aida marveled that normal life continued against the backdrop of a mean struggle for life by the indigenous in the countryside. Not to mention a dirty war against the Zapatistas, with assassinations which people in the safe city read about. Nobody in the city was indigenous, although many people she met spoke their parents' language—had two parents of Tzeltal or Tzotil stock who migrated to the city and assimilated.

So is Aida going to run into Constance? Sure, what else. Here they are in a tiny town, with one main gathering place. Americans were far from their Thanksgiving holidays, and most treated the day like any other—except, one by one they drifted together in Alvaro's Café.

Aida first became aware of the older woman's back. It was identifiable as old by some sense Aida had, perhaps of the curve. No excess flesh showed around the bra line, and the back rose from slender hips. If the woman carried any spare weight it must be on her stomach, hidden from view by the computer table. The woman's hair was a mouse and gray streaked combination when she removed her cotton hat—whoa, that hat was a giveaway—Aida's mother wore one just like it despite her daughter's pleas. Yo-ana (as Aida's father referred to his wife) claimed the hat protected her skin from the sun's rays, but since San Francisco has precious little of that, Aida finally concluded that her mother simply avoided the necessity of washing and arranging her hair daily.

Constance set her hat on top of the monitor.

Aida enjoyed older women, they fit the category of female, in a prototypical kind of way, right? When Constance finally stood up and moved to a table opposite Aida's, Aida smiled.

Constance recalled Merwin's smile. She found it didn't take much more among foreigners to establish at least a speaking acquaintance, and better yet, she could distinguish now who was American and who not, although sometimes Canadians fooled her. American showed in the confident glance around as if they expected homage, the set of their shoulders, their long stride. Of course if they wore Tevas that really clinched it.

Aida didn't need to speculate about the nationality of her new acquaintance. Her roused curiosity focused on why an older American woman came here. It was a hard life without wealth, and Constance did not appear wealthy. If anything, her clothing bordered on shabby—worn jeans and tee-shirt. No make-up. Horrible hairdo. Yo-ana looked snappier than that!

"I'm an English teacher," Constance admitted. Something in Aida's frank brown-eyed appraisal left her defensive. Harry was away, but that was no excuse—she wondered if she needed to tweeze her moustache hairs again. Sometimes she forgot, when he was away. Anyway, English teachers always looked like teachers.

Older Mexican teachers looked like middle-class women from the '50s, with high heels and bee-hive hairdos. But Aida didn't pursue that line of conversation. She really wanted to discuss the gossip with a fellow-American, somebody who must be here for a reason. The military build-up was reaching proportions impossible to miss, even within the city.

"Have you seen this?" Constance showed Aida a communiqué published in La Jornada. The Zapatistas again called Civil Society to come forward as the only force able to save the country. And incidentally, themselves. If no public outcry occurred, the Zapatistas were doomed.

The government was, as Aida put it, not only murderous but fucking useless in serving the population. Government inability to function showed in the huge Mexico DF earthquake of 1985. Citing that experience, the Zapatistas held up Civil Society as a model of self-governance, a competent force which without aspiring to public office, could organize politically without a political party. It was the model for their communities, and although neither woman knew it on that day, the model for the Zapatista's future.

"That's making the government assholes mighty uncomfortable. It leaves them out."

"Government functionaries don't just step aside, do they?" Constance spoke quietly, but nobody in the café was looking at them. They were just two Americans with their inevitable coffee, and Aida smoked a cigarette, which Constance wished she wouldn't do.

"Do you know something specific?"

"La Jornada says there're plans to assassinate the Human Rights lawyers working in Chiapas. They've all been threatened, and their children."

"I know the most important one," Aida admitted. Her low forehead frowned in horizontal lines. "A woman. And she has a little boy. Her husband was murdered but they never caught anybody, probably because they know who the killers are."

Constance raised her eyebrows. Aida could see the unplucked hairs between them. The eyebrows were untweezed too, so her new friend wore a silver frame above her eyes.

"Abducted," Aida went on. "The corpse turned up in a ravine. Tortured, naturally. They all know. Maeda is scared shitless for her little boy, but she hasn't left. Too stubborn. Is this today's?" She pulled the newspaper closer. "I think I should encourage her to go while the going's good, don't you?"

Constance assented. She would protect a child of hers, at any cost to her principles. The Zapatistas were into Principles. She wondered if that was equally true of their women, not the ones who joined their army but the ones who lived in the communities. "Are you involved with Human Rights workers?" she asked Aida.

"Only peripherally. I'm doing investigation on Women's Issues. About a million of them. Issues, I mean. Like, there's an epidemic of cervical cancer among indigenous women in their twenties out in the pueblos, did you know that?"

Constance was shocked. "How could that be!" she exclaimed. "I know about houses with dirt floors, no windows, no running water. I know parasites create big medical problems." She wanted to tell Aida her husband passed on to her some pretty grim descriptions of life in the pueblos. But she was learning not to mention Harry. Period.

Aida added, "Cooking smoke vented out front and back doors, not good for lungs. Etcetera. Sure. But for cervical cancer it's gotta be something sexual. They marry real young, so whatever it is that's getting them invaded years before they hit their early twenties. Some doctors say it's a virus transmitted along with genital warts by their men."

"That must be detectable and curable, genital warts!"

"You don't say." Aida's lips curved in a mirthless smile.

Constance felt like the idiot she was. Of course no routine exams were offered, no pap smears—in fact, nothing. The women lived as isolated as women hundreds of years ago. Warmth by open fires. Barefoot. Incredible bearers of burdens. Carry, and nurse if possible, toddlers of two or three; carry wood, water, charcoal, corn, chickens. She'd seen it.

Aida had obtained hard statistics for Chiapas. She knew how many illiterates among each language; out in the countryside most don't speak Spanish. A family may send boys to school but girls traditionally do domestic chores. Often they don't receive even the primary grade education of their brothers. Result: girls remain monolingual in Tzotil or Tzeltal, and illiterate, while many boys learn Spanish and reading.

"So what's to be done about this." Constance didn't think these women needed English lessons?

"No, I guess not! But for the moment I'll focus on worrying about Maeda. I'm sure she's been warned." Aida's coffee cup was empty. She stood up. Clearly she thought another warning was in order. She opened her shoulder bag.

Constance said, "No, my treat, hija." Smiling, she used the common Mexican familiar word, daughter. She extended her hand to shake goodbye, but Aida bent over and kissed her on the cheek. Constance returned the air-kiss in the Mexican way which did not offend her here as it did in Ann Arbor among faculty wives. She waved as Aida left. For some reason tears pooled in Aida's eyes. She must be worried sick about her friend the lawyer. It never crossed Connie's mind that she had reminded Aida of Yo-ana and Thanksgiving. Aida was homesick.

18

Billy Explores and Meets Merwin

The language school arranged for Billy to stay with a "family", and since Billy could think of nothing more repulsive than someone else's brat brother or sister, he was relieved to discover his temporary hostess was the mother of the owner of the language school.

Nothing like a little honest nepotism, Billy surmised. The mother was a coffee colored woman with dyed black hair stiffened and deployed to cover all possibilities. She wore the usual mother's makeup—eye rims and cheek circles. The overall look was America 1960 like his own mother who, Billy complained, never gave up and never wised up. Grennich undertook her perpetual upkeep. Like this Chiapas dame, his mother always went out in high heels and short skirts which made Billy avert his eyes. Both women showed veins traveling like ropes around their knees.

Billy slunk around the language school and then the town, checking out younger specimens. He figured that among the San Gregorio women, class showed. Start with bare feet and legs; upgrade one level to plastic shoes; then to pantyhose; then to high heels. High heels on the cobbled streets of San Gregorio? Braver than he was, man. His hostess drove a new Toyota. He didn't see any American cars, a few VWs. Señora Vasquez steered her car into the downtown, if that was a downtown, a walk which Billy enjoyed daily, less than thirty minutes for checking the scene.

In the economic disaster of Mexico, Señora Vasquez suddenly thinks she's poor. Ha. Her Indian servant still came every day to cook and wash clothes by hand no less, and clean—for a salary of 150 pesos per month, like maybe twenty bucks. Billy asked the girl to do his laundry too, but Señora Vasquez squashed that. It cost a lot, the Señora claimed, to run the electric water pump, she would prefer Billy take his laundry out.

The room he rented was cluttered with cardboard boxes and clothing, odd baskets and china heaped in a corner. This stuff remained from a shop the Señora ran for a few years, before the tourist trade imploded. The bedroom walls in the bright morning light tracked dark mildew from the rainy climate, while the living room of her modern bungalow imitated Home Beautiful 1955, with doilies and ashtrays.

While Billy sat alone in the kitchen with the thin shy girl who would not look at him, he tried to explain to her what American coffee was and how much money did she make. His Spanish was awful and hers wasn't much better, so conversation didn't go well. Billy ate quickly, hunched on a stool behind the tile counter that served as table. Rosa carefully wrote numbers on a napkin with the ballpoint pen he pulled from his pocket. The coffee came out of a jar, powdered instant.

The widow-mother-teacher was short on conversation when Billy met up with her each morning before he took off. Clearly she didn't know what to do with a boy who was not like her boy, her boy who called her daily and maintained respect. The guy was like, into his forties and lived for making a success of his language school business. The mother sat with Billy for a few minutes in the kitchen—never in the Home Beautiful living room. She asked him if he was hungry and instructed Rosa.

Billy preferred the mornings when she slept in or went out, he didn't know, and left him alone with the girl. Rosa was seventeen, and compared with Billy's twenty, plus his sparse but fervent sex life, she seemed like a child. Rosa arrived at the kitchen door with bare legs and plastic shoes. Rosa could print her name, and numbers up to 100. The Señora assured him Rosa never wanted to learn. But Billy thought maybe she did. She was patient with his own bungled pronunciation, and often asked for the English word, which he wrote on the napkin she saved. He gave her his pocket dictionary as a farewell gift, and moved to a small hotel, a posada in the center of the city, to study Spanish until he was eligible to head out as a Witness.

He slept in a center of a maelstrom of casual noisiness: the lady of the posada stood on her balcony every morning and shouted down into the central courtyard. One of the half-dozen boys who seemed to belong to the hotel responded, "What? Mande?" Then would begin the routine of fetching a bucket of water and sloshing it from a plastic bowl onto the tile floor. With a long handled squeegee whichever skinny kid pushed the water out the front door onto the sidewalk. The remainder of the water in the bucket he hurled onto the dozens of potted plants. The rest of the morning he minded the front desk, or watched Daffy Duck cartoons on TV.

Billy couldn't say if the boys were sons or nephews, but for sure they were related, because all business is kept within the family. The boss lady every morning shouted, "Pepe, Pepe, venga, venga!" It was seven A.M.

The daily celebratory rockets and fireworks had already blasted off in salute to whichever Saint's Day this might be when Billy, answering to the same call, struggled out of his room, shivering in his tee-shirt, shuffling in his sneakers, still untied. The church bells sounded; the roosters crowed. Along with the roosters he clearly heard the TV playing downstairs; the boy already had flipped on the cartoons. The water truck sounded its bell along the street.

Dutifully at noontime each day Billy began to take notes, to read the coffee-stained newspapers he found in the language school café. He could sit at a scarred wooden table, among fellow gringos, with almost a sense of comfort. Improved Spanish. That was required; he was always panicked that he'd misunderstood something really important, like life and death. Some effort for the distant university committee, to gather material, he was obliged to do that, in reality he liked to do it. He harbored an image of himself sounding forth with facts and data. Where and when he would show that authoritative command, he didn't know. He wasn't going back for exams or even the fall semester; he took the investigation money pretty much under false premises, sending reports he hoped the rest of them could use. He never wanted to screw his fellow students. Like, maybe he would go back for the spring semester. He'd be some kind of big shot, maybe. Like, respected, maybe.

He sent his mother a postcard of Mexican flowers, and another to Grennich of half-dressed barefoot children. He let his hair grow. It came in thin and lank, and looked like orange juice flowing over his skull. Disgusted, he opened his army knife scissors and chopped it back.

"Expulsados," he read, "were driven out of their own pueblos, bereft of house, of land, of belongings." Billy guessed these expelled people provided Rosa, and small boys who sold chewing gum on commission. Probably likewise the shriveled woman leading a blind man whose hand was permanently cupped by arthritis or by begging, he didn't know. It's always in the interest of the rich to keep around lots of poor.

Restaurant managers continuously shooed away children and elderly beggars. After the first day or so in San Gregorio Billy gave up eating sitting down; he bought an empanada or an ear of corn, and ate walking around back streets behind the language school where the children didn't beg. Although in the restaurants he never heard any manager talk mean. A determined silent encouragement to leave did the trick, like a cue from the wings from your third-grade teacher. Better do it. Or like his mother staring at him steadily when he used his thumb to push mashed potato onto his fork. Better not.

"The indio expulsion of fellow villagers is now twenty-five years old. It was one of the first effects of the conversion of Catholic indigenous people, usually led by the women, who saw hope in the Protestant fundamentalist religions which didn't permit drinking.

"Those with PRI support were the ones who confiscated belongings, drove out dissenters who wouldn't go along with the costly Catholic calendar of saints, the obligations to buy rockets, candles, fresh altar flowers and feasts."

The husbands drank the income. The PRI ruling party ran the show in the villages by doling out government food and money. For a few extra bucks PRI town leaders claimed they only expelled religious dissenters who didn't show up for their community work, and then grabbed their land and houses and whatever the expelled couldn't carry away. Lots of bad shit like shootings and beatings. The local bosses were called caciques. 25,000 Expulsados lived in colonias on the hills ringing San Gregorio. Got it.

Billy hiked across town to the outer ring. The traffic kicked up dust that settled on the food-stands adjacent to the main road. He crossed.

The mountainside was a steep deforested slope awash in mud. Colonia Mazariego in another time and place—like, for example Sausalito in California—he figured would sell its view over the city for a fortune. But here Colonia Mazariego looked like a slum. Even from below Billy could spot tin roofs hanging awry, with cinder block construction listing to one side.

He approached the dirt path with a determination to get all the way up, climbing as best he could in his sneakers, flapping his arms for balance. He passed women wearing the wrapped wool skirt and embroidered blouse of their pueblo, like they brought their town with them. Many walked barefoot. All the women carried babies, and some smaller kids were toted by sisters of maybe seven or eight, hard to say. Half way up he ran into a guy with a camera, poised on a plateau above the view.

"What're you shooting?" he asked in English before he had a minute to think. Surprisingly, the answer came in English, although the guy looked Mexican, whatever that means. Well, he didn't look like the Pillsbury Doughboy, like blue-eyed Billy. Billy kept his ragged orange hair under his cap and his face covered with sunscreen, but it was pretty hopeless. This guy had a permanent tan and sharp dark eyes, scant beard stubble. Tall for a Mexican.

"The cathedral." The photographer pointed out over the roofs into the town, where twin tiled domes were clearly visible, a kind of double yellow onion effect. "It's a colonial cathedral." Billy raised his eyebrows. "That means construction started in maybe 1560. When the Conquistadores got hold of the gold."

"Whoa."

"Yeah. So last year the United Nations declared it a Cultural Patrimony, which means they'll get some money to restore it."

"Cool."

Billy sensed he wasn't contributing much to the conversation.

"You here to do architectural photos?"

"Some. I also do other stuff." He fished in his jeans and handed over a small business card.

Merwin Jiménez, PhD.
UNESCO Investigator
Cultural Patrimony Project

"Awesome," Billy said. He felt stupid. Merwin nodded. Calmly, with a small smile, he replied, "Yup." He picked up his tripod, and waved.

Merwin for the briefest moment considered asking Billy if news was seeping in from the communities, or from the Human Rights organizations. Anxiety plagued Merwin, and although he looked cool he was climbing more to burn off unusable adrenalin than to accomplish any photography.

Billy headed up the hill behind Merwin Jiménez who did not look back. It was a hot climb, dry and dirty. Rocks and sand shifted underfoot with scrabbling sounds. Finally the guy turned as if he took pity, and waited.

They ascended the top of a ridge. Laterally, another colonia of equally homely houses clung to the hillside.

"Well, we might as well go together." He signaled with his tripod, lifting it casually in one hand like a cane. A shift of sentiment on Merwin's part; he concluded Billy was important because every Witness was important, and no other sane reason existed for Billy to be here.

The neighboring colonia was separated from the one they stood above only by a change from jumble and slum to neatness, a kind of home poverty held together by willpower.

"They get piped water over there. Did it themselves, laid the pipes right over the mountain."

Next to Colonia Mazariego the area called La Hormiga looked almost developed; it boasted a cement stairway, 500 feet high, built to the hilltop. Laterally, dirt paths lined with cinder block were marked "calle" or "avenida", with sticks supporting cardboard placards.

Billy followed the photographer. Jiménez was much better out-fitted than Billy, with an Australian canvass bush hat that shielded the face better than the cap Billy pulled down over his eyes. The sun caught him at the wrong angle; his pale chin burned beneath its red stubble.

Two men standing in the doorway of the cinder block church saw them pause, and waved. Apparently they were invited to enter. Billy muttered to Merwin, "Like maybe they think we're wealthy missionaries."

Nevertheless they stooped through the doorway. Merwin made no move to use his camera. Inside the church, plank benches divided on either side of a center aisle strewn with green pine branches. Women and children sat on one side, men on the other. The men's benches stood just a little higher off the dirt floor than the women's; the planks were supported by cinder blocks. Billy amended his mental picture of the inside of cinder block houses. Living in the dirt like his grandparents in Ireland, some.

He sniffed the pleasant pine resin. Seated on the men's side Billy gazed across at the women while the catechist proclaimed in a language not Spanish, and someone squeezed an accordion. The seated women sang hymns while children ran up and down and crawled and nursed. Not Billy's childhood upbringing. Less pious, somehow better. These folks were the converted, the non-Catholics. He wondered idly if they supported the Zapatistas—an unarmed army of sympathizers. And would stand up to be counted, if Civil Society was called on.

They listened for a while to the music, Mexican versions of hymns Billy didn't know, but apparently Merwin recognized them all, relaxing on the plank, his knees under his chin. Billy tried to do the same. The bones in his ass couldn't take it. If he tried to stretch out his legs they met the plank in front of him.

After ten minutes of torture Billy got up to leave, trying to smile in an apologetic, beneficent way, like he was on his way to write an enormous check for Latter Day Saints, which God knows, was sorely needed. He wanted to continue the climb up this face of the hillside to check the lay of the land. As he passed through the wooden frame, he looked briefly back into the dim interior. Merwin sat quietly, gazing at nothing.

Shop-keeping, hotel and restaurant keeping, and taxi driving looked to be the only sources of income in San Gregorio. And the language school. The Zapatistas chased away the tourists and then 60% of the value of the peso vanished. A tough scene.

"Everyone in San Gregorio has a cause," declaimed Billy, "and every cause is just. There's a strike going on tonight." He sat in the language café again, drinking cappuccino. A faint odor of cigarettes hovered in the air, wafted from the table of French students.

"Let's take a look, huh?" He pulled his classmates away from the scattered groups waiting for the Dietrich-Boyer flick to start at eight, and stepped into the street.

Ordinary explosions of night fiesta rockets and music, and then a sound of breaking glass. Shouts. Blows on the door of a house. They passed, trying to look inconspicuous and disinterested. The strike seemed to involve taxi drivers (tiny VW Beetles), combis, (small vans used as buses), larger buses, shopkeepers and street vendors. A dented van blocked the cathedral intersection; a wood-fire smoked in the middle of the stone street. A portable card table balanced on thin legs, coffee was served to strikers who ambled past, in no rush to go no-where.

"What's the skinny?" Billy didn't ask anybody in particular and one of his classmates replied, "So far the mayor didn't do anything. Hey, like what's to be done anyway? The mayor's a PRI puppet."

Billy grunted like he understood. He suddenly knew how un-committed he made his life, busy avoiding the commitment that ru-ined his father, and how totally stupid he was, some kind of baby asshole. His adventures up to now—that was playing. Playing like putting on his father's boots. Oh Christ, had he really done that? Kids did stuff like that, and the dimmest of memories settled into a con-viction in Billy's mind. This rebellion fitted his father's boots on, all over again. Whatever the fuck that meant.

Did other foreigners here hold convictions, and if they did, what convictions, beyond government = bad, and Zapatista = good. That wasn't convictions, because Billy knew from somewhere that a person should have informed convictions.

"Light a fire under a pot—the whole pot boils," he ventured, re-turning to the discussion. The second student shrugged, like a rebel-lion meant nothing more to him than it did to Billy the baby asshole. They were cool, man. But if they were so cool, what the fuck did they come here for?

They made it a short night. Trouble on the streets. In the morn-ing when Billy strolled into the cafe he picked up a newspaper. Over his coffee he read, slowly decoding the Spanish:

EDITORIAL
Shop owners are pitted against street vendors, mestizos and whites against indios, old residents against the Expulsados who play ring a ring of roses with slums, taxi drivers against market vendors, bus drivers against taxi drivers, the rich and formerly rich against the

poor.

The government is militarized, corrupt, useless or worse. The largest source of employment for young men of Mexico is the military, or local state and city police. These armed groups, along with private armies, are continuously named for human rights violations. The men are killing, torturing, disappearing their fellow poor. When a village confronts them the villagers shout, You are one of us. But this is their livelihood!

Billy re-read the last sentence with a frown. The contradiction. A trick question. Like a trap. Or what is justice, anyway? What's right? For Mexico the uprising of 1994 said, Guys you ran out of time to figure it out. "Now the end of silence has arrived." The Chiapaneco indios stepped forward with their grievances. Kicked off their territory, shoved aside in use of their lands' resources such as mines and energy and crops; nobody asked their opinion in the government processes either. The Government never came through with services like roads, hospitals, electricity and telephones. Shut out, shut up. They didn't receive the means of communication even among themselves, let alone a national voice. But 'Now the end of silence has arrived.' Wow!

"And I'm in on it," Billy spoke softly to himself. "Awesome!" Without warning, a surge of exultation flooded over him. The memory of his father, well, his father's golden red beard, his work boots with laces hanging over when Billy stood in them. What trite shit! Billy remembered little of that strange Irishman, the tiny inheritance he could claim was piss-poor and paltry. So be it.

He rubbed his own chin and vowed to learn more exactly what it was he was in on.

19

Martin Gets a Visa

Martin submitted to a bureaucracy to try the patience of ashram novitiates, circling from matins to dark, in obedience to instructions from polite people who responded to questions with the assurance of Masters, and never admitted ignorance of correct answers. It was all one koan. Each morning and evening as he sat for his meditation he found it impossible to just let go. In his inner being he wanted to smash somebody's face.

In banks, in offices, in the Telmex office, the notary, the immigration office—hundreds of invalid pieces of information fluttered about him like feathers. Information as to the whereabouts of any particular place, the hours it's closed, the days it's open—sometimes true, sometimes false. Martin perceived he felt anger for the first time since he left rural Georgia to become a disciple of Holy Master. Despite his spiritual practices he felt as he had in high school, when more affluent boys, their backs damp and broad in the spring heat, drove past him on their way to the beach.

At such moments Martin comforted himself with the memory of funerals he attended. He never wished guys would drop dead, although he shouted it, as receding cars spun dirt beneath their tires into whirlwinds, leaving Martin behind. He meant it only rhetorically. But the boys always drove drunk. Sometimes they died with a not-so-invulnerable girl, or maybe another friend on the right side passenger seat or sprawled in the rear. Often the guy in the back seat survived, paralyzed or brain damaged. On such days of enduring his condition as unloved pedestrian, Martin arrived home safely. He climbed upstairs directly to his room. Seated on his bed he practiced breathing and yoga postures to rid himself of bad karma such thoughts might bring. He had learned about karma from a Sanskrit video on Hindu practices.

Twenty years later Martin did the same, in a hotel room in San Gregorio, Chiapas, Mexico, December 1996.

He walked to the bank where he was supposed to pay for his resident visa, a permit mysteriously called an FM3, sin actividades lucrativas. Benches filled its interior space. He took a number, and sat down to watch the illuminated signs above the teller windows flash up and up, to his. He stood humble and reticent in his laundered cotton chinos and walked up to the open teller's window. He peered through bars at the woman seated inside beyond reach, shielded by marble and plexiglas. He smiled because he wasn't a bank robber.

Slender, humble, white: he was present as a Religious, supported by documents stating he would have an income from Meditators for Peace, an important NGO based in the United States. He carried letters, bank statements, assurances that he would in no way aid or abet or interfere with or assist any rebel anywhere ever. He was not political, he was not a worker. In Mexico the Constitution guarantees religious freedom, but the bureaucracy extends no respect for the religious. Perhaps even some ire. Historical resentment, Martin thought as he gazed across windows, bars and desks, into earth-colored faces. Yet they were mostly Catholic, he supposed, or converted Jehovah's Witness. Perhaps their ancient deities returned in other incarnations, pissed off. He wanted to tell them he was a Hindu, but after silent consideration decided it wouldn't help.

In silence he shoved beneath the plexiglas the form with the exact fee required, including two pesos in coin. The woman took it and began doing something official. She wrote in ink, in several small squares. She pulled out an official stamp, and after carefully inking it, stamped a red circle in three places. Martin smiled, supposing his goal accomplished. But no, despite Martin's prior instruction from the immigration office (where four uniformed men lounged around declining to try their English) the bank clerk abruptly shoved the form back under the glass barrier that separated them.

"We cannot proceed; you must have three originals."

"Where do I get them?" He was too thunderstruck to argue. Anyway, a man of peace does not argue.

"The originals must be purchased at a papelería. Go," she commanded. She reminded Martin of the biblical injunctions of his childhood, left behind him. "I will wait with the one form which is correct."

The manager was a fellow in a western shirt and necktie, an unusual sight. He stalked behind the women tellers and sometimes behind the male tellers also. He supervised. He expressed displeasure over Martin's printing in ink instead of typing on a machine. When he stepped down the line behind the next seated teller, the clerk assured him in a whisper that first, typing was not necessary (no-one has a typewriter, the nearest one in the bank gathered dust in an obscure office upstairs); and second, that the papelería would be open although it was then mid-afternoon.

Of course it was not. Martin panted in the hot sun outside the locked door. His canvas hat shielded his blue eyes, but left his large protruding nose exposed to sun stabs. Most shops closed at some (un-stated) hours between two and four-thirty in San Gregorio. He set off in search of an open stationary store, before the bank closed at four o'clock.

With his loose shirt flapping on his shanks Martin sped through disintegrating streets, avoiding rubble from a forgotten earthquake, accepting directions toward places destroyed or long shut down, and finally in the most innocuous place, a tiny shop whose glass display cases offered ball-point pens and gum erasers, he discovered the of-ficial form.

Martin purchased seven, just to be sure. He dashed back to the bank, where he paid the fees again, without bothering to mention that he had paid before. Not worth trying to get his Spanish around that theft.

Anyway, now all was well. He received his stamped forms (one for the bank, one for the immigration office, one for himself, and four to ward off evil). He checked his watch, and checked the bank's clock. There was no agreement, but by either hour he was too late to return to the immigration office.

Pressing his precious forms beneath his arm, Martin strolled back toward his hotel. Small upright fellows streaming toward him from the direction of the zócalo passed him, two in front wearing starched sombreros. On their feet, huaraches. Very poor.

Martin remembered rural poor, although he hadn't returned to Georgia since his baby brother smashed up himself and another blond teenager. He recognized their feet, the thick callous that be-spoke going shoeless when shoes were too tight, or too hot, or had to be saved for Sundays. Idly he wondered at the destination of these determined-looking men. Possibly another demonstration to block the street in front of the government offices?

He hoped not. Tomorrow without losing another day he must return to the immigration office for the next lesson in obedience. In a Catholic culture one prays routinely, and sooner or later some saint intervenes. Martin, in his Hindu incarnation as disciple of Holy Master Ragadam Baram, felt as if he mistakenly undertook a cross-religion self-flagellation, self-sacrifice, and a vow to remain courteous and well-humored. It was horrible.

Giving up expectations. Of anything. Ever. Just moving from one assignment to another, office to office, bank to bank, shop to shop, as directed. Totally un-American!

By American he meant Baptist, like his parents who farmed their vegetables, raised their own chickens for eggs, and kept cows for milk. They pretended to submit to the will of God, but in actuality never did. If God blew down the barn He surely made a mistake. They needed the barn, and promptly rebuilt it. When Robert John died his mother looked like she would never give in to it. She haunted the rooms of their house determined to find her dead boy, her baby, her favorite.

Martin was baptized on his twelfth birthday and had the faith. The faith of his fathers to accept God's will but do the opposite, resolutely and sometimes with force. For which he himself lacked the physique, damn all. He was ignored; his mother doted on Robert John, the pretty baby arriving six years behind Martin. Martin, taken for granted at home, the one who would get the chores done and cope for himself with a quick breakfast, found that being the occasional butt of jokes was his strongest pleasure. It served as clear recognition of his existence.

He was already at the University of Georgia establishing a new identity when Robert John smashed up. He made the thirty-mile trip back for the funeral in a borrowed car, driving forty the whole way.

After he met Holy Master at a Hindu lecture off-campus, that all changed. It was much better to vanish into the Absolute than go to Heaven, because with practice you could vanish right now. He remained very Baptist in that, one might say very American, like his parents. Now was better than later. His new life, of course, was not based on renunciation. His mother stood against renunciation and still wouldn't renounce her lost boy. His father stood against renunciation too, and wouldn't leave his wife although he wished to. Although Martin quit the university without finishing, he quickly assured himself that renunciation of worldly gain was justified, in order to spend his hours perfecting himself in the ability to retrieve from the Absolute waves of generous loving kindness, like catching minnows by hand. He would be recognized as a Spiritual Force. He would be bigger than everything, a free-style swimmer in the Absolute.

Only in the omnipresent sunlight of this strange country it felt—how—it all felt very unlikely. Dimly he sensed that all these people, with their neat driving spinal columns and black eyes, involved themselves in something quite different. Although in the appearance of things he recognized certain similarities. Poverty, for one thing. Pride, maybe.

Shouldering his doubts he entered the internet cafe to check his e-mail. Sometimes he could rely on the ethereal transport of Holy Master's thoughts, but in doubt he wanted to receive them in writing.

The cafe was crowded. He ordered a cappuccino while he waited to use a machine. A tall lanky youngster was mumbling over the keyboard of the pc Martin had his eye on. The kid couldn't keep at it forever, nodding his orange head and red face, luminous above his blue tee-shirt. Martin himself wore white shirts whenever possible. They were usually smeared and stained with colors rubbed off from painted walls and wrought iron fences. He looked at the kid with orange hair. The kid looked clean and calm. Quite competent, Martin thought. It was a state he himself yearned to display in his own person, a badge of manhood.

At last the kid went off to pay his ten pesos and Martin occupied the computer chair. No message from Holy Master after all. That must mean he was doing okay. He scanned down his messages—two from his mother who insisted on remote electronic communication. She thrived on it, he sensed, a wonderful development in her life whereby she imagined her lost son was somewhere out in heaven speaking to her by e-mail. Sometimes Martin wasn't sure his mother remembered that he, not Robert John, was alive. Martin fortunately was immune to heart injury since his affiliation with Holy Master twenty years ago. But now and then he wished his mother worried about him, or at least thought about him and remembered.

The other message was from Laurie Afflick whom he met briefly at a meditation center and silently yearned to touch, in an imminent, material sort of way. But although they drank many cups of chai together he never had. He read:

Dear Martin,

I am usually adamantly opposed to letters that tell you to forward them to people for good luck--your basic chain-letter-guilt gambit. But I got this from a friend of Mother Divine who had something astonishing happen after she sent it. A coincidence? Maybe. But, a little luck and miracles couldn't hurt while you are bringing peace to a difficult world! OK, I broke down just this once. I hope it doesn't annoy you, and who knows? maybe it'll work. All the best to you, Martin.

Ganesh Prayer. Peace. "OM"

Just send this prayer to seven people or more and let me know what happens on the fourth day. That's all you have to do. This is a powerful prayer of Ganesh. Do not fail, please.

Prayer is one of the best free gifts we receive. There is no cost but a lot of reward. Let's continue praying for one another.

Make a wish before you read this prayer. Did you make a wish? If you don't make a wish, it won't come true).

(Last Chance to Make a Wish).

Let us start:

SHREE GANESH VANDANA

CHUKLAAMBARADHARAM VISHNUM

SHASHIVARNAM CHATURBHUJAM

PRASANNAVADANAM DHYAAYET

SARVAVIGHNOPASHAANTAYE

AGAJANANA PADMARGAM GAJANANA

MAHIRSHAM ANEKADANTAM BHAKTAANAAM

EKADANTAM UPASMAHE

Send This to 7 People within the next 5 minutes and your wish will come true, somewhere, somehow. Do not keep this message. The mantra must leave your hands within 96 hours. You will get very a pleasant surprise.

This is true, even if you are not superstitious!

FORWARD THIS MANTRA E-MAIL TO AT LEAST

0-4 people: Your life will improve slightly.

5-9 people: Your life will improve markedly.

9-14 people: You will have at least 5 surprises in the next 3 weeks.

15 people and above: Your life will improve drastically and everything you ever dreamed of will begin to take shape.

Love and hugs,

Your friend,

Laurie

Martin stared at the screen. He felt exactly as he did in chemistry class one grim Friday when his steady date, the otherwise unclaimed Anabelle Sausalito, copied from him on a test, implying that he would soon be permitted to feel her breasts. But the next night when they paused in the shadow of a building after leaving the movie theater, Anabelle pulled out of her blouse a cross on a gold chain. She waved it in front of his quivering fingers, and flipped it up and down, almost striking his too large nose.

"I'm Born Again," she asserted. "I'm saving my love for Jesus." She peered at him. "Marty, anchu you happy for me? Doncha wanna get baptize so's we can be together in Christ?" She was wheedling him from at least twenty-four inches away.

It was probably just then, at age nineteen, that Martin felt betrayed by Jesus for the final time. Never mind Robert John was smashed up. This was personal. In church on Sunday when the choir sang What a friend I have in Jesus Martin laughed in rage, not gratitude. His friend could take it and shove it. He was long gone.

Now as he sat in a café in Chiapas and stared at the computer screen, a miracle happened. A new message appeared. It carried the return address from Holy Master: hmragadam@earthlink.net.

Martin wiped his damp face with the back of his hand before clicking open the message. It directed him to proceed out to the pueblos to spread waves of goodwill. Holy Master didn't need to tell Martin anything about the Zapatista uprising, nor trouble Martin with anger against oppression endured for five hundred years. That was ending.

Immediately, Peace soothed him, rolling in like sugared heat from his cappuccino. He followed the right track, he knew it. He was redeemed, he was uplifted. He was soaring on toward the Absolute. He could almost feel his body lift off the hard wooden chair.

20

Frank's Group Gets Intercepted

Most Americans in Mexico finally figured out that the term municipio translated better as "county" than as "municipality". Each Zapatista municipio formed a headquarters serving many, maybe a dozen or more, tiny pueblos in a fifty-mile radius. These centers were what Frank might've called a county seat, but for communities in rebellion, tiny and poor, each was more like a county courthouse, or county camp. Each Zapatista "county seat" consisted of a fenced and guarded area where visiting witnesses were received and meetings held. The area often enclosed the school, and a rudimentary clinic staffed with volunteer civilians from Mexico City.

Beyond and outside the gated municipio headquarters the rural Zapatista families lived in their thatched chosas, with damn near everything outdoors except their bedding. The animals, if the community owed any, strolled around the little settlements, and bamboo or cactus fences to protect chile and tomatoes enclosed tiny gardens. Populations of refugees from pueblos threatened or assaulted arrived on foot, and were taken in and fed.

On the morning of December 5, 1996 a delegation from Estación Norte, five nationals and four international volunteers, traveled in two vans toward the besieged community of Miguel Alemán. One van was driven by Tomás, and the second by Frank. The five Mexican nationals, riding in Tomás's beige van, were professionals: a doctor and a dentist, and three teachers coming to teach Tzotzil youngsters how to run Primary School classes. With Frank rode four international Witnesses, two American guys and a French couple.

The two vans carried, in addition to humans, nearly a ton of humanitarian aid destined for people displaced from outlying villages by paramilitary violence within the last year. The vans rolled along slowly with that weight, low on their shocks. Frank, navigating dirt back roads, spent most of his wakefulness focused on avoiding potholes. He wanted the van to survive; its tires were new and so were the shock absorbers but shit, this was way overloaded. He felt like his ass was dragging.

It had been a long night. Most of the passengers napped, and Frank, rubbing his red-rimmed eyes, wished he'd been napping too. The inside of his collar felt like the road-grit settled there specially to rub his neck. He stuck a finger into the collar to try to ease it.

At 9:00 a.m., at the turnoff for the road leading to Miguel Alemán, a swarm of men surged out in front of them. Later Frank thought he should have run over the bastards, gunned the van, but Tomás led, and Tomás knew you don't gun a van carrying a half ton of food and half a dozen people. He stopped.

About two hundred men closed around the two vehicles. They appeared very much like the locals, armed with machetes. Frank's new rifle hid beneath his seat. Neither van's doors were locked, and as he debated how to respond several men roughly slid aside the door and invaded the front van where Tomás sat. Grabbing his arms and legs, they yanked him out of the van.

Frank held his breath. Tomás regained his feet. He said nothing, and Frank hoped that when the marauders became aware of Tomás' age they would ease off. He knew if they knocked Tomás around he, Frank, would pull the rifle no matter what, and waste a few. The others in the van ahead got down, which Frank thought was a mistake, but the men, holding Tomás from behind around the neck, were threatening to cut his arms off. It happened too fast. His own van was surrounded, he was visible, and the rifle was useless.

He guessed the attackers were Paz y Justicia thugs. No rifles, just expertly wielded machetes. He and his passengers in turn reluctantly descended from the protection of his dark green van. He couldn't leave Tomás and his group isolated. He began to move toward them with a firm unquestionable stride, and his passengers like baby ducklings followed at his heels. It was better if they stood together, with all the women inside the circle.

"Bastards, sons of goats, foreign whores!" The attackers, small dark skinned men like any people of the area, screamed at the delegation members, waving their machetes within inches of the faces and feet of their silent hostages. Give them credit, thought Frank. They'd been trained. But the real target was the humanitarian aid, cartons of food and medicine their captors rapidly began to offload into trucks. The parked trucks waited disguised behind bushes on the side of the road. They were ordinary farm trucks with slatted wood sides, often used to move cattle or corn. The fuckers were recruited pirates.

As the men formed a line, heaving boxes from one to another, Frank guarded his flock, if standing with his back to them and his front facing the pirates could be called guarding. Tomás spoke quietly in English, "We will stay calm, no? Let them take the supplies. Supplies can be replaced."

The leader of the Paz y Justicia band shouted into their faces.

Passports! Visas! Identification! His aides snatched the passports as the foreigners brought them out. In the usual small scruffy notebooks they wrote down each name. A man with a camera photographed faces of every captive.

"We know you!" the leader snarled at the Mexican nationals. The men began a search of vehicles, throwing the delegation members' duffle bags and knapsacks onto the dirt beside the road. The heap of bags vanished like cake under the feet of ants. Cameras, recorders, documents, passed from hand to hand and vanished. One guy appropriated some raingear, sneakers, sweaters. A second man, his lips stretched in a grin, sailed white cotton shirts toward waiting hands. As the shirts vanished into the back of the pirate truck Frank wondered who the hell brought along white shirts. A pair of athletic shoes, black with white stripes on the side, went immediately onto waiting brown feet. No socks. Frank waited for them to find his rifle.

The leader shouted at them, leaning in toward the circle and breathing in Frank's face. "You go nowhere, not continue down the road or turn back. We keep you hostages until you rot, son of a whore!" Beyond the circle the men pulled at their trouser fronts and pumped their hips. Fingers and hands made obscene gestures and the men shouted threats of rape at women in the group, who at Tomás' calm instruction said nothing. "We'll slash your throats!" They waved machetes. The group stood. Frank tried not to sway on his tired feet, or indicate that his bladder was stretched. For sure, not be jostled into pissing himself. In three hours the attackers had inspected everything and moved everything moveable, threatened the Mexican nationals, and jeered at the Witnesses.

Strangely, no other traffic appeared, no normal file of women bent under loads of firewood, no men with donkeys, no cars. Three khaki vehicles of the Mexican Federal Army, including one of the Federal Security Police carrying a colonel, passed by in both directions several times during the three hours the group stood hostage. Uniformed Army and State Police troopers waited laconically on a hill two hundred meters away, passing around an unnecessary pair of binoculars. Any moron could see from where they stood exactly what was going on.

"You see," Tomás reassured his charges, "if murder were contemplated they would do it alone, hours ago. This is harassment only." Frank grunted assent. This would not lead to slaughter unless somebody made a bad move. Like himself.

"I'll kill the motherfuckers," Frank muttered. It was his first time accosted, and he discovered his antipathy to war didn't extend to these motherfuckin' criminal thugs. The troops witnessed the events calm as eating a picnic lunch, despite the fact that the previous day the Chiapas State Government promised to provide police protection for the group while they transited through this zone. So much for protection. Too bad Estación Norte was so dumb, telling the police they carried food and supplies. Naive fucking morons.

Frank increasingly chafed under his self-imposed exit from warfare. His basic instincts were to step up to the plate, take a stand, some thousand other clichés he learned in high school. Be a man. But he hated war, he knew war. And his mind argued, Yeah but that wasn't for anybody who needed help: that was for rich oil-men and the US government. He controlled his breathing as if he were running a twenty kilometer race. Easy does it, he told himself. He stood.

After the last of the spoils were transferred to their new owners, the Mexican Federal Army finally intervened. The colonel, his bad ear clearly visible beneath his hat, waved. The guards stepped back. The group was released. The paramilitary drove away in their loaded trucks, still shouting obscenities, leaning out the windows. Nobody mentioned recovery of the group's belongings. The supplies were gone.

Back in the driver's seat of his van as they prepared to resume their trip, Frank felt with his foot beneath his seat, and his heel whacked the rifle. Unbelievable good luck. As the vans finally moved, the Paz y Justicia members left at roadside shouted after them. "Next time we shoot you bastards! Don't come back!"

Frank resisted the urge to flip the finger and held onto the wheel like a life preserver. If he were alone, the situation mighta been different. His eyes burned worse than before, dry with fatigue and rage. He knew that guy, that bastard in the Federal Security Police, with the twisted stump of ear. He asked over his shoulder if everyone was okay? The Americans were fine, they each replied promptly. Somebody reached forward and patted Frank's shoulder. Their voices rose high-pitched but not hysterical. Just thin, like caught in the neck and pushed out through the nose.

The French guy grunted, and the young woman with him remained silent. Frank looked into the rear-view mirror to glimpse her face. It was white, and wet with tears. But she was quiet, thank god. Violence in the northern zone of the state was commonplace, that's what they were here for, right? This wasn't a fucking game. "The campesinos if they're displaced even once never can get back to their communities. These are good people here, taking in refugees. So we'll do our thing, right?" Everyone nodded. He could see them in the rear-view and almost feel it when their heads bobbed. Right. He felt like a hypocrite, but exactly why he wasn't sure. Maybe because for the first time in his life murder lodged in his heart, uncommanded, unsummoned, at nobody's bidding. Furthermore, they were driving into the community empty-handed. At least the people Tomás carried would be useful.

Tomás left a day ahead of Frank, heading the Estación Norte van south, at three A.M.. For the next twenty-four hours Frank tried to help men and women in the town finish building sheds for their new clinic and school. They used no saws but sliced the wood with machetes clean as a whistle, and the memory of the Paz y Justicia gangsters kept popping up in his head. Machete use was acquired early, as common a skill as a handling a car wrench in Akron. They went about the construction with no wasted effort, and Frank conceded his best assistance was dragging logs down from where they were cut on the hillside. As helicopters flew over low, the fierce blades roaring, these men, slight and sinewy, their dark faces genial, worked without breaking rhythm. They had balls.

"Keep on keepin' on", he told them when he drove away the next morning. The guards opening the compound gate nodded. Frank spoke in English, but the good will was evident in his face and body. He still had his rifle, and he knew the way.

Not many mistakes of this sort occurred, nobody could afford it. Furthermore, by now the towns in rebellion communicated regularly, with warnings and queries. Supply sources would send goods as long as Subcomandante Marcos emailed news of refugees in dreadful need. Then the Mexican government would blockade. Too bad, once in a while an individual stopped at the Guatemalan border was relieved of a package of aspirin or other medical supplies. That was hard luck, hard to take. The rage was contained.

And for the pacific volunteers, the witnesses, they had just Witnessed. That was what they came here for, right?

Part Two: 1997

21

Maeda Escapes

Constance, despite vowing never to do so, descended to the status of rich American: she paid a ragged old man ten cents daily to take away each small bag of trash, of garbage in a recycled plastic bag, and used bathroom tissue. To wait for the truck, to listen for the bell, to say yes no did you hear it was that it wait here's the trash, run! had become a chore, not fun. They bought their way out of it.

While Constance agonized over white guilt the old man happily accepted their business. He rang the courtyard bell and waited patiently while either the Señor 'Arry or the Señora Constancia brought out the bag of trash and a peso. With Harry away, Constance saved her loose change in a little straw basket in the kitchen, and waited for the bell.

When the ring sounded it was still quite early. Constance, glad she was up and dressed, went to the gate. She opened it without looking through the security peephole; she never looked. She was alone too much and determined not to act paranoid, although Harry once or twice suggested that she take precautions. But she didn't.

It was not the little old man.

Aida quickly pushed through the metal door and all but dragged with her a woman carrying a little boy. Without thinking Constance opened the inside courtyard gate and then, after her guests passed safely through into the patio, turned back, opened the door again and looked out. Nobody. She pulled the automatic lock as the door clanged shut.

Relieved, she returned to the patio. The child seemed to be about six; when he dutifully said Buenos días, Señora Constance could see spaces where his upper two teeth belonged. Tiny nubs of new teeth were pushing through like grains of white rice. She wanted to ask if he put the lost teeth under his pillow, but such quick thinking in Spanish was beyond her, and anyway she didn't know if people here did that. She smiled instead.

"These friends of mine would like to visit you," Aida said. She didn't offer any name or introduction. Constance knew the exhausted woman must be Maeda.

"How nice," she responded. She smoothed the front of her shirt in a pointless motion. Without waiting to be asked, Maeda, her dark skin filmed with a sweat, sat down in the patio chair, and Constance said to Aida in English, "Can we get her inside? She can sleep, while we entertain the boy."

"We're planning to leave as soon as it's dark," Aida told Constance before she spoke to Maeda, who like a sleep-walker stood and ran her hands down her skirt in a smoothing gesture oddly mimicking Constance's. She followed Aida indoors without a word.

"What's your name?"

"Ricardo." The child was gazing after his mother with anxious eyes.

"Well, Ricardo, I am thinking of making some cookies." That

was a bad reflex! She had no idea of how to make cookies in this city—she never bought flour or even tried her oven! "But first, I think I'll draw some pictures!"

"I'm thirsty," Ricardo whispered. Glad the boy relieved her of inept cheeriness she shepherded him inside to the small kitchen. Constance feared he might cry, and as a grandmother she felt totally inadequate. A brown baby—that fantasy! She wasn't up to it. But certainly she didn't want Maeda to rush out in alarm. The woman needed rest. She began to pour water from their jar.

Aida reappeared from the bedroom. Constance breathed in relief. Aida, in their month of their friendship, was more of a mother to Constance than the other way around. Aida was enormously competent with human interaction. When Constance commented on it, Aida discarded the compliment and simply told Constance she was born that way. She spoke three languages and now advanced a fair way toward learning Tzotil. Calm and in charge, Aida went to the refrigerator and opened it without hesitation. Immediately Ricardo brightened.

"I suppose you're hungry, too?"

The child nodded shyly. His mother snatched him from his bed at five o'clock, and they moved for three hours without breakfast. Ricardo, Constance could now see, still wore pajamas, with sweat pants pulled over the bottoms. The cord at the waist dangled; the pants drooped. Constance could see his small belly button where the pajama top pulled loose.

Maeda called on her cell phone. Thank god Aida owned one—line phones were rare. Maeda wore hers around her neck in a pouch, on advice of those who knew what might happen. She slept at home with the phone at her hand when the call came. The Human Rights office was vandalized.

Only by a fluke someone was there, sleeping in the back. The lawyer was badly beaten when the intruders discovered him. With no effort to be silent, they smeared the office floors and walls with pig blood and shit. They grabbed computers and cables, joking among themselves they emptied file drawers and burned papers in heaps on the floor. The lawyer, still conscious when the intruders left, reached his phone and made the first warning call. Their organized chain reached Maeda at four-thirty. A month ago she put aside a shoulder bag with what she thought they must have, if they needed to flee.

Could Aida come to her place and get Ricardo. Maeda said nothing more over the phone. It took Aida half an hour, and when she tapped at the door they stood ready. She was to take Ricardo by a pre-dawn bus out of the city, wait an hour and return.

"I'll meet you in front of Sangre de Cristo. You know?" Aida knew. The church's deep recessed doors sheltered on the north side.

San Gregorio was a clean city; no trash lay on the streets. A few skeletal dogs slept on the sidewalks, and occasionally dog mess lay in a mound. Aida never saw anyone follow after a dog, it would be too ridiculous. The dogs themselves seemed so near exhaustion it was difficult to imagine them ever moving, even for natural needs.

Sweepers had begun to clean the gutters when Maeda appeared, half running and half trying to look unconcerned in her dark skirt and hand-embroidered blouse. When she stepped into the church portal and saw Aida with Ricardo she lurched to one side and Aida grabbed her.

"How are you?" Aida stretched her arm around Maeda's shoulder, but Maeda wasn't ready to collapse, she needed to get her boy to safety.

"I moved what I had to. That's done. Two men in a Public Security vehicle pulled up outside Estación Norte while I was inside.

I couldn't leave by the front door so I went by the back window. I jumped." Aida saw that she was holding her arm. Her blouse was ripped on the shoulder, and blood discolored the flowers.

"Just a scrape. Nothing broken." She moved out of Aida's embrace, tightened her black hair in its roll on top of her head, and took Ricardo's hand. "We need a place off the street until dark."

"No problem. I know just the woman."

Householders, both women and men, appeared on the sidewalk to sweep. Aida approved the pride they took in their clean city, with no sense that anyone was too busy or important to tidy up. Thank god for these calm early risers. Several sloshed the street from buckets or plastic bowls. The three skirted the wet areas as they began to walk toward Constance's home. After ten minutes Aida picked up Ricardo and carried him on her hip.

Inside the apartment Constance began to chop chilies and tomatoes to make an omelet. Lucky that Harry was away—one less person involved. It was Carmen who worried her. Carmen would show up to fuss with water and plants. Carmen had a husband, and by now Constance knew that her husband worked with the Public Security Force. He never accompanied Carmen, but what if she told him?

Aida would pretend Ricardo was hers, and Maeda would stay indoors in the bedroom. Constance spoke softly to Aida in English, over Ricardo's head.

Ricardo watched her cook. Constance donned her apron, and except that she wore her usual jeans instead of a homemade dress, she supposed she looked quite normal. The child sat at the table. He needed to be fed.

"Can you make enough for me? I'm famished." Aida filled the chair next to Ricardo, and like magic pulled from her bag a set of cards with animals drawn on one side and a word printed in red on the other. She held up the red word for Ricardo. Caballo. Horse, he read.

"Are we going home?" He seemed to know the answer, and merely confirmed what Maeda prepared him for. "Is today the day we go to Aunt Tila?"

"That's right, mi amor," Aida replied. "Today we go. At night. Maybe you can take a nap first."

"I'm not tired!"

Constance listened. It could be any child any place. She knew Ricardo would nap by noon, so that would offer a break when she wouldn't have to worry. It was certainly going to be a long day.

"Where does this Aunt Tila live?"

Aida nibbled her upper lip. "Listen, Constance," she finally said.

"The less you know the better off you'll be. Someone's coming around nine o'clock. We'll get out of here, and you can forget all about it."

"What makes you think I can forget it?" Inclined over the cooking fry pan, she was deeply offended. Aida must think she lacked ability to understand anything!

"I only meant, let it go. Let it go, Constance. You have only just so much energy, and there's no point in wasting any of it on things beyond your control. You do the helping now, and after, it's handed off, it goes in stages; someone different for each stage."

"And you? I suppose you're going to turn it all over to the next person?"

"I don't know," Aida admitted. "I'll think about it."

"Well, so will I!" Constance was furious. That the government could sponsor this kind of thing! As surely they went hand in glove with the local PRI landowners. But in truth she didn't know what she could do. Write a letter—to whom? How? Complain to the US

Embassy? Huh!

She thought of the several Human Rights workers, who like Maeda, were Mexicans defending their own Constitution and the San Andrés Accords which supposedly would include indigenous people in basic ways—for example, publish their rights in a language they could understand! Unlike Aida, Constance knew she herself didn't have much chance of learning an indigenous language. She struggled with Spanish. By empathy, she understood that most rural people, at least the women, were in the same boat.

"I can pack a few things for a supper, so they don't have to stop for food."

"Sandwiches—good idea!" Aida smiled. "A couple small bottles of water would be good, too."

They settled down to wait for the hours to pass. As she had guessed, Ricardo went into the bedroom to find his mother, and Maeda returned to the kitchen without him. Mid-afternoon Carmen came as expected, and Maeda silently retreated out of site into Harry's workspace. The boy still slept.

The hours dragged, as if the hours themselves were housebound and could not fly out. The desultory conversation refused to move toward any destination. A few facts—suspects arrested and tortured, with no charges. Land appropriated, wages withheld. Constance knew it all, and if she hadn't known, could have guessed, it was typical of repression and terror in the Western Hemisphere. The Chiapas thugs didn't invent it. Nor their determination to retain power.

At four they ate again, more eggs because that was all Constance had in the refrigerator. She made rice to accompany the eggs, and sliced the final tomato. Not even milk for Ricardo, who, still in his pajama covered with pants, asked for soda and settled for more water. Constance watched from the corner of her eye while she cleaned up the kitchen, how Aida calmly played reading games and word games and number games - infinite patience, that woman.

At eight forty-five Maeda's cell phone trilled. Constance breathed a sigh of relief. The driver would come for her and the boy in fifteen minutes. Constance offered Maeda a sweater to throw over the one she wore – in case they headed into the mountains. Maeda shook her head. Constance offered pesos. Maeda hesitated, and then accepted two hundred, all Constance kept in the house. Twenty dollars US. Nothing.

Aida stood inside the unlit gate and waited for the sound of the vehicle. She signaled. Maeda and Ricardo slipped out the door and into the open van instantly. It rolled away in the dim street. Constance caught a brief view as the interior light went on and off. An older Mexican man with a moustache. Satisfied, she turned and locked the gate behind them.

Aida would sleep here and leave in the morning. The two women returned to the kitchen. The bag of sandwiches lay forgotten on the table.

Constance felt her stomach lurch. Sandwiches were nothing of course. But the boy would get hungry, and his mother would want to feed him.

Constance looked sideways at Aida, who seemed for once not to be miles ahead of Connie. I don't know how to discuss this fucking business, Constance thought. I figure there's two choices: say something or keep my mouth shut.

She kept her mouth shut.

22

Darkness

It was as dark as Emily had ever known darkness to be. Blindly she stared toward the windshield, an undecipherable black wall. Next to her she sensed rather than saw the rough hands of José holding the steering wheel softly, delicately, as if moving in darkness would be easier for the van if it felt gently handled, like a woman in bed. Emily inhaled the closeness of José's woven cotton shirt, the blue jeans he wore. She sensed his foot in an American sneaker on the gas pedal. It was so dark.

The van snaked out through the opening made for them in the gate. Four Authorities of the barricaded Municipio Autónomo en Rebelde had admitted the van three days ago, holding them inside it while passports were checked, and good and sufficient reasons for strangers entering were verified. The same men opened the gate at four this morning, sending them without headlights into the blackness.

Nobody spoke. The van settled into ruts on the dirt road and climbed out again. Emily rolled against Billy on her right, trying not to interfere with José's hand on the gearshift as he guided the wheels through the darkness. Behind her she could hear the group shifting, trying to keep their balance.

"Christ," whispered Aida softly.

A military vehicle loomed in front of them, abrupt lights blazing. José stopped. Beams of several flashlights walked toward them as they sat pinned in the truck's searchlight.

"As we planned," José said calmly.

The idea, Emily knew, was to drive as far from the municipio as they could before the military stopped them. She was briefed, as were the other five foreigners, to say absolutely nothing, to pretend not to understand Spanish, to do nothing. José would explain, their tour guide. They were coming or going to the ruins of Palenque. In panic Emily found she couldn't remember which. But it didn't matter. José would do the talking.

The captain put his head alongside the van door. His flashlight butt rapped. Obediently José rolled down the window into the mouth of several rifles. José opened the glove compartment to show his registration and document of Tour Guide. Billy shifted to get his lanky knees out of the way, and at his motion the captain stepped backward on one foot and raised his rifle.

"It's nothing," José said before Billy could speak. "He only makes a space." Emily clutched Billy's knee with her right hand. He wasn't always bright about keeping his mouth shut.

"Hiya," Billy waved to the captain. And he lifted his waving hand to smooth his hair, visible in the spotlight as an aura of reddish gold. His white skin and pale blue eyes. The captain stepped forward again, and gestured for José to get down.

The two disappeared beyond the blaze of lights. Inside the van no one spoke. In Emily's nostrils she could sense the fear Merwin felt.

He holds a Mexican special visa, she thought. Of all of us, he's authorized to be here on United Nations business, traveling

Mexican roads. The lights of the military truck swiveled.

But it wasn't like that. Merwin's investigations for UNESCO permitted traveling in Mexico. He could hardly pretend a Cultural Patrimony hid inside a Zapatista municipio in Chiapas. What were any of them doing, at four in the morning? Getting an early start to the lakes? They would have to explain Palenque, the ruins, the studies. Then, with American passports, they would be held, threatened and expelled. That wasn't what Merwin's grant paid for. He wasn't allowed to do anything political, such as bring aid to rebel communities. Or take notes or videos or witness or report. Or support them in any way. All of them were in violation. Grounds for expulsion.

Emily knew her letter credentialing her as a journalist wasn't worth diddly. She wasn't employed by Reuters or La Jornada or The New York Times. In fact, she wasn't employed by anybody. Her letter of authorization in English from Mutual Community was a joke.

But the Mexican government can't go in for physically abusing Americans. We're privileged, Emily thought, with some relief. She didn't like stories of assaults and injuries foreign peace workers suffered at the hands of paramilitaries. Mexicans were kidnapped and killed. But thank heaven, college kids, and journalists like herself with nothing but a bribe and an American passport, could enter the jungle war zone and be protected. God bless America.

José returned to the window. The captain and guards with their weapons pointed at them loomed behind him. The dark faces receded indistinct beneath green helmets.

"We'll show our passports. Although they have no legal right to ask. This is not a good time to argue."

Emily unzipped her waist pouch. The zipper sound was strangely loud. She looked into the light and blindly smiled, pushing her passport into the air outside the window. It was taken. Her visa was good for another two weeks. She had no idea what she would do after that – become an undocumented alien, she supposed.

The captain looked at the photo of the woman, her clipped blond hair and pixie face, her blue eyes. Another with blue eyes. He grunted. Billy went next. From the back seat Frank handed his up front. Twenty-nine. Brown hair. Brown eyes. Tanned but fair skinned. American.

Frank, undergoing his first trial as a passenger rather than driver, kept quiet. His van would arrive with Tomás by a different route, with supplies. Their plans involved an intricate hand-off because of weapons and communiqués Tomás brought. Frank wasn't employed for high-level Zapatista business. He knew, but it wasn't his business to know. He held his body straight, without moving.

The captain became impatient. Aida's passport was American also, although her apellido, Elizondo, could be Mexican. The captain spoke to her in Spanish. "What are you doing here?"

"Learning about the country of my ancestors," Aida, in front of him, replied to the captain. "We are tourists as you can see." Her Spanish was formal. She forgot José's injunction against admitting they understood. It seemed not to matter.

The captain spun on his heel. "Get in."

José climbed back into the driver's seat. Around them lights began to withdraw. Emily made out faint shapes in the mist, a military convoy. Dawn overtook them while they waited in the van for José's negotiation with the captain.

"The military in this situation has no power," he addressed them all. Emily felt his hand on the gearshift brush her jeans. She was acutely aware of his thigh next to hers. "They wanted only to delay us until the migración opens."

"Anybody want some chips?" Frank offered cheerfully. Suddenly they were all cheerful.

"The hard part is still to come. You will remain quiet and let me do the speaking, no?"

"Forgive me, José. I forgot. Next time I will remain silent. You did excellently." Aida spoke in her deferential and courteous Spanish, her role as social worker foremost, giving off an aura of calm appreciation on behalf of all, sending the proper apology and thanks. The van moved now at as good a rate as the road would allow, jouncing when José couldn't avoid the potholes, swaying where he could. Billy put his arm around Emily, and although she began at that moment to plan how to shed the kid, she rested her head against his armpit.

Their journey constituted a strange secret game of musical chairs. A group would show up at a community in rebellion with papers, and be admitted. Another group would leave; the Zapatista men would slip in mysteriously at dusk for night patrol to guard the encampment; their women would emerge from the mist at dawn to prepare food. Even the horses appeared mysteriously in midafternoon, charging through the opened stockade gates. The children, little boys in ragged clothing, materialized in ways and at hours too mysterious to comprehend. Their life hid from her, Girl Reporter. She asked about the school and yes there was a school. And she asked about the clinic and yes, a clinic. She knew the women met for women's decisions. She knew! Yet her notes were meaningless. She couldn't get it. No matter how many times the music played and they shifted chairs, always there was one person out. She supposed on a new mission. She hoped on a new mission.

Billy had arrived at the last compound in a different vehicle, with Frank. Billy looked somber. She wondered if he understood more than he let on, or if he traveled solely on instinct, going wherever he could. He latched onto her as if she were a girl, a girl-friend. Okay. She didn't want to scandalize the village by appearing not only unattached but sniffing after José. She had to admit. Frank came with aspirin and ampules of something. Frank traveled on a mission, she knew. Aida and Merwin rode in her vehicle when José drove over the mountains from San Gregorio. On the harrowing hike into the village she never inquired about their sponsoring organizations. She didn't know, and she didn't inquire, Girl Reporter! Well, shit, who could she report to? Who could she tell about all this, the silent night patrols, alarms of assassinations in the next pueblo?

Now they all stank of sweat, of slept-in clothing, dried mud. They had camped within the community, not on the dirt floor because of snakes. On wooden benches, in one of the sheds, for three days. When helicopters roared over they ran out to document the Hueys with video cameras. Everyone knew they were there. It was part of the game, this harassment.

Emily rubbed her hand through her crew cut and tried to relax. She breathed slowly, as if by sheer willpower she could select the fresh morning air instead of the tired stink inside the van. She could see José's hands, and they soothed her. She wondered if she could stop in one place long enough to learn something. Anything. Real.

José, oddly, was wondering the same thing: if any of this felt real to the gringos, or if they pretended like actors, in a film by that Oliver Stone. At each encampment foreigners were briefed by a Zapatista authority. Whichever man was designated, he came to the meeting masked, and sat opposite the wide-eyed Americans on a rough wooden chair. They were not allowed photographs, only questions. The Zapatista answered through a translator, in this group fortunately both Aida and Merwin. The Europeans understood English. The leader announced figures of how many killed or numbers of military troops. It was dry information. He signaled when time was up, and departed. That was all. No discussion of organizing the communities. No reasons for why or how they gave up permitting any government presence, disguised as assistance for schools, or doctors. How the people in the community gathered to speak. How they agreed. They were Zapatistas. For the briefing, the designated man wore his mask.

With special permission Aida walked down among the huts to interview the women. One woman was a dentist, on three month enlistment. But she did no dental work, no equipment or supplies were available. And the doctor, also a woman, received aspirin brought in by the man Frank, and could do no more than hand it out. They attempted to teach the mothers to keep the children out of the dirt, entirely hopeless. Children must be allowed to move about, not be hung in trees like fruit!

There was a widow, whose husband fell on the first day, January 1, 1994. She lived with her son in her parents' home, and her task was to prepare tortillas for the others. A younger child had died. The widowed woman could not re-marry, there was no one to take her. Nor could she support herself. What could she hope for? Aida asked, what do you hope for, for your son.

"That he die for the Zapatistas, like his father."

Aida stared at the woman. The child was five or six years old, and rachitic.

Perhaps Aida believed the woman was instructed what to say? But how the widow woman, perhaps older than twenty by now, could live—how? How, her child? She had no education, no idea of what peace might be like, no experience of a decent income for the community free to work without expulsions and crop burnings.

José recalled his life before the paramilitaries came. Brief, the time with his wife and boy. And hard, and poor. In his village the women worked in a cooperative, sewing blouses. None of the shared income was allotted for private needs. They were preparing, both the men and the women, according to the plan, for several years.

Now with his son dead, his woman and boy both dead, he could not afford to wonder. It was too late for wondering. He had no answers to give this bold one, Aida. He did not pretend to have a future either.

Two days later the gates were opened for them before dawn. As the van bumped along in early dawn light the ignorance of Emily offered a strange comfort, a soft strange comfort. He hoped the orange-haired man was not going to hold her. José sensed she was willing, Emily, in her ignorance, to give comfort. He could feel her warmth on the seat next to him.

First they must travel. If the gasoline was sufficient, they could pass on another road where the migra would not yet be on duty, he knew those lazy bastards. So let's see.

He checked the side view mirror, and turned off onto a narrow dirt road.

23

Aida in the Mountains

Aida requested permission to visit the communities. Estación Norte was sending observers, the Wandering Witness Troupe, she called it. Songs, dances and funny stories. Only the stories weren't funny.

The Witnesses were supposedly both visible and hidden, a neat trick. Their presence intended to deter the military and paramilitary from excursions into the communities, but since excursions to aid and abet the rebellion were forbidden, the group didn't want to be stopped and deeply questioned. Some observers feared expulsion. Like Aida, they did other work here, and while she in particular tried to carry out women's research in a war zone, others dedicated themselves to unspoken political or private obsessions.

The nationalities spoke courteously to one another and mixed very little. Aida tried to become acquainted with the Germans, and found them disinterested in her. It was not in Aida's nature to worry about whether men found her attractive, so she soon concluded they thought of themselves as on a stricter mission. Somehow this group didn't suit them—they needed more militant business.

Those of other nationalities, and women too, were soft and looked soft, like grown children wandering around in wonderment. The tougher ones, dressed in the best gear, carried the best cameras, and wore the best boots. Sterner stuff, those.

Aida was something of a softie, but not a child. She slid like water, spreading into all crevices, as if water were sentient, tasting and sniffing the smooth and jagged surfaces it crossed. She watched members of the communities. The men came or left at dawn. Men's meetings. The women gathered by themselves in the evening. Women's meetings. She wasn't invited.

Maeda and her child were gone, and Aida hoped that if they were apprehended or harassed news would get about. Beyond that, she tried to follow the advice she gave Constance, and let it go. Easier said than done, she worried ruefully. Maeda was a special person—a woman who risked a great deal for principles. After her husband was killed.

After your spouse or kids were dead, was it easier to stick with principles? Or was it just a case of nothin' left to do, some hideous freedom?

Uneasily she kept close her minimum of clothing, soap, a towel, a hammock, her notebook.

NOTES:
Two week tour:

Municipios of the Zapatistas.
Low-intensity war against Zapatistas continues.
Foreigners witness, gov afraid to kill off tourist/investment dollars.
Increase in militarization evident along with malnutrition of

children in towns under siege. Spoke with woman whose husband was "war-hero" killed on first day of uprising. Maria had two children, one died at age three months. Six-year old boy living.

Here Aida paused to think of little Ricardo, who despite his troubled life, was fed and cared for. She recalled his small hand tucked into hers while they waited for Maeda to appear. He didn't cry, but looked at Aida with so much adult anxiety on his face Aida could imagine him at age forty.

What dreams she has for her son? Answer: "He's going to continue the struggle, and die like his father."

Is this a normal mother? Did someone teach her to say that?

Maria tries to earn her keep in home of parents and extensive sibling family—prepares noon-day corn gruel and evening tortillas, the food they subsist on. Was given a sewing machine by a sympathizer, and thinks of earning some cash; parents can't cope. Maria's nieces and nephews look half-starved.

Resident health provider reports all children suffer malnutrition; diarrhea common cause of infant death. Among women, cancer of cervix and ovaries common at age twenty-three. No prophylactic explanation offered to local women.

Who is supposed to tell them about genital warts?

Sewing machine gift is source of concern to Authorities. Will set Maria apart from other women working by hand in their cooperative. Unity of struggle paramount. Autoridades must discuss dilemma of war widow whom village cannot support. In communal struggle, private income not allowed.

Beautiful rich land, plentiful water, cattle, horses. Starvation?

Military patrols. Gov increased numbers and intimidation.

Women out in fields risk rape, water polluted by military wastes, crops randomly destroyed. Cattle butcher themselves on military razor-wire fences.

We brought food and water, they have none to spare for guests. Current visitors/witnesses include journalist, American college boy, NGO medical provider who is nice but a wimp, UNESCO nerd, etc.

Went to 2 of 5 Zapatista municipios. Fenced and gated. Two resident volunteer foreign observers permanent in each. Sit all day at road-side and count military transport vehicles and over-flights of helicopters and observation planes. Little awning on sticks to keep off sun. (The UN team also here) Most of them French or Spanish. Recreation consists of soccer or basketball among the men. Foreign observers play chess with children. Evening meeting to make necessary decisions.

It was new to Aida. Others on the van routes were old hands. They could speak about the Zapatista network, their determination to survive despite clear intentions of the government. The uprising entered its fourth year. The communities honed their survival skills. They accepted the assistance of Civil Society and that of NGOs who made two or three or four trips a year, some taking foreign witnesses, some like that fellow Frank bringing supplies. Some this year brought cameras and video equipment. Sophisticated support for the Zapatistas grew in step with the military repression.

Aida was sturdy. She could sleep in a hammock, she could eat rice. She felt worn out and exhausted.

Toward sunset the mountains grew cold. Aida wore heavy jeans and a sweatshirt beneath her windbreaker. Spooning hot soup she was grateful for the sharp chili and heat that warmed her hands as she held her plastic bowl. This feast was prepared for them, and they had to eat or insult.

She looked into the bottom of the bowl. Pulled molars lay scattered among scraps of carrot and parsley. Torture! But no, these weren't teeth, only kernels of white maize. Aida sipped, then like a deer raised her head from the bowl into the sharp mountain wind. A nervous wreck, she surprised herself by her bizarre reactions. She stretched her neck backward and brought it down again, tucking her chin into the shelter of her shirt collar. The view gradually faded, purple mountains merged along a line in the distance. No news of Maeda meant all went well. Among these intense small people things were going on. Things not random nor undirected. The people planned, they discussed changes which might alter the way Mexico thought of itself and its people. This was not pointless misery.

The cold air calmed her, and as a lady calm and in control as she always was, Aida knew she'd reached her limit. No wonder volunteers came and went in rotation. She was glad they could at least leave some supplies, flour and even the store-bought canned sardines that sustained the travelers. She flattened the page of her notebook in the breeze.

Volunteer teachers from Mexico City teach local teachers to teach the children. The Mexico teachers vocal re trauma to children living in war zone.

Student teachers: 2 young women, ages 17, 23.

Now here was part of her research. How did these young women get assigned this task? Did they volunteer? Or was it part of their community obligation to serve in whatever capacity? But they seemed to have aptitude, so more likely it was a choice.

Children may already speak Spanish; young bilingual teachers help children who are not. Support children in maintaining indigenous cultures.

Zapatistas refuse gov "support", seen as divide and conquer, to create splits in the communities. Bring in their own nurse practitioners and dentists, all very youthful volunteers supported by various NGOs, for six months or a year.

Dentist equipment rudimentary, likewise doctors. Aspirin, penicillin. People only come from the campo to municipios for special occasions, combined with trip to dentist.

First medical supplies in four months brought in on the van after us. The wimp, no less. Clark Kent.

The wimp was Frank. He was not a wimp, she now knew, but an angry non-combatant. Tension in his body and face shot sparks back at Aida's queries. In better circumstances an outright pacifist, but how could anyone be a pacifist here? He had served in the Gulf War and regretted it bitterly. He'd enlisted. Aida asked him why he did it and received no reply. She looked closely at his square, simple face, a face which matched his square simple body. But people are not so simple.

Diplomatically she skirted around classic reasons: a broken romance? A father dead in Vietnam? None of the above. Then it must have been economic. There was no way someone as good-hearted as Frank would have fought for oil. He wasn't dumb enough to have bought into US propaganda about saving Kuwait.

"Were your folks able to afford to send you to college?" She asked him in an offhand way later, when the discussion was about her, her proposed doctoral work. And that was it. We are so accustomed to those economic factors among black kids. But here was a nice white boy who wanted to attend university and medical school, and couldn't. So he'd signed up to maybe kill people, for money. And he killed them, Aida was sure, remembering the planes which killed helpless people fleeing on the ground, and troops on the ground dealing with blackened war trash.

"When you got out, didn't you have the GI Bill or something like that, education bill, whatever they call it?"

He didn't seem bothered by her ignorance, although she was ashamed of not knowing what benefits GIs got. But it made a safe line of conversation to pursue. She wasn't into accusations or guilting people.

"I have benefits. The problem was me." Aida watched his face. "It wasn't a nervous breakdown, if you're thinking. Not like that. It was more like—." He stopped, tucking his chin down. "I'm too tired. That's all. I am just too fuckin' worn out."

"Ya no puedo más." Aida repeated the common refrain. She wondered what it was about United States lifestyle or culture or what – that he couldn't stand any more. Maybe it was that nobody admitted to military murder. They said it was serving your country.

"Right." And he got up and moved off into the encampment.

Aida would have taken him to rest on her splendid wide hips, if he had asked. Instead, she watched the sun tip over and fall behind the fading hills. A strange wistfulness permeated the twilight, as if the air itself could yearn for something, some succor for the people. Social work was not succor, it was just telling women to get off their asses, and of course the ones who could, would do so anyway. Like for the Zapatistas, days of victim-hood were passing out of style. Get off your ass. Take control. Aida herself needed no urging. But then, maybe she did. The sky spread huge distances. Slowly stars began to stab it. Before it became completely dark, she scribbled on.

Significant: though minimal, Zapatistas set up own infrastructure in their own villages. Since the first two weeks of the insurrection in 1994 they have been in non-violent resistance. Much use of slogans and songs. Women stand face to face against soldiers in the roads. Will struggle until the last person dies.

One woman in this latest village on her tour could speak Spanish. The others spoke only Mamey, and some had never left the mountain. Only men, who walked ten hours into San Gregorio or Tuxtla, learned a little, enough to work. And perhaps a little arithmetic.

Aida didn't know if anyone here could read. Lower down, in Tzotzil villages lived several literate men, and since electricity was brought, the Tzotziles knew from television that a world existed beyond their visible world. A couple of men went and returned to tell.

What if they believe what they see on TV is reality? Or maybe they understand none of it, but believe it like a legend in pictures, a story of creation and the gods. Without the language Aida could not guess. She mulled the possibilities, chewing kernels of molar-shaped maize left in the bottom of her bowl.

A fact-finding trip. She'd lost about ten pounds, she thought, no such thing here as a scale. Her pants sagged in the waist and seat. Despite her jacket and hot soup she felt chilled again.

Gov seeks access to petroleum reserves, biodiversity/forests, water/power, land. God knows what.

Spokesperson Subcomandante Marcos says true situation is not just that Mexican gov wants to exploit oil - but that because of globalization, gov wants to sell Mexico's land/mineral/biological resources to foreign companies. This to be accomplished without consulting indigenous inhabitants.

Time to get indoors.

The group moved mostly at night, as best they could, to avoid confrontations at immigration posts. Immigration troops could detain them.

Stopped seven times by immigration and military. Finally refused to turn over passport. Sat in van with others. Looked like tourists who would complain to American embassy. In Chamula vendor charged me more than local people for a soda. Turista!

My problem – what am I doing here?

They arrived in Chamula around mid-day, in time to do tourist shopping and eat something

Chamula PRI stronghold. Nasty little village. Gov succeeded in fragmenting community. Bosses get fat with concessions - Coca-Cola, poche, candles. In return, deliver PRI votes every election. Okay, fuck them.

Preparing for 2000 election, village received new buildings, new facade on church, very nice new houses, a museum. Bosses sold independence. Village is museum village for tourists. Begging children still visible. Viva the Zapatistas!

Capitalism, neoliberalism, globalization have won????

Aida, plunked on a bench doodling on the pages of her notebook, hated Chamula. She waited impatiently for the others to finish shopping and sightseeing. This wasn't what she came for, Chamula living high on the PRI hog.

"Think of the others," Frank sat next to her, also waiting. "Those who were kicked out. All along this area go the refugees." He chafed, needing to deliver supplies.

Zapatistas refuse to participate, create their own new social structures. Those in power willing to starve those with no power, murder, intimidate. Those with no power will not support the power of the elite which depends on their acquiescence.

A final stop, final day and night to witness, final delivery of Frank's supplies. The return journey to San Gregorio bone-breaking and dry. The group of "tourists" dozed or when they thought it safe, brought out their notes, shared and compared. Some conversation, mostly anger and outrage. Frank said nothing. He worried about getting his vehicle back again, to return to the countryside. He was the quiet one.

When they reached San Gregorio Aida pulled her gear from the van and looked at Frank. She was filthy and her hair was matted in a braid which hadn't been combed out for two days.

He got out. He followed her along the street, and when they reached her place, through the metal door into the patio. Her apartment was only a kitchen with one all-purpose room off it, and a functional bathroom.

Before she could open her door she saw the tree, the one she greeted coming and going. Its bark had been horribly mutilated. The broken trunk and sawed-off branches remained without a whisper of leaves, a war amputee.

The landlord, sawdust on his head and shirt, was hauling away branches littering the patio. "The tree demanded too much water and invaded the cistern. What a pity. It is necessary to kill it."

She turned to Frank with a wail and for once the guy knew what to do. He placed his arms around her while she bawled into his shirt collar. Too much!

He took the key from her hand and unlocked the door into the kitchen and they moved into the second room, where her bed and desk occupied all the floor space. Frank stood and, unable to move more than a step in any direction, looked up at the ceiling.

Aida's benign resident lizard waited in its corner, where it kindly kept down the population of mosquitoes.

"Hola, legartito," she waved to the silent creature. "I'm crying because my tree is dead, and this is my friend Frank."

Frank waved to the lizard. It looked sympathetic. Since it didn't move, he assumed it was okay with Frank's presence. As non-judgmental as their mutual hostess. He put down his duffel and waited.

"I'm like completely exhausted. Let's shower and go to bed."

Clearly Aida kept no booze in the apartment. He peeled off his shirt.

24

Billy Gets Laid

The Witness and NGO excursions, differently designed and planned elicited wildly different responses. The Zapatistas were creating, on the foundation of their original communal practices, a politic that refused to seek or accept power. Those who arrived with political convictions—those Billy met—often were Marxist Socialist types, but for sure this wasn't Marxism or Socialism. The Libertarian Left was troubled by tight quasi-military control under which the pueblos in rebellion lived, but consensus didn't excite them. The Big Government liberals felt equally baffled. No way would any Zapatistas form a political party. Billy, instructing himself in a course of Chiapas 101, couldn't sort it out. He had trouble concentrating. He propped himself up further on the pillow. He wanted to have all this info he was reading under his belt, but something else under his belt was stirring and giving him flashbacks. He read again:

NATIONAL PROFILE OF THE INDIGENOUS PEOPLES OF MEXICO:

Conclusions and Recommendations

1.   Mesoamerica was and is formed by a series of regions with cultures that continue to inhabit it today. In this region specifically, one can distinguish Mayan, Zapotec, Mixtec, and Huastec areas. This region has seen many changes in the past five thousand years which are a part of the history of contemporary Mexico.

2.   The indigenous peoples can be defined by their condition: colonized and excluded from the national society. There are no "indios" in real terms, there are ethnic groups and the "indio" is a national cultural construct. The formation of an inclusive and democratic society would lead to the disappearance of this colonial construct, to recognition of the indigenous peoples, and to elimination of prejudices about racial superiority.

He experienced two seconds of sincere doubt, and then it all became a blur again.

How he got so lucky, he couldn't imagine. Sure, she didn't really give a shit about him, but he was in the right place at the right time. Chance. Fortune. Fate. The way things work out. He got lucky, despite his unlucky childhood and his unlucky patrimony, and his unlucky scrawny appearance.

"Hey," Emily whispered. She had knocked on the door of his space – he could hardly call it a room. They inhabited wooden slatted mangers, the best the "hostel" could offer. At least he was grateful for being on the second floor, where he felt the cold less than downstairs.

"What's up?"

"I can't sleep. I'm freezing. Can I get into bed with you?"

"Why sure," says Billy, imitating an old Robert Redford movie.

He pushed his bones back against the frigid wall and lifted the blanket. She was wearing sweat pants and socks on her feet. Billy wore his socks to bed also. He hoped they didn't stink but probably they did. They all lived pretty rough.

For ten days they stopped off in various communities. They didn't do much but watch the fucking helicopters overhead, and video document the presence of US army equipment circling overhead. Evenings he played soccer. Some foreigners had more purpose—Aida, come to find out, was doing research; Frank did his thing with medical supplies. Billy heard the presence of foreigners like himself and the other tourists protected the pueblos from attack.

He sure hoped so.

He was wiped out from fear and poor food, and despite the crudeness of tonight's accommodations, glad they finally came into a town with a hostel and a hot shower in a bathroom. Only there was no heat.

"What did you think?" Emily whispered, "About the village?" She was consulting him, consulting Billy. They'd been through some hairy times. He thought maybe some other visitors did missions, maybe courier, and dropped off when they came to where they needed to go. Emily always said she was a reporter. Billy had no mission. If you asked him why he was doing this, he couldn't reply. His obligation to his university studies vanished without a whimper.

"I'm not sure what to believe." That seemed innocuous enough.

"Like that guy who wore a ski mask during the briefing. Was that fake?"

"I guess not. Although who's to identify him? None of us could bring cameras into the room. And I think they're all Zapatistas anyway."

It's like a spy movie, Billy concluded lamely, thinking of their journey. They toured their way through Peace Camp settlements in the

Lacondón, a long tedious trip only three-quarters done, punctuated by "secret spy" scenarios like escapees crossing frontiers in World War II. Like, he sensed their danger but after the first time it felt melodramatic, and almost fake. Not that it didn't get to him. It was the contradiction in his perceptions he couldn't reconcile, a cinema verité unrolling beyond his comprehension. His head didn't grasp the big picture. He couldn't get the logic of the rebellion, what it all meant, because there was no goal specified. Like, how did you define dignidad? Who fought a rebellion for dignity anyway? Or what this meant. He was definitely warming up, and Emily must have been, too. Anyway she took off her sweat pants, shoving them with her foot down toward the bottom of the narrow bed. He held his breath.

"Well, well, well." Emily had found something interesting under the blanket, inside Billy's sweat pants.

"Off they go!" She pulled herself on top of him, and he could feel the damp drippiness of something inside her.

"What's that?"

"Just think of it as a mine disaster," She giggled. "All those little guys lost forever." It took him a minute to realize she was a.) talking about spermicide, and b.) she was fully prepared. She had come to him for this. Oh god. He clutched her rocking buttocks, each a handful. Oh god.

And after, she rested with her small frame fully spread out on top of his, covering all but his feet which fortunately still wore socks.

"Listen, Billy the Kid," she said kindly, with him still inside her, "I have a case of raging hormones. You understand?"

"Like, don't take it personal?"

"Exactly," she agreed. "Ya wanna know what forty year old women go through? Think of yourself at thirteen."

Emily was thinking of herself thigh to thigh with José. She suffered a bad case of lust, and figured this would be less damaging all around than putting the make on José. That was a guy with serious responsibilities, and although Emily lacked grand values, she understood the small ones—like don't get yourself or your team-mates killed.

Billy, as instructed, dutifully thought of himself at thirteen, eighteen, and now twenty. He was still a bag of raging hormones. He wondered when a guy got over it. If ever.

> 5. The states having the most indigenous populations are those that also have the lowest level of development due to the social policies that have excluded these peoples from state and federal investments. This has led to a wide gap between developed states which have relatively low densities of indigenous people, and the southern tier. These gaps illustrate lack of investment and interest on the part of the State and private initiatives in the indigenous population, and lack of recognition of these peoples as part of the national social and productive capital.

Yeah yeah yeah. His eye slid down to number five, and he didn't go back for three and four. It seemed to him the government and land owners liked having a pool of low-wage workers. Why would they want development?

It was hopeless. He had one thing on his mind, and that was the slight warm body which last night had moved over him so urgently, and then rested upon him like a cotton blanket.

> 6. The exclusion has determined, in many cases, the failure of development projects executed in indigenous areas, because they were based on attempts to change indigenous culture rather than develop and enhance it. The indigenous communities combine traditional with "modern", and have dynamically modified to include different elements in organizational and communal life and

behavior. The dynamic evident in indigenous communities is a clash of two forces: on one hand the traditional that bars the penetration of the modern, and on the other, the modern intrusion into the life of these communities. Within this context it becomes essential to understand the contemporary indigenous reality to make them effective participants in the development process with their own identity.

The guys who wrote this essay hadn't ever been where he was. What was barring the penetration of the modern? Marcos with his internet bulletins? The Indians followed their own path, so make them participants in a development process? That contradiction Billy connected to money, bulldozers, new bungalows shaped like Monopoly pieces. The indigenous people he saw wanted something else. Like, get off our backs.

Development.

He brooded for a while on that word. The Zapatistas use of the internet to rouse support wasn't exactly a development process, it was more like marketing, at which Subcomandante Marcos was a master. He refused government development, which could only benefit the big international capitalists.

Development process? He'd ask Emily. And then he realized that he might not see Emily many more times. People seemed to slip on and off their group as they moved across the state, always unexplained, always without surnames. He was getting familiar with the format: ride, hide, glide. Glide in, glide out. He visited four communities arriving at night, in a van rolling through gates with guards armed with flashlights to inspect their documents. Then sitting in an arranged tiny audience while somebody in a ski mask welcomed them. Then making themselves visible to the army.

On departure they did it the same way, quietly at night. Sometimes a person among the group would leave money with the leaders, for communal use. Billy didn't have anything to spare, so that decision was a no-brainer.

Sometimes a van driver dropped off cornmeal or rice or beans in fifty kilo sacks. Its origins remained mysterious, and Billy couldn't ask the men who spoke no Spanish. If they even would tell.

Between coming and going, he walked around the compound and played with the little kids. They wanted to touch his hair and rub his beard, the bright brush that grew on his face in thin patches. Billy shaved when he could, but a cold water shave with soap left him raw. So he avoided it.

When the helicopters clattered over, anyone with a camcorder rushed out to take pictures. Billy took off his hat to make himself more visible. Probably somebody in the government had a file with this oddball carrot-top walking through the mud. He wondered if their cameras used colored film. Damn waste if they didn't!

Of the original group this week—of tourists? Of sympathizers? Of Witnesses for Peace? Hell, he didn't even know what they were— who arrived in the van on his first day, only he and Emily remained, with their driver José. Frank and Aida got off in San Gregorio, talking about another route to check out another area, not under immediate threat. Aida forthrightly stated she couldn't get work done while she was shitting her pants. Merwin went off by himself.

8.   The low level of investment over the past 50 years in the indigenous areas has resulted in a lack of opportunities for employment with fair wages in contrast to the northern region of the country. This has contributed to the existence of thousands of persons reduced to peons in large ranches and other properties. These conditions have led to significant migration from indigenous communities, lower levels of medical and nutritional assistance, and the lowest levels of education, all of which further

accentuates the asymmetry of the relations between indigenous and non-indigenous peoples and is translated into disadvantages in the system of justice.

He hated this shit. Besides, he had a hard-on again. Forget concentrating. He rolled over onto his belly and waited for it to subside. By then it was time to go down for the main meal. They were "resting" for two days, which permitted everyone to bathe, and take care of their various intestinal problems. Shop if they needed warm shirts or underwear. For sure, some of his clothes just rotted. He discarded a tee-shirt he snagged on a fence splinter. Big hole. When he placed it in the waste basket he knew somebody poorer than him would take it out and use it.

A rest stop meant supplies were purchased, drivers changed off, people joined or left the van group.

Ah.

He grabbed the booklet and jogged two at a time downstairs to the tiny restaurant across the street. He grabbed a table in front of the window facing the street. Emily was not in the restaurant.

14. The land continues to be the basis for the existence and re-production of the indigenous communities. Production of maize, beans, squashes and chili are their subsistence base. In addition, most of the indigenous people also have cash crops, including coffee, sugar cane, wheat, tobacco, vanilla, cocoa, and citrus fruits. There is a growing trend to this production.

He figured that was written before the uprising. If they had cash, why did they need an uprising? Because NAFTA undercut corn prices? He bet the ones who still had cash crops were sticking with the PRI.

15. Relations between indigenous peoples and the nation state have been asymmetrical. In the indigenous regions, production and marketing, justice, education, and power are controlled by the small and large urban centers. Relations have always been characterized by a profound discrimination that blocked development in these regions. The democratization of Mexico can only begin with a change in these relations in order to legitimize the indigenous identity and make them participants in the development process.

There it goes again. These guys were into the development process in a big way. So where was Emily when he needed her? He tried not to look desperate as he checked the street again.

16. The use of natural resources in the indigenous regions is characterized by a non-materialist view of nature inherited from their cultural tradition. In their view nature is a living and sacred entity with which people interact, dialogue, and negotiate throughout the production process. This concept of nature is contrary to that of the urban, agro-industrial world designed to produce food, raw materials, and energy required by the dominant enclaves. The maintenance and protection of protected areas can only occur with the recognition of the indigenous knowledge and techniques that have made these areas sustainable, and by enhancing this knowledge to avoid ecological degradation.

Billy groaned. Must be the essay was written by university students with a point of view. In the US they'd be off at tourist sweat lodges in North Dakota. As far as he was concerned, two absolutely boring things were university students and points of view.

What he really wanted to know was how come the Irish were not only still at it, but bitter and angry and never past poverty? That rebellion seemed damned near immortal, and his father rotted in prison for something which had no resolution because fact of the matter, the people had no vision. Killing your oppressors wasn't a vision. Billy was developing a respect for the Chiapas communities, or at least for community autonomy. They didn't need nobody to come at them with fucking development.

> 17. The three types of property in the indigenous communities: ejidos, communal, and private, registered in the Ejido Census of 1991, are controlled by 6,298 indigenous communities and about 1.1 comuneros or ejidatarios. These communities control an area of over 22 million hectares of which 230,000 are irrigated lands; 1.1 million are rain-fed; 9 million hectares are natural grasslands, and 7 million are forested or jungle areas. Other uses cover 340,000 hectares. The per capita income varies according to different regions and communities.

> 18. Collective forms of labor within the indigenous communities are a characteristic element that has contributed to their survival and continuity because this work contributes to organized productive activities even at times of crisis. Reciprocity is an important element among the households and community members.

Bingo. That was it, reciprocity. He wanted a little reciprocity in his sex life, and swirling his cold coffee in its cracked cup, he could foresee he wasn't gonna get it.

He rubbed his hand over his freshly scraped face and sighed. He felt sad, but not sad like he wanted to go home. More like it was a sad business to learn stuff, and a sad business to grow up. Like, he knew the mysterious Emily was gone.

Tomorrow he'd get into another van with another driver leading them through the countryside, to one fenced outpost after another.

He felt like a traveling freak-show.

Momentarily disheartened, he thought about his father. Another traveler. And then before he had time to wallow further, his unmistakable new fellow-travelers came into the restaurant. Maybe there was some new female in the group who wanted to get laid.

25

Constance Accepts a Student

The doorbell rippled once and then again. It was an unexpectedly pleasant bell in San Gregorio, installed high on the kitchen wall. Her heart thumped. Standing at the sink, Constance quickly wiped her hands on the delantal she had taken to wearing as routinely as the women of San Gregorio who spent many hours on the streets and at the market, selling their tortillas or fruit. Getting laundry done was no easy thing; the few laundromats never separated whites from colors and apparently had no idea that Clorox was a laundry product. Most of her white camp shirts showed stains under the armpits and on her bosom. Maybe she was going to be one of those old folks who always dribbled on themselves.

The heart-thump indicated a fear she didn't express. Lately, the militarization had become so tense she wondered why she wasn't in Florida with other senior citizen dribblers. Maeda and the little boy flashed through her mind.

She was still pulling the apron over her gasping face when she realized her visitor was a man. For a moment she couldn't recall, and then with deep relief she recognized Carmen's husband. The landlord. He had entered the gate without formality.

She peered through the glass and then opened the door into the living room. She managed a courteous stretch of her lips she hoped resembled a smile. "Pasele."

He stepped in, and Constance was newly struck by how handsome a man he was, except for the strange ear. His features were not exceptional, but he carried an expression of competent pride that seemed to justify them like margins on a printed page. He looked regular, orderly. His clothing, civilian cotton trousers and shirt, looked militarily clean and well kept.

She remembered Harry's absence, like a child instructed not to open the door for strangers. But just as when Aida had brought Maeda and the boy, Constance was glad Harry was away. He never knew of that episode.

"Perhaps you would prefer to sit outside? The patio looks lovely. Carmen is a wonderful gardener." In her own ears she sounded bright and false. Maybe her lame Spanish would cover it. Ignacio, that was his name. They stepped out into the warm sun, Constance pulling the door shut after carefully checking for the key in her pants pocket. One careful measure after another. Better to have him out of the apartment. While she indicated to Ignacio to sit down under the umbrella affixed to the patio table, she caught him looking at her. Confronted with Ignacio's swift male up-and-down glance she flushed with a sensation she hadn't felt in twenty years. With Aida's gentle hint she had modified her hairdo, getting rid of the plastic headband that held the hair off her face, in favor of two side twists clipped together on the crown of her head. It was in style. The high sides accentuated her facial bones.

With no prompting, in simple celebration of living in a

permanently warm climate, she indulged her vanity and no one noticed—her feet were small and elegant, with high arches. Her sandals
showed off bright pink toenails, a bit of silliness. She hadn't pulled on
sneakers or boots for months. Many women here owned no shoes at
all—but she doubted Ignacio was thinking of that.

After all, she was much older than he, and she noted how he
looked away satisfied that there was nothing to look at. She smiled to
cover her grief.

Of course she had been a pretty girl—at least Harry used to call
her "my pretty girl". Then one day when she looked into the mirror
she saw—she felt—wronged. As if she had been robbed.

"Well, Mom," Judith said cheerfully, "I guess now you have to
rely on your personality!" Indeed. She wondered if other women felt
this grief, perhaps men, too. She was long past menopause, and yet—.
And yet she found sometimes that she was expecting a particular man
to flirt with her. Which of course was not going to happen. Which of
course never happened anymore.

Nevertheless, she quietly yearned. A man who perhaps knew her
twenty-five years ago might magically appear in Chiapas, and in the
exotic environment, find her exotic again. Like Ingrid Bergman in
Casablanca, only she, Constance, would be the person waiting.

They sat in the shade of the striped umbrella. Ignacio waited until Constance placed her hand on the back of a chosen chair, and
then he sat to her left. So the bad ear was not visible. Constance said
nothing. He seated himself in a way which made it necessary for her
to turn her torso to speak to him. That wouldn't do. After all, he came
here for some reason, she supposed.

"I was thinking perhaps you would accept me as your student."

"Excuse me?"

"I want to learn English. Quickly. Privately. I have eight months,
more or less."

Now she did twist to look at him. Her appraisal of a prospective student. Her eyes narrowed and relaxed as she briefly wondered.

"Would that be possible?" He glanced at her sideways. The posted sign on her door stood out in bold red ink, so she could hardly claim she didn't teach English. Really, she wanted several students, if possible. One she had already accepted was a young woman who worked in a tourist hotel. Very sensible. Another who rang the bell was a student at the preparatorio, with one year more before he departed for university in Tuxtla. Both were able to pay the minimum she charged of thirty pesos an hour. She didn't need the three dollars; it was more a question of establishing value for the lessons, and respect for her. For her time.

"I charge forty pesos an hour. All my lessons are private." Of course working here for money was illegal. She made her statement in reckless disregard for consequences.

"Muy bien." He fell silent.

"For what purpose do you need English? I mean, I need to know what kind of vocabulary you want. Will you be speaking, or reading or writing?"

"Yes."

"Formal English? Academic English? Street English?"

"Yes." He looked at her sideways again. "I am a military officer. I will speak with American military and study from them."

"That's fine," she replied blithely. It sounded to Constance like he might learn specialized military vocabulary, maybe tactics. She wondered if she could ask Harry what phrases they routinely used in the army. All she knew for certain was motherfucker, and probably that was not what Ignacio had in mind. Suddenly she grinned. She felt cheered by her own profound knowledge of men, no doubt.

And an instant later she frowned.

Deliberately pushing to the back of her mind the question of tactics—where and when he would apply such tactics – she stood up. Chill out, she instructed herself. Tactics is your own word, he didn't say that. Before Ignacio could rise too, she stepped around to the opposite side of the table and sat to look him full in the face. There was the ear, there the browned Mexican skin, the regular handsome features. Okay.

"Ignacio, if I am to teach you, you must follow my instructions." She spoke so firmly she surprised herself. It didn't cross her mind to refuse to teach him—she never refused to teach. Nor did she ask for credentials or occupation before accepting a student. She only looked at the face, for willingness to learn.

"First, you must look at me. And I must look at you." She waited while he met her glance. After all, this was a military man, not a schoolboy. Not a wimp. Not at all, she saw that now. "I will teach you English like a mother teaches her child to speak. First without a book, without a dictionary, without grammar. You must look at me and listen to me and repeat what I say."

"Yes."

"And when I smile, you smile. And if I sing, you sing." He nodded.

"And when I sing the alphabet and clap, you will sing and clap." His eyelids fluttered, and he nodded. "And also I will give you written materials to take for homework. Together, the fastest progress follows."

"Very well. I believe I understand your method. When shall we start?" He didn't know how a foreign language should be learned or taught. He accepted her firm expertise.

They arranged two afternoons per week, for two hours, during the afternoon dinner hour. Constance supposed he would eat his comida after the lesson, and she would also, although she had not yet made peace with the Mexican mid-afternoon dinner. She hadn't asked him where his military duties were based or precisely what he did. She wasn't sure it was any of her business, but perhaps later on as their conversations progressed in English he would tell her. She was in fact a rather good teacher, and sooner or later he would talk.

He said goodbye, and Constance led him out to the patio gate, as if this house were hers instead of his. In truth, she wasn't sure whose house it was, it was not uncommon for women to buy property as economic backup for themselves or their children. Harry paid their rent to Carmen. But since it was always in cash, that explained nothing.

In the living room Constance carefully wrote down in her small calendar the lesson dates and times for the next month. Maybe she should have refused, but how—that would have been as much as to say she didn't like him, or the military, or had something to hide. It never crossed her mind to state she was too busy! She very much wanted to be busier than she was.

And of course she enjoyed contact with an attractive man. Damn. Constance knew perfectly well it was a reflex—was it biology one never recovered from? Were dirty old men matched by dirty old women? Sadly she recognized that although it was never spoken of when she was young, it must be true. She heard often enough of rich older women who kept young studs.

Somehow she couldn't see herself like Tennessee Williams' Mrs. Stone. She didn't have the money! And besides what would she do with Harry!

Without the necessity of cooking for the absent Harry, she puttered around the sink washing out her coffee cup and juice glass. The news coming in from the countryside was scary. No wonder her heart raced when the bell rang. She not only had no way of knowing who was safe and who not – not just that Maeda vanished, but where was Aida, where was Merwin?—or if she herself was safe, or soon to be singled out by the immigration police.

People came and went, she reassured herself. She must think first of Harry, her lifetime companion, her husband. Something about Ignacio's visit left her uneasy. She recognized a dual anxiety creeping over her. The militarization of Chiapas lurked in the back of her consciousness. Does the body confuse emotional anxiety with sexual desire? Or does anxiety push us toward sexual desire? What a way to appease. Young women didn't do that. It was a leftover from pre-Lib days, for sure.

Anyway, she wouldn't be jumping into bed with Ignacio. Worse luck. It was pretty long ago that she had been unfaithful to Harry. Once or twice. Maybe three times. Innocent Constance! But Constance never felt guilt about her one-night sexual flings. They took place when she was in her thirties, and once in her forties, each time when Harry was overseas and she was sole parent for Judith. They were anxiety driven, not love driven.

She never cheated on Harry. Perhaps Harry had done the same with other women. She never asked, and truly believed it was none of her business. One had to manage, somehow. Principles weren't pragmatic.

Now she faced the realization that men would not approach her, not approach her as a wife left unattended, a pretty, anxious, and lonely wife. Having or not having principles had been rendered meaningless!

Nor, she guessed now, would Ignacio request her passport in order to receive English lessons. In fact, here in an informal economy and culture, nobody asked to see a CV or a credential. Somehow being American was all the guarantee required. And Ignacio as a military man – she suspected they all maintained several lives: one professional, another life in which bribes, and murders as favors, or advancement might play a part, one life for private contracts, yet another reserved for family and friends—assuming a man like Ignacio had friends. No doubt he cultivated contacts, but that was quite different.

He had Carmen. Carmen's face and body seemed molded like Adam's from clay, primary and beautiful. But often, as Constance watched Carmen's features when Ignacio's wife felt unobserved at work in the garden or on the roof, an expression emerged which Constance could neither like nor exactly identify.

It certainly wasn't the rosy bloom of a well-bedded woman. Constance knew that expression from looking in the mirror, and although the years fled, now and again she saw the glow reappear. She still was capable of feeling a pulse throb in her groin. In this moment, thinking of Ignacio. Power and control turned her on. That must be the other side of the coin from anxiety, she told herself. She couldn't really admire him. He was confident, and she would be a long time in knowing what ideas or abilities held him so firmly.

26

Carmen Works

"How hard she works," Constance thought, listening to the dogged scraping on cement as Carmen scrubbed the new bricks of the patio wall.

Harry returned from the mountains tired and dirty. He yearned for peace and quiet while he gathered his thoughts. The project was going well enough. Each trip brought in more of the necessary materials, and god knows the men worked their butts off, making their decisions as a group and quietly following without demure his instructions for elevation and angle. Even the women and kids worked, mixing cement and carrying loads that Harry wondered at. It was a community project; they all wanted this dream of water

Leaving his coffee and juice on the table in front of him, he stretched his legs and leaned back. He enjoyed the solicitude from Constance who brought him juice she squeezed herself, joking that her biceps were as big as his. It would be perfect if he could take his breakfast out into the patio. But the noise.

This project—he wanted it, too. It was his encore, his final show. Maybe not. He smiled briefly. Maybe there was more to come, if.

The *if* he couldn't yet think through. If they were stopped by Immigration he carried no work permit. They overstayed their visas without a moment's hesitation. Constance knew that. A quick examination of legal regulations informed Harry, and he explained to Constance. He couldn't work for pay, and he would need to claim he wasn't working. He couldn't volunteer. As a foreigner he would be condemned by the government in Chiapas as aiding and abetting, if they were investigated. So no matter what, they fell outside the law. Ignoring it for the moment seemed like the best option.

At first he didn't worry over it. Now he realized their project was no secret. Out in the pueblos he was watched with keen interest. Not only for the water. For his attitude. One evening Tonatín asked him, in the quiet off-hand voice that hid serious things, if he could train some men to do engineering. So that after he was finished others could go to the far-flung tiny mountain towns. He almost laughed in pleasure at the suggestion, but recovered.

"People here understood irrigation a thousand years ago. I bet they can figure out pipe-lines for themselves."

Tonatín shook his head. "Everyone wants science these days," he responded smiling. He rarely spoke of the commonality underlying the Zapatista vision. They were traditional yes, but not frozen in time. They wanted the benefit of new technologies also.

Harry frowned. So his activities were widely known. More than he liked. Despite his trust in the people he knew, others saw and heard. He and Constance often read about indigenous men betraying, even killing, for money. The corruption arose from centuries of poverty, but regardless of causes, betrayal came with no warning, and it often meant torture or death. Pride and fear fought for his attention.

Beneath his eyes brown hollows had appeared since he last slept at home in San Gregorio. Constance noticed, and recalling her own despair at seeing herself aging, said nothing. It didn't occur to her wakefulness produced the smudges. Nights half asleep half alert, monitoring sounds outside his one-room house.

Now, sitting at the table with the repeated scrape and bang in his ears he monitored the area which was supposed to be home, safe, quiet. "Doesn't that woman ever go home? She never quits." His eyebrows drew together and his hands clutched the cup.

It was true, more or less. Lately Carmen seemed to work from eight in the morning until ten at night, not steadily, but leaving and returning like rains on the mountains. What could she be wearing down, rubbing and rubbing at the facts of her economic life, her personal life?

Constance, waiting for the fresh pot of coffee, stood at the window and watched the clamorous birds that flocked to the patio. They were blessed with hummingbirds, a rather larger species than Constance had imagined, somehow more rapacious, if one could call a hummingbird rapacious. A black body stood on the air while the pinwheel wings thrummed. It thrust its long beak into the pink blossom dangling from vines outside the window.

Half hidden by the window Constance watched the woman. She was strong, built for work when she discarded the foolish outfits she wore to accompany her husband in public. This represented her private life, perhaps, working and working, scrubbing and scraping, pounding, painting, building, arranging, a never-ending busy-ness.

Constance realized that earlier—when, at dawn?—Carmen relocated plants in the patio, brought more, placed some of the pots on bricks to drain properly. And then of course she watered them, fetching water in bowl after bowl, striding back and forth. The brown and gray speckled tórtula which usually snacked seeds from the ground beneath the vine fled to its upper reaches.

Constance inspected the woman's face. It was drawn, lightly filmed with sweat. Yes, sad. Something within her kept her rubbing.

The new patio wall was constructed in the strangest way. The bricks stacked carefully one upon the other like Leggo blocks. The usual small brown workmen spent three days while Carmen supervised, apparently satisfied. But no structure connected to it—no house nor construction. Just a wall, free-standing in the patio. It served as a room divider, to separate the Skelbas' pretty patio from the laundry area which contained a large cement block. On top of the raw rectangle stood two soapstone ribbed sinks with drains. The drains connected to nothing, and let water drop onto the cement through two contrived holes, one beneath each sinkdrain.

Harry strung clothesline for Constance, so she could rinse manageable items of clothing without the expense and bother of dragging everything to the laundromat. The laundromat existed, that was very nice; the heavier sheets and towels could go. Sun and her own Clorox comforted her. She washed clothes by hand, as her mother did before washing machines were affordable. And as the campesino women all did, in tubs or in rivers; Constance watched them kneel on stones, with their dark arms obscured by moving water.

So Carmen put her behind a wall, doing work which was not middle-class American lady's work. Carmen aspired, Constance knew that much from her neatly clipped hair and stylish clothes. Or had aspired when she was younger. Perhaps before she knew the price? Carmen commented only that when people came to the patio for English lessons, or to chat and drink coffee, it would not be nice to see the estanca and their intimate items strung on the line.

Constance opened their door and stepped outside to ask Carmen what she was doing, how long, could she wait perhaps, until later in the day.

Harry followed her, and sat down at the patio table. His fatigue level troubled Constance. She chatted briefly with Carmen, who quickly apologized. Then Carmen, without sitting down herself, turned toward Harry, and asked him something in her quick Spanish.

"Are you sure? It's a long trip, and not comfortable. The roads are bad," he added as if this would be new information.

"Yes, sure. I must go. I must."

"Pues, bien. We'll leave Friday, by 6:30 A.M. Meet the truck behind the cathedral. Be sure to bring food and water." Harry's voice again after a pause, "Something warm to wear. And a flashlight."

Carmen's answering laugh struck Constance with a jolt. She never had heard Carmen laugh. And anyway, why would she?

As if Carmen heard Connie's unvoiced thoughts she answered, "That was my home, you know. I am of the Ch'ol people."

She stepped back, and seeing Constance's expression change from curiosity to dismay as she understood the Spanish, Carmen diverted the conversation, saying cheerfully, "Now I'm going to fix these vines. They drop flowers into the estanca water and that's not good. The rot. It's very quiet work! You won't know I'm here."

Effortlessly she propped on her shoulder the wooden ladder she kept against the rear corner, and gripping a handle-less knife, she vanished behind the patio wall.

Constance perched on the edge of a chair and faced Harry across the table. "Would you like me to bring out fresh coffee?"

"That'd be nice. The air is wonderful. A sweet bread, if we have any?"

But she didn't move. Finally, she spoke softly in English, despite no likelihood that Carmen would overhear, or understand. Harry responded, "You don't really want to know, Connie."

"I do. I'm not a child. Naive, not stupid. You look like shit and I do want to know."

"There's trouble. Cuates is okay, but towns along the road lower down have been harassed." He didn't add, and they all know a gringo is working up above. If he were snatched. Kidnapped into a military vehicle and like gringos before him, driven around day and night incommunicado, unable to contact the US embassy. Bundled onto a plane without so much as changing his socks, and lucky at that.

"Harassed by the government? By the military?"

"No, by the White Guards. Armed by the military. Set afoot by the military. They stir up trouble over land boundaries and water. I think only to maintain the illusion that government control matters. To keep rebellion from spreading, or more towns from declaring autonomy." He sighed. "In reality, there's not much up there. That's not oil country."

"Forests?"

"Yeah, maybe. American and Japanese investigators getting their bio-specimens. Universities with contracts. Supporting the pharmaceutical empires." He shifted forward in the chair and placed his hand over hers. "This is about resources, yes, but more about autonomy. No government lets chunks of its country drop out."

Finally Constance put aside the warmth of his hand and stood to fetch the coffee. She leaned over Harry and kissed him.

When she returned with their mugs she brought other questions. Harry resigned himself to telling her. Truthfully, it was a relief. Sometimes Connie saw things. In people and events. Which he missed completely. For example, she told him Carmen was unhappy. Carmen's upper arm was bruised. Well, that was no surprise, but he hadn't noticed until this moment when she paused to speak to him. Carmen needed to go up. Which town, he didn't know. Up. They all came from up. But although Connie would quickly spot Carmen's unhappiness she wouldn't know, unless he told her, that most likely Carmen's own husband was the military figure directing raids, a colonel in the Public Security Forces.

He would keep that to himself for now. One more thing for Connie to agonize over—she didn't need that. At least not yet.

Constance had not yet informed Harry about her new student. Maybe this was the time. She hesitated, sitting quietly and watching Harry's face.

"I'll be taking a few other people," he continued. "It's better for hiding materials, more non-indigenous tourist types makes it easier. There's Tonatín, of course. That American, what's his name, of Mexican descent who's investigating ruins, you know who I mean."

"Merwin." So Merwin was back in San Gregorio. He hadn't yet stopped by to visit, but Constance hoped he would. He was a good source of information.

"Harmless," he nodded. What Harry meant by harmless, he couldn't have said. Not a spy. On the other hand, Carmen would learn his route, his comings and goings. Did that mean the military, via Ignacio, also would know? But she already knew! Or at least enough to know he would pass her village. Was her source maybe someone from Cuates, whose kinship net must cover most of the Sierra Corral? Info flowing in the other direction?

"At least I won't have to feel jealous of you and Carmen alone together." She left the political content and moved right on to the personal. She'd always say something flattering to cheer him up. "A handsome dude like you and a young unhappy woman. That sounds like trouble to me!"

They both smiled.

Privately Harry imagined there was plenty of trouble to go around, without any flirtations. His gut felt like he played with forces far beyond his ability to confront. And the network. Talk about smoke signals—these indios communicated by telepathy. Or they traveled. Incredible distances on foot, hour after hour. Carmen might be going to warn them. But they knew what was coming. Maybe not when. Harry doubted she was going to visit an aged mother! Something more important. No, deeper. A bond, maybe. Her childhood people, before she descended to the town, where schools and shops seduce you; where she accepted the courtship stroll on the alameda with the handsome cadet. Risky for her, betraying Ignacio. Because that's what this visit would be.

The sun moved to place its hand on the back of his shoulders. He relaxed into the warmth. He and Constance married young enough, after a couple years of dating and horsing around at the university. Their cultural similarities made bonds fall naturally into place. Their marriage held together on a glue of historic similarities. That was how most long marriages worked. Well, sex too. He never doubted the fidelity of his wife, nor gave her reason to doubt his.

It worked like that before we all became so damned mobile.

Divorce existed here in Chiapas. It was rare. More likely abuse, alcoholism, abandonment. Go off to the US to pick lettuce. Carmen and Ignacio had no children. That was good. He basked in the sun, letting his thoughts slide along. What held together a marriage, when those bonds of similar background weren't so reliable. What, then? Similar goals? How about whole communities? His head dropped onto his chest as he dozed. Who stays, who leaves?

Constance carried their coffee mugs back into the apartment. She hadn't told him yet about her student, but she would.

27

First Lesson

Friday morning Harry rose from the breakfast table at five-thirty, preparing to leave. He slung his pack and bedroll on his back and hung over his shoulder by the strap his rolled maps in their straw carrier. His backpack sagged, bottom heavy.

Connie hoped he planned as carefully for warm clothes and dry boots as he did for his supplies to work in Cuates de Santa Ana for two weeks. At least he looked somewhat rested, his jeans and denim shirt freshly laundered, and his curly mop of silver hair freshly washed and shining like a helmet on a Spartan warrior setting forth.

"I'll be off," he said, "and leave you with your guapo." It was the best face he could put on the situation, referring to Ignacio as handsome. He knew Connie thought the guy was good-looking.

Finally she told Harry about her new student. That he had come to see her asking for lessons for his forthcoming trip to the United States. For a long moment Harry simply stared at her. School of the Americas! That guess determined everything, told Harry everything.

He was appalled, and then stone-faced, immediately blaming himself for not informing Constance about the suspicion surrounding Ignacio, the probable director of militia attacks on indigenous communities. And what could he tell her now, so as not to scare the wits out of her. Only that he worried about their lack of visas.

Neither of them knew how to undo what was done. Furthermore, Ignacio's motives were unclear. Constance thought he truly intended to learn English, and took the easiest and safest opportunity—with someone who could not gossip with his fellow officers. She doubted he would ask questions; and Harry, supposing Ignacio knew he was more than a retiree, agreed. Games within games. Nevertheless. If it came up, she must tell Ignacio that Harry investigated ancient irrigation methods found in archeological ruins.

"Be careful," he instructed her.

"He is handsome," Constance admitted, brightly misunderstanding. "But compared to you—eh! Nada!"

She was sorry to see Harry leave. Often she wished he were dead, but that was no contradiction. If he died she would be free to begin her life afresh even if that meant no more than volunteering at a public library in Ann Arbor. It was odd, she knew. She couldn't possibly leave him, nor did she want to. Only this odd yearning for something different. Chiapas of course was different. She herself was different. Harry, her lover, was not.

She felt herself literally absorbing new ideas, a sensation of swelling or re-taping in her brain, something beyond description. And even stranger, they spoke between themselves of these new ideas: autonomy, decisions by consensus, leading by obeying, self-sufficiency; and yet Constance supposed that only she, not Harry, actually altered her American liberal democratic ideas. Harry, for his part, did not often introspect. That wasn't his way; he simply acted. Yet he had changed also, and often wondered why Constance did not seem to soak up what was going on. Had not changed as he had. Could it be she was too old to modify her beliefs? But Harry and she were the same age.

"Do you think he's sinister?" Connie lifted her face to kiss him. "I can manage him! And you, stay safe," she whispered against his lips, as if some Fate might have heard private thoughts.

"Military men are always sinister. It's their job," he flung over his shoulder as he unlocked the door. "Will you be okay with the apartment? I mean, you won't have Carmen to call either, if something goes amiss."

Constance was self-reliant when Harry worked away. She took quiet pride in being masterful with leaking faucets when her engineer-in-residence moved beyond call, and she rarely mentioned problems when he returned. Only when he was home did she ask him to do repairs for her, or lift ungainly water jugs. What might go amiss neither of them could express. They lived hidden in the interstices of the Chiapas oligarchy, past their visas, in the midst of a rebellion, with sinister forces directing not only the military but federal and state governments. So what's to worry about?

"I'm due back on the 24th. If I'm not here by the 26th, call the American Embassy in Tuxtla."

She nodded. "I'll be in deep trouble if the water heater conks out." He returned her smile, and was gone. At the patio gate she stood for a moment and watched his receding back. The trivialities she pretended vanished, leaving her face somber. Then she shrugged and turned.

Precisely at two, Ignacio Ayela Ramírez stood before Constance like a boy showing up for dance class, impeccably dressed and combed. His dark hair, brushed and shiny, covered his head like a smooth dark helmet.

She invited him, "Pásele".

Although Constance once again stood near the gate, it was Ignacio who closed the metal door firmly behind him and moved toward her. Awkwardly she offered her hand. Ignacio hesitated a fraction of a second, then grasped it with the slightest indication of a bow.

"Maestra."

In the moment, she knew she would not mention Carmen. After all, this lesson did not concern the wife. She must have told Ignacio some lie to disguise her trip, and Constance didn't want to know it. Or did Carmen tell Ignacio the truth? Mentally Constance switched off her image of Harry on the road with Carmen and Merwin while seven thousand soldiers patrolled. On his way, while she remained alone with Ignacio. Was that double danger a betrayal? Of what, or should she ask herself, of whom?

"Oh, my name is Constance," she replied firmly in English to indicate the lesson had started. She gave her first name, as a casual American. "Sit down." And she sat to demonstrate. Quickly he sat next to her at the round patio table, so that she could not entirely see his face, but sensed how he turned toward her for confirmation.

"No." She was firm. If she could not guide him, nothing would work. She pointed to the chair facing her. For a brief moment he paused. Thinking it over? Okay. Take your time. She waited, with her arm lifted and her finger pointing.

He stood up and moved, sat again. Again she looked at him squarely. And wondered which of them had more reason to wince under inspection. She looked into his eyes, forcing him to focus on reading her thoughts, not the lines around her mouth, not the furrows between her eyebrows or the loose skin beneath her chin. Her mind, her mind which would lead his mind.

In this game, she must keep him on the English, where she would betray nothing.

So they began. I am Constance. You are Ignacio. man woman

child house. He repeated. Food water. She brought out for its pictures an old English As A Second Language text carried pointlessly, she had supposed, from the United States. From her collection of books and charts and cards, all left behind, she brought this one only, as an unrelinquished symbol of her status as a teacher. Michigan and graduate school. Her leap beyond the small town high school where girls wore straight pageboy hairdos and plaid skirts, where girls wore white bobby socks and loafers, dainty strings of pearls over cashmere sweater sets, they all wore—.

Then. When she bloomed, the way teen-age girls will. Still in bloom when she enrolled in graduate school and paired off forever with Harry. Then.

The book cover in red white and blue with an American flag on the front signified a new language in a new mythic land which surely didn't exist, neither now nor then. And here she was using it after all.

Despite fifty years gone since her last purchase of a cashmere sweater set, she felt girlish as Ignacio studied her face. But that's what he was supposed to do! To learn! She wrestled her feelings back into the right frame—she was an educator.

He made a quick student. Businesslike, determined. Once when she corrected his pronunciation of "her" which he repeated as "hear" she watched his left hand rise toward the side of his head. Then she realized she had forgotten the deformed ear, and simultaneously she knew by the way his lifted arm firmly returned to the table that her correction had not hurt his pride. Not seriously, not enough to slow his pace.

After forty-five minutes she offered him watermelon juice, and without waiting for his reply fetched from the kitchen two glasses and a pitcher of pink juice. "We must rest. Would you like some juice?"

"I don't choose to stop." He spoke in Spanish. "I must learn as quickly as possible."

"During our lesson I don't understand Spanish." She knew she must sound like a fussy old school teacher. "Besides, I need to rest. I'm rather old, you know." Immediately she was glad he didn't understand her. What if he interpreted this unnecessary statement as a request for a compliment? Oh, no, Teacher Constance, you are young and lovely. But his face remained blank, and because she didn't immediately return to the book, somewhat dark. The darkness lent his demeanor a sexual charge, a power Constance struggled against.

"I am drinking. You are drinking." She gestured to indicate he should repeat. She drank. "I am tired." She touched her forehead with the back of her hand to indicate "tired."

Immediately he leaped to his feet. "You have a headache with a student so stupid. I apologize for my thoughtlessness."

"Oh, no! I only meant that a rest period is necessary." Unwilling for him to be uncomfortable for even a moment, she responded in Spanish.

A tiny smile twitched his lips. "It's all right then."

He had won, won back a tiny slice of control, manipulating her to speak Spanish during an English lesson. He held his trim upper body straight, with shoulders squared.

She leaned back. To hide her chagrin she responded in Spanish,

"In English we say break. After forty-five minutes I need a break. And so do you. Despite your intelligence."

She tilted her head sideways as if appraising his intelligence. There was no doubt he was sharp. But what impelled him was a different matter altogether.

"The mind absorbs only so much at one time. We can speak Spanish during the break but we must speak English during the lesson. Are you ready?"

Constance asked herself the same question. Thank heaven she

always started with naming.

He put the glass to his lips and drained it, childishly wiping the protruding upper lip with the back of his hand. "Sí, Maestra."

"Yes, Constance," she said for him in English.

"Yes, Constance."

When he left she didn't protest his taking with him the book, and she wondered how many days would pass before he'd have it by heart. So he was off to the US in eight months for a training period. In what, she wondered. It was clearly something he didn't care to discuss. He hadn't alluded to it again, merely mentioned his hurry to learn English. His concentration and impatience were evident.

From her side, she was unwilling to approach anything not in her lesson plan. An old teacher's trick to maintain control and stay out of trouble!

Harry supposed the training was purely military, maybe horrible. School of the Americas! Ah, no, she sighed. Ignacio was so well-mannered, and repeated after her so earnestly, like a child, glancing up like a child for her approval. More likely he would receive some quasi-diplomatic experience.

She found comfort in that notion. Learn to interact with the American command which commanded—. But she wasn't stupid. Her fear and loathing surged anew. She was afraid to estimate how much of this attempt to put down the Zapatista rebellion was American inspired, to keep options open for foreign investments. Ignacio would gravitate toward the powerful, of that she felt sure.

Her ambivalence twisted her. She recalled Ignacio's possessive hand resting on Carmen's nape. She reached and touched her own neck beneath the hair. Her hair was almost white on the newly caught up side twists which adorned her head like a silver coronet. Attractive, she knew. A strange shiver raised the skin on her arms. He's so mannerly, she repeated to herself. He learns so quickly.

Abruptly she decided to walk down to the zócalo. It was early enough to sit in Alvaro's café for a while and enjoy a cappuccino. She hadn't treated herself to a cappuccino in a long while. Like a girl, she impetuously grabbed her purse from the bedroom and briefly touched her lips with a pale lipstick on her way out.

In the zócalo a few French tourists sat smoking over beers at the sidewalk cafe. They spoke quietly among themselves, ignoring a four-man group in wool serapes who serenaded with Andean wind instruments. The sound of the reed pipes came to Constance's ear on a plaintive breeze. She thought she recognized "Guantanamera" from Pete Seeger days when liberals in Ann Arbor supported Cuba against the evil imperialism of the US.

Mixtures stranger than that became common. Peruvians in Mexico, Mexicans in Los Angeles. In Chiapas the state orchestra played Gershwin tunes and the Guillermo Tell Obertura. Plenty of mariachi, mostly Tex-Mex.

Culture shifted almost daily, small seismic ripples despite efforts by the Chiapas aristocracy to hold onto the status quo. Their own daughters, the pampered rich presented in white ball gowns at their quinceañeros parties, zipped themselves into tight jeans like the rest of Mexico's young; playing Britney Spears albums like the global teen population.

The young will leave, Constance thought. Go to learn computer technology and agro-business. Well, why not? Why shouldn't Mexican teens enjoy malls with Kentucky Fried and McDonalds hamburgers? Globalization, Harry would shout. He hated the invasion. But even Harry admitted that people should be free to choose for themselves. That was part of the impact the indigenous rebellion made on every Mexican member of Civil Society. Some sense of change, and possibilities. Novelty would lure them all, young and old. How about Marcos communicating by internet.

Seated at her favorite table she drank her cappuccino and felt dissatisfied—why? A little consumer therapy as Judith used to call it, was definitely in order. Whatever it was she yearned for had no name. Aida was not here to chat.

She left her tip. Across the square she entered the only shop that sold foreign goods, and purchased a second set of "nice" sheets to supplement what Carmen supplied for them: 100% polyester sheets. Their joke was that every time Connie rolled over, Harry slid out of bed; the pillows followed onto the floor, and the blanket skidded sideways. When Harry climbed back in, Connie skidded sideways. No sex life possible!

This joke survived several nights because Constance determined to use what the apartment provided. Finally Harry began to refer to her as his teflon bedmate, so she gave it up. It was one night too many of grappling the edge of the mattress.

Their sex life was important, she knew without specifying why – hadn't it always been important? Hadn't she always waited for the gesture of approach Harry made in the dark? Why think of it now? Should she have been more often the one to reach out? Styles of lovemaking change as certainly as the shape of eyebrows or hemlines. She solved the hemline problem by giving up skirts altogether.

Not possible for sex!

She held her package of new sheets under her arm, and began to walk toward the lavanderia to have them washed before use. So nowadays they'd rebuke her for being the passive female. True. She had no defense – but then, why should she defend herself? Harry was of her own generation, and never expected her to make the first move. Much less Ignacio. How did that sneak in? He'd have a heart attack of shock!

She moved along a level street, as most were in the San Gregorio basin, toting her concerns like the bulky bundle which now began to tire her knee. She was not young. She was not young, the hair rolled on top of her head was white. She could hold it with a butterfly or flower clip, but arthritis pinched her right knee. So having youthful thoughts—outside of marriage!—was permitted, but not useful. Not cost effective, Harry would say. And besides, she hated these military bastards.

And that was that. She passed her image in a window. Briefly she paused. Ignacio was responding to her exactly the way a student should, after that moment of brief conflict. He was her student. So that was that.

28

Carmen in the Mountains

Gratefully Merwin unfolded and jumped down from the truck when it halted. He and Carmen were dry as sand, sitting in the back on top of a canvas covering Harry's materials. Carmen jumped unaided although Merwin stood with his hand outstretched. The men in the back of the truck waved, and immediately the truck rumbled off. They hadn't been stopped, and Merwin knew Harry wanted to get higher quicker.

Here he was, nowhere. Riding together, Carmen told him about her pueblo, the place she left to find work in San Gregorio. The old story, no way to earn a living, too many children to feed, eroded land, irregular water. She was fourteen. Her choice was marry or leave.

In her destination, the modest city which to her eyes appeared huge, the difference was Ignacio's mother. Who rescued her. If you call that rescue. Sealed her life in a debt of gratitude.

Carmen claimed that ruins up here on the mountains lay as common as cooking ashes, scattered every which-way. Merwin wondered.

The UNESCO catalogue hardly began to list, that was sure. He could explore. He wasn't even clear which ethnicities they referred to. He could start by identifying the local language.

They began the hike from the road along a dirt path into the pueblo. The land sprouted occasional blue agave, huge and sharp, interspersed with scrub bushes and sparse grasses. The soil looked as dry as he was. Merwin trudged along with his gear, his tripod, his backpack, his bedroll, his boots covered with dust. God knows what he'd need.

Carmen carried by their makeshift handles two big plastic shopping bags, secured with rope. Food. They always needed food. She carried a backpack also, and Merwin wondered if she needed help with the load. But she didn't seem to. After a while she paused to peel off her sweater, and so did he.

He felt lucky to have an intro to an intact village like this. Remote and impoverished, with nothing to attract outsiders, such tiny outposts were rare. More rare still, if they remained undamaged by the military incursions throughout Chiapas, seeking Zapatista sympathizers. Had to happen soon, he knew. No wonder Harry looked anxious.

Carmen halted among the pebbles and rocks that weighted the path. Slowly she rotated her head, side to side, and then looked upward, as if aligning her position in relation to the mountain. Finally she led him to a low choza, a thatched hut with a hole in the roof issuing smoke.

This was the home of her tía, her mother's sister. The tía was the only one left of her family. Carmen's brothers vanished like many men, north toward the United States, and nobody knew if they lived or were dead—the crossing was very dangerous. No money ever arrived, no letters, nothing. So it is.

Carmen preceded him. He stepped inside. The ceiling was low, the floor dirt. A dim light filtered in behind him, through the door. No windows.

An old lady wrapped in a rebozo sat near the fire, her hands and head directly above the warmth. The scarf wound around her neck and over her head, and it took a moment for Merwin to realize she wore two or maybe three different cloths. Her face and hands seemed not to feel the heat from her comal, nor heat of the cooking tortillas. The old lady paused in poking at the wood embers and looked up, the stick still in her hand. She peered through the smoke, saying nothing.

Her face was brown and grooved like a walnut, her nose prominent between fragile cheek bones. Finally, she nodded. Her expression shifted the flesh around her mouth. She recognized her niece. Her thin arm rose and she crossed herself. Tears filled Carmen's eyes. The aunt made the sign of the cross again, in the air in front of Carmen. When finally the old lady spoke, it was not in Spanish.

Merwin waited. Carmen exchanged several clicking sounds with the old lady, kneeling at her side to embrace her. She gestured to Merwin to place his belongings on the rope bed suspended on a frame six inches off the floor. Merwin balked. It was the only bed in the one room, maybe the old lady once slept here with her husband; she slept alone now. He supposed Carmen would sleep with her. Merwin indicated that the floor would do, and showed Carmen his nylon drop cloth. That was settled.

He looked around. A small wooden altar, no more than a shelf nailed onto the wall, held a plastic virgin painted blue and rose, and a white candle. Other than the bed, no furniture. Above them, from hewed beams darkened with smoke, two burlap sacks hung. A cooking pot. A string of garlic, a string of onions. Several dried bunches of herbs fixed to the thatched wall with nails. Hanging from two other nails the old woman's clothes—another wool wrap skirt, he supposed it was. A wool rebozo, one embroidered blouse.

Leaving the women, he stepped back out through the choza's doorframe. A sort of door, of rotted wood, hung suspended by thongs. A few hens squawked and scrabbled. Along a dirt path other huts stood, just like this one, he imagined. How many? As far he could make out four streets lay arranged on the four cardinal points of the compass, leading to a central dry watering trough of stone.

It didn't take much imagination to reconstruct Carmen's life. She appeared at age fourteen on the streets of San Gregorio wearing long braids, a wool wrap skirt sashed and bunched at the waist, her best blue embroidered blouse. She walked door to door seeking work.

As they rode she told him. The embarrassment of being indigenous. The fear that never left her. If she were raped or robbed of her few pesos nobody would intercede. The shame of being illiterate. Oh, yes. It was Ignacio's mother who taught her to read while she kept house for the family. Ignacio's mother was also Ch'ol, from a different village, but she and Carmen more or less understood one another. The mother learned and so could Carmen. The father was from failing coleto stock, if not pure Spanish close enough so that he could pretend, and hold social aspirations. He refused to permit Ch'ol to be spoken to his children. The mother was ailing, lonely, starved for her language.

Carmen owed Ignacio's mother everything. She owed Ignacio, who after all wasn't required to marry her. A servant girl. Maybe she was pretty. Maybe it was Ignacio's tribute to his mother. He loved his mother, Carmen was sure. He was born with a deformity the father would not forgive. Although it had no effect on Ignacio's intelligence, the young girls of good family did not smile when they danced with him.

The father represented status, power and pride, which the son imitated. Then the father sickened. He required eighteen months to die, in much pain. Ignacio's young military career supported them all.

Merwin wondered how. Even an officer with a cadet's formal training. How much money came from the government, how much from extortion and bribes? The obligation to support his family would lie heavily on his shoulders. Merwin didn't ask. Carmen said, "In our culture, the highest obligation is to family." He wondered if she meant herself to her mountain people, or Ignacio to his parents. Or her obligation to Ignacio. Clearly, whatever obligations to church or God existed, they stood secondary.

Merwin understood these old customs, especially male dominance. Ignacio was her husband, and in Carmen's mind that meant for a long time that she was his property, that he could instruct her not only in Spanish grammar, in manners, in sex, in style, on how to assimilate; but also he could strike her when he felt it necessary as punishment. Or worse than that.

Merwin counted. This was 1997. She was fourteen, when? How many years have you lived in San Gregorio? Twenty. So that was the situation just twenty years ago. He nodded.

For the rest of the afternoon Carmen disappeared, and Merwin understood he was not invited to follow her. Men appeared slowly, one by one or in pairs, from fields surrounding the crossroads or from the animal corral. In their shabby dust-covered clothing they drifted in the direction of the tiny church in the center of the village. Not that Merwin could understand in any case, although he realized that most of the younger men spoke Spanish. But not in community meetings.

Alone, he wandered around in the high clean air above the settlement and photographed the hills seemingly stapled back to back around them, the narrow dirt road that brought them up, and its distant extension visible like a finger-streak across dust, rising into the distance. That's where Cuates hid, in its crevasse up there.

The next morning they gave the old aunt the bags of coffee and boxes of milk to supplement the corn meal and beans from the previous night. Merwin slept surprisingly well, aware across the small windowless room of the faint breathing of Carmen and snores of the old lady. The room was warm, despite chill on the grass when he stepped outside at dawn to pee behind the house. Hens cackled. When he re-entered Merwin lifted shut the sagging door, and in the darkness fell asleep once more. He woke to the sensation, more than sound, of women moving about him.

The land is peppered with ruins, and ruins built on top of ruins. Civilizations last just a brief while, and vanish into rocks and soil. Carmen assented, that's so. She was taking him to look at one spot precious from her childhood. Two decades ago, the "ruin" was well known to every resident. Lovers went there when the moon was full, it was said.

He followed once more. Along the path they passed a man coming down with a load of wood braced against his forehead by a mecapal. Buenas días. They passed no one else. Carmen climbed as easily as if her acquaintance with high heels and tight skirts left no impact, held no importance. Climbing behind her, he admired the architecture of her ass. She was not short-legged like most indigenous people in San Gregorio, and the equality of her torso and legs focused his attention on the fulcrum. Rounded, with generous muscles. Nice.

They reached a plateau, and to Merwin that meant the ruin was neither a sacred high place nor a fortress against attack. A village then. The Spaniards' labor conscription left many towns like this one stripped of inhabitants, fallen into disrepair, decaying back into the soil.

They waded through long grasses, interspersed with low thorn bushes and two biznaga cactus, short and rounded like small fat women. Few trees survived in the wind. This was not an archeological ruin, but a remnant of the Conquest. A Catholic ruin.

One wall of the old church had crumbled. If it had been of stones, they were gone, appropriated for other needs. The soil mounded where the wall had stood. The other walls rose more or less intact, perhaps away from the wind-lashed rain. Yes, they were stone, he could see the greenish cast and lines of dirt that surrounded each. Here was some priest's disciplined faith, the shape of it. Drawn with no doubt. Local labor, of course. The roof was gone. Inside the outlined shape the shelter of the remaining structure kept off wind, but not sun. It was warm. They sat down to drink their water and chew cold tortillas they carried.

Merwin saw she felt a bond of some sort here. Her open face was smoothed of worry, and serene. But it was not sacred space; the town permitted the church to fall to pieces. Carmen pointed toward one corner of what had been the altar stone. After a moment he could see other stones. Beneath the church a different temple stood, the original temple of her people. He sprang up.

Then squatting, he scraped aside a square meter of rubble in high excitement. He wanted to take photos, he wanted to document and report and bring here experts to unearth buried gods! He grinned at Carmen, and jumped back up to his feet.

She smiled. Yes, later for that, her smile responded to his rush of enthusiasm. It will be here forever.

Merwin looked up at the revealed sky, at mountains swelling beyond the missing wall. Buried gods remain here; people remain to watch over them until once more they can be brought forth to show their strength. He filled with love for the site, for the tiny town, for Carmen. He loved it that she was alive, and had been alive during centuries of abuse and neglect. He loved it that the church was dead, its ruins vanished, but the people lived.

She took his hand and led him to a far corner of the broken nave.

She knelt, and he knelt again, now beside her with his small spade. Working together, they uncovered some kind of plate, a mosaic of rose and turquoise stone fragments. She placed her hand on it, and then took his hand and laid it palm down, flat on the colored chips, as if on a person's cheek. It was warm to his touch, as warm as Carmen's own hand. He leaned forward and kissed her mouth.

"You understand," she said, "Me, he possesses. This—we can't let this be trampled and changed."

Merwin gathered her and kissed her again. How could stone chips beneath the earth be warm? The soil did not feel warm. Only Carmen, her mouth and breast against him, should be warm. As they were. He could taste the warmth of her lips, laughing and weeping at the same time.

After the kiss she wept a while longer, for relief and joy. Merwin held her quietly. He imagined he was kissing and blessing the past; she was kissing and blessing the future.

29

Massacre at Mocotlán

José heard branches cracking uphill where the cliff rose to meet the road. The crickets went silent. The horses shuffled away from the dry grass beside the house, as if to indicate this was none of their business.

Down the slope from the roadway, into the town, men swarmed. The town hid in a cut in the ground, a crevice into which the refugees and residents of Mocotlán secreted themselves like grass seeds. The men carried automatic weapons and rifles and the crackling sound of breaking branches raced with them over treeless grass. José gripped Emily's wrist.

"Run. Get as far up onto the hill as you can. Go!" He pulled her to her feet. The wooden chair, wobbly as most of the hand-made pieces of furniture, tipped and fell soundlessly onto the dirt floor.

Emily turned her head toward the armed group sprinting down, through and on top of tiny new orange trees, trampling indiscriminately frail stems and young corn stalks planted on the slope. Random bullets cracked cement and pomegranate trees. Splinters flew into the air. Next door a woman screamed.

"Go Go Go!" She leaped across the floor and around the side of the open wall called a house, and saw to her left and right along the narrow dirt road other women dash furiously back toward the opposite hill, which marked the further side of their declivity. The sun had slipped behind the mountain, diffusing a lurid pink light streaked with clouds. She turned her head. José left a gray shadow, loping doubled over in the opposite direction. She wanted to see his face, maybe his hands. Blindly she began to run.

Ahead on her left a pounding figure carried a baby in one arm and a toddler in the other, his legs jutting like sticks. The spurt of blood from the woman's back amazed Emily. It was like a bag burst, a small fountain of red hanging in the air above the fallen woman.

The green ribbon to tie the woman's black braid turned black. The woman's blouse was red. The skirt she wore, tied with a red sash, twisted over her legs as she twisted, trying to rise.

Not bothering to crouch, Emily overtook her. The little boy lay next to his mother, the back of his shirt red. They lay like poppies thrown on the ground. Emily heard the baby's cries as if they came from beneath a field of flowers.

Without thinking she shoved the woman's shoulder. It was Maria Luz the wife of Donaldo. All the women were named Maria.

Emily kneeled, bracing herself, and shoved again. The zinging noise around her along with screams and answering shots receded. Before her she saw Maria Luz the wife of Donaldo was dead, although she was trying to move. The legs exposed beneath the wool wrap skirt were still running. Emily heaved with all her strength and with her left arm reached beneath Maria Luz the wife of Donaldo and pulled out the screeching baby. Quickly she pulled free the bloody skirt, leaving Maria Luz nude from the waist down. She set the baby girl on the hem of the skirt and rolled her like a cigar, creating a bundle.

She tucked the bundle under her arm football style and lurched again toward the hill, one arm outstretched as if to ward of tacklers.

The grass was eaten short by horses and goats which found little enough to eat in this crevice town. The vegetable garden beyond the row of houses was trampled by running women and children, tomatoes squished red under foot, also red, everything was red behind her eyes as she tried to breathe. The sound of gunfire was punctuated by yells and screams of men. The town owned almost no firepower, probably the Mocotlán men fought with machetes and sticks. That was how they practiced military drill. Some of their sticks were carved to resemble guns but they still were only sticks. Emily witnessed those drills for the month of preparation, when they feared the attack would come, when they knew the government hired paramilitary from a nearby town to do the dirty work. The small dark men of Mocotlán running and turning to shoot, running and turning to shoot with their carved sticks and slash with their real machetes.

Her breath heaved in dry gasps. The hidden baby rode silently, and Emily tried to hoist the bundle upright on her arm, but it was too difficult to run bent over with the child's weight against her. To her right a shout came from Maria Carmen the wife of Adolfo. Maria Carmen pointed with her free arm toward the hermitage, a stone construction called holy, a place where Dominican monks hid and were cared for during the Revolution. Maria Carmen the wife of Adolfo turned toward it, dragging her tiny daughter by the hand. The little girl wore only a soiled dress, its buttonholes empty down her back; beneath the dress her naked legs and buttocks were visible ahead of Emily's upturned face.

The hermitage was a cave built of stone, unlike cinder block constructions called houses, really most of them four walls around a dirt floor, with neither doors nor windows, but often they had openings in the walls suggesting doors and windows in the future. In a worst case the tin roofs could be shoved off from within.

Emily balked. The hermitage, totally enclosed, no exit windows, terrified her. She hesitated a split second, and then continued her sprint uphill.

Why had the Mocotlán guards not alerted them? Guard posts stood at the road, at both entrances down into the dirt path that served as the main street. The men must be murdered, and Emily supposed that meant all of them, by stealth, simultaneously. The guards carried no weapons, their only function was to sound the alarm.

Now as she gained some altitude on the hill Emily paused, her breath ratcheting. Hunched over her knees she made out below in the twilight the paramilitaries who attacked from both the road opposite where she and José had sat, and also from behind the north building which served as infirmary, and the south building, housing the school. Shrubs and plants were flattened.

Growing gloom obscured the attackers who swarmed overground, pounding from house to house. Firefly bursts revealed their path as orange flames leaped; so little to burn! Furniture, food, clothing. Directly below her in the clearing she could see nobody unarmed, only the flock of moving shooters, and scattered forms stretched on the dirt, which must be the dead. It looked like all the still-living village people had fled, some women and children who scrambled uphill pounded past and around her through trees and bushes, or raced toward the hermitage.

Emily heard her breath screech in an asthmatic rhythm. The baby remained silent. She stopped and held the bundle to her chest.

Climbing more slowly now, toward the remaining light, she gained the hilltop. She placed the bundled infant on the ground. As soon as she unfolded the skirt the baby waved its arms. One tiny wrist wore the seven plastic yellow and green bracelets Maria Luz put on her daughter, for each week the infant lived. The baby began to squall.

On her knees, Emily wiped her own face of tears and sweat and looked around. Firewood long since claimed what few trees grew up here. Some bushes remained, of a dull green sort Emily couldn't identify. Three women also kneeled, half hidden on the ground. Below them they heard high screams and machine-gun staccato. Emily could discern small figures running from the hermitage, leaping into the air and falling as they ran. The women watched. A silence.

Finally the blackness of oncoming night hid them. There was no water, and the five children able to walk gathered among the three women whimpering.

"Shu-shuhhh!" One woman was naked from the waist up. Without self-consciousness she put her breast to the lips of her boy, and then let her arms hang at her side, as if folding them across her body would require too much effort. None of them carried blankets or rebozos. As the darkness grew colder the women circled the children and drew them into their bodies. Another woman pushed her blouse above her breasts and nursed first the child Emily carried, the child of Maria Luz and Donaldo, and then her own toddler.

Emily took one of the other children onto her lap. She rocked back and forth. The child, the bare legs told her it was a girl, fell into sleep like a stone.

By late night Emily's arms ached. The half-cup moon shrank away. They heard dry sounds of men climbing the hill on dirt and stones below them. Nobody moved, and then came a soft hoot and then another. The women instantly began to softly keen, followed by the children. Emily giggled with relief, and clamped her hand over her mouth. She recognized José's voice. When she stood, the only one among the women with shoes, José gave a sharp grunt. Emily was easy to spot in the faint pre-dawn moonlight, in her jeans and boots. Despite her cropped hair nobody would take her for a man. He said nothing to her, nor did Emily offer any words. He touched her arm briefly.

The men each picked up a child and began to walk, choosing a path along the top of the ridge. Perhaps they would find a safe area by full morning.

José and his companions carried children and rifles, while the women, whose stamina amazed Emily, carried smaller babies and stepped along the trail with bare feet immune to stones and thorns. Three hours later by the first light of dawn Emily was silently weeping from fatigue and exhaustion. She tramped midway in the line, her head down, the tears running down to her chin and off onto her shirt. The shirt was dirty, stained with blood and grass. Inside her boots her feet burned and squished wet at the same time.

At the emergency room of the field hospital two government doctors washed and bandaged treatable injuries. They made no comment nor asked questions. One child from Emily's group had lost a lot of blood, seemed barely alive, his upper arm in shreds, shattered by the expanding bullets the paramilitary used. Of the four other small children another showed an arm smashed, one a broken collarbone, two with skull wounds opened by high caliber bullets. The hospital lacked blood for transfusions, and the doctors sprinkled sulfa powder onto open wounds. Emily stayed with other women while the boy they carried to a table screamed. His side oozed.

The women folded onto the floor next to available cots where bandaged children whimpered, and in a few minutes both women and children fell asleep. The boy did not sleep. His dark eyes remained open and fixed. Emily assured the doctor that she needed no care, and went out into the early morning air.

Amazing. The world remained. Mountains she loved loomed in the far distance decorated with cloud forms in light and shade. The field hospital of the IMSS apparently was located beyond the outskirts of a town; she stood next to a blacktop road. A white Red

Cross ambulance sat on the gravel, waiting for State Police protection to finish their work. The driver slept in the front seat, his head thrown back. Emily, to her own amazement, began to walk once more, toward the onion dome of the cathedral visible in the valley a dozen kilometers away, its splashy red and orange tiles caught in the dawn sun.

Mentally she began to count how many dead, how many still in the village. She plodded on. Maybe fifty left behind. She could take fifty more steps. A battered truck pulled up beside her. She glanced briefly, while her legs continued to move of their own accord.

"Get in," José ordered. He sat in the front seat next to the driver. He opened the door. Emily stood paralyzed, staring at him. She could not lift her leg to the high step, could not lift her body. José got down. He lifted her from behind, under her armpits, and she could feel his fingers near her breasts on each side.

"Do you know who attacked?"

"Oh, yes. We expected them. Paramilitary from three PRI villages, deployed by El Jefe Tornilloreja." Emily was already asleep. José, half holding her on his lap, looked down into her face. He touched her fair eyelashes, on her right eye, then the left. She was not shot, he believed, despite the blood. It was not her blood.

He put his head back against the seat. The driver glanced over.

"Better luck this time," he said. "You didn't lose your woman."

"We lost many."

"True."

Emily woke in a shabby hotel room. Probably it was evening—or maybe the following day, she wasn't sure. She picked up the newspaper folded on the table next to her bed and looked at it. Yes, someone had come in and out. She had slept twenty-four hours, and the nearly noonday sun bathed the splendid cathedral dome beyond her window.

Twenty-five wounded by firearms and "many" dead, according to the testimony of eye-witnesses who managed to enter last night the village of Mocotlán. Early on some residents took refuge in the local hermitage, which afterward was machine-gunned. The attack, according to witnesses, was organized several days in advance and with the participation of at least sixty heavily armed men. The Chiapas Public Security forces are known to be behind the attack. Very likely men were recruited from at least four neighboring villages.

Killing their own people for food to feed their families, the small money and favors they received as paramilitaries. Emily was already too learned in the ways of rebellion, the whys and wherefores, to register any surprise.

Among the indigenous from Mocotlán many were already refugees, originally from Tzajalucum, Chimix and Quextic. Residents of the first two villages were attacked the past month by the same PRI group, who burned houses and stole part of the crops. Since the beginning of December PRI partisans have been threatening to attack the refugees sheltered in Mocotlán, but dialogue for peace had begun, suggesting to the government that no protection was required. Then the conversations were broken off.

A commission is investigating a claim that elements of the Public Security force remained 200 meters from the attack site without intervening.

She read the newspaper account and tossed the paper onto the table. She was clad only in her panties, and felt ravenously thirsty and hungry. Who undressed her and put her to bed she had no idea, but hoped it was José. In the month she spent with him in the village he never acknowledged her openly, although people seemed to know they were lovers. She was not officially his mujer, his wife, his woman;

his woman was dead. She didn't blame him for maintaining priva-cy—after all, she was a foreigner.

In fact she was more foreign than José, with his firm culture of rights and wrongs, could ever imagine. Unthinkable that she relieved her lust with a boy twenty years her junior. Unthinkable she aban-doned her husband because she didn't like the way he spoke to her, or thought about her. Unthinkable she would choose to satisfy her own sense of self, leaving her mother behind in a distant city.

José, unlike David, was good to her, and she to him. Sometimes at night in bed, as he moved slowly above her, she grieved as he wept. He married a girl many years younger than he, before the uprising, perhaps as a final gesture toward peace. A girl of seventeen. His tears wet her face and the hollows in her collarbone. She wept also. Her loss did not echo his, his was external, a real woman, a real child. And hers was internal, a complaint of lost opportunities, lost youth, lost motherhood. Deeply she felt her freedom, a freedom almost unbear-able in its senselessness. They comforted one another.

Cautiously, she opened the door into the hotel hallway and found outside on the floor her boots, cleaned and shined. A head appeared at the stairway and a young woman carrying clothing over her arm.

"Muchas gracias," Emily managed a smile. Great. She was alive with clean clothes. But uneasily she wondered how she could man-age with no money, no passport, no identification. Those things were always kept in her waist pouch. She never left the sleep house without it, until now. What was the chance that José thought to grab it, or did the paramilitaries take it. Or by now the government. Shit.

Dressed, she perched on the edge of the bed trembling. Some aftershock of nerves. She wanted to bend over and put on her boots. She needed to lace her boots. In her own ears she heard her voice mewing. She clenched the edge of the mattress. José better show up pretty quick.

30

Caught Between

It was a rare Sunday they enjoyed by themselves since Harry began to travel up to the mountains. He returned at dawn on Friday, on schedule. In her dream Constance heard his pack drop in the outer room, his boots drop alongside the bed. She woke as he lowered his body next to her, stinking and still wearing his clothes. By the time Constance fully woke, Harry slept.

Cautiously she left the bed, showered and dressed. He wasn't going to wake up. She unzipped his jeans and pulled them out from under his butt and off his legs without him stirring.

In the workroom she found his drawings, pieces of polyvinyl tubing and clamps, even cement samples he removed from his pack and placed on his work table. The pack still bulged half full, on the floor. Careful, she touched nothing. But gazing. How these artifacts could indicate some deep difference in the lives of indigenous people, in the lives of Harry and Constance.

He slept all day Friday, and into Friday night. Finally, when she slipped into bed next to him, he woke. He pulled her against his side. The pungent odor of his body surrounded her.

"What happened?"

"Another attack. Very bad. Not at Cuates. We avoided the military on the roads. The fuckers."

"Who?"

"Paramilitaries did the dirty work. Women and children, blasted to pieces." He groaned into her hair. "Twenty-five wounded and a pile of dead." Constance placed her hand on his shoulder and rolled her warmth against him. "They gunned down women and children trying to hide. Maybe sixty men came down into the ravine blazing away like Marines invading Managua."

"What happened to the civil protection Albóres promised?" Constance asked with a tight throat. She shared Harry's anger, or he would be alone. Her heart thudded against his.

"None. Paramilitaries were recruited from neighboring villages. The Public Security forces stood by and watched."

"Oh, Harry." She was relieved none of her fantasies came true and he was back safe. It was all too horrible.

"They were trained and armed by the military." She heard bitter condemnation in his voice. "Somewhere in the background, you can bet your ass, the Colonel was standing by."

She said nothing. She didn't know and didn't want to know.

Instead she asked if Carmen and Merwin returned safely with him and Tonatín. No, they went to another village. He didn't know how or when they came down. Who brought the news. Had he seen the wounded. She encouraged him to talk, and finally he filled in as much as he knew—once again Cuates was safe, beyond the circle of killing.

Constance felt his sweaty body tense with fury as he gripped her shoulders and squeezed her breast. He pushed at her knees. She couldn't describe it as making love. Nor as making peace.

Afterwards he wanted to get up and eat and work. Constance heard him moving in the kitchen, and then in his study. She knew it wouldn't help to get up with him, and she didn't.

At his desk Harry chewed a piece of cold chicken and concentrated on the plans. The pipes were extended and now the community had to work to camouflage or bury them along their route. Harry warned, when the high end was connected to water the force might shake loose segments further down, requiring them to excavate and rebuild. But they voted to hide the pipes for now. Not to be seen by intruders, or the throbbing helicopters inexorably ranging closer with their cameras.

Harry didn't argue. Those pipes represented incredible effort and money, pesos saved from god knows what labor. They also represented the participation of an undocumented foreigner.

From here on the job became harder, and Harry hoped against hope they could build some decent dam or reservoir before he got arrested and deported. The Cuates men understood the plan; together they explored the cascade which made a small pool five feet below a ledge. Only what sort of container? Where the main tube would feed from. He wanted to create at least a sound blueprint. In case he wasn't here to finish. He began drawing on his blue paper.

The next morning after breakfast they walked down to the zócalo, and listened for a few minutes to the marimba band tap out its wooden notes. "Marimba sounds great in the thin air of San Gregorio, have you noticed?" Connie asked, light-hearted, as if by agreement they put aside fear and anger it was not possible to sustain.

Harry snorted.

Giggling, they clasped hands, and abruptly, with no prior plan, jumped onto a bus heading out of town. It was like their past, running off with no further provision than keys and pesos.

The echo of old adventures, the same abandon. Harry wouldn't tolerate restraint on him now. Constance felt his spirit transform itself from anger to energy, and fly out, like it used to. Not yet traveling up into the high Sierras, thank God—she could enjoy their day together close to home, filled with freedom like their college days, when they rode a tramway or bus and pretended they were traveling in a foreign country. As they were!

Looking up at Harry's blazing face Constance remembered youth and love again, although she'd never doubted Harry's love. What she doubted was hers, her ability. She yearned in the tense darkness for younger firmer flesh to overwhelm her, to enter her, to solicit the passionate lift of her womb. Not that bitter angry dumping of rage.

Youth meant innocence, and giving over to the other. But truly she didn't seek or want a lover now. She wanted only to understand. She felt the pangs, and the mourning, grief for her lost body, her vanished face. And the grief Harry felt—for what? Being helpless in the face of massacre? Being helpless, period? For death? Coming too soon, coming sooner or later?

Each year they lost; each year they had less to lose. But if years weren't the most important measure, each year they gained. In that moment of their lives, they ran off.

He helped her cram into the sway-backed bus, and for most of the journey they stood hanging on seat backs admiring the scenery over the shoulder of the driver. From the plain of San Gregorio the road rattled through the valley with mountains rippled like cake frosting on every side. Harry peered upward once through the window, and thereafter looked straight ahead.

Finally the road met the "international highway" two lanes wide and choppy, although the driver denied the ruts were caused by a recent earthquake, or by its thirty-three aftershocks. Just Chiapas road in ordinary disrepair. Harry nodded. They clipped along. Connie's knee made her glad to sit down when another passenger got off, in the middle of somewhere known only to him and the driver. A hidden place below the trees. She didn't want to imagine the village.

After a jouncing hour the bus parked at a bus station, which contained a remarkably fine bathroom with toilet seats, and doors on the stalls. Constance took serious note of public bathrooms. In late-morning it looked clean. It even included a long trough sink, with water running in two of the four spigots. The toilet-paper person on duty asked for two pesos, and handed over supplies. Normally Constance was well prepared and carried her own, since few facilities were adequate.

"This must have been a big tourist destination," Connie surmised when she rejoined Harry, "before the rebellion." If one judged by the bathroom, and the enormous market.

The bus station emptied directly into the middle of a street of stalls and wares of every variety, like the Five&Dime stores of her childhood. Vegetable stands and pastry stalls overflowed the sidewalk on both sides, making passage slow. They were stared at and smiled at. Constance missed her hat. Foreign tourists were few. Her face and hair gave her away. Outsider.

A woman wearing a woven Tzeltal scarf wound around her head against the sun picked up another, and wound it around Connie's head like a turban. Enchanted, Constance paid the twenty pesos.

"Harry, what town are we in?"

"Don't ask me! Didn't the bus depot have a sign?" Cause for more giggles. There was no way to get lost, since buses ran only between outlying towns and San Gregorio.

A man behind a large table auctioned pots and plaid wool blankets, the high-pitched running words the unmistakable call to bid. People thronged past, eating honey-soaked fruit and hot enchiladas, to examine stiff sombreros and cheap shoes, finger plastic tablecloths and buckets, admire dishes and ceramics.

This richness represented life as Chiapas was supposed to be but was not, and how this one town maintained itself like a movie set, baffled her. Police stood quietly on corners without threat, and it wasn't until Harry spotted military vehicles at a distant intersection that she understood. It was a showcase.

Determined to enjoy herself regardless, with Harry in tow she toured the market. It wasn't one of Harry's usual gifts to her. Usually he wanted to look only at what he needed—a claw-foot hammer, batteries. But today in Disneyland he was gifting her.

Because he knew last night he used her. He was not insensitive.

Or perhaps she was gifting him—because she knew he endured a deep rage, and was more noble than the man she had half a crush on.

They bought lunch at a stall and ate sitting on a wall. Afterward they walked again, realizing that the town, confined within its military restrictions, was smaller than they thought. A few unpaved streets with painted stucco houses bordered the market. Taxi-bicycles pulled high square carriages topped with a canvas roof for shade. The passengers sat quite upright, proud as New York tourists in horse-drawn carriages, their brown faces closed and unsmiling.

"Horse shit," Harry remarked. "They can't get vehicles into the theme park."

Constance understood. Nevertheless she held onto his arm. She wanted to stroll with her aging and companionable escort. Her lover. Her husband.

They found the cathedral by sighting the round Moorish domes, their ceramic tiles of green and yellow catching sparks of sunlight. Inside, a cool twilight floated. High overhead the arched ceilings were baroque, intricately gilded.

They sat in a pew for half an hour out of the sun. Harry rested his hand on her thigh. She imagined that his fidelity endured so that no effort would be required on his part to find a sex partner. He had one.

Harry would not have been so dismissive, had he known Connie's thoughts. He was faithful because for him making love to Constance was touching home base. He appreciated the enduring architecture of her bones, the engineering of her marvelous slender feet; her face, structurally perfect beneath aging flesh, was the Brooklyn Bridge of faces. He frightened himself last night with the near-rape that came with rage. Not at home, he didn't want that at home. He doubted he could work well with constant fear and anger. He would be used up soon, depleted by this over-rush of unusable adrenalin. He would make mistakes.

In the silent church parishioners floated through like dreams, carrying long-stemmed gladiola and carnations. Delicately they brushed the flowers against the legs and robes of the carved saints.

"Dusting for blessings," Harry explained, "and when the flowers release their scent at home, the blessings scatter into the air."

"Now how did you know that?"

"I asked. They do it everywhere."

Constance wanted to do it. She wanted to bring home a flower full of blessings for their apartment and their patio and her English lessons. For herself, with Ignacio. So no evil would come of it. For herself, with others. For herself, a slight aged women in jeans and camp shirt, with fallen breasts and painted toenails. Wearing an indigenous headscarf like a turban, add that, she admonished herself.

They rested in their thoughts. Families entered. People genuflected and then sat. Some prayed in a nonchalant way. How can one pray nonchalantly, Harry? She was praying earnestly and pointlessly, that Ignacio was not involved in the massacre. She didn't speak. It all went on inside her head. She looked at Harry who sat with his eyes closed. Maybe he was dozing. A man in the pew behind them was reading something, a book? She thought back again to how they arrived here in Chiapas. Her friends agreed she was losing her mind. Judith understood, though. Thank heaven Judith had grown to a pleasant maturity. Of course they didn't see one another very often. Still. She wasn't nuts, she insisted to her friends. Just think of it as socially pro-active retirement. They all laughed. Constance re-used the line several times. But she herself wasn't doing anything so great. It was Harry. All she could do was learn.

When they left the cathedral they bought popsicles, and Coca-Cola emptied into a plastic bag with a straw emerging from the knotted neck. That way you didn't need to return the bottle.

In the tiny zócalo a concert was in progress.

"I'm a fool for mariachi. Those falling notes, that whine for love, those falsetto cries of pain! Me encanta!"

With Connie leading the way they sat like they belonged in the strange audience, half captives, half shoppers. Harry idly stroked her hand. Three musicians at three microphones, unreal in suit jackets and neckties, sang while plucking guitars and bass. Even better were the guest singers, two men who strutted on to wild applause. The local loyalty was divided. Each segment of the audience cried out for its man.

Constance and Harry vigorously applauded every song. Twice during a sustained falsetto note the crowd cried otra, otra, more, more. Constance yipped. Harry whistled through his teeth. Again the high crooning.

Harry free-floated. He seemed to have fallen for the show, or at least he didn't mind that they had stumbled into Disneyland. After the music ended he suggested they purchase the embroidered place-mats she admired. Harry wasn't ordinarily so thoughtful of Connie's thirst for home decorating. She was touched, and pleased.

Although she wondered exactly what he was telling her.

They selected placemats with brilliant embroidered flowers.

"They're perfect, aren't they?" She smiled with delight at the colors: red, fuchsia, orange, purple. Harry agreed. Home is where you place your placemats.

On the crowded return bus two elderly men jammed in with the rest. The one who sat next to the window lugged several bags secured with strings. The old gent who sat by the aisle refused to pay his fare.

"Seis pesos, por favor!"

"No lo tengo!"

"Por favor!"

"No lo tengo, hombre!", for the perfect reason that he had no money. The collector shrugged, and the old gent settled in. As the bus rolled and jostled he pulled from a string bag a tangerine, spat the seeds and skin onto the bus floor. Then he took out a yellow apple, and across the aisle asked the American to cut it for him—no teeth. Constance opened Harry's pocket knife and carefully dropped into her husband's cupped hand the dark seeds and pale core, which Harry tossed out the window.

"Biodegradable!"

The old man offered each of them a section of the apple.

"No, gracias," Harry replied, and said to Connie in English, "We took our risks for the day."

When they reached San Gregorio the senior next to the window stood, ready to get off. The old apple-eater next to the aisle refused to get up; perhaps he couldn't. He muttered something in a deep rock-rattling voice. The window man handed his packages over the heads of passengers in front, and then began to hoist himself over the legs of the gravel-voiced gent.

"Fuck your mother, accursed son of a whore" he growled, and more of the same which happy Constance understood perfectly. The passengers laughed, except the man trying to get out. He succeeded finally, listing badly with his bags and bent skinny legs.

Constance and Harry jumped off at the next stop. They jogged toward home with Constance clutching their purchase, laughing and repeating the curses in mimic of the baritone growl. She pretended she was spitting tangerine seeds into the air, and Harry jumped to catch them. They laughed.

Huffing as they crossed the small park in front of San Gregorio cathedral Constance saw approaching them a man in a buttoned khaki shirt and neatly belted pants, accompanied by a woman in high heeled shoes. For a moment Constance, still giddy from their freedom and pleasure, failed to recognize the unfamiliar woman as her landlady. She stopped.

"Is that Carmen? With?"

"Looks like." Harry never could understand why Mexican women endured cobblestones, floods and mud in those silly high heels. It was incapacitating. He saw Carmen when they were ready for the journey up. Women should wear boots, or at least sneakers. Sensible. She had been.

His happiness slid away like jello down the sink, leaving nothing behind.

Carmen approached on the arm of her husband, clinging in a way unexpected from this tireless landlady, dueña de la casa. She had returned from her trip to the mountains somewhat thinner, but otherwise unmarked. Once again she was ready for picking and pounding on their apartment roof. Her face was tightly controlled, her hair freshly cut.

Deferential and formal, Carmen and her husband paused. Ignacio stood at the same height as Harry, lean and straight, with smooth burnished skin a deep contrast to Harry's pink and white face with its drooping white Zapata moustache.

Constance immediately assumed her teacher role. She spoke to Ignacio the few words of English she knew he recognized: "Hello, how are you? Let me introduce to you my husband."

Carmen stood quietly. Neither she nor Harry alluded to what both had on their minds; they avoided eye contact. Ignacio shook hands, and in English remarked on the weather, the coming fiesta. Well done. He placed his left hand on the nape of Carmen's neck in the gesture Constance had seen before. Carmen braced her head back against his hand. What was he suggesting? Care-giving? Domination?

Constance felt disoriented. Just a few minutes ago she and Harry were laughing.

Harry stared at the man's black hair cut short in a military brush, the neat face with upper teeth protruding slightly. Harry guessed the man appealed to women. It was only when Ignacio turned his head that Harry noticed the deformity. Standing opposite them, Ignacio's left ear jutted shockingly out of place, low on his skull and no way a normal ear. It missed soft fleshy parts and stuck from the side of his head like a thick bolt driven into his skull. Harry saw the ear before. It hadn't registered; normally he didn't notice another man's physical features. Somebody remarked. About the colonel of Public Security who deployed paramilitaries. So he'd been right.

Harry's expression froze. Ignacio, unaware, looked at Constance frankly, and showed his large white teeth. They were damn near perfect.

Harry's were yellowed. Abruptly Constance was reminded again of age. Some days the curve of Harry's mid-back alarmed her, his head forward like a picture of Cro-Magnon, a thick neck, a small stare. He held his arms elbow bent, his backpack dangling by a strap in front of his waist in a womanish way. As for herself, she simply didn't care to dwell on the slack skin along her jaw, the crosshatching where once it was smooth, the drooping jeans.

We were having fun, she silently accused the spoiler.

Constance dismissed the military vehicles from her mind; the recent massacre was less real than her feelings.

We were enjoying life and vitality, the way a country should be.

And, I was a beauty once, her mind ran on. In the face of Ignacio's frank stare she corrected herself. I was pretty enough. Her flesh aged without her consent, she wanted to say, leaving her an innocent young girl surrounded by worsening decay.

She saw Ignacio's glance skim her loose jeans and camp shirt, the new salsa stain on her front. His eyes rested briefly on the scarf slipping on her gray hair, and her distressed face.

A handsome man accustomed to having his way.

Well, so what. They'd enjoyed a wonderful day! She touched Harry's arm, grateful for their unplanned excursion, for foliage and fruit on the trees, bursts of flowers flung recklessly down onto the soil of San Gregorio. This contrast to death and oppression. The respite. Surely good for her. Good for them both. Don't spoil it.

Beside her, Harry's body leaned as tense as the night before. Their day was over. He was consumed again with what he knew of Mocotlán, and she feared he might confront Ignacio with questions.

But Harry was not stupid. He placed his backpack on the pavement between his feet. The men shook hands again, as if sealing a pact. Constance knew well the calluses on Harry's palms; he often dug irrigation trenches alongside the laborers, sifting soil to assure himself of its consistency and dryness.

Ignacio's hand taking hers was different, strong and smooth. "Maestra! Hasta mañana." Tomorrow was Monday, a lesson day.

"A pleasure to see you." Harry lied, to Carmen and Ignacio.

Carmen's face revealed nothing. She knew Ignacio went to the Skelbas' patio for English lessons because she saw him there. He might not otherwise have told her.

"Why do you need English?" She asked at the dinner table later that day.

He was slow in replying, "Perhaps I will be ordered to the United States for advanced training."

"If you do well. If the General of Public Security likes you and the Governor likes you."

"Of course."

She fell silent. He must not learn that she knew his role in recruiting and training the paramilitary. It was a short step to knowing her betrayal. When she visited her community, he worked not fifty kilometers away, directing murder.

When she let Merwin kiss her, when she kissed Merwin, her husband gave orders not fifty kilometers away.

Carmen doubted he knew that people behind his back called him El Tornilloreja, even his own troops. She heard it in village meeting. Among women, more than one old crone wondered aloud if the mark on him signified evil within. When Carmen was fourteen she too wondered. Then she understood how his father believed the same superstition, and that Ignacio's mother refused to accept it. How not, she loved her son.

In time Carmen forgot and scarcely noticed the deformity. She was indebted to him for her food and clothing, her smart haircut, her status as the colonel's wife, her property. Now, Tornilloreja sprang to the lips of those who hated him.

She echoed the farewells of the American couple.

Harry's quiet rage thickened like cooked masa. They must go. Hasta luego, pues.

They turned down the street toward their patio gate. Along their path the flaming red and orange of bougainvillea bushes faded under sudden cloud cover. Harry, as he often did, took her hand with his free hand, and carried it like another parcel, carefully, fending off anger. So Carmen returned to Ignacio. They were partners in silence, he and Carmen. They knew evil and couldn't accuse.

31

The Corridor

Harry could trace in precisely which ravines and valleys the Zapatista National Liberation Army kept a presence: the few hard invisible men and women going about daily labor but waiting, ready. He knew in which areas paramilitary groups, also known to their villages, waited, hard and ready. The two factions occupied the same territory, in villages marked and separated by the military patrolling dirt roads in their vehicles. All the people were poor, brown, grim in the struggle for land and survival.

The paramilitaries were bought by the government, the Zapatistas would not be bought.

Harry flattened the map on a rock. It ruffled slightly in the breeze and he palmed it while he tried to locate Cuates de Santa Ana. The map was updated by the Dioceses of San Cristóbal in Chiapas, then copied and circulated. Harry knew the Zapatista rebellion irrupted after Bishop Samuel Ruiz trained a decade's worth of Catechists, who went from village to village encouraging the indigenous population to employ the Testament as a way to examine their own plight. Ruiz went beyond Liberation Theology, connecting with Subcomandante Marcos in ideas if not in outright rebellion. That would make interesting history some day. So if Harry didn't know precisely how information moved from the Cathedral to the Zapatistas, and into the communities, he could guess. A two-way exchange, for sure.

This map came a week ago, from one of the men who carried it on a computer diskette until it could be printed out in the relative safety of San Gregorio. Harry lifted his reading glasses out of his shirt pocket. He stared at the tiny red and blue lines. About 5,000 Federal troops occupied military barracks in the so-called fourth zone, one of the most important in the region, the location of many Zapatista communities.

Another 4,000 sat in six bases in the corridor serving the Copolar airport. Another 4,000 military held eight bases along the route from Palenque to Marqués de Comillas, part of the municipality of Ocosingo, to the west.

He tapped the map with his forefinger. According to information from Tonatín, one month ago the Mexican Army arrived in Cañada del Euseba. The soldiers remained after carrying out a "social service", transporting the coffee harvest for free, along the highway in the community of Arrollo Corozal.

Arrollo Corozal was one of the few zones previously free of military. Where the principal guerrilla encampment of Subcomandante Marcos was probably located.

Harry shoved his glasses up on the bridge of his nose. You didn't need rocket science to know the Chiapas government under Albóres intended strangling the rebel communities. Low-intensity warfare terrorized without disturbing international opinion; another public massacre would be impermissible. Thank God for the internet, and the Zapatistas' clever public relations.

And what about Harry, if they caught him? He worried off and on, a kind of recurrent reminder to himself that he was breaking Mexican law. If he was picked up Connie understood what to do. He doubted he'd be harmed, just deported. The harm came to Mexicans like that Human Rights lawyer and her kid, discovered by the side of the road in Tabasco.

Connie hung in there. She coped with Ignacio in a way he more or less admired. A good teacher, she was never judgmental; she loved her students in compartments, separated from their lives outside the classroom.

When he took on the Cuates job this rebellion receded to way in the back of his mind. He operated on vanity; he loved being sought out. He admitted it. An old fart like himself. Somebody acknowledged he was good at what he did. Not over the hill yet. Other cultures are better at aging than America.

The Zapatista rebellion was something else, remote, having to do with poverty, illness, desperation. Normally he left background research—who the people were, security issues—to the firms who contracted him. This time, he should have done more himself.

He had become part of it.

Harry pulled off his cap and dropped it into his lap. He roughed his hand over his hair, letting the sweat dry under the bright sun while he straightened and stretched his neck. He perched on a good overlook, and before him the cloud-marked angles of distant hillside forest carved designs. The birds chirped overhead, and in the peace he could hear crickets thrum. Far away, a thin brown line of road.

The military, the young brown soldiers beneath the daily sun constructed new highways. One principal road would surround the communities considered Zapatista, with a terminal point running parallel to Guatemala, uniting Palenque with Comitán, and passing through two regions of vital importance: Marqués de Comillas and the hot zone located in Amparo Agua Tinta. That lay south from here.

The construction would cross the Zapatista heartland, where the indigenous people launched their rebellion, and the first men to fall shouted Ya Basta.

The stretch of road looked to be in excellent condition. The lack of two bridges—one over the Jataté River and the other crossing the Euseba—still left the two areas isolated, but the completion date was not far off. Harry guessed the distant Cuates water source also fed into the Jataté, from a height he fervently hoped the military wouldn't bother with. There was no real reason to pursue people up in the Sierra Corral Chen. Their mountain rose midway between the Lacondón and the city of Ocosingo; they were autonomous by virtue of occupying remote land with no real roads in and out, and no valuable resources to entice capitalist exploitation. The Cuates men themselves had carved out their dirt access.

The governments, both state and federal, had a bug up their ass. Other rebel groups sprouted in Oaxaca and Guerrero, also poor, also dominated by corrupt caciques in the pay of the PRI. Foreign investment caught wind of uprisings and shied off. Zedillo was pursuing an ounce of prevention, read: a ton of trouble.

Better to eliminate foreign investment. It's usually preceded and followed by US intervention. But fuck, Americans were here already, with their damn Hueys and advisors. They pushed el Presidente to stomp the rebels—make the world safe for Mexican petroleum.

He was referring to the American government as "them."

The war was close, the paramilitary striking hard. A single man or two, alone on the road were doomed, a single van or truck ambushed. The claim was always that the victims attacked first, and it never became clear who the hell shot them. Left them dead on the side of the road like so much trash. Like the lawyer and the boy. Impunidad, the Mexicans called it. That meant, scot-free.

José was bringing up additional necessary supplies for the reservoir. Harry was toying with the idea of linked vinyl containers instead of cement and was anxious to test it. The men created cement pylons in some areas to support the pipes across declivities before they buried, and good sand was a bitch to bring in. Bricks were out of the question.

And what more did José carry, from place to place? The communities needed food, cable to highjack electricity. Most of them were building extra wood structures to house visiting Witnesses and hold town meetings. They brought lumber down from their own hills. On their backs. Materials didn't arrive by burro, that was for sure. Even here in Cuates, expecting nobody—he hoped!—they built a room which served as meeting and dining area. But Harry figured the most important thing José brought was the network. These people knew that without binding together the small communities they would in the end have nothing. Slowly, painfully, they created ways to interact, to agree on goals and methods.

Reluctantly, Harry folded his map and adjusted the bill on his cap. The pickup, pulling its low-lying dust carpet beneath it, entered the mountain pass into Cuates de Santa Ana.

José brought a woman with him. Clearly, an American, in her forties or maybe thirties, Harry wasn't a good judge. But old enough to know better.

She shook his hand and claimed to be a journalist, and he had to believe her. He glanced over at José. The woman carried a camera and a notebook. No way would he let her investigate his project. American women were a naive bunch, in Harry's experience. They believed in a US passport the way some campesinos believe in the Virgin.

This one, Emily, also appeared to Harry's eye like she had the hots for José. That was bad news. That meant José was compromised in what he would or wouldn't do. Harry knew enough of José and his lost family to understand. He wouldn't give up another woman to slaughter.

Harry cursed all women. At least Connie stayed out of the way, out of contact with all this shit. Safe. Women made it too hard on the men. Macho honor. José's wife was at home—shot in her own front yard, while José went out in the field. Even so. They came on purpose to get José and his family and it was only luck that José moved beyond range that day. Harry could guess why, before the actual uprising. José was that kind of man, to be on someone's enemies list.

And this one—what the hell did she think she was doing? A nice piece of ass in her shirt and jeans, despite her clipped hair—you could almost smell privilege on her, the way she stood with her chest raised and her pelvis forward. Expensive boots. Expensive face, despite her sun-dried skin and absence of makeup.

The object of Harry's disgust, whose eyes hid behind sunglasses, was far away, thinking about the truck route they had traveled along the coast. While José's mind focused on avoiding confrontations, she and Frank, jammed together next to him in the cab, gazed out the window with delight. Humped shapes like prehistoric cave drawings with serene vertical faces, watched them pass. The heavy animals were pale brown or dove, as if milk-washed as they strolled by the milk-topped sea. Across the lagoon distant mountains loomed, a sweet purple. On the water fishermen cast their nets. One could believe in a different world.

"Idyllic, right?" Frank asked, as Emily hummed softly.

"Yes."

"No." Frank was distributing two hundred kilos of medical supplies, mostly aspirin, penicillin and iodine he received off a transport from Peace Now. Frank felt like the little Dutch boy with his finger in the dike. Medical facilities down here were almost non-existent for serving indigenous groups, including Guatemalans fleeing north across the border, coping with pervasive poverty and damage by the USA's interminable meddling. He tried to vary his routes and the population centers, not so much for tactics as for coverage of neglected areas. His third trip this month. He wondered how long his luck would last. The bullet with your name on it, the guys used to say. The bullet here could be anything, anybody.

Emily pulled her notebook off the dashboard. "So fill me in." She was all business.

"Put the notebook away." José's voice, soft as always, commanded. She obeyed instantly, stuffing the notebook and her camera between the seatback and the seat, trying to lodge them securely so if she had to get out of the truck they'd stay hidden. Up ahead was a retén. The soldiers stood armed at the side of the road. The truck stopped.

José took out his tourist guide license. "I'm taking these Americans to see the Reserve." She and Frank posed as a couple touring on a wildlife vacation. How many times would that one work, Emily wondered.

The soldier, a youngster with a pale impassive face, asked for documents. José repeated words in Spanish for the benefit of the soldier. Both Emily and Frank understood and pretended they hadn't. Ignorant foreigners.

They took out their passports. Estados Unidos.

Emily spent a week in Mexico City harassing the US Embassy to get her a replacement document for her "stolen" one. God knows who grabbed the pouch—they could only hope her name wouldn't show up on a list. But José guessed whoever found the passport kept it to sell on the black market; it was a valuable item. He told her to say she was robbed.

Agreeing, she bussed north with pesos he loaned her. Her bank card and credit card could be Fed-Exed to Mexico City. And she'd be back in business. She booked into a decent hotel and went shopping. She needed time away from José and away from Chiapas, to regain her equilibrium—if ever she would. Sleeping alone left her at the mercy of nightmares. In her sleep she was gazing down at José's boots, darkly stained with blood.

She surprised both herself and José by returning.

The passport looked brand new, unused—which it was. The sergeant passed it over to his captain, who looked at the photos and grunted.

"When did you arrive? How long is your stay?"

"A ninety day visa." José indicated with his thumb the date on her form.

The captain grunted.

Two miles down the road the van turned at a right angle, north.

Harry, striding in for the meager supper the town's communal kitchen offered, washed his hands in the standing water of the sink. That's not going to work forever.

By which he meant the tourist routine. Frank kept his NGO visa current—his tourist visa was way gone. Many of the sympathizers crossed into Guatemala to renew theirs every ninety days, but that was tricky. Too much depended on bribes or the whims of border guards. The Mexican government recently snatched two Americans and a Frenchman right off the street. As in past episodes the captives were driven secretly from one post to another for two days without communication, while the American and French ambassadors made a dozen phone calls. Mysteriously the captives turned up at the Tuxtla airport, were hustled on board, and adiós. Apparently not hurt, but who knew if they'd been roughed up, or what if they'd been female? What then?

After the meal Frank disappeared in the direction of the tin-roofed shack that served as dispensary. Emily vanished into the women's area. José lingered a moment. The chill mountain air blew through cracks in the wood planks of the room.

"I see in your face you believe the woman is a bad idea."

Harry admitted as much.

"I agree," José surprised Harry. "There is nothing to worry you about reporting. She will be discreet as needed. It appears she has a charmed life. The women trust her. They know she ran with the infant." He continued briefly, explaining.

"She asks me for nothing, you know? She won't stay. But for the moment she comforts me. You know the smell of animal blood? Horses, goats?" His gazed wandered and returned to meet Harry's. "This smell recurs in my dreams. They slaughtered the animals also. Uy, uy." The soft lament killed Harry. "She tells me I comfort her also, for the nightmares. I could not marry again, you know?"

Harry nodded, yes he knew.

José left for the meeting area to speak with the community's men. José no way was obliged to explain anything to Harry, and Harry, touched by the confidence, couldn't get over it: Emily survived Mocotlán, with José! Never mind the blue eyes and blond hair, never mind the class outfit. She was alive. The finest credential available. Uy, uy, he repeated to himself softly.

Alone, he sat down, and by the single overhead naked light bulb the eating room offered, he studied his maps again. He extracted his pencil from his fatigue shirt pocket and reached to his cargo pocket for his knife. Carefully he sharpened the pencil, and blackened the pale blue lines indicating the two rivers. They formed a pincer. Cuates lay beyond the grasp of the two thrusting fingers. He wondered what José needed to communicate to the men outside the pincers.

Well, for now it was the military's call. He better focus on his work here and now. Different map. The topography up here was a bitch.

32

English Lesson

Constance collected a cleaning rag and broom, and stepped out into the patio. A fine dust of pollen settled overnight on the table and chairs; she wanted the space clean for Ignacio's lesson. Even his civilian chino pants maintained an aura of spit and polish.

She wiped carefully, and then went back inside to fetch her Spanish-English dictionary, the Oxford picture dictionary she ordered for basic words, the English grammar, and an ancient Time magazine in English she found abandoned at Alvaro's.

She worked on automatic. Inside, the bitter anger at news of Maeda's death, and the boy's, swelled like a tumor. She learned about it at Alvaro's, of course—news and gossip roosted there, vultures whose sharp beaks stabbed the tiny group of foreigners who stayed on.

Aida wept. Maeda must have been grabbed outside the bus station in Tuxtla where her friend delivered them during the night. Why the hell didn't she go directly inside, or if she had, stay there? Constance said nothing. Aida guessed Ricardo got hungry, and Maeda decided it was safe to walk to a cafeteria. They were followed.

The bus would have taken them to Veracruz, to her sister. Instead, the bodies were dumped over the border in Tabasco. The authorities offered no information—bodies found. Period. No personal identification. Although both were clad, the corpses were barefoot, Maeda's feet swollen and purple.

Constance gripped Aida's hand. At Alvaro's café they could commiserate and compare the fragments of information trickling in. Neither could swallow the coffee, which cooled to mahogany pools in their cups, abandoned when they left.

Constance carried paper and pencils out to the patio. Everything sat neatly arranged on the table, and she went to work with the broom.

Usually Carmen swept, but tacitly they agreed that Carmen would not appear during Ignacio's scheduled lessons. The day's fallen bougainvillea blossoms rustled ahead of her broom. Faded and thin as the skin of elderly women, they still retained their colors. Among the petals she swept fallen seeds in their dainty transparent packets, gifts in cellophane wrappers. And leaves, although those were fewer, from the ficus.

Such gifts from nature. She herded the debris into a pile in the corner, and carried the broom back into the kitchen. Her chest constricted with rage.

Ignacio arrived promptly as always, and he sat without being told, opposite Constance so that the view of her face was full and clear, and hers of his. Once again she realized how handsome he was. Apparently in his late forties, his skin remained firm and clean. His white shirt folded open at the neck, and a few dark hairs sprouted below the hollow of his collarbone. Constance caught the whiff of after-shave.

She loved him. She yearned over him. Not because of his physical presence. Because he learned, rapidly and with few repetitions. She loved that he verified her teaching skills. She could explain grammar differences to him in Spanish, and these he was well-educated enough to grasp. She was unable to explain to herself the sexual pull. He commanded it without wanting it. The mere thought of him sent a pulse between her thighs, an old familiar throbbing.

But today other ideas compelled. In firm control she pulled her chair around the table so they could look at the same page. She opened the picture dictionary to a picture of policemen, firemen, waiters, different people both male and female in uniform, sailors, pilots, surgeons in green scrubs. She began to name the occupations, and he repeated. She saved "soldiers" for last. Uniforms. He understood the concept.

Cautiously, she picked up on the soldiers. She mimed shooting a rifle, and then toppling over dead onto the table. She was a good mime; she had years of experience.

"I shoot, you shoot, he—she—it—shoots," she conjugated. "We shoot, they shoot." He repeated and she paused. "This is the present tense, correct? You understand?"

Yes. He already knew the gerund with be, and the simple present. He knew the regular simple past for verbs ending in ed. She was ready for the irregular past.

"This verb is irregular: I shot, you shot, he—she—it shot. Ok? We shot, they shot." Ignacio looked at her carefully. She lifted her arms as if holding a weapon, sighted and pulled the imaginary trigger. She flung out her arms and fell onto the table.

The same performance, a bit more energetic. She straightened up and with her right elbow back aimed her invisible weapon at Ignacio and pulled the invisible trigger.

"I shot you," she stated. "This is the simple past tense, something done in the past. The verb 'shot' is irregular." She repeated the conjugation. "You see how simple it is. In the past the verb doesn't change its ending, no matter who shot.

"The word order gives the meaning. 'The soldier shot the man' is not the same as 'the man shot the soldier'."

Momentarily terrified by what she was hinting, she halted and then resumed, " 'He shot the man.' 'The man shot him.' Now you see by the pronoun it matters who is subject, who is object. Who shot, who received the shot. The action is the same. The shooter and the person shot exchange roles. The rules of grammar structure show the change."

She had violated her own teaching rule by explaining grammar. She didn't trust herself. She violated her own seating rule in order to show him the picture page, and now they were not face to face. She stood to realign her chair, and when she stood Ignacio did also. His thigh was half a meter away from hers. She felt the warmth of his body.

But his manners were so exquisite.

She sat down again, and so did he. Now they were eye to eye again. Constance forced her lungs to expand. Her chest burned. She waited, to regain her self-control.

In her silence Ignacio spoke in English. "I shot a man. I was twenty years old." He switched to Spanish, watching her eyes watch him. "I don't shoot anybody in the present. I am a Colonel of Public Security."

"Why did you shoot the man?" She asked it twice, first in Spanish and then in English. She steered the conversation in the neutral realm of instruction, it was only a lesson.

"Because I was young," he answered in English. That much he could manage. She wouldn't drop her gaze, and he was obliged to meet it, or look down like a shamed boy. So he switched to Spanish, "I was young and I obeyed orders. Now I give orders."

His face revealed pride, not shame. "I am in the service of the Armed Forces of the Republic of Mexico. If all goes well, I go to the United States for more training. Ojalá." One hopes.

Across the table she saw how he held his head with scarcely any motion. It lent his eyes a predatory, forward-gazing focus. He entertained no worry about his moral position, he was employed by the President of Mexico, by the thirty-three states, by the flag with an eagle seizing a serpent in its beak. He had no patience with her female American sentiments. She must know the American government also supported what he was doing. How could remorse be appropriate, if indeed remorse was what she wanted? Or perhaps, he was mistaken and she desired a recounting? Women often wanted to know intimate details of his service, and of death. At such moments horror and curiosity warmed their faces like sex.

Constance was useful for acquiring English; he would go to the US with adequate preparation. She understood that by his manner, and wondered if he felt about Carmen, she is useful for fucking. Or, more likely, she is useful as the presentable wife. Constance guessed that in Ignacio's career useful was important.

For the briefest moment while time balanced between their separate worlds Constance knew herself to be alone. Unsought, her mind spun toward bringing Ignacio to her in bed. His bronzed back, the same color as his face, his butt and thighs. If he allowed Carmen any pleasure. Or if Carmen allowed herself any pleasure. Some women separated themselves, aloof from an act they didn't acknowledge. Constance never did, with Harry or her few lovers. She would swell, and at the moment lift upward and seize within her the cascade of sperm, as if she wanted the sperm itself, wanted it to succeed.

Ignacio afforded her a different pleasure. If she laughed at his attempts to pronounce the unpronounceable th and initial h, he laughed also, and tried again to imitate. If she laughed with delight at his correct phrases and increasing vocabulary, he laughed, too. He accepted her laughter because his own mother exhaled the same laugh forty-three years ago when the toddler Nacho spoke. Gratified, he recognized Constance's loving appreciation of his accomplishments. He accepted it, and in the same moment believed his success in directing both paramilitaries and regular troops was equally praiseworthy. Naturally he must guard from civilian knowledge those achievements. But he was confident of his strength.

Constance closed the dictionary on the page of uniformed men. Nacho's pride in his abilities, whatever he was doing, was unshakeable. It followed the desires of his superiors, political and military. She was not only an aging woman, but a foreigner and a fool. What did she expect, that he would be remorseful over his success? Oh, no. She opened the old Times magazine, and reading upside down, pointed to headline words. Most of them referred to killings, shootings, wars, death by drowning. The lesson ended.

After Ignacio left she gathered her books and pens and went inside to the bedroom. She kicked off her sandals and stretched out on top of the bedspread. She wept deeply, wiping with the palms of her hands the tears that rolled down her cheeks into her hairline. Uy, uy, she wailed, while Harry in Cuates a few hours later, repeated, uy, uy.

They had been married so long, no wonder miles apart they shared the same tide of grief.

33

Martin Brings Peace

Martin was trying to meditate inside the shed where he and other observers slept. He sat cross-legged on a string hammock suspended on nails between one side of the plank wall and a post supporting the roof. The shed's only other furniture was crude board shelves onto which each person placed personal belongings. A jumble of pink, green and yellow plastic cups held toothbrushes; clothing jutted from knapsacks. A bra suspended by one strap to dry on a nail dangled next to mud-crusted boots suspended by their laces on the wall.

Martin sighed, and his sigh made the hammock sway. He hated that. Assuming the lotus position on a net wasn't so easy to begin with. The hammock curled like a banana peel. When he slept he lay across the net to keep it open. He hadn't mastered rolling over onto his side the way Mexicans did. They wrapped themselves in the hammock and slept in any position they wanted to. Martin, on the other hand, frequently tumbled out onto the floor, and finally settled for sleeping on his back rigid as a stick, pushing with his toes against the net's border.

He felt slightly seasick. Briefly he contemplated getting down onto the dirt floor, but his hosts warned him many times about snakes. Poisonous, of course. They never told him about fleas, which were much worse. The one time he sat on the floor bites appeared all over his feet and face, and gazing into his tiny shaving mirror he wondered if he had contracted some tropical fever like measles, only fatal.

Young chickens often strolled in beneath the rough walls. They casually pecked the fleas, but they didn't protect him, nor did the lizards. He suffered less on his miserable hammock.

He recited his mantra, and as HM instructed, when thoughts intruded he gently came back to it. Gently. Thoughts intruded in raging torrents. This indicated stress, and why not—here he was god knows where, locked in a compound with half a dozen other foreigners. The compound they were "guarding" as Witnesses for Peace extended the size of a football field. Pigs ambled between wooden sheds every afternoon, and raggedy-assed boys chased after. Tiny men marched in with loads of wood on their backs, and marched out at night to stand guard. In the afternoons helicopters chattered overhead scaring the children, and each time the helicopters passed over Witnesses ran out with video cameras to document their harassment. Martin suspected their reports wouldn't make a big splash in the US where the media pretended that military over-flights were part of drug interdiction. His task was to count how many over-flights passed daily.

During his alternate shift, he sat next to the dirt road and counted military vehicles raising dust. He carried with him his pocket Vedas and his pocket English-Spanish dictionary. The morning shift was chilly as fog on the mountain drifted vaguely toward the sun. The afternoon shift was hot, unless it was raining. He was also supposed to count how many soldiers, but usually he lost track, and anyway, when the trucks returned he needed to count them all over again—

each soldier passing by counted as one, even if it was the same man twenty times.

He shared this convoy count with a young couple. The French Witnesses brought an apparently endless supply of coffee and cigarettes which they carried out to the makeshift booth by the side of the road, and enjoyed while playing gin with a ratty deck of cards. They also occupied their own hut, a nice bit of privacy. Their tour of duty was one month, Martin's was two weeks. He wasn't sure he could make it. His favorite drawstring pajamas were drawn to a tiny knot around his sunken belly, and above the area where his beard grew his cheekbones jutted like rocks in a plowed field.

Anyway, being here as a Witness wasn't his main task. His duty here was to spread good vibes, thoughts of good will toward all men, as Holy Master instructed. He tried to meditate four times a day. The hammock swayed.

Abruptly the two German guys burst in, humming and stomping. He tried to maintain his mantra and then gave it up.

"Want to go with us?" Karl asked, oblivious to Martin's closed eyes. "We're going to cross the road!"

Leaving the "security" of the compound was forbidden, Martin knew. Outside, if they got picked up or shot down it became their own problem—no protection at all. Not that inside offered much— what, a chicken would flap onto the automatic rifles of the White Guard?

Nevertheless, he was intrigued. And pleased that they responded to his peaceful demeanor this way. Probably they really felt safer with him along, Martin surmised. Within his balding head and nearly weightless frame, he was a man of peace. He resembled Ben Kingsley playing Mahatma Gandhi.

"Be prepared in five minutes, if you're coming," Heinrich informed him. "Be sure to bring your documents because if we meet anybody they may be necessary. Also, wear your boots." He glanced disdainfully at Martin's thongs on the floor beside the hammock. The thongs' shade of Ramah blue was obscured by dust and dried mud. Since it rained every afternoon, Martin felt thongs were practical. But the Germans worried about snakes and wore expensive stitched leather boots laced above the ankle, and like long-distance hikers, tucked their pants into the boot tops. It was a mistake to appear so military when they were Witnesses for Peace—Martin knew his thongs made a better statement. He would go barefoot like HM if he could, but the dirt of the compound was likely loaded with parasites.

They waited for the morning troop truck to pass, and then waited another five minutes. Waving briefly to the French on duty, they ran. Across the road a forested area dropped off out of sight. A declivity revealed a path, and they plunged down, each of them carrying his waist pouch with passport, and a water bottle. No identification linked them with the encampment.

One hundred meters down the path they came to a tiny river. The temptation to bathe, to swim, was erased by fear of leeches. The Germans feared unhygienic events. Bravely Martin cupped his hands around the trickle of water and washed his face. Blinking, he looked up to see three little boys splashing at the nearby turn in the river. They stared aghast for one moment at strange white men and fled, their narrow haunches visible through thin white fabric. "Wait a moment," Karl called in Spanish, but they didn't look back.

"Probably don't understand Spanish," Heinrich said in English. Martin was grateful. His Spanish wasn't too good either.

Another descent, and now they rested on a plateau opened to the western sky. They entered the fields, unplowed, covered with grasses. Peculiar, almost eerie, to see land abandoned where it was so precious, so desired. Then as they stepped through the grass they saw directly ahead the ruins of a house. A large house which had burned. Or been burned. The busy earth wrestled its mosaic tile floor into unaligned fragments, and a vast ruined fireplace littered the ground with stones. Small blue and white ceramic shards gleamed in the green growth. The landowner's abandoned house decayed, its remains cursed.

Perhaps the rebels' horses came from here when the hacendado was killed or fled. They were handsome animals, with fine manes that flew when they ran. Milk cows were scarce in this part of the countryside, but an ox-like animal might be used for plowing. Martin didn't care to approach—loitering untended on the other side of the plateau a bull grazed, whipping flies with its tail.

Nobody. Silence surrounding the ruined farmhouse fell so deeply Martin heard, he was sure, vibrations of the wings of butterflies, or perhaps the clicking of grasshoppers. The three men stood quietly, as if awaiting an explanation. Since none came, they retreated.

They climbed back up toward the road, somber and aware of emptiness left by unresolved conflicts: no men worked here, no women pulled herbs from gardens or tended animals. Surely the little boys lived somewhere nearby, perhaps in the eastern declivity. Between the trees they spotted a few chozas with palm roofs, and smoke from a cooking fire. The adventure, exploring outside the compound, assumed a cinematic sense of doom.

They followed the upward path in silence, stopping twice in the noon heat to drink their water. The climb was much harder than the descent, and in the absolute stillness their footsteps on the dirt sounded clamorous.

Achieving the road's edge they could see the French couple still sitting at the booth, with their tally-books propped open beside their deck of cards. A coffee mug had tumbled onto the grass. Overhead, the clatter of a helicopter grew louder until it cleared the trees. Inside the compound Martin knew, men with video cameras were racing to get their films.

He felt his arm yanked with a brisk pain. Heinrich pulled him down. Karl moved on his knees, crawling toward a small tree, while Heinrich and Martin scurried behind him as quickly as they could, to get under its cover.

Martin was appalled at himself. He left his post, his place to send forth peaceful thoughts into the environment. And look what happened. A bright red stain already congealed upon the table where the French couple awkwardly leaned, and red stained their shirts and hands. They didn't move. Was the helicopter shooting? No. It dipped noisily and circled. In the open cab door Martin was sure he saw the military uniform of a man taking photos.

Martin never saw his brother's mangled body, and never asked to; he was glad the corpse was displayed neatly clad above the chest with suit, collar and tie.

He knew about human women's monthlies, something so secret that knowledge was deduced only by comparison with bitches who came into heat and left trails of spotting in the yard. His personal experience of blood consisted of stepping on a tack at age six, away at camp for the first and only time, to make way for Robert John to get born. His tiny puncture wound showed the same red. This was different. This was very different. He saw redness as broad as poinsettia leaves.

"Shit," Heinrich whispered. "What happened?"

"Drive-by shooting, American style." Karl looked at Martin, to see if Martin was offended, but Martin had fainted.

"Somebody in a vehicle. Not long ago." Heinrich left Martin as he lay, and sat quietly.

"Better to wait until dark." Karl extracted a handkerchief from Martin's pocket and wiped Martin's forehead.

"He's coming around." Karl spoke in German. "Just an excess of adrenalin, I think."

"Good. I don't relish carrying this guy. Even skeletons weigh. Me, I faint only when the blood is mine."

As if he heard, Martin regained consciousness. He briefly held his left arm, and then let it rest against his ribs. Later he would check for finger marks. The helicopter was gone, somewhere behind the mist of cloud smothering the mountain. It was men on the ground they should fear.

The motionless air was so quiet Martin knew that before, on the plateau, he hadn't heard butterflies and crickets. No.

They gazed across at the compound from under their bush. Karl swallowed some of his water, and offered it to Martin. Martin unscrewed his own flask, thanking Karl politely. He needed to drink something, and feared he would soon need to piss. First he would watch the Germans and see how they managed without standing up. They were very efficient. An enormous wall in his mind shuttered the view across the road.

Six o'clock. Neither the helicopter nor the road patrols passed again, and finally the small men inside the compound appeared, or maybe these were men who entered from the other side, as the scout contingent often did. They moved toward the edge of the road where the French couple still rested, as motionless as before. The men lifted the woman first, under her arms and by her feet, and placed her on the grass.

Karl stood up, and then Heinrich. Finally Martin managed to get to his feet, his head light and his bladder aching. How strange to feel his body alive. He hadn't felt his body as a body, a weighty thing of substance and matter, for a long while. But here it was, and here he was, inside it just as he experienced it as a kid, peering out.

Into his wavering view approached two more small men, and they steadied him on either side. They crossed to the compound. He was momentarily glad he didn't need to explain to them his failure to keep them safe, his jaunt to escape boredom. Nor did the men of the community try to speak to him of the murders, more warnings that they would not be left in peace. They would take their discussion elsewhere, to their own councils.

Martin feared that nothing he could ever do hereafter would compensate. His shame, Holy Master would know instantly. HM wouldn't discard him or drop him from his embracing love. That would not be the Way. But Martin had failed. Dimly he sensed purgatory ahead, and the need to redeem himself. Shame endured forever.

The Germans went off with the community men to discuss the practical facts of what had occurred, and who would accept the task of summoning police, and how to notify Witnesses and the French Embassy. No easy matter. There was no telephone line, nor vehicle. Somebody must walk. Bodies wouldn't wait in the heat.

Part Three: 1998

34

Tomás is dead

It was hard to imagine that a war of attrition could get worse, and yet it got worse. It was hard to imagine that an unfocused fear pitted against the huge well-equipped and often invisible militia and government enemy could be sustained, retained inside the fist like a whirlwind, and yet it was. And for Frank, hardest of all was to comprehend how the Zapatistas remained committed to holding the high ground, no reprisals. Sure they fought and killed on that first week. Got the government's attention by knocking their officials upside the head with a two-by-four. Okay. And thereafter, no more attacks.

Calls for justice, no calls for revenge.

Frank didn't even bother to get drunk, so certain he was that nothing could dim his rage and pain when Tomás was shot eight times, in front of his two grandchildren.

The children reported only that they were playing with their dolls in the living room of their Ocosingo house, while their grandpa read in his usual lumpy chair. An unmarked car drove up and paused in front. Two men got out, the driver and another man stayed in the car. The man who stayed wore a uniform, and beneath his hat, the seven year old reported, his ear looked broken. The eleven year old girl, Luz, ran out to the rear yard where they kept chickens and two goats. The animals along with the van the grandfather frequently drove were out of view from the street.

The daughter of Tomás heard the shots and raced back toward the house, meeting Luz as the child ran to get her mother. Alvira knew how to shoot, and a loaded rifle hung inside the kitchen door. But it was of no use. The two men executed her father quickly with many shots, bangbangbangbang. They turned around and jumped back into the waiting car. It squealed away before Alvira placed both feet in the living room.

Frank heard the report by telephone. He drove down to Ocosingo at a calm pace, keeping his van as inconspicuous as possible, his head as clear as possible. The newspaper reported that the Attorney General of the State claimed Tomás accidentally killed himself while cleaning his rifle. The official version reported one shot. Frank stood over the body as it lay arranged on the kitchen table and looked at his friend, washed and dressed for his burial as was customary, by his daughter and sisters.

"I counted eight wounds," Alvira told him softly. She stood beside lighted candles at the head of the table and twisted her hands. The table was surrounded by white flowers in vases and jars. The faint aroma from blossoms of lilies and carnations made the air drowsy. Wide awake, Frank lifted the shirt and looked. High caliber weapons, from a distance of five to ten feet made those volcanic wounds. They blasted the hell outa him. He wondered how Alvira stood to deal with the body, returned to her after the "official investigation." They might as welluv give her a package of chopped meat, bloodless now with dried purple flesh gaping unsewn.

He sat on a wooden chair away from the body of his friend. Around him, lined against the walls, more chairs supported silent figures. Among the men sat the three elderly sisters of Tomás. The Human Rights workers entered also, placed another bunch of white flowers on long stalks, looked at the body, sat a while and then departed. The two grandchildren, Luz and the younger one, Carmela, sat on chairs alongside the adults. Their feet swung slowly as they waited. The little one cried and stopped, cried and stopped, because she couldn't grasp the bad death but knew it was bad. Luz's dark eyes gleamed blank and bottomless as nighttime wells. Frank had seen that glaze before.

After the burial Frank returned with several others to the Dominican convent courtyard where he met Tomás for the first time. Several neighbors heard the shots, and one woman saw the vehicle and its license plate. It was not an official car but a Toyota, with a license plate CH04940, registered to no one.

The statements by the stunned children were repeated and shared. "I saw my grandpa jump up and down in his chair, and I heard the shots," Carmela wept afresh. "I saw who shot my grandpa and I don't know who he was. I saw out the door the man in the car watching. He wore a military cap and his ear was broken."

Luz still had not spoken nor wept. Alvira held her, rocking gently. An elderly weeping brother-in-law reported all this to the committee.

The newspaper from Mexico DF was contacted; objections given by the Community Committee for Human Rights were sent and printed. Evidence contradicted the official statement. The Committee stated the assassination was committed by elements of the Public Security Police. "Whoever examined the body," they stated, "did so without a forensic doctor. They carried away the body without permission, and brought it back to the daughter's house on the following day." Like garbage, thought Frank.

The committee members once again circled in the quiet sunshine of the patio. Outside, the town streets showed a few tense men, but Frank didn't care. They could do what they had to do to defend themselves, but probably it would remain quiet now. The Zapatista fury simmered outside the town, and they would not attack town officials again—shit, who could they attack anyway? The indigenous community in the countryside vowed to obtain justice, but they didn't say when or how. They could make vows all day and all night. It was expected, a mark of honor. But no reprisal would follow. That wasn't the justice they sought. Justice will come when the indigenous are permitted to live as they chose. That was their way. Not Frank's way.

Frank put his head in his hands, bracing his arms on his jeans. Discussion floated around him and over him. He grieved for the children, and for Alvira whose husband was killed in '94, and now her father. He accepted a shot glass of mescal from men who brought bottles. He accepted a second and a third. It was wicked booze, and he couldn't say if his hurt was the burn of alcohol or the burn of hatred. It moved down from his throat to his gut and stayed there.

He didn't want to see the burial. He stood blindly staring at nothing in viewing range of the freshly opened family grave, into which Tomás' body would be placed wrapped in a sheet. The older bones made way for him, in this crowded old panteón. Frank didn't want to talk with anybody, about what happened to his friend. He lived isolated despite the influx into Chiapas of Americans—he did work that went beyond, aiding the rebels.

The others Witnessed. That meant they stood and watched out in the communities, placing their bodies in visible line of view. Frank was no Witness, he carried supplies, the less visible the better. An outlaw. An apprentice. A revolutionary.

From where he stood he heard the keening of the old sisters, and worse, he heard the silence of the men, punctuated only by the scrape of shovels and falling dirt. He turned and walked back into town to the convent.

He sat as before, in the convent patio. He poured himself another glass and threw it down. Lousy stuff, you needed a cast-iron gullet to get it down and keep it down in its pool of hate. It burned away.

Hours later in the cool evening he still sat, although no other men arrived. After attending the burial they went to the home of Tomás' daughter to show respect. Frank knew Alvira would respond to his comfort, and likewise the children. They knew him, as part of Tomás' extended family. Perhaps they loved him. Nevertheless he didn't go.

It was José who found Frank, his legs extended and his shirt pulled loose to expose his hot belly to the air. José gazed in front of them as he sat down next to Frank's inert form.

Frank turned his head with slow difficulty. "You shouldn't travel aroun' down here," He muttered through his alcohol mist on recognizing the dark form next to him.

"Of course not."

"It's dangerous."

"Clearly."

The stars had emerged, and the moon with the Mexican rabbit loomed over the roof. The rabbit leapt upward, as if to escape from hunters, an image Frank could understand better than any benign man in the American moon over Akron.

"Is this your life, José? Is this my life? I am enlisted forever? Does this continue forever?" His voice grated in his throat. He hoped he wouldn't weep, although among these men he had seen many weep. But sober, not drunk.

"My life, yes. You are free to leave." José paused. "Many Mexicans come, many foreigners come. They stay as long as they can stay, two weeks or two years. They learn what they can learn, and report to the world what they believe they understand. This is not a perfect process." He moved his shoulder closer to Frank's, without actually touching it, as if warmth from his body could warm the other. "It's like sowing a field. Not every seed will sprout, not every stalk will yield ears of corn. Some will fail, but the majority will grow. Or so we must believe if we hope to eat."

"Tomás was no stalk of corn."

"No. The stalk I speak of is you. And the others, those here and those who will come. These are the ones who must grow and yield."

"Oh, no. Don't give me that shit myth of the future, José. I won't swallow any shit right now. Tomás was my friend. They blasted him to hell and gone, in front of little girls. Me, he took care of me, you know. I can't function without him. And why should I anyhow? This ain't my fight!"

"If you think it is not, you should leave, Frank." José repeated gently. His voice was not angry or dismissive, nor did he say the words Frank said to himself—grow up and be a man, Frank. This is where we understand the old man can't hand you everything you want. Like home style love forever. Beneath his mescal and rage, he knew José wouldn't judge him. He blew out his breath in a huff. He pulled in his legs and hunched his shoulders inside his sweated shirt. After a few minutes he raised his head and found the moon again. It was less than full, as if somebody sliced a portion off the side of its pale loaf. These were José's people, and José's moon, the dark leaping rabbit upon the moon's bright face.

"The bastards killed Tomás!" Frank heaved the cry like vomit. Against his will tears shot out. "I need to think, I need some time!"

"The time we have," José replied, "is until the earth dies beneath the feet of the last man." He sat quietly beside Frank, now placing his shoulder against Frank's shoulder, waiting for his warmth to penetrate.

35

The Caravan Arrives

In the darkness Harry sat up. The mosquito's buzz woke him, and finally compelled him to act. He braced his back against the wall behind the bed. He wasn't going to tolerate the bombardment of an insect. Dependent on blood. Like an army officer! He pressed together his lips in readiness as his eyes adjusted, and his head shifted slowly to follow the insect's noise.

What a day. The streets of San Gregorio were thronged. The Zaptista caravan passed through on their way to Mexico City. Harry, while applauding the PR coup the Zapatistas pulled off, tried to remain unnoticed—one more person among thousands cheering and shouting.

The caravan followed the route Emiliano Zapata took in 1914, during the Mexican Revolution. Like the Zapata whose name they used, the Chiapas rebels focused on the poverty and mistreatment of the country's diverse Indian groups and their calls for economic and democratic reform. Harry remembered the movie with Marlon

Brando. The current uprising played equally romantic, that is to say, glorious.

"We go to Mexico City to demand the rich share with the poor!" shouted a woman who joined the caravan.

"You are not alone!"

"Never more a Mexico without us!" responded speakers on the makeshift platform of a truck bed. "Never more a Mexico without us!"

If President Zedillo wants peace, he better get on the stick. A Zapatista leader, high on the platform fixed on the truck bed, cried, "The Zapatistas know how to fight!"

Sheer balls, Harry continued in his internal monologue, more propaganda than reality. They might know how, but they had no means; anyway it wasn't in their interest to lose the moral high ground. The growing concern of Civil Society that would turn the tide.

The list of murders and assassinations blazed on wall posters: human rights workers, Mocotlán, Acteal, the French peace witnesses. Global attention favored the Zapatistas, and Harry felt goodwill rise in the atmosphere as palpable as sweet cake in the oven. In the countryside, hidden from UN observers, the same old shit and increasing tension.

He gazed around at the mestizo Mexican crowd. Civil Society, plain and simple. Many wept, tears following the eroded creases in their faces. As always, women stood with babies slung in knotted rebozos. Men perched small children on their shoulders, their long backs straight and their short legs planted.

"Zapata lives! The fight goes on!" the crowd chanted in the zócalo of this worn-down impoverished city, hot in the midday sun. Paint peeled in bubbles from stucco walls on the municipal palace, flaking and falling where bodies and hands rubbed. PRI officials watched behind high windows, smiled, and acted like they loved it.

Harry looked across at the military trucks, loaded with soldiers in combat gear. Also on their best behavior. Nobody was going to fuck up this demo with a bad move that would grab the public tonight on international television. The massacres of a group or of one man like in Ocosingo, swollen to mythic proportions. The class struggle in living color.

"The Zapatistas are not alone! Long live the Indians of Mexico, long live the Zapatista army!" the man next to him shouted to the crowd's applause. Several boys shot bottle rockets into the air and waved Mexican flags. The man might be a PRI plant, his shouts and his gestures struck Harry as rehearsed. He tried to move away. The crowd walled him unyielding.

The soldiers climbed down from their vehicles and stood lined up opposite the Zapatista sound truck in front of the church. They held their rifles vertical and stood stiff as lead toys. Most of them were dark-skinned indigenous boys. The same old story. Harry spotted Ignacio and checked him over. Their landlord reigned in full uniform, sporting gold bars and stripes.

He and Constance knew Ignacio's time for departure to US training passed months ago. Harry hardly believed it himself, that a year in San Gregorio had passed. Not just that Ignacio hadn't left for his mysterious trip to the United States. But, more importantly, the Cuates project was nothing like done. They still struggled with how to create a holding reservoir. Mexico. Harry grimaced wryly. All those jokes about Mexican time!

Some things couldn't be moved faster. Clamps for fixing the pipes never arrived. The project stood on hold for two months during the rains. Tentatively Harry suggested they tie the pipes, using old-fashioned fiber, against the day when the reservoir would fill and the pipes be connected. The community refused. They wanted the best.

Like Harry.

Standing in his worn jeans and frayed cotton shirt, Harry recognized the discipline in Ignacio's meticulous figure. He resembled every military man Harry ever dealt with, in the army and out. Guys like that showed up in unlikely places, in out-backs, deserts and jungles. Flagpole up the ass kind of guys. Commanding and obeying, opportunistic aggressive personalities ready to join the right side.

In contrast, the rickety rumbling buses in which the caravan arrived, and the caravanistas themselves, looked like what they were—ramshackle, held together with Mexican fiber. No stainless.

But goddamn. They didn't give up! The community of Cuates wasn't an isolated example of—of—he searched for the right word—perseverance. They'd stick it out until the last man fell, until the last segment of pipe, the last meter of interior copper tubing, clamped into place. Until the reservoir he designed held water against infrequent rains, and gravity brought them water, until the pipes were properly installed so they'd hold up when pumps operated, off their own town electricity. Which they high-jacked! A long process, an endless process. That was life everywhere, that was okay.

Harry gazed around again, wiping sweat off the back of his neck with his handkerchief. Constance should be here, he thought, and as he craned she appeared, coming into Calle Noviembre wearing her canvas hat and sunglasses. For a moment Harry viewed a stranger, a slight woman past her prime dressed in the kind of get-up you knew right away was American. Despite their year and a half here. Despite how, with no conversation, they accepted remaining here indefinitely.

Who she really was, he wasn't sure. A woman he'd grown old with in forty-five years. Threading her narrow path through the crowd of onlookers and vendors, children peddling bracelets, women with baskets. He waved.

Constance saw the caravan first, surrounded by bouquets: pink, yellow and purple flowers. A display which usually appeared heaped in churches for weddings. And then she noticed troops across the square in front of the church, with Ignacio upright at attention. He wore his flat dress hat, and the black brim shaded his eyes. She was accustomed to how her heart lurched.

They never obtained visas. Nobody ever asked for them, in fact —Mexico was casual faced with the presence of American money, except out on the roads and inside autonomous communities, three and a half years into armed rebellion. Some blessed negligence allowed it. Ignacio never asked if she taught students legally or illegally. She accepted his thirty pesos per hour in cash; most transactions used cash, the informal economy kept Mexico going.

Without documents. Harry must know Ignacio must know— boxes inside boxes. She shook her head. The bottom line was, don't disturb what you don't have to disturb. Go for the goal.

Constance turned away from the troops, from Ignacio. How her heart beat for that man. And her groin. She had no proof of anything really bad on his part, she lied to herself for the thousandth time. She pretended not to understand the frequent gossip. She introduced no further direct conversation about his career. Instead, she yearned over him. Her best student. He spoke almost fluently now, with the same Middle America accent Judith used. She recognized it. His duty hours weren't her business. She spotted Harry in the crowd waving at her, and she crossed to join him.

In Harry's peripheral vision from the light of the patio, the huddled form of Constance stirred. She pulled over her head the thin bedspread. But that was too hot. He wasn't gonna sleep defensively. He listened to her muffled breathing. Curled like an unborn child, that wasn't his style. He waited palm open and hand raised, for the mosquito to find his naked flesh.

Constance was awake, wakened as Harry had been by the insect's buzzing. Unable to see, she sensed Harry sitting upright beside her. He always slept nude, a substantial target of old savory flesh. Lots of rich-looking skin there, the color of good bread pudding, sprinkled with freckles. He stayed in good shape for a man of sixty-eight, still active, still sexually motivated. When the inevitable slap on flesh resounded, Constance permitted herself a small sigh.

Harry sank down next to her and immediately she wondered what he did with the dead mosquito. Was it still stuck to his body somewhere? Rubbing off onto her when Harry pushed into her spooned back? Or on his hand, now inserted between her thighs? She didn't need to think about it, did she. Only to roll onto her back and make welcoming sounds, as she had for forty-six years.

Darkness cradled their bed. The patio's dim capture of the outer streetlight cast only the faintest aura. This was how Constance preferred sex at their age, non-visual. Behind her blind eyelids she imagined a young form, bronze and muscular, smooth of skin, maybe somebody like Ignacio? Ah. Thinking of his strut, the open neck of the bright yellow shirt he wore last week, the brown throat revealed. As often the case, a fine curl of hair, almost invisible, showed at the top button, leaving her to wonder if more hair grew below, if it was soft, if... She let her thighs fall apart.

As Harry penetrated her she hoped he wouldn't make any disgusting noises, male noises of chuffing and snorting. Her connection to her body dimmed. She was aware only of Harry's weight pressing on top of her, struggling in his kind way to hold back for a minute, so that she might come also. But it was spoiled. Why did he need to stalk the mosquito? Because today she read to him an article about hemorrhagic dengue spread by mosquitoes, she supposed. It was her fault, her information promoted the killing.

At the end neither of them made any sound at all.

Harry opened his eyes slowly to faint light penetrating the drapes. It wasn't light that waked him every morning, but church bells, a sonorous and uncountable clanging every morning, repeated every evening. This morning as usual he began to count, to try to make sense of pauses and sequences, to decode the system. As always, he lost track, forgot if a pause was the first or the second, forgot why he was counting and drifted backward into a brief morning dream. A dream of dawn, with birdcall and bells, cockcrow in the adjoining yard, the bleat of a goat. He was asleep yet awake, in a first innocent pleasure at being alive hearing so many sweet meaningless calls to his waking consciousness.

It was a country he could love without thinking. The problems, my god a million: corruption, inexcusable neglect of basic needs, unceasing paramilitary murders. The Zapatistas might win the propaganda war, but on the ground when the caravan departed last night nothing was changed. The Zapatistas could go to Congress, could make their cause known all over the world. In Chiapas, war against the people continued. The dirty low-intensity war the United States encouraged. He didn't say that to Constance. But repeated that she not go outside town without him.

She was a good sport. He admired her willingness to giggle at his witticisms, to be adventurous, to jump onto buses without a plan… To take him, always, without a minute's hesitation. He was lucky. He knew lots of guys whose wives played at headaches. Not Constance… like the bougainvillea, she was… stepping onto a plane to Mexico. Carrying her knapsack, wearing her canvas hat. She was forever innocent in his mind, learning whatever literature, magazines and encyclopedias offered. As if they explained the game.

He lay awake. Automatically he began to calculate. Ten meters of mountain trench required huge labor in the rock. Hand labor, the kind you never saw in the US. He decided it was necessary to sustain water pressure. In San Gregorio he saw men shovel dirt through a window when nothing existed behind the aperture but a vacant lot, for chrissake. The building collapsed or crumbled or who knew what. Wouldn't waste the one standing wall. Teams of three men with one wheelbarrow, two shovels, one bucket. Shoveled sand through the gap to make cement. Not a backhoe, not a Cat, nothing.

He saluted them. He felt chosen, to participate in this water project, and grateful that they understood the slowness of the process. Uncritical. No cost over-runs! Life was slow.

A few thousand dollars to do a task that in the US would pay fifty k every six months. They lived on his pension, it didn't matter. Connie's Social Security arrived in her bank every month in Ann Arbor. They didn't need to draw down their savings. Harry got mail from non-governmental organizations which formed part of the networks that reached into Chiapas. They were getting mail. Addressed to him by name. He sympathized with the uprising and didn't pretend otherwise. His own immigrant grandparents escaping poverty. Whatever shit in Lithuania a hundred fifty years ago. His grandfather told him stories of his grandfather Skelba. The mountain people in Cuates didn't want anybody who came on to them White. Just show them how to do what they wanted done, with modern materials. No clay pipes. Copper connections. Polyvinyl tubing. Stainless steel clamps. Where the fuck did the clamps go. The reservoir fashioned from 5,000 liter tinacos, lined with polyvinyl. Hydraulic pumps convertible from burro power to electricity.

Although clay pipes worked, maybe a thousand years ago. But the community expected traffic, trucks, in the future. Thinking ahead to when truck vibrations would crack clay or cement! In the future! Highways with trucks! A fairy story. Somebody had read somewhere about vibrations. Amazing, how people initiated a future, in this state.

Connie always claimed the future starts with a word. Like, in the beginning was the Word, and the Word was with God. Mystical. But goddamn. Something to it. Look into somebody's eyes and say vibrations. Harry remembered how his grandfather always wanted to buy the best. Poor as stale beer, he always demanded top quality. Or nothing. An attitude Harry appreciated and shared. Built into his work. Stainless steel clamps. They wouldn't budge on it. He'd have to reorder. Pay for them himself. Funny. He hadn't thought of his grandpa in forty years. Others would buy second best, as if second best is good enough for the likes of me. No way. It won't last, his grandfather fingered the fabric of a cheap shirt. The old gent acted like he might live forever. Died before the shirt was washed twice. No future with that shirt. Harry remembered him, though, an old man with a neat beard.

Harry didn't know how or when the future starts. Had started. Maybe with the uprising. Their own pueblo, their own usos y costumbres, their own system of assigned public service, tequio. No waiting for the government of Chiapas or the Federal government to help them. Throw the bums out. Get rid of the PRI-imposed caciques. No more bosses. After five hundred years. Ya Basta. Hard working little bastards. Incredible the labor. On practically no food, just atole, that corn flour mixed in water. Whatever water. Even after the pipes connected it would be necessary to boil. Animal run-off. The men didn't seem to suffer diarrhea the way babies did. Or they didn't say so.

Finally he hauled his naked torso around to swing his feet onto the cool tile floor. For a moment he paused, waiting until his stiff body told him he could rise. The morning chill sometimes didn't leave his bones until after his second cup. Constance still snored. He would be in and out of the shower before she woke. Now that infant diarrhea passed through his mind he remembered Frank. Find. No damn telephones in these NGO houses half the time, or if there were, they didn't function. The workers slept on cots and floor mats. It irritated him. Too fucking righteous.

Dried off, he zipped his jeans and pulled on a sweatshirt. Frank was a do-gooder. Harry corrected himself. Frank was good. A post-Gulf War victim. Once he shook off the booze, he knew. Harry fished in his mind. He knew—blah blah blah. How could you articulate something like that, when you were sent out to kill, blot from your mind, those rolling trains of ants, only they were men. And wake up sober two years later. In Frank's case it was a post-battlefield conversion. They were all damaged, all Americans, with a new war every damned decade.

Harry sighed.

Frank was only one of the sympathetic foreigners working alongside the Mexicans, taking up the cause of Good. Justice. Dignity. Human Rights. All those words. In the beginning was the Word. It was Connie's job to figure out people. Harry never could. He couldn't take a word the way Connie could, and make it bridge between one mind and another. Marcos could. Harry read every word put out by the subcomandante. He knew it was great stuff, and Constance claimed she was madly in love with Marcos. All the women fell in love with Marcos, like Frank Sinatra. It was the words, like that Cyrano movie, in love with the words. Justice. Dignity. Marcos used them all.

Harry preferred that Constance swoon over Marcos instead of Ignacio. Her student. He knew how Connie's mind worked, with these students. Like each was her child. Connie's mother died and Connie reincarnated her role, as a teacher. Once one student, a middle-aged Chinese cop, relocated by the British from Hong Kong. Told her he tortured the prisoners, for the British. Constance repeated the story to Harry. The man assumed the name Johnson. Johnson had brown eyes. When he told Constance about his former work he expected her to approve his loyal service. She felt sick. How could she have taken that man into her—her what? Heart? Mind? Loved him into English? Johnson betrayed her, with his crimes committed many years before. The British government moved him to the US ahead of the Communist takeover for his own safety, Connie explained. Harry snorted. Another democracy. Sent their criminal trash to Constance. He shared her distress, but his was anger, and hers a cut to her soul.

The man Ignacio put Harry's nerves on edge. He looked like razor-wire. You couldn't go there. How could Constance continue, like she never learned? Taught, never learned. Was that it. Yet everyone knew. Sure as shit she knew. He emptied his coffee cup. He heard Constance shut off the shower and open the bathroom door.

"I'm thinking of bussing up to DF. No, not with the caravan," he told her raised eyebrows. "It was long gone before dawn. To visit the American Embassy. We should apply for FM-3 Resident Visas. We're retired foreign senior citizens with guaranteed income."

"Will that make us safer?"

"Nope. But once they issue papers they might be embarrassed to expel us." He didn't add, or shoot us.

"I like the idea of having legal status, anyway," Constance said. "We might be here for a while?"

"As long as it takes," Harry replied.

Takes for what? She didn't ask.

36

Martin is Guilty

They were kind to Martin in San Gregorio. Witness for Peace gave him an empty room, a rarity. The house sat parallel to a main street, on another with less traffic. It hid behind an iron door, and opened in the sun of an interior courtyard. The room they led him to contained no furniture – an office occupied it previously, and Martin's amenities consisted of an unusual number of electric outlets, and wires running along the walls like snakes. The office recently relocated to a safer place, but the Witnesses didn't bother Martin with that information. He was already in a state of shock.

They looked at his emaciated form and glazed blue eyes and left him. Martin used his sleeping bag as a mat on the tile floor. His meditations took on the quality of four times daily penance, because the tile refused to shape itself or yield to his bony backside. He endured it. At night, without changing his loose cotton pants and shirt now definitely giving off a certain ripe odor, he simply stretched out, with his head pillowed on his backpack. He didn't mind being ascetic. In fact, he relished the punishment.

No way to bring the dead back to life, as Holy Master whispered in his ear from a telephone in Iowa. Whispering on the telephone ruffled Martin because he used to associate the breathy quality with perverts and sex. But HM was sexless. His disinterest in the physical body, full of blood and juices, was precisely what Martin, in his failure and guilt, most craved. Disembodiment for himself was high on Martin's list of desires. He wanted out.

Instead, the authorities, first Mexican and then French, requested reports on what he knew about the couple's assassination. He recounted hearing gunfire from the overlook across the road, and failing to recognize it. The Germans verified as much. They could offer no further information. The community dispatched a man on foot to the nearest town. When police officials ultimately arrived the following noon, they had to summon a separate vehicle to take the dead. What Martin remembered best was the length of time, hours that ticked by while the French, shrouded in wool blankets, suffered the heat. The odor began by dawn, and by evening Martin was frantic.

Now he suffered his own aroma, and inhaled his collapse.

Out not being a physical option, Martin launched his mind into the atmosphere above San Gregorio, and hoped it would connect with the minds of other Meditators for Peace—sort of like running into your best friends on the train platform to Des Moines. You might. There aren't that many trains. From Holy Master he wanted simple absolution for his appalling failure.

Holy Master whispered something about karma. In one of Martin's previous lives he failed to protect, and he must redouble the dimension of his spirit, to do it now. Martin visualized his spirit as a balloon, a stretching skin he blew air into. Then the air released into the atmosphere. The air had to be full of love, like flowers Mexicans claimed were loaded with dusted blessings. Martin's entire life until now was devoted to offering love in penance for wishing Robert John dead, but apparently he didn't understand the mechanics well enough. The flowers probably worked; the balloon, he was sure, was properly inflated; something in the release wasn't taking effect.

In a sullen non-meditative blaze he told himself, "Well, I didn't hurt anybody!" But the anger passed.

In the Witnesses' house they brought food to him for one day, and then wisely ignored him, assuming hunger would require him to open his eyes and unfold his legs. He must go out into the market, let himself be seen by the multitude.

"You must have patience," Holy Master breathed.

"For how long?" Martin all but cried aloud.

"Love will support you for seven more years. Seven after seven makes a good number." It didn't sound that good to Martin, but on the other hand, he didn't have a job elsewhere.

"Not hurting others has not sufficed," Holy Master whispered. "Life requires that you do more than abstain from harm—be positive, send forth love, smile on your brother!"

The tune, as if obedient to Holy Master independently of Martin, ran through his head and then faded like a poor radio signal. Martin liked the Beetles and often wished he could carry a tiny CD player. He must travel on and on and on, a spirit in the wilderness, and it would be real nice to have some music.

He began by going to the zócalo.

Then an earthquake struck.

Martin lay himself down in the center of the cobble-stone road, his arms outstretched like Jesus'. It was the wrong image, again. He was supposed to turn blue, like Krishna. He held his breath, but then a man leaned over him.

"C'mon, Martin, get up," Frank was saying. He took Frank's outstretched hand and got his legs under him. He brushed off his laundered jeans and smiled weakly. Frank clearly wasn't afraid.

"Take the long view," Frank offered as they walked toward the market. "Like, you won't live to the next ice age anyway."

Martin accepted that. Frank was profound, although a decade younger. He'd lived more life outside the Golden Dome. Frank for his part took in how scrawny Martin became since their last trip together. They hardly knew each other, but Frank recognized the look. Death passed Martin by, as it did Frank. But its passage left a mark on your forehead.

They strolled into the market. The buzz of frightened and exalted people hovered in the air. Frank purchased staples in bulk: rice, beans, corn meal. The usual. Martin stood helpless.

"How about cornflakes?"

Martin nodded. Yes, he knew how to make cornflakes. You put them in a bowl and add milk. He could handle that. "With bananas," Frank prompted. He didn't have time free to deal with this poor scarecrow. Let's get him down to Constance Skelba's. She'll normalize him. Therapists were lacking in San Gregorio. People just coped.

37

The Ground Shakes

For two minutes the ground shook. In the deep silence she heard only the urgent whisper of a man behind her in the immigration office corridor: Get out. She expected screams, a crushing rumble of walls, or at least the rush of wings as the Angel of Death hurtled past her toward another place.

But no. So silent, such an intense dream. The morning when her mother announced she was dying of cancer. A silence like that, in her heart where the noise of its beating had stopped.

Others emerged into the sunshine. They gazed around, at walls, sky, and waited. Nothing more happened. Every vista looked the same, but different. Everything altered. Her mother was dead forty-six years.

The immigration officer ordered tea for everyone in the adjoining café. The function masked his fear. At the patio table a woman with very blue eyes wept herself red. She had been in San Francisco, she announced to everyone, and she knew.

Harry, in the bank across from the zócalo, heard women scream. He grabbed the precious stamped forms from Mexico City and rushed outside. He stationed himself in the precise middle of the intersection, as far as he could get from each building. People ran. By pure chance he was back in San Gregorio. What timing! A bank could fall on him! How a big quake like this one affected the mountains he had no idea. He guessed at a massive shift, maybe eight Richter. And it lasted. The epicenter must be pretty damn close. If all their work was undone—Jesus. He couldn't deal with it. Polyvinyl composites and copper tubing have a certain flexibility. What they'd demanded, to hold up against truck vibrations. Damn! The damage if there was any, he calmed himself, would be in three sectors where pipes tunneled through cinder blocks into the community buildings. The buildings might fall.

When the shaking stopped he trotted back to the apartment as rapidly as he could, knowing Constance would head back whether or not she'd picked up the next set of required forms. Pieces of granite lay tossed on the sidewalk like the innumerable pieces of paper they were filling in. Not much structural damage, as he assessed it. On one street a facade collapsed onto a garden. Bird of Paradise lay beneath it, in broken stalks.

Constance was already home. She was unhurt. The apartment appeared intact. He rapped on a few walls and nothing fell. Harry finally looked at her ghostly face and hugged her. Nothing more could be done.

Carmen arrived. She climbed up onto the roof—well, she does that every day anyway, said Connie—and checked for cracks, for breaks in the structure that kept the roof waterproof.

In the aftermath, various friends strolled by to share their excitement at being alive. Frank introduced Martin, and went into Harry's study to compare notes. Constance brought out food, leftover tortillas, cold chicken. She couldn't believe Martin looked so shell-shocked merely from surviving an earthquake! She sat with him while he chewed, and encouraged him to swallow. Her jaws made little chews, and then made little swallows. He understood.

On the street later Constance saw police everywhere, and the usual soldiers, only now they cleared fallen stone. Just ordinary boys, bending and lifting, joking with one another. Maybe they laughed because they were alive, untouched, untouchable. Like young people at a funeral.

Townspeople stood inside the safety ropes police strung, pointing up at precarious facades over their heads. Around town a dozen saints perched adorning public buildings, gazing sternly or benevolently, depending on their mission. Today their parishioners returned their stone gazes, relying on magic to prevent the leaning shapes from toppling onto their upturned faces.

A bareheaded fellow with a camera stood in front of the Catedrál. He took pictures from several angles, moving his tripod. Several saints of the rococo facade had lost portions of their sacred persons—an arm, a foot, lying shattered on the patio beneath.

Constance smiled at the young man. It was Merwin Jiménez.

"I didn't know you'd returned," she called as he recognized her. "How's your study going?" Constance tilted her head upward for his kiss on her cheek, a custom she now enjoyed.

"This is the first part of it to suffer an earthquake. Unless you count the Zapatista uprising in 1994!" Merwin's personal earthquake was his own business. Did you feel the earth move? He shared his earthquake only with Carmen.

"Absolutely, it counts! It's ten on the political Richter! I'm always scared to death for Harry when he goes up. He might be in the wrong place at the wrong time."

"Me, too. Some close encounters! Bloody battles go on between the old guard and the new. Literally, death squads. San Gregorio looks like the earth opened to show the shakiness beneath. Everyone in Mexico's on edge."

She nodded to indicate she understood .

"My big discovery," Merwin continued, "is, I don't give a fuck for the Cultural Patrimony the Conquistadores built on the backs of slave labor." He hesitated. "Excuse me." He looked at her sideways. She didn't blink. "I did once care. It's remarkable and beautiful."

"Can't you think of it as a Mexican heritage, given who hauled stones and framed ceilings?"

He put his camera into its case and folded the tripod. He took her arm. "You're right, of course, that's what UNESCO says. Along with all Mexico. You know what the indigenous say? Every conference they go to they haul out a Mexican flag and the slogan, No more a Mexico without us. That's like these damn cathedrals. 'Include me in', is what the indigenous say. 'Factor me in. Because it's mine as much as yours.'"

"And these indigenous are present and alive."

"Yes, finally everyone notices! It took a rebellion, plus magnificent PR efforts." Inside Alvaro's the conversation buzzed, people at the table hailed one another. They ordered coffee. "Museums are fine. But survivors of five hundred years of colonization—man, that's something, isn't it!" He smiled at her. Better to change the subject. "I hear Marcos likes contemporary music. He listens to Pedro Infante. Only twenty years out of date!"

Constance sipped her hot coffee and waited for sweat to break out on her forehead. Alvaro's coffee was always worth it, even in a hot climate. Her own tastes were formed in the sixties and seventies. She sympathized with Subcomandante Marcos.

"Marcos is smart." Merwin pursued his thought. "Never mind his taste in music—he's onto the destructive side of neoliberalism. Take a nation, undermine its leaders, bomb the hell out of it, and then charitably rebuild it in the capitalist image. Unless we let it rot like Haiti. That's our US government I'm talking about." His face pulled into a bleak stretch.

"Many times over," she agreed. "And weren't we all grateful immigrants to the US at some point. Excuse the cliché! So I know what you're thinking—is this what we bought into. What are you, second? Third?"

"I'm second generation US born," Merwin said. "Unless you recall it was all Mexico's to begin with. And I wasn't raised to detest my government."

"Nor I," Connie affirmed. She knew only too well Americans unlikely to criticize NAFTA. Sally wrote to her about how great development plans would be for Mexico!

"A thousand people stood and cheered the Zapatistas right here, you know."

Constance nodded and sipped the mountain coffee. She remembered crowds surrounding the caravan. "And they sold books signed by Marcos," she added. "Tee-shirts with his picture, the whole commercial thing. Don't oppose the economic model!" Although she recognized the pulse of hope.

"They'll grab the land."

"The communal land? The ejidos?" A rhetorical question to keep the conversation alive.

"You bet. An earthquake makes a great excuse to get in and explore. Oil," he ticked off on his fingers, "water resources. Biodiversity. Precious woods. Minerals, who knows. The technocrats will swarm up from the cracks in the earth." He poked the sugar at the bottom of his cup. He wore a short sleeve cotton shirt tucked into jeans. Constance admired his forearms and strong wrists. Lately she found herself looking at young men more closely than ever. The flesh called and called.

Unaware of her wandering eye, Merwin went on, "You know what Marcos calls them? A cybernetic species, bred from mediocre humans, mathematical knowledge, and political stupidity."

Constance smiled ruefully. After they'd finally gotten that poor wreck Martin on his way, she heard as much from Harry. Again. He wasn't quite ranting, Constance reported. With neoliberalism as their sword and shield, irreparable harm cut the environment. They already murdered one another in half the world, for fresh water, Texas siphoning the Rio Bravo, Israel robbing Palestinians, Chinese contemplating insane damns... Indigenous cultures who tried to live in communal rather than privatized cultures got hacked to death. Never mind the damned earthquakes! And then small farmers and businessmen...

"You know this stuff," Merwin said, His dark eyebrows curving upward.

She flushed. "You know I listen to Harry. I even can learn by myself."

"Sorry, not what I meant," he lied, taking her hand. She looked at his. Several abrasions, scabbed over like a boy's on the back of his thumb and hand. He'd been someplace. Those marks weren't made by a camera.

"So you know the government screws them over, out in the autonomous communities. Zedillo will never honor the San Andrés Accords, nor any peace agreement. That would mean ceding rights to develop land to people who belong to it. No way."

"No way," she agreed. She looked across the open patio; the zócalo was nearly empty. A quiet time, of dropping blossoms and faint breezes. The silence of an earthquake. She wondered how long that sense would hold her. Not that her life flashed before her eyes. Not at all. Nor her mother's death. No. It was the silence of change. The tectonic shift. She sighed. Ignacio went on duty most of the time. He told Constance his role was to keep the peace, and she surmised that meant arresting Zapatistas—or anybody the government wanted rid of. "So have you been out in the war zone?" She looked at Merwin in a maternal way. Nobody wanted to confide in anybody, she knew. It was too tricky.

"Mmm." That was noncommittal enough. "The feds won't withdraw the military. It's occupied country out there. No secret. Harry sees it each time he drives out. Him and three thousand Mexicans from four hundred organizations and twenty-seven states. Add twenty-eight rebel commanders who see it, plus every person in the Autonomous Communities sees it. And me."

Merwin trusted Carmen with his life. Her life, she entrusted to him. And to Harry, if Harry got caught in a rebel community. Torture was a strange thing. Someone needed to know the key question before they went about it. Or key results. It wasn't random. Not at all. It was purposeful, businesslike. Gutting the Zapatista leadership. They were tracked.

"Add me, too. I haven't gone there but I understand," Constance echoed. The newspaper reported threats to Human Rights workers right here in the center of town. They continuously moved their offices. Maeda got kidnapped and murdered, and the others threatened with the same, and their kids, too. Ignacio referred to it, just last week. They were enjoying the mild sun in the patio, both of them casual in short sleeve shirts. Constance straightened her books on the table, and brought the usual glasses and a pitcher of sandía for the break.

Ignacio spoke carefully, "These people bit off more that they can chew, sometimes. It's a pity."

Constance watched him carefully. He was using badly an idiom she gave him last week. She didn't correct him.

"Maestra, you should understand. Not worry about these things." He looked boldly into her eyes. "Some actions are necessary."

Inevitable."

"Why?"

"Chiapas cannot remain in the Dark Ages. Progress is necessary."

It was not her task to argue politics with her students. Constance wondered who ordered assaults on Human Rights workers. For progress! Really, she was glad she had teaching to occupy her, with the few private students like Nacho who came regularly and seemed eager to learn. Ignacio of course was special. He was so intense. They were communicating; tiny conversations like this. She elicited from him a description of his two older brothers, of his stern father and bronze-skinned mother, all now dead. Carmen was his family. No children. That counted as another defect, the unresolved blame. Constance realized more sharply that his bright skin and cruel ear constructed his personality. Ambition replaced family. Sometimes she was sure he would reveal more intimate facts about himself. Was on the verge. Wanted to. She had only to wait. The other things—.

Meanwhile, Mexican people must do what they could to bring justice to the indigenous. She believed in justice, the way she believed in hanging laundry out in the sun. It was clean and good. Ignacio said people must obey laws and look ahead to progress. Not prevent progress. What did he mean by progress? Not what Harry meant. Her stomach bothered her, she realized. The lesson ended early.

And today, post earthquake, she accepted a pleasant moment for coffee with Merwin, who showed surprise because she wasn't a complete dunce. Nor unduly rattled by the temblor.

Or perhaps she was. She felt tired now, and looked forward to getting home. She smiled at Merwin as she stood. She could take a hot shower and let water run on the back of her neck. It felt like a hand, and when she let water stroke her, her whole body gave over to the comfort.

She needed to think. When earth beneath your feet splits or

clashes. That's like when your mother dies. And afterward, life re-builds. If better for all, that's progress. And if you look more care-fully where you step, and assess what you step on, that's learning. She walked home on soil laid over shifting rock.

The evening news reported little more than bare details of the earthquake's aftermath. The epicenter was not in San Gregorio, but east toward the Lacandón. "Help" would be on the way, yeah yeah, by helicopter where no roads existed.

Listening, Harry muttered, "Another fucking excuse."

"But surely?" As Merwin had told her.

"Yes, no but. Absolutely."

38

Day of the Dead

The Day of the Dead arrived. No recent murders broke the calm of the city neighborhoods, few were reported out in the countryside. Some towns suffered houses sliding off the mountains. That happened in rainy season, too; an earthquake wasn't necessary. Most families prepared peacefully for the day of reunion with their departed.

Doña Consuela, almost as broad as her broad table, leaned out of her doorway where she displayed her sweet breads and dulces. She was neighborly, and if Constance asked what something was or how one cooked it, always helpful. "Are you expecting guests?" Consuela inquired, in a tone almost coy. Her neat gray hair bundled in a grandmotherly bun with a turban over it. Constance paused.

Four years into the rebellion, two years of their own stay—Connie and Harry discussed the holiday. Maeda, little Ricardo, the people at Mocotlán—those Mexicans weren't theirs to claim.

Neither of them wished for reunion with their own American dead. Their generation grieved in silence, privately, stiff upper lip and all that. For Constance the concept of welcoming the apparition of one's deceased with food and flowers carried a certain charm, but since her mother died in 1958, chances were she long ago reincarnated elsewhere, and hence was too busy to attend Day of the Dead festivities.

"A prior engagement," Constance replied to her neighbor. She didn't specify whether it was the dead or herself, too busy to meet.

Doña Consuela's brown face folded into disapproving creases, as it often did when Constance failed to grasp the old lady's common Spanish or, as now, made some inappropriate reply.

Nevertheless she handed Constance an extra piece of sugared fig. "Then go the panteón and listen to the music," she suggested.

"It's very nice. Muy bonita. With beautiful flowers."

Out of Doña Consuela's sight Constance gobbled the sweet herself, like a greedy child. The three Nights for the dead to appear passed without incident.

Thus it was a shock when Constance's mother showed up mid-November, thirteen days late for the holiday. Despite the war of repression, Constance began to regard their time in Mexico like two years at summer camp, when you complained if the weather wasn't perfect, and expected the food to be awful and the other kids mean.

"I'm going to call my mother and tell her to come get me," Constance joked to Harry. "I want to go home; I have nothing to wear, either." They laughed in despair over torrential rain flooding the streets, a daily diet of stewed chicken, the way clothes disintegrated under the sun. But her nerves filed to an edge. The intensity of balancing disconnect—of why ever she lived there, the brilliant spill of unreal flowers, colorful street life, dark edges of poverty and harassment out in the countryside.

Constance heard footsteps in the patio. Carmen was back, to work on the roof or rear of the apartment, or maybe just to sweep petals fallen from the bougainvillea.

"I was about to get worried," Harry chortled. "She doesn't miss a day."

And at that exact moment Connie's mother appeared in the center of their living room, sitting on a wooden Mexican chair taken from Connie's childhood bedroom. The white-painted chair was decorated with a design of pink and blue flowers on its crooked back and down its hand-hewn legs. It was much too small for her mother, and Constance wanted to ask why she sat on it; after all it was Constance's own chair from the bedroom she shared with her sister. But what a ridiculous question to ask a dead woman.

"Couldn't get away any sooner, I suppose," Constance remarked instead. "And I've been wanting to go home for weeks!" And abruptly her silly laugh inadvertently blurted turned wild, and she wept. Harry got up and moved to her side of the table. He stood behind her. He failed to notice his mother-in-law, whom he met just once, when she was already dying. He leaned over and kissed Connie's neck. "What's wrong?"

"Carmen. I think Carmen must be hiding from Ignacio."

"But you told me there's no lesson this week because he's out on patrol?"

She remembered. Ignacio indeed had told her. So he wasn't even home; yet Carmen came here. Constance thought she might go out and ask, straightforward ask, why Carmen came to the patio daily, every day, to do some invisible chore she couldn't identify, to tap on the cistern with that senseless hammer. To peek furtively into their kitchen window, with averted head.

Instead, she looked for an answer to the ghost of her mother, who was fading piecemeal like the Cheshire cat. "Wait a minute, Momma," she whispered. Her mother gazed at Constance and smiled. And then she moved her lips, and carefully mouthed, say Momma. Momma,

Constance whispered again. She made the sound exactly right. Her mother's voice exactly like Judith's. Judith pronounced Momma that way. Constance imitated her five year old daughter.

I'm sorry I didn't prepare for you. If I'd known you were coming I would've cooked a nice meal and put marigolds and candles on the table. She wondered how her mother got away from wherever her spirit presently resided. Apparently it was easy enough to visit Mexico. No long air flight, she surmised. Just show up.

Harry held her shoulders from behind her chair. He stroked them gently. It wasn't like Constance to suddenly break down weeping, certainly not in the last decade as she'd moved beyond hormonal storms. He hoped it had nothing to do with Connie's attacks of intuition—those didn't seem to change. He was familiar with how they grabbed her, and even when he laughed and discounted her imagination, she usually held on until contrary proof arrived. Well, she was a good sport. She never sulked when she was wrong.

Maybe now something to do with Carmen? Harry guessed Carmen acquired her new determination since their trip together, having to do with the mountain people. It was not peculiar to her, either. All over the nation indigenous people sloughed off ancient constraints, as if they never forgot who they are but held the information quietly under wraps. Not anymore. 'The wind from below' was blowing off the covers. Harry stroked and stayed quiet, waiting for Constance to snap out of her funk, whatever it was.

Her mother was vanishing, and Constance feared the last thing to go would be her child's Mexican chair. And so it was. Momma, she murmured again, and that was that.

She reached to her shoulder and patted Harry's hand, acknowledging his kind silence. Then shrugging, she rose and moved toward the patio. At least she could ask Carmen if she'd heard from Nacho. Constance didn't really suppose Ignacio kept rushing bulletins back to his wife. But she could ask. She wanted to watch Carmen's face.

She wanted Carmen to watch her face.

What a strange notion; she amazed herself. What she wanted was for somebody to see if she was physically altered to such an extent that now she resembled her dead mother. But that wouldn't be possible; Carmen never met Connie's mother who died in her fifties, and Constance was already sixty-six. She outlived her mother. She lived out her mother. The words circled in her head while she looked about for Carmen. Decades of her adult life in which she didn't reconcile to the loss of her mother!

And what about Carmen? Was her mother dead? Was she reconciled to the death of her childhood culture? Was she disconnected from her indigenous people because she wore high heels and modern haircuts?

Finally Connie spotted Carmen behind the brick patio wall, patting the soil around a small sabilla set in a clay pot. The thick leaves leaned, and Carmen adjusted them in their container. She looked up.

"These grow only indoors, in my city." Constance spoke in her stilted Spanish. She indicated the aloe. "It's too cold in the north."

Carmen nodded, and stood up, holding the pot. "I'll put it in a nice place for you."

"Thank you."

"The women of my family never saw these plants either. They don't grow in high mountains."

"Does your mother still live there?"

"She died when I was thirteen. Life is hard, and there was no medical treatment, no more than local teas from herbs. Afterward, it was necessary for me to leave my village and find work here below." Carmen met Connie's glance. "Perhaps you know that my employment was muchacha for the family of Ignacio?"

But Constance, instead of pursuing the role of Ignacio in

Carmen's life, asked, "And on Day of the Dead, did you put out a welcome for your mother?"

Carmen shook her head. "This custom is too superstitious for Ignacio. He goes to the church to pray for his mother's soul and I for mine, and if I light candles, that's permitted as well. But it does not trouble me. I carry my mother within me."

"Ah."

"Perhaps for that reason I never gave Nacho a child. My belly is already full!" She began to carry the potted aloe toward an empty corner. "Do you like it here?"

Constance wasn't sure if Carmen meant the sheltered place for the pot, or San Gregorio. Or Mexico; or for that matter, life on Planet Earth. So she took her time before nodding yes.

She wondered what Carmen's full belly would produce. Perhaps like all the indigenous cultures waking in these years, it would produce something rare and strange, like communality. No more isolated visits from the dead, no more wondering what she struggled with, alone although with Harry. But no, all that pertained only to Connie's life. Although Carmen often looked grim, she now carried beneath her skin a blush of something new. Assertiveness, maybe. Self, maybe.

39

Billy in Mexico

Billy had a temp job. Awesome! He wouldn't have believed it himself. Here he was in Mexico City at UNAM, hanging out on the famous university campus with the students. He knew students. Like, they had something in common all over. Dope. Sex. Figuring out who you are and why. Rebellion. Maybe here rebellion was more real, because their history of student movements was fierce, more violent for them than even the Kent State killings he read about. Same era, though, more or less. The good old days!

Just kidding, man! The Mexican government was famous for massacres. Like the US, when you get right down to it.

Billy marched in demonstrations, hung in the villages as Witness, scouted San Gregorio and San Cristóbal. So he felt ready to pitch in and work a repetitive daily job whose very repetitiveness gave him a rest from emotional swings and the always-ready attitude.

Billy coordinated the weekly student journal, collected articles they wrote, cartoons, whatever. These were radical activists, he knew that. Some kids went about their business getting law degrees, and then there were kids like these. Like him.

Info from Chiapas came via e-mail, from the Frey Bartólomeo Center that paid his pitiful stipend—couldn't say salary, that was illegal. They wanted him there, an American untouchable. Billy downloaded material and turned it over to the Zapatista Student Support Committee; the students did rewrite. He formatted on the computer, and passed out newspapers back from the print shop. Some far-out cartoons, some small inky art he didn't go for. Video stills, but they couldn't print them in color. Too bad. He'd seen the originals, indigenous women standing in dirt roads of their villages, chasing away soldiers. Fantastic. Part of Billy's job was to make sure those same videos showed in the Anthropology building every week. If nothing new came in he showed the old, nobody minded. The high was like, terrific.

Frey Bartólomeo in Chiapas coordinated a lot of the info circulated around the country. They knew student support was important. Billy agreed. Mexico was an ocean of kids, he could see that without reading statistics. Hell, he was a kid himself. Or he used to be, last year. He giggled. That giggle repositioned him: still a latent kid. He figured if he went back to the US right now, he would be out of the closet as an eternal kid. So he didn't go.

It didn't take much for a kid to live around here, and he hung with students who knew where to go for beer, frijoles with tortillas, free wine and snacks at gallery openings and author readings, free chocolate with sweet bread in the main building. He had his eye on a chica named Rosa, a toughie whose indigenous blouses dangled over her jeans, and whose hair in long braids dangled down her back. Despite his shameless mooching, he was as sharp-boned as he'd been down south, but he bought a pair of new jeans, and sandals to replace his ruined sneakers. She smiled at him.

As the anniversary of the 1968 student massacre approached the campus bloomed with Zapatista signs, slogans, murals on the walls. Zapata's big moustache showed up everywhere; likewise Marcos in his black ski mask and pipe; likewise EZLN tee-shirts. He felt pretty much at home except for his white skin, but lots of kids looked as white as him. The difference? Like, most of them had somewheres to sleep, and he didn't. Out of what Frey gave him, he put aside a few pesos by sleeping on the floor in the computer room. He stashed his bedroll in the supply closet, and was up and out before the cleaning crew arrived at 7:00 A.M..

Thank God Mexico was still a place where people used public baths.

Nobody caught on when he stayed late, doing newspaper layout and design. In fact, he earned a rep for staying on late after others left, long hours, dedication, whatever. And he didn't let anybody smoke in the computer room, no breaking that rule, so at least he slept with clean air, closing his eyes on the endless lines of twisted computer cable, in his own sleeping bag.

His Mexican was pretty good by now, and he sent e-mails in English translation back to Texas. It was weird how he felt a surge of change at his back, well, lots of people, thousands of people, pressing behind him like fans at the fence of an important game. He couldn't predict what might happen, but he figured he'd see it through for a while yet. And there was the chica. She was a couple of years younger than Billy, not too innocent. These girls no way were the simpering Catholic virgins he'd imagined. The necking on campus gave him a constant hard-on, all those mouth to mouth gropes going on in every corner and even on main paths. They just stopped where they stood, and did it in the road. Whew! As soon as he got up his nerve he was next. This was no Emily who would come on to him in a knowing way. But she might accept him in a knowing way, right?

He hung out with a small group of scruffy Socialists who draped themselves over the tables in the local bar. He learned names of men who supported the student massacre in 1968. Luis Echeverría—that guy knew genocide, and he owned responsibility. Only Billy didn't know what genocide meant. Like students were a race of people? Maybe so. President Diaz Ordaz assumed responsibility for what happened in `68 but did nothing to the guilty. Probably thought it wasn't necessary. The army obeyed the civil mandate, even when the order was to kill, but that didn't excuse them from the Geneva Convention. Nowadays who knew who they obeyed, anyway.

The group of kids who took on communications, finding space, setting up machines, getting material in and out, those guys talked like it was yesterday, not thirty years ago. Figured it could happen again, like it was happening in Chiapas. They forgave nobody.

"Yesterday it was repression of students. Today it's repression of indigenous people, not only in Chiapas. Tomorrow they'll prepare the way for neoliberal fascism!" proclaimed Rosa. She stood nearly at his own height, nearly hip to hip, thin like him. Her bones looked frail. Billy liked the way her mouth moved, tasting words. He still had difficulty following more impassioned speeches. Her words spouted full speed like water from a faucet. Cute, though.

"The struggle goes on," Rafael affirmed. "Governments never learn."

Billy could have written the script himself. How about the Gulf War? What was that? It could be any one of a dozen US horror stories, and Socialists everywhere the same.

Rain fell like tanks of water onto them, kept falling. Tlateloco at six in the afternoon. A multicolored waving roof covered the crowd that completely filled La Plaza de Las Tres Culturas. "Today we come to demand justice!"

The garden filled with umbrellas and faces. A black banner in a corner waved its silver letters in spite of the rain. "Only three weeks ago the criminals who run this government hid under the pretext of business secrets." Alvarez Garín was solid. "Today they want to hide crimes they commit under pretext of military security. The illegal repression in which the armed forces of this country participate!"

Billy wasn't born thirty years ago and didn't know anyone here who was. But today's repression. He knew that. He'd been there. 1968. 1998. Then and now. Lies were lies, repression was repression, murder was murder. The faint image of Billy's father floated through his mind. He wondered if his Dad absorbed crimes committed by the Brits before his Da was born. Long memories, they said of the Irish. But look around here! Their feet were soaked, the bottoms of their jeans like sponges absorbed water from the pavement. Long memories.

"Until victory! With justice and dignity!" The crowd shouted. The Polytechnic contingent began to dance, a crazy splashing around, couldn't get wetter. "Zedillo isn't with the Poly, the Poly is Zapatista!"

Tens of thousands swarmed through the street beyond. At 6:05 the Moment of Silence happened, like the world suddenly stopped. Families waited, grandparents, children and grandchildren waited out the minute. Students, teachers, workers. Kids who weren't university but maybe indigenous, maybe remembered with that strange memory of events they never experienced. Billy knew. Generation to generation.

For a moment he felt, like, a time warp. Then as the crowd moved, he spotted Rosa and Rafael moving alongside a student waving a banner. "Why are we feeling nostalgia? We're celebrating the change that's coming. This rally is a wake-up call!"

He tagged along with them, pushing through the stragglers. Marshals still lined the streets, umbrellas making a colorful party under the drizzle. The faces in the street were solemn, serious, happy.

"The presidential power under the PRI always is one boss man, pseudo-democratic," Rosa lectured him. But he already knew. What did she think he'd been doing the past two years? "Corrupt. Supporting caciques who help buy votes."

I know, I know, he muttered in English. Before '68 you hadda ask permission to demonstrate, or to organize. Even to meet in the university cafeteria you needed permission. To use the smallest meeting space you needed a permit. To read different books than what the syllabus offered. To think outside the box. He knew, he knew. Jesus, wasn't it like that everywhere? Today where were you if you objected to Market Capitalism?

Billy was drenched. Rosa beside him lifted her umbrella over him in a kind way, but too late. Even his hands in his pockets were wet. He enjoyed the warmth her body gave off, and tried to decipher the conversation.

"We have to continue the struggle. We have to finish the transition to real democracy." His sandals sloshed in the rain, the leather stretching and flopping. He was not Mexican. He was not Irish either. He was American. But maybe lately he knew he wasn't

American either. Too narrow, too confining. He'd like to call himself a citizen of the world, but it sounded pretentious, fake. Who could he say that to, out loud, Well, I'm a citizen of the world. I don't think so!

A banner beside the road read, "Remember! I remember! We remember! Until there is justice, we are one." So maybe you don't need to say anything, or declare anything. Maybe just be there, like today.

On the other hand, Billy knew it's a pretty big world. How the fuck could anybody support every fight for justice? Man, you couldn't even learn about every fight for justice. All you could know was, when bad shit happens, it happens to poor people. There were a lot of claims out there waiting on his righteous indignation. And he didn't hardly feel any, at least not when he arrived. Some people come born with it, born angry. Not him. But he couldn't remember himself two years ago. Left out of all the fun, whatever fun was. Now he was included, more or less, shit, here he sloshed along the street with thousands of people.

Arm in arm, they were skirting groups with umbrellas jammed together overlapping and buckling, chanting EZLN, EZLN, and Marcos, Marcos.

"The message of the Zapatistas is a gift," Rosa informed him. He tried to keep his feet out of puddles. Many of the placards disintegrated, buckled with rain. On the street as he picked his way he could read crumpled and muddy identities of those who passed ahead of them, the Movimiento Urbano Popular, groups of gays and lesbians, high school groups, vocational school groups. One sign read *Today and always, the anonymous are here.* They passed kids wearing black pasamontañas. Billy wished he'd thought of it. His lank hair lay plastered to his round skull. He was chilly. Maybe wet wool wouldn've helped.

As if Rosa shared his discomfort, she whispered "Let's get inside for a coffee?" A contingent dressed in black ran past. They were toting a huge cloth that read, "Remember the massacre at Mocotlán". They carried a coffin.

"Yeah," Billy agreed. Inside his head spaces opened up like windows into rooms he'd never been. It was too much. From the third floor of the building opposite he could hear shouts, and answering shouts from groups surging past. The monument to the fallen, he could see now, was covered with dripping flowers and wreaths.

"For the rights of indigenous people!" someone shouted. "Education for everyone! Down with militarization, genocide, impunity!" Conversationally Rafael asked, "How are they going to stop the crimes?"

Billy leaned behind Rosa's back to answer, "Don't ask me, you'll just make me cry." He said it in English. He usually reverted to English when he wanted to be snotty, but he always wanted to be snotty when sloganeering got thick. Privately, he preferred quiet discussions of the Zapatistas, where talk stayed calm, and from his post in the yard he sensed how words spiraled upward until consensus came to a head. The emerging leaders had not been hoarse or sweating.

Billy and Rosa ducked into the café and made their way through the crowd to the rear. Rosa's umbrella left a trail of water on the tile floor. A café girl followed everyone with a mop. The tiles were slippery. One young guy stood on a table reading at the top of his lungs, like a theatrical piece. Rosa told him, "He's quoting Marcos."

"'The paint sprayed on walls, the brigades, the lightening-quick calls for meetings...the street as territory for student politics, the other politics, that from below, the new, the struggle, rebellion. The street speaking, discussing, pushing to one side automobiles and loudspeakers.'"

Billy knew the names of Tlateloco, Acteal, Chavajeval, Unión Progreso, Aguas Blancas. He wasn't a leader. The people out in the street weren't leaders either. They were ordinary. The young guy was declaiming, "...at home, at work, in the bus, in a taxi, on horseback, at the machine, in the classroom, in the factory, in church, in a wheel chair," Billy didn't try to absorb the catalogue. Just ordinary, "...in a bar, in the beauty shop, in the football stadium, in the doctor's office, in the laboratory, in offices, in movie studios, in the metro, on radio, on television, in the closet, in whatever colors, with those who painted silently and daily, they raised their hands, an image, a sound. A ticket, a vote, a fist, a thought, a voice to confront government lies and say, 'No, ya no. Ya basta. We don't believe them. We want something better. We need something better. We deserve something better.'" The chanting took on a swollen rhythm like a creek run too high.

Next to him Rosa whispered, "The people. They're following us. They're coming together. You'll see. The Zapatistas won't be alone."

Billy felt it, the wave of energy in the coffee shop. Only, his common sense told him ordinary people wouldn't follow students; better if students followed the Zapatistas. The people would too. The performance guy wasn't much older than him.

Rosa managed to fetch two small cups of black liquid topped with white frothy stuff. It wasn't worth drinking, if what he wanted was to get warm. He looked across at Rosa beseechingly. Thousands marched, from the Zócalo to Tlatelolco to commemorate thirty years. Nobody forgot. Couldn't they go home now? Next to them at the crowded tables an older guy in a wet blue denim shirt proclaimed, "I was there, on the steps of the Chihuahua building, below the orators, and I heard shots. I felt like a trapped rat, I didn't know what to do, where to run…"

"Nobody dared stop to help the wounded," Rosa told him, as if she too had been there. "They didn't have the balls to stay and help." She stirred the white stuff down into her cup, producing a grayish muck. Billy seriously wanted to leave. He wanted to get warm and dry. This was like the ice cream party after the senior prom. It didn't add a thing.

In the front of the café a group began to shout, "Che! Che! Che Guevara!", "Ho Ho! Ho Chi Min!" and "We don't want games we want revolution!" and then "E-zeta-elay-enay! E-zeta-elay-enay!" and "Marcos! Marcos! Marcos!" and "No-que-no, si-que-sí, los asesinos son de PRI!" The noise jarred, rising full blast, taken up table after table in a kind of ecstasy. "I gotta go," Billy said.

He stood. Rosa looked at him with her elbow on the table and her face open for shouting. She half waved. He pushed his way out.

When he passed in front of Garibaldi to cross to Paseo de la Reforma a woman who was not yet born in the year they commemorated, with a red carnation tucked in her cleavage, took the hand of her boyfriend and asked him, "Doesn't this make your skin prickle?"

"It's history," her grinning boyfriend affirmed. Billy shouldered past. "Part of our history, the beginning of the search for democracy, the parting of the waters for Mexico!"

At the entrance to the Anthropology building Billy realized he was locked out. A heavy guard of students on one side faced police on the other, and neither were about to let him or anyone else enter. He hesitated. Across the plaza he saw a guy run with a camera, filming as he went. Impulsively Billy took after him, under the rain which had returned full force.

The man turned and thrust the camcorder into Billy's hand and posed in front of him. "Just keep it going!" he shouted. "I'm trying to capture this!" He began to speak in a deepened announcer-type voice, his hands pocketed in a casual pose.

"The people relive their memories. That's how history is made. Think how people suffered in those years, it's like now. Maybe now it's more overwhelming, or maybe because we stand here in our own living flesh, in this moment. Thirty years of history is nothing, an eye blink."

How had he got back into this? Sucked back into the undertow? Rhetoric with no result? Exhausted to the point of tears Billy held the camera in the rain, and centered it on the speaker, and then on the crowd still streaming past, and then on knots of police. He was in it. Their struggle, my struggle, anybody's struggle. I know, he wanted to say, I know. The softening drizzle fell steadily on candles and wreaths, the crowd, letters placed to remember the dead.

"When we students saw the tanks," the sonorous voice continued,

"We thought they were only to frighten us, but when they began to fire one of my friends fell with a bullet in his chest. He fell at my feet." I know, Billy said.

"We didn't know it was an expanding bullet until he tried to get up. His back dripped a huge bouquet of bloody meat." I know.

"We all began to run. The tanks moved. It didn't matter if you were a kid, if you were old. They came on, and people fell and were crushed. We kids ran, and they took out their bayonets." I know. "They stabbed us like sausages. I owe my life to one of the soldiers who at the moment he was going to stick his bayonet into me he pushed me down into a bush; he whispered to me, Get going. He turned and I saw he was covered with blood. Really, I don't know why he did that." I know, Billy said, I know.

The man went silent, looking around as if he expected to see blood. Was that it? Billy panned over to the banner at the man's left, "Martires del Movimiento Estudiantil de 1968." The rain had penetrated the fabric and it hung motionless, dripping from its bottom hem.

"The defense of authority," the man revived, speaking to nobody in particular. He and Billy stood as if in the center of an island, people still streaming by parted on each side. "The suppression of anyone who questions it. Same for the railroad workers' strike in March of 1959, or the universities of Michoacán and Sonora, where they brought in troops. Defending at all costs the antidemocratic regimes, restrictions of liberties, abolishment of constitutional rights…" He looked as dazed and wiped out as Billy. It was a speech he must have given many times before, coming out by rote.

"The technocrats of today don't hesitate to use armed force to face political problems like the conflict in Chiapas. Thirty years after the massacre in the Plaza de Las Tres Culturas, terrorism goes on. Today, now. The army follows illegal police, on their own or by the president's command. Officials deny responsibility, want to cover it over. Bloody repression!"

He gave out again, and in his silence Billy muttered I know, I know. The knowledge felt heavy. He had to lie down pretty soon. Or fall. "Like in Mocotlán."

The man's face cleared, and he was back in the present, looking at Billy who still held the camera. So that he saw through the lens the pale face come into focus. "At eighteen years of age I was absolutely sure I could help this country change, not to mention the whole world. Justice and democracy. I understood people needed it and listened for it." He shuffled toward Billy, and removed the camera from his wet cramped fingers. "You look frozen."

"I am, for sure. I need a place to dry off and sleep." The man made a gesture with his head for Billy to follow.

In the tiny apartment on Donceles the man introduced himself as Paco, and brought a dry shirt for Billy to change into. Paco was still someplace else, as far as Billy could see. He wasn't finished unloading. "Because we were the anonymous, we did paintings, we went to secret meetings in markets, hung banners, got out propaganda mimeographed in the University in one school or another." Billy raised his eyebrows, that's what he was doing. "We took risks. We weren't fooling around. We found a level of reality we didn't understand, not really." He pulled a wool blanket out of the closet while Billy stared at him. There was no bed, but the ceramic tile would do, as usual. Paco seemed unable to stop talking. Billy's open face sucked out of him all his words. "We were the nation's activists. No classes, but it was a time when we studied, investigated, discussed change, all that. Information got around, you know? Yes, he knew. Every believer carried news. "Because it was serious, it wasn't school stuff. We had to comprehend politics, the social situation, wealth, poverty, family, religion, everything," Billy nodded. He spread the blanket, avoiding the area where he and Paco tracked water. "We questioned everything."

"And what you did, that had an effect?"

"The Movement grew, the government threatened us, but we continued. The Movement existed. Most of us moved out of our family homes."

"And it was really great, right?"

Paco grinned. "Yes. It was marvelous. We were sure we could pull it off, the changes, the strikes. A dream like all dreams."

"Well, it sure ended rough," Billy agreed. What else could he say? His eyes were closing despite his best efforts to remain an alert audience for this poor shit from the old days. If you could really distinguish. That was the scary part. Nothing changed. At least they won't need to shoot me to wake me up.

"Thirty years later it doesn't feel like I won or lost. I'm alive, right? And free of blame."

"You did what you thought was right," Billy mumbled.

"Every time a helicopter goes over I duck, you know. We never get over these things. If someone describes the history of Tlatelolco I start to cry. But now I see we lost, when they shoot at Acteal or Mocotlán. The Indios shoot their brothers in the back in the cañadas or inside churches."

"The caciques have them by the balls," Billy smothered a yawn. "In the interest of eating. The government announces a new economic crisis every six years why they can't do anything for the poor, and denounces the thieves. The thieves never are punished, naturally."

"Worse! There's never any crime! Stuff disappears, nobody knows where, books don't arrive, medicines don't arrive at hospitals, there's no work for months at a time." Paco merely glanced at Billy whose eyes were closed. "People have to tighten their belts, they say. They say it while they're at the movies, or concerts, while they're at discos. They eat, they have houses and they say people must tighten their belts. Their children don't live in the streets. They don't work in the fields."

On the floor Billy was profoundly silent. Paco spoke on, amazingly upright. "The country never takes care of the hungry. Democracy and voting don't effect privatization of workers' pension funds, the breakdown of the national education system, all the inequities. The young people, they don't struggle for anything, they don't want anything. They're apathetic," he informed Billy, who slept like a fallen hero after the day of student frenzy. "Because among other things, they have no future, no jobs." He lowered himself into the room's only chair.

Paco bent and unlaced his wet shoes. He pulled them off and set about stuffing them with newspaper pulled from a pile on the table. He placed the plumped shoes carefully in the center of the remaining papers. "I'm forty-eight years old now," he informed his unconscious audience. "When I was eighteen my mother told me I couldn't have children and at the same time maintain my dignity. I believed her. I still do." He stood and moved to the door of the little bedroom. "We're afraid," he flung back over his shoulder. "The government opted for a final solution to the student movement then, and to the Zapatista movement now. The exemplary assassination. Jailing leaders. Terrorism. The fear was as justified as the indignation. So was the impotence." He vanished into the dark room.

In the dim dawn light Billy climbed to his feet groaning. He found the small bathroom with the usual naked light bulb and pissed into the stained bowl. There was no sound from the other room. He folded the blanket, took off the dry shirt and exchanged it for his own, still damp. He could make it back to campus.

By seven a.m. he stood in front of the Anthropology building, where guards were unlocking doors for the cleaning crew. He moved inside hoping he could grab a dry shirt and a few more pesos from his stash, without being noticed. There'd be a lotta news to put out, but he felt totally starved, and if he couldn't find a free breakfast he'd hafta buy one.

40

Woman in Red

It was raining in the late afternoon.

Mildly annoyed that she hadn't worn her tevas and the rain would surely ruin her leather sandals, Constance clambered up the stairs of La Catedrál. Her wet hat-brim flopped. Above her she viewed women and children sheltering under the church portico. They looked in turn at her get-up and perhaps laughed, laughed quietly behind their faces, until she made eye contact and grinned. She pulled the hat off. Much better. She acknowledged she looked like a plucked gray bird, and they agreed. Smiles all around.

The domed interior of the cathedral resonated with sound.

Gilted paintings of saints and bishops gleamed in the half light. Constance loved the Tree of Life motif, despite saints and bishops whose pitying glances implied nothing could be changed on earth. Along the walls original scroll designs, work of indigenous artisans, still lingered, faded, eroded by the centuries. She secretly believed the vibration of deep organ chords washed away some of the paint.

On Sundays the massive doors stood open. People who took refuge from the rain or from their worries quietly occupied the pews, and when she craned her neck to see the organ in the high loft, several seated people of San Gregorio craned also, as if never before they wondered where the booming chords came from.

It was an antique instrument, 1639 if tourist propaganda could be trusted. She placed her hat beside her on the pew and stretched her throat backward. A woman in the loft played changes of keys, pulling aging levers with obvious effort, sliding sideways along the bench. Her dark cranberry dress bunched under her as she shifted. Perhaps practicing. A concert was scheduled in two weeks, masterworks. Constance calculated the date. Harry would enjoy attending.

The silence of the cathedral lived beneath the throbbing music. How could that be? The silence of side chapels, prayers, statues of soundless saints. Then she realized the music had indeed ceased, and the woman beside the organ stood aside for a man to replace her. The lights behind the organ pipes revealed him briefly, his compact figure and rounded head. His dark hair was held back in a pony tail with something invisible, an elastic perhaps. He didn't look Mexican but perhaps he is, Constance thought. That's Merwin. He's in the loft with permission to play their three hundred sixty year old organ. I didn't know.

In the quiet pause between compositions a steady throb filled the loudspeakers, spaced as evenly as a heartbeat.

It's God's heartbeat, and then she felt embarrassed, although she hadn't spoken aloud. Harry so constantly lived in her mind she imagined he knew her waywardness. God's heartbeat indeed! Her attention followed the woman in red now descending the narrow stairway. She carried a square cloth bag with cotton tassels dangling from its bottom corners. As Constance watched, she slung the strap over her shoulder and moved toward the church portals. Her walk and the shape of her cropped black hair were familiar. Of course. Why do we never recognize people we know well when they appear in unfamiliar roles?

On whim Constance followed, pausing at the doors to watch the lithe figure descend the stairs and cross the patio. On the street a car waited, a long black vehicle. The woman, folding her dress under her, stepped neatly in as the door opened. The light changed and the car pulled away while Constance stood on the pale green squares of granite.

What had she expected? Behind her the organ rolled triumphantly over a Bach prelude. She contemplated returning to the cathedral to speak with Merwin. But suddenly hundreds of indigenous people swirled around her like a dust storm. A march appeared from somewhere, from nowhere, in the city streets.

Constance was astonished by the relentlessness of these people, repressed for five hundred years and now not a damned minute without protest. If ever she'd wondered how people walked on hot coals, this left her equally dumbfounded. She just finished digesting news of the massive protest commemorating the 1968 student massacres in Mexico City, and here came more, in San Gregorio.

Hands thrust placards into the air. They protested the illegitimate governments of Zedillo and Albóres. The banner read MILITARY OUT OF CHIAPAS. The limo had pulled away only a moment ahead of the crowd.

Dozens of blue-clad police in front of the Municipal Palace cradled automatic rifles at their chests. The marchers shouted. Development Crumbs Buy the Conscience of the People and Divide Them. Thank god no military were present. The police were one among half a dozen other special uniformed forces, but at least not military. By which she meant, not Ignacio. He must be in the limo with Carmen, speeding away from the area.

The government was opening roads across Chiapas, to make the isthmus accessible. Soon. Harry said it meant that personnel and tanks could enter the Zapatista zone. The international outcry against repression forced the government to be more clever. They claimed it was development.

Zedillo and Albóres Prepare for War and the Destruction of Our Towns. A man placed a flyer in her hand as she stood.

Constance shook off the deep organ chords pulling at her heart, and the revelation of Carmen in a role Constance did not expect. La lucha sigue, sigue! the crowd chanted. Ignacio whisked his wife away. Not so Constance, who clutched her canvas hat and gawked. Her legs felt thin, her arms heavy. The flyer in her hand read: They speak of peace and dialogue but at the same time they attack indigenous communities, assassinating, persecuting, torturing, throwing in prison innocent people. They have prepared a grand war of extermination.

Constance folded the flyer. Its content long-since loaded onto the memory board in her head. She turned toward home, swept into the stream of chanters. Students from UNAM down from Mexico City walked alongside the protesters. When did they ever find time to study?

"Three hundred PRI men are waiting for us in the park," a tall skinny redhead warned her. He spoke English, and clearly knew she did. "Be careful." Mexican law forbad foreign participation in Mexican protests, so what was he doing?

The organizers led the crowd down another street to avoid confrontation. Gratefully Constance turned the corner with them. "We didn't come for trouble," her informant shouted in Spanish over the heads of marchers. "We came in peace!" Many protesters wore Zapatista masks and kerchiefs over their faces. A banner with the image of Emiliano Zapata floated by with its message: "Albóres no es gobierno sino un asesino de campesinos."

Constance kept pace behind a dog, the thinnest and oldest dog ever seen in San Gregorio. The dog carried a small banner around its neck, dragging it in the dust. Constance could make out the letters, which she thought meant, "Albóres, don't be what I am!"

The crowd surged and shouted. "If there's no solution there's always revolution!" "Zapata lives, the struggle goes on!" "Viva el Subcomandante Marcos!" "EZLN, EZLN!"

She felt breathless and roused, as she always did in crowds and demonstrations. The power of the people moved her. But she mustn't appear involved. The visas were in the mail, the immigration officer told her; yet with or without them she better be careful. In the middle of the block she detached herself, leaning against a wall. Her pulse raced. The dog ran ahead, and abruptly the march turned a corner. If she waited they would all pass and turn. Why on earth had she walked along in the first place? But how could one not, she slowed her breathing. How could one not follow.

The wiry men marching were short, brown, shabbily dressed. The covered their faces defiantly with red kerchiefs. Some wore stiff hats she thought of as campesino hats, some were protected from the sun—when had it quit raining?—by baseball caps. Their feet in sandals showed thick flaking calluses. Women marched alongside the men. Some wore traditional wrapped wool skirts, some a scarlet ribboned dress. Most wore ill-fitting nylon hand-sewn dresses and skirts. Many carried babies in their rebozos. Many also hid their faces with the trademark red bandana. How could one not.

Several thousand marchers flowed by, circling four sides of the central streets and back to the zócalo. On this street no police were visible. Half a dozen shopkeepers stood in their doorways. Nobody was working. Some nodded. A few raised their fists. Others watched in silence.

"The government thinks the Zapatistas live in the jungle." A woman paused beside Constance, resting her back against the same wall. "But they are right here in the city, no?"

Constance nodded. Her Spanish didn't let her enter a discussion, but she understood. The woman's gray hair was braided with the usual campesina ribbons, but her clothes were those of a vendor, a dress covered with an apron. Constance checked the woman's feet. Yes, she wore plastic shoes, did not go barefoot.

"The government thinks all the indigenous are backward." She looked boldly at Constance. Her dark eyes flashed. "They don't oppose progress, but military encampments keep them hostage. And where no Zapatistas go, they can weep for years, because nobody will ever enter those towns to build a road!"

"Yes, I know," Constance responded in English. "Because my husband is laying water pipe up in Cuates de Santa Ana, and he says roads are hardly passable in the rain. So I know." She looked at the woman beside her in sympathy, and at the blank stare she suddenly remembered. The woman couldn't understand her. Relieved, she put out her hand. The woman put down her basket and took it.

The woman said, "I am a Tzotzil woman." Constance nodded again. The woman continued, "In our village nobody could survive. There was not enough money to buy even a kilo of tortillas for the family. We came here to eat." She held up her basket of embroidered cotton blouses. "That is the justice I want. To live in peace, and have food to eat."

Again Constance nodded. How could one not. She forgot the black limousine rushing through the zócalo. The street was returning to normal. Young tourists with backpacks and ankle-high boots moved toward the square in the wake of the marchers. The students with placards were peeling off. She noted other Americans among them, like the tall boy, but not Merwin. She wondered if music still resounded in the cathedral.

41

Martin Buys a Moto

Lifting her hand in a goodbye salute to the Tzotzil woman, Constance made her way along the street. Shops were re-opening and daily occupations returning to normal. She spotted Martin ahead of her, and wondered where he might be going. It was unmistakably him, the thin torso and pipe-stem jeans beneath a long white flowing shirt.

Martin stepped up into a doorway and vanished. Constance came abreast and peered in to see what Martin could possibly purchase on this street in San Gregorio. It was a Honda motorcycle shop! Well, my goodness! He was a whole lot crazier than she took him for, if he planned to travel around Chiapas by moto!

Despite thousands of delegates marching to celebrate the new emergence of the EZLN to meet with COCOPA, Connie's judgment wobbled, confronted by so much unreality. Or unverifiability. Or misinformation, propaganda, lies. Endless bombardment with no certain truth. The endless crowds and shouting swept her away every time, but what for? The more the Zapatistas called Civil Society to rally, the more frequent the expulsions, more mysterious deaths on the roads of local people like those poor Ch'ol men, more interference with international observers. That she knew. And now Martin? Up to what? If Martin planned some wild escapade, well, he surely added to her sense of unreality! A religious Witness? On a motorcycle? Martin?

Really, as she gazed up and down the street, she and Martin were the only visible foreigners. Few natives, or foreigners either, patronized the shops. She glimpsed gleaming chrome and bright red bodies and fenders of motorcycles. They startled, like bodies from another planet. She shook her head, and continued walking.

Martin in fact decided to travel through Chiapas. Partly he followed the dictate of Holy Master: get out there and do it, as HM would say. HM was giving him another chance to merge with the Absolute, to send his spirit into the atmosphere with its call for peace and brotherhood. It crept into Martin's mind that he'd always wanted a cycle. And if HM was paying… Various fantasies appealed to Martin. Certainly travel by levitation was one. But the Lone Ranger was an all-time favorite because he could ride away into the sunset with everyone wondering who was that masked stranger.

Most of Martin's time he wasn't inventing himself as a biker armed with love and goodness. Mostly he wrestled with guilt pounding on him. It ground down his flesh and bones. First Robert John years ago slain by Martin's powerful thoughts, and now Vera and Louis who'd shared their coffee, slain by him playing hooky.

Martin, who in his youth received ample proof of the importance of thoughts, lived devastated by his folly as a man. He left to see the other side of the road! Two dead instead of one! Twice the impact!

Tears sprang to his eyes. Bracing himself with one hand against the stucco wall, he paused in the motorcycle shop's doorway to repeat his mantra. When he entered, his mind was calm. The gleaming machines shocked him. They looked made to show off, machines designed for fantasies, to maybe do trick stunts, death-defying leaps across an abyss between cliffs! Martin never rode a motorcycle before, and he suspected there might be a lot to learn, about maintaining the machine and not falling off.

Inside the shop the only other person was an indifferent seated young fellow who averted his eyes from Martin's emaciated torso and feet in cracked sandals. Martin didn't look like a tourist, except those druggies who drifted down from Estados Unidos New Yersey wearing rotted jeans and matted hair. The kid assessed Martin surreptitiously and decided Martin's hair looked too clean. Actually, Martin didn't have hair to speak of, he was bald except for the fringe tonsure. A bald man in Chiapas also was rare. The young fellow considered other diseases besides drug addiction, and came up with none that suited. The spectacle before him didn't look a maricón, with that kind of disease either. Therefore he reluctantly got to his feet and spoke to Martin.

He said, "Buen' día'." That sufficed. The next move was up to the customer.

Martin carefully circled the motorcycles. He ventured to pat one or two, like animals. They didn't object. Domesticated. Looking at the young guy he asked permission with his eyebrows, and receiving a nod in return, lifted one leg over a bike and sat on the leather. No, definitely not. By now the young man thought maybe he had a real customer and pulled around another model. This one had a wide seat, wider wheels. More like a farm horse than a race horse. Martin nodded. They were making progress.

"Have you experience with this machine?"

"No. Not yet. Can you show me?"

"No problem!" The fellow promptly locked the front door and gestured for Martin to follow, apparently out a rear exit. For a moment Martin felt a stab of fear and then, reawakened to how he so recently screwed up, decided his life was worthless anyway, and followed. His new friend handed him a large purple helmet. Martin sat behind the guy and clutched his waist, until the kid turned around and commanded from under his matching purple plastic, "Not so hard! You're cracking my ribs! Did you have a bicycle when you were a kid?"

"No," Martin replied, "my brother did. He let me learn to ride his."

"So it's much the same. Lean into it!"

Martin leaned. His teacher zoomed and revved and spun around corners. Martin, nauseous in the darkness beneath the big helmet, acquiesced. He figured he could learn by himself, if he could just get the knack of how to start and stop.

Finally his guide halted. Martin raised the helmet and blinked. They had halted above the city, gazing down from a hill into the streets. "It looks peaceful from up here."

"As they say. But don't be fooled" his friend said. His name was Pepe. His skin was lighter than Martin usually saw hereabouts. "CO-COPA and CONAI are a fraud. Zedillo wants to stall while the indigenous are exterminated. The Zapatistas call on Civil Society again. Perhaps you saw?"

Martin saw. Although he knew the Zapatistas rejected the government counterproposal, a gutted redrawing of the law upon which indigenous rights and culture rested. His own task was to encourage love and peace. But look at this guy—a mop of brown hair and a green silk shirt open on his chest, a Chiapas citizen involved in incredible events. To speak to Martin about it—hey, he must take Martin for a peacenik. Martin warmed with pleasure.

"Never mind the peaceful hill we sit on. Down there, life ends like a chili snatched from a vine. Zedillo acts so neither peace nor justice with dignity will arrive on indigenous soil."

Can you imagine anybody in the US spouting something like that? Come on!

"How do you know?" Martin asked.

"A three page letter signed by Marcos and circulated by the EZLN. It accuses Zedillo of authorizing the present low intensity warfare. All police and military and security forces in the chain of command understand el presidente!"

Instantly Martin, firmly enrolled in Meditators for Peace, joined Civil Society. Briefly he considered prohibitions against serving two masters, but probably that didn't apply. HM told him to get out there. Holy Master's incredible foresight at work again! Martin could meditate on the road, could emit his good vibes up close and personal. He brushed road dust off his jeans and sandals, and then for good measure polished the purple helmet on his sleeve.

Marcos wrote that a bridge between the Zapatistas and the National Congress should have been built by COCOPA, formed by the National Congress for that very purpose. But the executive branch refused to permit it. Peering out from under the fresh weight of his purple helmet Martin envisioned the road his mission would follow.

Respect! The Zapatistas earned respect from the people, no doubt. Even the moto salesman knew Zedillo broke his word, refused to honor the San Andrés Accords. So the bridge must be built between ordinary people and the Zapatistas. The national government would see how the people voted!

Pepe wheeled the motorcycle one hundred eighty degrees, scuffing his feet on the rough ground. Time to go. Martin remounted behind him.

"You want to buy this machine?" Pepe asked over his shoulder.

"Yes."

"Things are not so easy in southern Mexico right now, you know? Not so happy in Chiapas? You will be robbed and murdered. I just inform you, you know I want to sell this machine."

"Do you always read letters from the EZLN? From Marcos?"

"How not. They're everyplace. Very noble. Do you need to urinate before we start? No? Well, hold the moto for me a moment." He dismounted and for the first time Martin held in his own hands the metal steed he would ride into the distant sunset.

Pepe returned to his seat and took the reins again. He lowered his helmet, and turned briefly to Martin. "This war. This is a struggle for democracy, liberty and justice in Mexico. Every honest Mexican man or woman participates however possible. Not just indigenous people!"

"So how do you participate?"

"I sell motorcycles. To foreigners like you." Martin, behind him on the black leather seat, couldn't see Pepe's smile of happiness. "Do you need saddlebags? A waterproof case top class mounted on the rear? Tools? I don't sell boots, but I tell you in friendship you can't travel on a moto in sandals. Your feet will vanish off the ends of your legs."

"Yes," Martin said. "Yes." He was ready for whatever might come.

42

The Christmas Season

By eight o'clock Harry was up and dressed for nearly two hours. The bells, the rockets, the band accompanying the procession in the street beyond their patio roused him from a dream where he dynamited rock to lay pipe. He woke because he knew they couldn't get away with using explosives, and the men were already meticulously hammering and chiseling.

He heard the truck's bell at the far end of the street, and the high cry naranjas. He grabbed the plastic shopping bag from its place behind the kitchen door and stepped through the iron gateway.

"Here," he said to the woman, placing a ten peso coin in her open palm. As the truck moved away he returned through the patio toting the heavy shopping bag. Connie wasn't in the kitchen yet. He spilled the oranges into the dishpan and poured disinfectant water over them. They floated. He examined their star-form stems. The fruit rolled belly-up, gently bobbing like fat green porpoises, some mottled to a yellowish fade. With his index finger he set one after another spinning, the water a magic purification.

Little here in San Gregorio was as it appeared, or as he supposed when he agreed to come. Hey, he came to see oranges twirl. No way to live, one of those retired Sunday golfers safe at home mouthing platitudes about programs for the poor and downtrodden. He wanted to outlive dead Liberal platitudes. Well, living involved accepting an element of luck, beyond science. He hated luck. But was glad when it came his way. He didn't understand the life around them. It twirled like purification, it slipped between luck and magic. Death seemed more real. Less real. But it's all real, right? This mornings' tubas and drums, flags and flowers that appeared happy and light-hearted although he thought more likely death-defiant. The incessant banging of rockets and firecrackers, like kids. Because their lives were short and serious. They repeated old rituals, they tied their babies to their bodies in old carrying ways. They dressed up their little boys like the campesino Juan Diego who saw in a vision the Virgin at Guadalupe, they painted moustaches above tiny damp pink mouths; while children in the countryside repeated their fathers' slogans. Continuity glued the people together. Like everywhere. Half real, half smoke and mirrors.

He could contribute some science, gained from his years of dams and highways.

He set up the little plastic apparatus they used for juicing, and sliced five oranges. He placed two glasses on the oilcloth-covered kitchen table, and began to work for the sweet odor of juice.

He didn't have much faith in Connie's intuitions these days. For one thing, the guys she brought home to feed. Martin with his glazed blue eyes, Merwin with his grant from UNESCO—yuh. He couldn't guess what Connie was up to. Merwin hooked up with Carmen. What did Connie think of that? What was she meddling in? As he twisted the orange his eyebrows shot up at the futile question, ridging his forehead. They'd gone up into the mountains together. Carmen's village was in Ch'ol territory. Two Ch'ol were murdered on the road. Any cultural patrimony up there would have to be discovered by digging.

And that goofy guru, fresh from peace-keeping with a double assassination to think about. Then Ignacio to reckon with.

Harry stopped speaking about his work if Ignacio were present, or when Carmen was nearby, and finally he wondered if he should say anything to Constance. Was he paranoid? Ignacio was a bad apple. If Connie couldn't admit it, her problem shouldn't get him.

Constance emerged from the bathroom with her hair wet, braiding the side loops Aida bestowed on her more than a year ago. He watched her clip them atop her head. A different look. The first time she'd gone with him to a foreign country on a job, and it changed her.

He was glad he fetched the oranges. Connie smiled when she saw the juice.

She sat down and held up her glass in salute.

Off behind them they heard a strange gurgle. Harry went.

"Water's pouring through the bathroom ceiling," he reported. "Weren't you just in there? Did you hear anything?"

"What's she doing up there?" Constance answered. "Filling the water tank, I suppose. At least I've already washed." She fluffed the ends of her gray streaked hair.

They listened for a few minutes to water dripping on tile.

"Did you move the towels?"

"And toilet tissue," Harry responded.

"Okay." Nevertheless she finally stood up and leaned into the bathroom without putting her feet on wet tile. The gush of water slowed to an evil trickle, making its way through cracks increasingly visible in the ceiling where plaster met the open roof windows.

Washing or brushing her hair, many days Constance heard

sounds on neighboring roofs or in patios or the street. And now as she listened she recognized, tapped in regular intervals, the muffled sound of a hammer on pipes. "She's a prisoner of this," Constance thought. "She's tapping out a message."

What this referred to, she didn't know.

Nor could she guess what the message might be.

She returned to find Harry chewing a bolillo, the crumbs from the hard crust gathering in the hair on his chest where the shirt opened. He followed her glance and brushed at them. They fell onto his belly, and some into the shirt opening above it. They'll be in our bed, Constance mused without rancor. The desperation of Carmen inclined her to appreciate what she had.

"Harry, you must be one of the most intrepid men I know."

"Why so?" He smiled.

"Because you not only sleep nude in an earthquake zone," she answered. "you work all day with bread crumbs inside your shirt." She was certain pale beige crumbs nestled on his chest.

"What's that to do with bravery? I'm no hair shirt!"

"Me neither," she agreed. "So I just thought I'd mention it before bedtime." He smiled, relishing her innuendo, and brushed at himself again.

"The ceiling? Nothing we can do. Later I'll tell Carmen it needs fixing."

"Fine. I'm sure she'll stay up there all day."

"Yes. Do you suppose she sleeps on the roof?" They laughed. But it wasn't funny. And this damn party was coming up. Harry didn't object when Connie said she wanted a party; after all, they'd been living in San Gregorio eighteen months. It crossed Harry's mind from time to time they might stay here forever. Connie didn't miss snow. As foreigners, they should be hospitable to others in the same boat and establish a social life. Saying so, she worried that Harry might think she complained about loneliness.

"Because it's Christmas," Constance implored, in the face of his unresponsiveness. But she was not transparent. A change took place in the past month that Harry couldn't put his finger on. He used to think he and Constance were alike. She was changing, and he couldn't be so certain he was, too. Dimly he understood that some people never change; they were set in childhood and more or less stayed that way, a lifetime of steady rewards for similar endeavors. He didn't want to admit it, he feared he fit that category. Even though he took on this adventure, there were a dozen similar well-rewarded adventures behind him. Yet his sense of rightness had altered. Dignidad, he supposed. Maybe it's not possible to live in a situation like this, in the midst of deep social change, without some change in yourself?

"Okay," he agreed. "Let's do it." They would send Judith and her husband a funny greeting card by e-mail. Gifts for the grandsons when they flew home to Ann Arbor. You wouldn't purchase anything here for an American child.

Around noon Carmen descended from the roof and knocked at their door. Constance took her in to look at the bathroom ceiling, and while Carmen's head was up-tilted Constance gazed not at the water but like so many times before, at Ignacio's wife.

Carmen's face showed the slow erosion of whatever was eating it. Her skin faded weekly, ever closer to the color of raw clay. Something was chewing out Carmen's substance, because for all that Carmen played the dutiful wife, she had a thing going with Merwin, didn't she. Constance didn't think Carmen would be eaten with grief if Ignacio disappeared. On the contrary. It couldn't be pleasant living with a man like that. Social obligations compelled every act.

Nevertheless, Constance herself could not shake Ignacio's sexual pull, a sense of long-quiescent internal tide flowing in his direction, sweeping her along. She felt it with her eyes closed while Harry patted her breasts, and made little huffy noises. She tried to not imagine him, but Ignacio's daemon entered her.

"Sometimes good guys do bad deeds. Sometimes bad guys do good deeds. It doesn't pay to look at the person. Just look at the deed. If you separate the doer from the deed, it's easier to evaluate. And reject or accept."

Harry told her that, years back when he came home from Saudi Arabia. Some local fiefdom run by an Arab who was building a university for women. Because he loved his daughter, who couldn't attend school with men. Was that a good deed? Building a segregated university because of his daughter, with money from oil, not exactly his, but his by the power to take it?

She guessed so, but wasn't sure. The university stood new and modern, superficially a good deed. That was the problem. All these Band-Aids. Nothing ever clear. Her sense of right and wrong, for example. Their vanished faith that governments could solve problems. Governments made problems. What did she really know of Nacho's deeds? She never imagined he did good deeds, but how could she continue teaching him if she admitted his bad ones? Would Carmen re-plaster and repaint the ceiling in time for their Christmas party? Although the party would solve nothing.

Abruptly Constance realized she spoke aloud. Carmen turned toward her with a glimmer of interest in her eyes. "A party for Americans?"

Embarrassed and trapped by good manners, Constance offered, "Of course you are invited." Carmen, and by unavoidable extension, Ignacio. She hoped Harry would cope with his fury when he found out what she'd done. Ignacio in their home wasn't the same as Ignacio the landlord.

In her young heart the aging Constance wrestled her infatuation. Of necessity she loved her students, her wards. In forty years

,only Johnson was evil. Because he didn't analyze. He followed orders. Constance knew right from wrong, she recognized evil: damaging other people, damaging life.

But something possessed her. Ignacio's will-power took her, or was it some natural force, like menstruating and ovulating. Producing sperm. Fucking. Marking his turf. Whatever it was, it lurked within Ignacio like a viper in a cage. His determination to go to the USA for training. It was postponed again to spring, but sooner or later, he'd go and return with even more power: external, recognized, hailed. Hailed. Because he has a deformity. But we all have deformities! Was his deformed ear a symptom of hidden will-power?

And then she was frightened. Because she liked that sense of power, and in Ignacio it engendered danger, maybe sadism. Yes. Harry avoided speaking to Ignacio. Harry would know she put them in jeopardy with her stupid invitation. Worse. Ignacio in their home.

"The wealth of the poor is community," Aida declared. "And community depends on women. They stay, they maintain the culture." She plucked at her simple blue dress. It hung loosely, and Constance noted that wherever Aida had gone for the past two months, she'd lost weight. Her full face now shallowed beneath her cheekbones. Other women present looked not much better. Certainly not Carmen, who as usual kept busy doing nothing. Despite her professed interest she ignored the American men. Merwin stayed at the far end of the room. He glanced her way and Carmen gazed at the bowl of chopped nopal salad.

The American reporter Emily resembled a war orphan, with clipped pale hair and colorless face. The party was advertised by word of mouth, an American open house to observe the Christmas season. Several Chiapaneco neighbors were included to mitigate the presence of Ignacio. Doña Consuela of the wonderful bread, the dressmaker and her husband and daughter. She hoped Ignacio wouldn't arrive in uniform. Harry told the neighbors Americans celebrated the winter solstice. Harry thought that would cover all their idiosyncrasies.

And he instructed her to find some good dance music. The less conversation the better.

"People think the indigenous organized to resist NAFTA, but it was a lot more and a lot sooner," proclaimed Merwin. "Armed rebellion doesn't pop overnight." Aida nodded. "I just hope they don't equate UNESCO with corporate terrorism, a là World Bank." He growled, holding his beer at shoulder height, and looked past it to the table where Carmen stood. Music in the background didn't drown him out. Other guests circled between table and sofa.

"There's a new kind of community forming. Seventy-three percent of the Mexican population believe in the Zapatista cause," Frank half-smiled at Aida. "They took a poll." The three spoke congenially, sipping their beer and chewing on nachos. The third man joined them, uninvited but not excluded.

"The sad lesson the indigenous give the world," Ignacio spoke carefully in his new English, "is that communality does not permit advances. Only one strong man, or a strong family, can pull a town into new and real progress." Dressed in a black turtle neck and slacks, he stood between the two American men. He followed Merwin's eyes.

Constance, on the other side of the room, watched as Ignacio turned his glance. It was impossible not to see. A faint rosy stain enlivened Carmen's skin. Constance felt her stomach lurch. It's gone that far. When had that happened?

"Show them progress is better than the old ways?" asked Harry, who despite all his promises to himself to stay clear, leaned into the group to hand another beer to Frank. "Maybe they know what they need."

"Or show them something worse," interjected Merwin at the

same time. He glared at Ignacio without looking again in Carmen's direction.

Harry had moved the kitchen table into the living room to serve supper. Carmen stood quietly by the table, using a spatula to move tamales from casserole to plates. Emily joined her, and they spoke. Everyone was drinking; more beer and two bottles of red wine waited unopened on the table. They were socializing, that's what mattered. The myth of friendship and peace toward men of goodwill. Doña Consuela perched like a tiny beaming Buddha next to her basket of sweet cakes. A successful party! Constance wasn't responsible for Merwin's actions.

The apartment looked nice, she thought. Two clay bowls stood heaped with fresh fruits, red, orange, yellow and green, on the end tables. On the window ledge flickered a line of three votive candles, with shiny tin angels flanking them. Flowers on the coffee table. It was nice, she applauded herself, without being gaudy. Too bad Mexicans equated American taste with crappy Taiwanese Santa Clauses. Is that the progress Ignacio is talking about.

Merwin asked, "And what do you have in mind, when you mention a new reality, Colonel? Many believe Chiapas remains stuck in a pre-revolutionary feudal model. Land reform, for example, never became reality here."

Ignacio appraised Merwin. "We think of bringing new investments, you know. There's oil. And of course our magnificent forest."

"Whose magnificent forests do you refer to? And whose oil?"

Constance interrupted. "Nobody's dancing, but I have a CD of some wonderful baroque organ music, shall I put it on?"

The men drew apart. Frank answered for them, "Yes, Ma'am! Please. Let's enjoy the Peace of Christmas, by all means. You know a young French couple were shot to death recently, out in a community?"

Martin, seated on the sofa said nothing. He looked wan.

"I'm keeping track," Aida answered softly, ignoring Ignacio. "After Mocotlán." Aida really wished Frank would dance with her, but fat chance. She linked her arm in his. He was sipping, not guzzling, and looked clear-headed.

Emily drained her wine. She'd scarcely spoken since she arrived, and wasn't sure why she came. She drifted from the table through small knots of men and women. Looking for Billy, maybe, her boy toy. He hadn't showed up, at least not yet; she didn't know if he was in San Gregorio or out in the countryside. She wasn't after sex now. She only wanted to say something to him. Maybe that he had been kind to her. Thank him, for when she needed him. She felt the weight now of following José. That need. That was sexual but not sex. It was heavy as the hand of fate.

"There'll be another uprising, sure as hell."

"But it can be averted by positive thinking." Martin stood up, back on the job, mindful of his obligation after failure to be the eternal optimist saving the world. His recovered benevolence showered on them. He encouraged it to flow directly from his Life Force.

"Let's not talk about rebellion right now. Frank," Constance drew him closer to the music. And she whispered under the throb of the organs, "This is a Public Security colonel. Ignacio." Frank had already seen. He knew that ear. He wondered why the man showed up in the home of Harry and Constance. "He's the husband of Carmen, our landlady."

Ignacio went to the table and picked up a plate. He murmured something in Spanish to Carmen, who nodded, and handed him another beer.

"The indigenous know how to solve their own problems. Land, education and health. That's the short list." Merwin, ignoing Connie's attempt to divert him with his cherished organ music, confronted

Ignacio. Frank kept out of the way. Merwin stood with his legs apart, his chest thrust forward. He was nearly even in height to Ignacio, they could have been brothers. Neither Ignacio's ear nor Merwin's pony-tailed hair disguised their features and bones. Carmen moved from behind the table. Constance's view was blocked, and then she overheard, "Because kids there die of curable illnesses!"

"The whole world looks for alternative education. Why stop the EZLN? They do something for their own people the government won't do." That was Harry.

"Land's the eternal problem in Chiapas. Business likewise; problems are worse because commerce is globalized. Nothing brings in enough income, not coffee, not pineapple, not sugar. Nothing. They need the local market." Who spoke? She couldn't see. Harry's voice. He sounded like a few beers. She wondered if she should divert him.

"When the Indigenous Congress organized, the indigenous created their own solutions. The problem is, nobody sees it like they see it. They only see neoliberal threats: Plan Puebla-Panamá, oil, biodiversity..." People moved and re-stationed themselves nearer the food and drink. A few other foreigners drifted in without formalities. Voices filled the crowded room.

Doña Consuela munched one of her sweets, and then recalling her manners, smiled and passed around the tray. Pockets of conversation swirled. Food vanished.

"The indigenous crisis began because anthropologists wanted to manage the Indians. For their own good."

"Yeah. They labeled them victims, never actors. Then came economists, planners, leaders, like always. They impose projects to save the poor. But they never think the indigenous are capable on their own!"

Constance gave up on the CD and responded to the end of the conversation, "Harry does, I think. He lets them set the way." In their corner Constance spoke directly to Aida. But the room was a bit small, after all. She realized with horror that Ignacio, not far away, overheard. His eyes flicked from Constance to Harry, and then back to Merwin.

"Yes." Ignacio recovered quickly. "The indigenous built San Gregorio; they're the builders of most Mexican cities," He spoke quietly. He gave Indians their due. He had loved his mother after all, he was mestizo. His skin was her skin. "The system of usos y costumbres is the resistance of five hundred years, with a system of organization that changes little with times and men. The challenge is, replace tradition with present possibility. This may be difficult to accept. But something must be done to provide jobs, and maintain public safety."

Constance smiled brightly. Damn herself for this stupid party. How many times could she blurt out everything in her mind without thinking. She simply never learned to monitor herself in the context of her surroundings, although she monitored the surroundings in regard to herself.

"The information I'm gathering deals with women's role in local government, a municipio here being a collection of tiny pueblos, each with maybe a hundred families, up to two thousand residents, rarely more." This was Aida shifting to Frank's side to address other foreigners as well. The room was comfortably full; two Germans stood eating tamales and drinking beer, a French woman sat nearby. God bless Aida. She tugged the conversation in another direction. "The campesinos tried to grow coffee and staples," she nodded at Merwin, "but NAFTA undercut prices. There's something terribly dangerous about making a population dependent on another country – let alone the USA – for its basic food, no?"

"Applied social change," Merwin growled. "Defines needs from the top down by professionals on behalf of the rich. It omits people's needs." He ignored Aida and addressed Ignacio. A dual.

"But one must honor men who rise to the top. Often it is because they have intelligence and ability, is that not true?" Ignacio turned away before Merwin could reply. He moved toward Carmen, and indicated with his head that she should come. He had learned more than he expected to.

Following Ignacio's lead she began to make her way toward the door. Merwin stood aside.

As the couple said goodbye to Constance in the patio, Emily turned to Harry. "Nice to see you again," she murmured. "Have you gone back up?"

"Next week," Harry said quietly. "José's going. He's waiting for a shipment, to bring up new clamps. Make sure they don't get lost."

Emily swayed, and Harry put his hand under her arm. "You okay?"

"Of course," she answered. "Why wouldn't I be? Where's our guru? I'll ask Martin to walk me back to my hotel. Nothing could be safer than strolling with a man of peace!" She laughed. And then sobered, "Look, I want to go up with you."

"It's not safe."

"I know."

At the door Martin pulled over his head a white wool serape that fell down over his jeans almost to his sandals. It was an astonishing transformation. It brought the Holy Master to life right then and there. Reincarnate, and Holy Master wasn't even dead. Better yet, Martin wasn't dead, although badly bruised from motorcycle tumbles.

"Thank you for including me," he said to Constance returned to the living room. He courteously draped Emily's rebozo around her shoulders, "Don't worry about safety. Depending on the direction of our gaze, we may see quite a different significance in unfolding events. Are we perhaps witnessing the death throes of outmoded philosophies, technologies, and world views?"

"Stay tuned," Emily quipped as they left.

"Stay tuned," Constance echoed. It was like saying Merry Christmas, only different.

43

Chistmas Eve

The clock on the south wall of the cathedral halted at 2:00 many years ago. Pigeons rested on its iron hands and nested on nearby cornices. Beneath the clock on the south side of the cathedral plaza, stood a Coca-Cola tree, a high green plastic cone tied around with red disks, labelled "Coca-Cola". A white iron rail surrounded it and a miniature cozy wooden cottage for Santa. An armed guard, partially visible, sat inside the hollow tree at a table next to a charcoal brazier, thumbing a girlie magazine and glancing out occasionally for signs of trouble. The air beyond his tent was cold and he hoped for peace.

The zócalo and plaza were thronged. Overhead the brilliant full moon, the year's last, illuminated faces of lovers, of cooks and crafts-people, of women embroidering blouses, stringing amber beads, weaving hats – the entire population of San Gregorio present: making, selling or buying. Housewives balanced their comals on top of charcoal stoves. Apron-clad women turned tortillas, picking them off the scalding discs with their fingers. Daughters and sisters with bent backs and weary arms fed the heavy iron tortilla presses beside the comals. The odor of grilled meats floated out. Bees trampled sugared fruits and cream-filled pastries.

Merwin gazed up at the cathedral and sighed. The first great Mexican church was built in Mexico DF, the second in Puebla, a third in Oaxaca. This one, hidden away in a remote corner in Chiapas, was late seventeenth century, of a colonial past no one cared to beautify. Except for its gorgeous organ, it stood completely neglected. Damaged by settling and earthquake. The weather-scrubbed statuary on the high frieze showed worn figures missing noses and hands; the mosaic of dark and light tiles on its domed belfry revealed beneath the moonlight odd dark spaces where tiles had fallen. Bullets gouged the painted walls. Merwin turned in pain.

Carmen, her crisp hair brushed, strolled down to admire the plaza filled with stalls of hand-made crafts, foods, sweets, and music. So she told herself. Not a square foot of the zócalo or surrounding streets lay empty. Pushing her way through the crowd around a stall she paused to pull ten pesos from her red tasseled shoulder bag and purchased a sweet made of pistachio nuts and honey.

On the other side of the square the best restaurant was filled, except for a large reserved table. The American couple sat enjoying a restaurant supper and the hum of Christmas. Three suited men entered and were ushered to an empty table. Calls were made on a cell phone. The waiter appeared and nodded. A copy of the local newspaper appeared on the tablecloth. Four more men entered, one of whom Harry recognized as the Municipal President of San Gregorio, and another surely was the Governor. The third man, dressed in an ordinary shirt and jeans wore a stiff campesino sombrero. Harry couldn't identify him. He was clearly an accessory to the fourth man. The fourth was Ignacio, his face suffused with pride, in full military dress. The men sat down and the waiter brought small glasses of mescal. Their heads nearly met over the table.

Were they inadvertent witnesses to a meeting of the cabal? Constance leaned back in her chair as far from the light as she could. Grief flooded her chest. Why was Ignacio meeting with the governor? Military operations came by official order, not in restaurants. Private discussion suggested indigenous militia, local massacres, orders to destroy the EZLN communities. She knew that. And here? Now? Nacho? So trim in his uniform, so bedecked with ribbons and stars. Could this meeting be something else, consultation on another topic?

Harry silently signaled for their bill. He wasn't sure if Ignacio saw them, but he thought not. Ignacio's cheeks were flushed a deep brick. He leaned over the table, with a map and a pencil in his hand.

Harry and Constance circled the restaurant wall, walking in silent agreement behind other diners as far as they could get from the men's table. When they left, another man stood braced against the doorway wall as if for a long night. "That guy's a bodyguard." Constance nodded.

The fireworks began as they squeezed their way back through the crowd and stalls. The fire brigade arrived, wearing yellow helmets and windbreaker jackets zipped to the neck. Each man was armed with a small red fire extinguisher, and strode between stalls and streets, alert and ready. The Skelbas stepped in behind one of the firefighters cutting a path across the square toward the cathedral. A viewing platform had been erected, folding chairs neatly arranged. Harry hoped they blended into the crowd, mingled with the scant busload of tourists buying embroidered blouses, draw-string pants, ribbon-bedizened dresses.

He looked about defensively, holding Connie's hand. Young people of San Gregorio wore Levis, the older folks basic polyester, the few wealthy wore Mexico City styles. They looked out of place in the moving swarm, but he hoped not unbelievable. The locals stood eating street food, linking arms, talking in loud voices to be heard over the general noise. "I need a Reality Check."

"What Reality Check are you referring to, Dear?"

"Questions for which I have no answers, THAT reality. Does Ignacio know I was invited to work in the mountains for the Cuates community? That particular community? Does he care?"

She needed to make her own reality check. Men in public restaurants plotting murder and mayhem. Before their solstice open house, Harry hadn't asked outright if Ignacio knew of Harry's task. Anyway, he doubted Ignacio, a military man, would bother to communicate with the migra about illegal American workers. Turf wars were the same all over. The separation of the dozen security forces would probably keep Harry safe. The question unasked, was there danger to Cuates de Santa Ana? His town.

Constance pulled her jacket closer. She lacked answers to Harry's concerns and to her own. Overhead the moon, somewhat worn around the edges, still gleamed. They heard music, and like children lured by the Pied Piper, turned and followed until they were caught up in a procession.

A ragged band of musicians led them. Constance as always merged into the crowds in this city, she was always drawn, pulled, assumed into, a relationship with people who had not been hers before. Leading the procession a round-faced child rode sidesaddle on a burro, her white satin mantle draped over her head and around the burro's flanks. Three men on horses followed, charming in fake whiskers and crowns to represent the Wise Men. Behind strolled the crowd carrying torches made of candles mounted inside cellophane shades on long sticks, and sparklers which threw darts of flame recklessly down onto the women's hair. From an outstretched arm Constance accepted a torch. The people smiled at them, spoke to them, assimilated them as part of the procession.

Together they paraded down and around the hillside street and back to the zócalo, their small troop meeting up with grander ones, float after float bearing toddler angels secured with ropes to tiny chairs on the open truck beds, bigger angels seated in front of Nativity scenes. The biggest angels of all stood serious with the Annunciation. The bands bur-burped, crowds lined the streets admiring illuminated halos and wings; shoulder to shoulder the couple swept along. When the crowd halted they halted within it; a small boy asked Harry for his torch. Harry obligingly handed it over, and immediately the candle ignited the cellophane. Behind the blaze of light as Harry stamped out the fire Constance saw Merwin and Carmen together in the shadow of the church. The red cellophane shade hissed like a special-effects devil in the movies, then curled and vanished.

In its sudden absence Constance blinked.

Reality Check, please. Constance is a senior citizen. Constance was enchanted teaching a man at least twenty-five years her junior, who very likely orders military incursions, who apparently terrifies his wife. Constance had no answer to her husband's query, had she in her foolishness betrayed him, was her betrayal putting the whole town of Cuates in danger.

The warm bodies of spectators greeting the huge dancing papier-mâché puppets milled around her, leaned into her, held her upright. Constance split in two. She felt it, she almost heard the earthquake cracking her bones. In the open area, twirling frames bobbed beneath painted mustachioed men and pink-cheeked women. The dolls approached her and circled as she clung to Harry's arm. The crowd clapped. Someone ignited the firework wheels. Constance gazed up. Beyond the shooting colored streams, the actual stars shone. She was exhausted, exalted, driven away from herself into herself.

They would not attend midnight mass. Silently in accord, she took Harry's proffered hand. They headed back toward their apartment, leaving behind the garish fair and processions, the warm crowds and warm foods. On a quiet side street they passed a small church where the congregation was already leaving, saluting one another with the Christmas Kiss of Peace, embraces, handshakes all around. Cries of Feliz Navidad. Igualmente. Explosions of rockets followed into their apartment, coming from every direction.

44

Emily Brings Alarm

Three weeks later Constance sat in their sala listening to the radio. Once in a while the tiny university station played old American tunes from the sixties and seventies, and behind them in her memory ran the many protests and causes she'd joined. "All we are saying, is give peace a chance..." It was easy then to belong, to feel part of something. It was so local. Hers.

She leaned her head back against the chair. A brown splotch where wall met ceiling in the corner began to move. She focused her attention. Maybe a leaf or a butterfly. After moments of fixed contemplation she called Harry. He took a kitchen chair and climbed up to look. Then Constance could make out splayed legs, the tiny eye of a lizard. No harm, but not in her house.

Harry went to the closet, and returned with a broom and plastic pail. Connie positioned the pail directly beneath the lizard. She dragged over the kitchen chair.

"I guess you expect that lizard to plummet ten feet into a pail, like a circus performer?"

Connie sniffed.

Harry raised the pail over his head, braced it against the wall with one hand. Constance lofted the broom, her sleeve falling away from her wrist and her back arched. Her hand held on too far down the stick to reach the ceiling; she didn't have arm strength or length. They changed positions. Harry stepped up on the chair, Constance positioned a second chair so she could make the catch, holding up the pail.

Too ridiculous, although Harry's strength never ceased to amaze her, if you can picture this old gent with his white Zapata moustache wielding a broom against a lizard, like tickling the government during an unending rebellion. Finally he touched the creature and it fled along the wall out of reach. Harry jumped down off the chair to give chase. The lizard fled into the hole in the wall surrounding the electric cord.

"It's outside safe now," Harry asserted. "These walls aren't hollow." He knew; the wires and cords and cables strung everyplace passed through holes drilled into adobe or cement long after the end of basic construction.

Constance jumped for the flashlight and unbolted the door. She wanted to see that lizard well on his way. They tumbled out. It was cold; Connie shivered, no wonder the lizard wanted to be indoors. So did she. A soft almost freezing January rain drifted down. She flashed the light along the wall—no lizard. Harry checked the inside wall and estimated the spot on the outside where the lizard's electric cable entry should be located. They stood outside in the chilly night with a flashlight, looking for a hole in the wall and a fugitive lizard. No lizard, no luck.

Indoors the radio announced the name of the primary election PRI winner, Labastida. "A corrupt nonentity," Harry asserted. "At least lizards are genuine."

"Is he irrelevant?"

"Probably not," Harry grumbled irritably. "The PRI pays good pesos for votes. If Cuates de Santa Ana votes wrong—well, in their case, they never get government money anyway. They're okay with that! just don't want militia up there shooting sheep and scaring women." They closed the door. "This cold spell at night in the mountains, it's below 40 degrees, serious trouble. A few pieces of wood and a blanket don't help. Although I don't know what the government could do, if they took it in mind to do anything."

Constance shivered in sympathy. Usually, the weather stayed tourist-pleasant, and many young people hung around outdoor cafés late into the night listening to guitar music and drinking. For Connie, like them, roughing it meant no hot water if the pilot on the water tank blew out; all things being relative, a far cry from having your house collapse, your sheep slip away in a mudslide, and getting rained on in freezing weather with paramilitary around the bend.

Anyway the lizard was gone off to wherever lizards go, and might not return until the next cold snap. Constance went to put on a fresh kettle of tea, and the door-bell sounded.

"Who is it? Come in, for heaven's sake! Pásele!"

Emily stood in the doorway a moment, and then entered. In an American ski jacket she looked small and washed out, her pale hair even paler under the electric light.

"The EZLN says there may be another attack on the way. Or an arrest." She put her hand to her lips to stop her mouth from trembling. She spoke to Harry, who put an arm around her shoulder and led her to a chair. He seemed to know what she meant.

"What?" Constance stood with tea mugs on a small tray.

"An armed attack on another community." Emily held out a flyer. Constance took it.

Clandestine indigenous revolutionary committee-general command of the Zapatista National Liberation Army of Mexico.

To the people of Mexico, To the people and governments of the world.

Brothers:
Today, in the early morning hours, troops of the Federal Army, Public Security Police and PRIistas cut the access road to the communities of the Sierra Coral Chen.

Trenches have been dug, trees were felled and huge stones deployed. The paramilitaries guard the blockade, stopping everyone.

We're waiting a possible attack on the community of Cuates de Santa Ana. The last bulletin we received from Subcomandante Insurgente Marcos this morning reported heavy land and air military movement in the vicinity of the road toward Cuates de Santa Ana.

The war goes on.
That's all.
Democracy, liberty and justice.

Comandantes Felipe, David, Moises and Daniel.

Constance looked at Harry. "But you passed there! Didn't it seem normal?"

Harry shook his head. "I didn't want to worry you. Since Christmas, military and police swarm all over the place. In maybe ten communities, but down below, in the valley. All Zapatista communities are on alert."

"They stop people on the roads. Not just at military checkpoints. Thousands of Public Security troops and police forces are out there. They harass the hell out of local people. Fifty families from Nazareth!

They fled and moved in with the refugee population camp in the next village." Tears streamed down Emily's face. "I'm at the end of my rope."

Constance looked at Harry. Since Christmas? Had her stupid remarks pushed the situation over the edge? What was going on, her eyebrows asked. What rope was it of Emily's? Harry shook his head and mouthed I'll tell you later.

"I'm afraid they'll pick up José," Emily wailed. So. Constance nodded. She handed Emily a tissue. Love sticks out like a fly on a dinner plate. Harry acted oblivious to her crush on Ignacio. But maybe he knew? Ah. Suddenly she wanted to put her arms around him and explain. But explain what?

"When soldiers and police forces arrest alleged Zapatistas, they don't just wreck the place and burn houses. They go for physical abuse." Harry patted Emily's shoulder while he told Connie. "You know Frank, who was at our party? On several occasions, they've intimidated or refused free access to NGO workers. Soldiers do police functions like detentions, and try to register and photograph foreigners. Frank was interrogated, roughed up but not tortured, if he knows any military intelligence, or has contacts with Zapatistas."

"What did he say? Of course he takes medical supplies..."

Connie closed her mouth. So much of her normal blurting of what came to mind now was worse than making her look like a foolish old woman. It was harmful. She bore some responsibility for Cuates. That damned party conversation.

Emily's voice was bitter. "They say dialogue but they mean war."

Harry paced away from her and back. Governments with force on their side always say dialogue just before they shoot. It was a fact of life. But what should they do? He worried more about José than destruction of his polyvinyl tubes and running water. If José got caught it was all over for everybody.

Emily accepted her mug of tea and warmed her hands on the sides, trying to stem her tears. She still wore the turquoise and purple ski jacket. Instead of looking chic, on the small chair she resembled a homeless child in Salvation Army clothes.

Constance sat down.

"We spotted a lizard in here," Constance offered. Emily looked confused. "It was kind of funny for a while. I mean with Harry trying to catch it. It escaped, though." She twisted her fingers, and looked at Harry. Foolish, she was. "But I don't think they'd do too much with American Senior Citizens watching. Would they?"

Harry frowned at her. With a Zapatista alert out, peace-keepers and witnesses would assemble and be sent up as quickly as possible. "They've done some damage to the French. And threw out one American, kidnapped another before they threw him out. Threw out a couple of Germans."

"But. That was for aiding Zapatistas. Cuates isn't officially Zapatista. You told me, Harry!" Her voice threatened. Like she'd make him regret the day he lied to her. But he hadn't lied. Cuates was autonomous by default, not by rebellion. Because normally nobody wanted to go up into inaccessible areas. They were ignored: no roads, no electricity, no telephone. The suspicion of harboring Zapatista rebel leaders—that was a different can of worms. Like José, for one.

"I've seen those photographs of indigenous women standing facing soldiers, shouting at them, and then chasing them down the road." She smiled at the memory. "Right, Emily?"

"That's right." Emily was unable to smile back. "But a whole village."

Ah, thought Constance. Together a whole village. "An old American woman, accompanied by a young one, of course—that would look bad on TV. They won't do that, I don't think? Shoot me or shove me?" She looked at Harry for confirmation. He was bemused.

"So you say you'll come up with us? And confront the military at the gates?" It was so preposterous Emily laughed, a high-strung gasp of noise. Who would hold the video camera? Hey, who would bring a video camera?

"Well, why not?" Constance demanded. "I can be useful. Age must carry some advantages. I hate these bastards as much as you do!"

Harry looked at her. She didn't comprehend the magnitude of the government's genocide against the indigenous. She just didn't get it. Even though since Christmas she'd regained her equilibrium in regard to Ignacio. Because Ignacio could speak English now. She'd done her job, and didn't need to hover any more. But she still didn't get it.

Somebody needed to get up there pdq, if the warning was correct. They'd need to navigate between checkpoints, and that wouldn't be easy. He'd talk to José. If José got back into the city safely from his next run, that'd be tomorrow. Harry didn't know where he was. And he wouldn't ask Emily. In fact, there was nobody to ask. He'd have to wait. He handed Emily the honey to put into her tea.

Constance brought out some sweet bread, and coaxed Emily to try a little. She'd learned something about women when she saw the video of actions in one of the villages. Old, and none too lovely, many with teeth missing, and hips splayed from pregnancies and toting huge bundles. Women. They were fierce.

Anyway, she was tired of never grasping what went on. It wasn't as if she never heard of the World Trade Organization or the history of oppression in Chiapas. It was simply not concrete for her. For two years now—or was it her whole life—she'd lived off fleeting glimpses and wild surmises, all connected to individual lives. She wouldn't admit how many times her supposed intuition failed, and her wild guesses crumbled into dust were swept under the rug. When she made a successful guess she thanked her lucky stars.

But why didn't she know? Other people seemed to know the

way things fit together. Because they made an effort to find out! They asked! They went! She didn't. She wrote letters home to Judith about clay pottery and woven rugs, the indigenous clothing! She knew she was timid, or if not timid, locked into some created world, like learning from movies. Her life consisted of an accumulation of events flicking past in the half-light. Well! Not for another year! No more! She would go and stand with the people, her people now.

And as for Frank, of course she knew Frank! How could Harry think she forgot? And of course she was sure Emily was involved with some man in danger! Emily clearly was involved.

But it wouldn't be polite to ask.

She sipped her tea and planned what to wear. She'd been with Harry before in rough places.

45

Arriving in Cuates

All roads were occupied throughout the five Zapatista Aguascalientes headquarters. River crossings and daily life of suspected sympathizers crawled under the eyes of occupying soldiers. They permitted, they ordered, they prohibited, where and when. The militia carried out the executions.

Harry, heading northwest toward the mountain pueblo of Cuates de Santa Ana, felt in his own bones the Mexican army's boot on the indigenous people. He tried to explain to Constance how difficult the trip would be. It wasn't necessary to explain to Emily.

In the truck, with José at the wheel and four five-thousand liter tinacos in the back, they rumbled across the Chiapas landscape.

The empty water tanks had been placed in the corners on the metal truck frame, and covered with the truck bed. It rode high, and placed on top, Harry's usual "luggage" was visible: a tripod, three nineteen-liter containers of water, a sack of rice, a sack of oranges, corn meal and beans, coffee, charcoal for cooking, a tent, a sleeping bag. Constance brought her backpack, sleeping bag, and a square cosmetic bag like movie stars carried on their trips. Damned if he knew where she got it. Emily's equipment included the video camera, paints and a brush case, a dozen small canvasses. He hoped to hell they looked like insane tourists going to camp in the winter mountains. He hoped whatever soldiers would tire of looking at stuff and quit without lifting flooring or crawling underneath. He had no plan for explaining the tinacos. He simply felt proud of the system he designed, of raised connecting containers, all vinyl lined, all with lids that could be lifted for rain collection. The reservoir problem solved!

Innocent tourists traveling through a war zone. Does this sound unlikely, or what?

As they rode, José pointed. Under an awning of leaf green stood raw artillery guns. "They hide them in clumps of trees and behind hills." He looked grim. "The rains are ending here, and people need to prepare the land to sow. But dry weather is dangerous for communities in resistance."

"Militia attack?"

"Yes. Open sky, more planes and helicopters in support. Dry roads."

"But the NGO's can get in too. Some aid from Civil Society? How about Witnesses for Peace?" Harry raised his voice in hopeful question, and José nodded. But he didn't look hopeful.

"If they can enter. They guard the bridge and both banks. Thank God the Euseba flows full."

José looked at Harry briefly and returned his eyes to the road. The Euseba River was running wild after three days and nights of continuous rain. Harry thought of the lowlands of Villahermosa in Tabasco—under water, of course. This damned country. He shut it out of his mind. Mud everywhere, slippery roads where roads existed. He'd seen it.

Military equipment, now that he knew how to spot it, lay every-where, like sleeping dinosaurs. The sky cleared into early sun, burning off mist. No rain today. Overhead he saw a hawk circle, heavy and slow. No wind to ride.

Their truck grumbled to a halt at the first retén. The soldier ap-proached the cab. Smiling cheerfully José rolled down the window and greeted him. "Buen' día!" He waited for the trooper to ask before he handed over his papers. Indigenous men on the roads, whether passengers or drivers, got a tough looking over. So much for the Con-stitution, Harry thought. Driving while indigenous.

Harry, freshly shaved that morning and pink-cheeked around his white Zapata moustache, held his American passport and new visa in hand when the soldier came round to his side of the truck. The two women in the jump seats leaned forward to the window and silently imitated. Constance wore her benign smile. Emily smiled dutifully. Behind them, two other soldiers inspected cargo, lifting and shoving bulky bags of food. José explained that the crazy Americans wanted to camp. Harry kept his mouth shut. It was better to let José carry the ball. Instead he peered around like a rubber-necker.

Beside the wood stand where the soldiers took cover from the sun, a huge placard proclaimed: "98.12 por ciento de los chiapanecos cuenta con servicios de salud". Harry snorted. Disinformation put out by Governor Albóres. It didn't have much to do with hunger, ill-ness and forced idleness in the Altos and northern zone where they headed. It was like in San Gregorio, where signs pasted on the walls of houses proclaimed Peace. Maybe people who never left the city believed that, believed in paradise on earth, maybe. While just a few kilometers outside the city the dirty war continued, and now grew worse. And more like 98 percent of Chiapanecos received no health care.

In the past few weeks San Manuel, Francisco Gómez, San Pedro de Michoacán, Emiliano Zapata, Ricardo Flores Magón, all towns in Las Cañadas, watched the army approach, gradually as a cat stalking a mouse, so visitors like Mary Robinson and the United Nations Human Rights observers wouldn't catch on. Harry guessed they had, all right. At less than a kilometer from the Aguascalientes a huge military encampment had been installed. You'd have to be blind. Rebel sites clamored on the internet with bulletins from San Cristóbal and the EZLN.

The soldiers finally waved them through. Harry sighed. He felt Connie's hand pat his shoulder. José looked a little less grim. The others wouldn't be as bad. They turned off the main highway and begun the upward haul. Emily braced herself. She hated these treacherous roads.

Their arrival at the town seemed different. Four men came out to the dirt road to meet them. There was only this one road, muddy and rutted. The truck halted.

Harry could manage hello and goodbye in the language the people spoke. He waited patiently for José to finish the elaborate greetings, find out what was going on, and fill them in.

The town, small as it was, had taken in refugees. They were from Mocotlán. No place for them to return to. Refugee camps had little food and almost no medical care against whooping cough ravaging the children. As soon as the rain momentarily let up, they left the camp.

Emily tried to look beyond the men. José moved a little closer to her. Without touching her he lent himself to be leaned on.

For chrissake, Harry muttered to himself. Did they walk here? "How many?" he asked.

"Thirty set out. Ten died on the way. Thirty-five arrived."

"The others?"

"Men," José said quietly.

So they reinforced the town with fifteen more men, willing to fight if needed. "Have they weapons?"

"It's better that you not ask such things," José told him. "You are a tourist, only." José suddenly smiled and gripped Harry's hand. "The best kind of tourist. Un tipo con tubas!" A guy with pipes. Like a guy with balls.

The women stayed in the truck. Harry jumped down and strode on foot toward the center of Cuates. He wanted to see for himself how it looked. And it looked pretty much as it had. Chickens pecked in front of straw thatched chosas surrounded by small trees and gardens on the outskirts, and in toward the center, where cinderblock created a few houses, he saw no changes. Perhaps the newcomers all housed in the school building or, more likely, in the church. Faintly he heard sounds from within the tiny building. More stucco on the venerable front facade had fallen, but the cross remained on top, and the bell. The bell served as siren, the most important object in the town's defenses.

Outside it on stone benches several ancient men sat, thin as copper wire, clad in white tunics over shorts. One held a tiny guitar fashioned from unpainted wood and strung with six hairs. The old man squeaked out something that might have been a tune when he saw Harry. They knew him.

Next to the church the town center sat inside its surrounding stone patio, and beyond the patio, the cinderblock "clinic", and then a cement basketball court. Proudly Harry considered the miracle of piped water from his clever and soon to be expanded interlocking reservoirs. It worked inside the clinic, and now was adjacent to more than ten houses, if you could call cement walls and dirt floors "houses." Additionally, a faucet still served the chosas, where women could come with their pails.

Beyond, to the north, the mountain plateau fell off into an abyss. Across the purple distance loomed other peaks. The truck had approached from southeast. They were well isolated here, well protected by their inaccessibility. Only it felt cold as hell. How could the old men? Ah, but they sat in the sun. Old men liked sun.

Harry found the truck parked in a yard, and José was already directing several men in unloading. Harry's own things were placed on the cement slab "porch" of the house he used when he stayed up here. It was the best the town could offer—the floor of cement, not dirt.

He had second thoughts about Connie's offer to come along. Not that she couldn't manage sleeping on rope cots or using the one room for all their needs. She was good natured about difficulties. But they would have to pose as tourists, or human rights observers – which, he wasn't sure. Witnesses. Only two gray seniors. It was ridiculous in any case, totally unbelievable. If military came, would they be deterred?

"Where's Emily?"

"She went to visit the refugees. She says she knows them."

"Ah." Harry sighed. He had near forgotten. Emily spent six weeks at Mocotlán. She wrote a report on how rural people lived, and sent it with photographs to the US. The story never made it into print. She couldn't speak of the massacre, José would not. Inevitably José wondered if the attack came because of his own presence. Anyway, that massacre was documented around the world. Yet from Emily's account, it was like it never happened. Blocked. Useless!

"Well," Harry said, "she'll find a place to sleep. We can make ourselves comfortable here. This is it, my lovely bride!" He gestured toward the narrow rope bed.

Connie looked at the swept cement and the bed. Her eyes met Harry's. "Okay, lover. But I want the bottom half."

He drew air through his teeth so sharply it hissed. She was his girl.

46

Billy in a Pueblo

He wasn't fading into the environment. He was strictly an American, an American guy, he qualified. Sometimes he heard news of Emily, the way the grapevine carried snatches of info. She was in Chiapas, a journalist, off in the villages. It was okay. He wasn't dying of a broken heart. Something else nourished his heart. He could hardly say what, but it wasn't a woman. Maybe he fell in love with himself. For the first time in his life he admired himself. Secretly he bought a pasamontañas, a black wool mask. Sure, he couldn't wear it. He shoved it down to the bottom of his backpack, hidden like a condom. In case he needed it.

Billy read in the local paper sixty-two earthquakes above 3.9 Richter happened in just this year. Exactly what he felt himself, brain and body, jiving in sympathy. To make it objective, he bought surge protectors for both electricity and telephone line. His cramped space where Estación Norte volunteers lived in San Gregorio allowed for nothing else. He was broke. His fund from the university gig in

Mexico City evaporated, and instead of heading home he'd come right back on down. Today the R&R was over. He was on his way again.

What a gas! Billy Boyd grinned and peered at himself in the small mirror, observing his peculiar image. The reflection shot him a high five. Billy Boyd Grennich, the Irish rebel, high fived back. Yeah, man! Billy Boyd follows in his father's footsteps espousing hopeless causes. Like his father, he had nothing much to lose. Or maybe his father thought Baby Billy and his mother acted like surge protectors for his wracked life and would keep him safe? Didn't happen.

Mexico is serious living. They don't call it Mexico Profundo around here for no reason. Chiapas functioned with unbelievable manual labor, plus machines and gadgets that didn't work or soon wouldn't. Makeshift was one possible word; another was cunning— they made it go! Before another repair. Nothing thrown away or wasted.

He met some educated folks, up to speed in water, agriculture, health, stuff like that. They came down from Mexico DF to enroll in the Zapatista cause—not like him, for escape, but for real hope. Teachers who trained teenage teachers in the autonomous pueblos in rebellion, doctors who served in cement block clinics. They were for it. They were his companions on the rusted van that took him back out to the country again.

For his two-week-long Peace Observer excursions to pueblos he carried water, and in case it ran out, a bottle of disinfectant to use in pump water. He bought the usual supply of beans and rice at the San Gregorio street market, a jammed and dirty place. On foot he dodged in and out of stalls, avoiding the meat area which stank, and the charcoal area which was the dirtiest you never wanna see. He purchased tangerines and bananas, two things you can peel.

The situation got worse and worse. Governor Albóres was

mouthing off about public security, his excuse to call out more military. Maybe ten thousand troops were stationed in the rebel area. Like a world war. The Zapatistas had few guns.

On the radio and state television Albóres asked housewives, shop owners, bus drivers, and loyal campesinos to join, to rally against those who prevented PROGRESS in Chiapas. That phony bastard. People worked much harder, seven days a week, man, to fix up and maintain their properties—small *comerciantes* clinging to the cliff edge. They had to defend everything they owned, which Billy figured was slightly worse than having nothing. They were nearly middle class. They wanted. But for all that, they were very nice people, aware of what affected them directly, like the water shortage and lack of city services. Not likely to fight Zapatistas. They weren't big landowners who hire guns, or PRI officials who use robbed government money to buy them. Their sympathy lay with the rebels. The type at the top of the heap, Billy didn't meet. The type who wanted PROGRESS for Chiapas—the neoliberal right to get richer, he didn't know those folks.

The van headed out at 3:00 A.M. in an attempt to avoid the military posts. Estación Norte was alert to the plea for help in Cuates de Santa Ana, but Cuates had no strategic importance, it wasn't on the road to anywhere. They'd have to get up there later. This run was headed to the village where the road would cross.

With city streets behind them, and the descent made to the highway, the road was peppered with military vehicles. Blockade posts monitored every fifteen kilometers. The bastards strode up to the van windows poker-faced and ramrod straight, sternly unaffected by what they were doing. They shot flashlights directly into the eyes of the van occupants. They inspected documents, and wrote down in little notebooks information which Billy guessed was bluff—they didn't have computer systems to process—what? Maybe names of those absolutely on the government's shit list. Billy felt safe enough. You heard horror stories. But were they believable? Stories about a colonel with an iron bolt screwed in the side of his head, who stood to one side while the troopers beat men on the soles of their feet to get them to sign confessions. You supply food to the Zapatistas!

Stuff like that, Billy asked his companions, was that true?

Politics as usual, they replied noncommittally.

The villages felt the pincers. Dirty tricks, dirty war. Billy, trapped inside a sixties textbook, groped for the next chapter to explain how it would end. Once the Berlin Wall came down, corporate capitalism blasted into the stratosphere, that much he understood.

But this was the nineties. The Zapatistas were waging the world's first internet warfare. Information flew all over the globe, against neo-liberalism or whatever. People grabbed the Zapatista spirit; in his gut Billy knew power to the people had an awesome media range. So how could this old shit still go down? These rebels were Mexican, right? Like in the USA, the First People, shoved onto the worst land and ignored.

But it wasn't so simple. Almost everyone in Mexico, like eighty percent, had indio ancestors. Like any minute, they could wake up and say Whoa, man, this is me you're fucking over.

Safely inside the municipio compound he found a spot to string his hammock and stow his backpack. Food and water, in the shack they called the volunteer house.

Billy saw solidarity for the first time in his life. Not like Irish Americans who drank endlessly and kept alive a fantasy of uniting Ireland by warfare. This was different. This was resistance, yes, but stoic, peaceful, determined to die if necessary; a sober, transparent insistence on the right to have their autonomy. A say-so in their destiny. Dignity, they called it.

The reality was, death wasn't dignified. Some medical guys weren't actually doctors. Like, his buddy Frank who Billy knew since their first trip, brought antibiotics when he could, and aspirin. That was pretty much it.

Maybe they'd seen pictures of flower children and hippies, putting flowers into the rifle barrels during Vietnam protests. Billy saw it once on a video. Before his time, but now this was his time, right? The army arrived. They claimed it was to build a road so each remote community could more easily get to market.

According to French Peace Observers, the governor established eight military corridors to squeeze the four municipalities where the EZLN was. He stationed 13,000 soldiers through the ravines and valleys. The German guy dug out some maps. Between where Billy stood right now, and the political center of the Zapatistas, six military bases got built, to hold 4,000 guys with guns.

They spread maps on the cleared wooden planks in the eating area where volunteers met for the afternoon meal. Billy kneeled on the wooden bench and peered over the shoulder of Jan. Another volunteer stirred something at the cooking stove, where pots and supplies for the community hung on nails on one side of the shed. Billy, on one knee, dragged a boot in the dirt floor. The two women observers smoked cigarettes and looked over Billy's shoulder. He waved at the smoke without eliciting any guilt. They smoked.

"One month ago," Jan told them, "the Mexican Army arrived in the village of Cañada del Euseba." He tapped the map with his pencil. Soldiers were posted there after carrying out a "social service", transporting the coffee harvest without cost to the growers. That was inside one of the few zones that previously was free of military. That's where Subcomandante Marcos supposedly hung out, in the principal guerrilla base.

Billy knew that all over Chiapas other people were doing what he was doing, staring at the damned maps, as if they could reveal the outcome.

Since 1994 the Secretary of National Defense pushed along construction of two principal highways to surround the Zapatista communities. Finally Jan put his elbow on the worn map and bent over his beans, shoving them off the plate and into his mouth using a tortilla for a spoon. There were no spoons. No forks, the only knives were machetes. Nothing more to be said.

In the eating silence that followed they heard the rumble. Billy swallowed. Everyone got up. They quietly stepped through the doorway.

The village women stood in front of the soldiers, holding out red, white, yellow and purple flowers.

"Brother soldiers," said Piedad, a square woman whose age Billy couldn't guess. "We come to tell you with these flowers that we love you, our hearts are with you. We think that someday you'll be soldiers for our country!"

The soldiers laughed. That was a break from the poker-faced crowd. These guys actually looked into the faces of women confronting them. The women were shabby. Their black braids, woven with colored ribbons, comprised their only wealth.

Piedad went on, "Serving the rich makes us suffer." Teodor from within the ranks of the men called, "Soldiers, you devour the flesh of your own family. You fight against your own people. They tell us you come for progress. You know you don't come for that!"

Billy watched. Foreigners were never included in village meetings when decisions were made. This was a well-planned resistance. Billy hung well in the rear, with his head covered. He wished he had the guts to put on his pasamontañas, but uh uh. That would make him an accomplice. But he wasn't hidden. His hands and arms were a giveaway with their display of freckles like stars on his pale skin. He only shouldn't be active. A foreigner in the front rank would be like waving an Orange flag on St. Patrick's Day.

They were blocking the building of a road. That was all. No giant machines to run them down, here just soldiers with shovels and picks. A man standing at Billy's side gritted his teeth.

"They do it so they can bring in the army when they are ready to."

Billy wasn't sure where the man came from or why he stood next to Billy. Were they protecting their protectors?

Another man, barefoot and ragged, stepped from behind the women's rank and shoved his face up to the soldier's. "Think, think for a minute, little soldier. Think about fighting for the people, not against them. Because you won't be so sad. Remember you're indigenous, too."

A girl called, "Soldiers, we're going to sing a song so you won't feel so isolated." And they began Cartas Marcadas: "Despite all the wrongs you've done me, today I want to smile, today I want to live." They formed a chorus, a dozen brown skinned women facing the troops. Another speaker took over, behind the branches and flowers. "You're held here, and we're free. You have the freedom to speak, but when we came here you responded to us with silence. Stop this bad thing you do, join us!"

The rebel indigenous men stood stolidly, playing their guitars in the mud. "We're going to give you a Tzeltal song," Teodor called out, "because we are happy."

Billy heard sadness in Teodor's voice. Teodor's last three kids all died before they reached their fifth birthdays. He gazed around the rank of women. They sure weren't young. Most younger women had left to join the Zapatista army.

"We reject the roads. We don't want them. We know what roads bring. First nothing, then the federales," Elías told Billy, suddenly appearing beside him. Elías wore a ski mask. It was a sign of rebel army rank. Billy envied him. It was impossible to tell if Elías were older or the same age as Billy himself. He stood quietly, his arms covered by a fatigue shirt. His hands showed manual labor—somewhere. The fingernails were rimmed in black, and broken. His shadowed eyes smiled with a kind of grief, a kind of anger. Billy felt the heat off the skin of Elías. These Tzeltales knew when they were screwed over. Maybe they didn't have much education, but they knew what justice should be.

"The road has not arrived but the army has," remarked another slight man, holding a meter-long stick covered with dirt. This was the outer rim, where Billy stood. On the ground next to the man lay a cactus stick, covered with tiny thorns. He left it lie, and nobody touched it.

"It burns," a little boy about ten years old informed Billy. A red handkerchief hung around his neck. It had slipped off his face. "No-one touches those things." A last resort weapon. A fucking plant. Oh man.

Elías stepped forward and joined the chorus: "Chiapas, Chiapas is not an army barracks, get the army out of here!" The cry issued from his black mask as if from the bottom of a well.

A few yards to Billy's right, across from the wire mesh that protected the work area and the troops, a group of young indigenous boys recognized one of the soldiers. They knew he was one of them, from a neighboring village. A kid called out to him in Tzeltal. The soldier flushed and looked away.

Behind them, out of view, Mexican artillery was planted on the hill. Standing unprotected, Billy's neck prickled. Shelling could fall onto them out of the sky. Only chickens and the old burro didn't get it. They strolled about in the compound dirt as unconcerned as a post-card picture. The boys, their faces covered by bandanas, continued speaking in Tzeltal to the soldier, only a boy himself, maybe eighteen, Billy guessed. The soldier answered in monosyllables, smiled nervously, chewed the end of a green plastic cigarette lighter. He tried to look casual, keeping his back toward his fellow troopers. They didn't understand Tzeltal; probably spoke other indigenous languages. Few pale faces showed in the unit.

"What do they say?"

The boy soldier didn't answer. One of the kids translated into Spanish, "They're telling him he should return to his village, he should be ashamed to come and fuck over his brothers, dressed up in the uniform of a soldier."

Who knows what they're really saying, Billy thought. Their voices shifted from friendly reproach to outright hostility. It was getting uncomfortable. The soldier turned and shouldered his way back into his patrol. Another came to take his place. This one was brown-skinned also, but nobody knew him. They fell silent. Finally one of the women began to harangue them again.

"You take your orders from a dictator!"

"You clean the latrine of your boss!"

"Little soldier, you are indigenous, remember that, and you stand behind that wire like a piglet in a pen!" Some of the community men had brought atole. The majority had nothing to eat. The day wore on.

Billy's duty hours. That meant he should count and note whatever he saw across the open field. He took out his camera. The officials who arrived by jeep in the last few minutes glanced over. An MP held a camera, and as he was about to snap Billy's picture, Billy took his. A helicopter lurched overhead. Billy hoped they had no gas grenades up there. Finally the chopper rumbled away, and hung in the distance, circling the hill.

The day wore on. The village people stood planted like trees in the path of the new road. Billy admired them, fearless little pissants.

Justice is what they wanted. They stood under the white sun. Two women appeared carrying a bucket and a plastic cup.

This village owned one rusted hand-pump. All their water came from it. Billy didn't need to think twice about the dying children. He strolled back to the village store and bought a bottle of orange Fanta. In the near-equatorial sun he felt thirsty all the time. He wouldn't be missed.

At five o'clock the church bell began to ring, and clanged without stopping. Everyone stood his place outside, women in the front rank, men behind them. Nobody moved but children running on the concrete area that passed for a basketball court. Billy's tongue clicked still dry although his gut protested the idea of more soda. Evening was coming.

It might be a long night, and a long two weeks.

47

Confrontation

A different town, a day later. They came to stand in the mud, some with plastic shoes, some barefoot, some with torn rubber boots flopping at their shins. Their cotton garments hung ragged, colors faded from many washings, buttonholes lacking buttons. All the faces were covered. A declaration of war in a peaceful town. The church bell clanged without stopping.

The few men in black wool ski masks stood out starkly among the red bandanas. But the stance was the same. Only eyes showed, a hundred women's eyes staring out above fifty bandanas that hid nose and mouth. A lot of kids, most of them too thin, their wrists, as they held up their fists, no thicker than small branches. Behind the rank of women, each holding vertical a staff or stick with one end planted in the dirt, ranged more men, also masked, some wearing tall stiff cream-colored sombreros over their bandanas, some bareheaded. Women, kids and men stood, and as the small clean uniformed troop ascended the mud slop, the people began to shout a rhyming shout, like college kids used to shout, like Harry heard during the Vietnam War, something anti-American and threatening. He turned to look at Constance. "What are they shouting?"

!Ya los vi! !Ya los vi, los que matan son del PRI!

!Tornilloreja nos escucha, ya seguimos en pie de lucha!

She repeated in Spanish as well as she could. Translation was easy. Probably Harry knew, and merely let her speak it. "They're shouting that the killers belong to the PRI. Screw Ear, they call him. 'Listen to us, we keep on fighting'."

"Screw Ear? Ignacio?"

"Yes. Screw ear. My Nacho." She stood quietly. "I guess he's famous." Through her flooded vision she looked around at the people. Red, an occasional blue or green, the kerchiefs emphasized their eyes, dark and determined. Harry's town had enrolled Zapatista. But any indigenous town was forced to choose, PRI or Zapatista. People who tried to be neutral or pacifist suffered for it. For or against. What a simple world war makes.

"This is what you came for, Connie. It's not too late to get back inside the church."

She didn't bother to reply. Emily walked next to her on her right, Harry on her left. The three moved slowly, in front of the front line.

"I hope they're not offended," she said to Harry, as if they were at a Faculty Social. "They may think we're interfering?" But now there was no way to retreat. She saw Emily turn, and for a moment thought the young woman would bolt, but no, she was only seeking José. Who was—where?

"A few men have weapons." Harry often read her mind. "They're higher up on the hillside." He jerked his eyes sideways with a cautious glance. "If the military shoots, they'll shoot." Harry didn't doubt now that José was a lead organizer and courier from the onset of the uprising. And Cuates was a rebel hideout. If they had told him, where would he be now? Ignacio came here to arrest a Zapatista leader.

That explained why the townspeople let them stand in front. Up here, the road wasn't an available excuse. There was no product to move to market. Their product was Zapatistas. Above all, José needed a way out. The approaching troops wore full military gear. It was official business, and when a man was arrested by Security Police it was all over for him, interrogated, tortured, locked up forever. No way.

"So we must dissuade them from entering. Or shooting," she added as an afterthought. She gripped Emily's hand. They strode ahead, three gringo faces in a line. Constance began to giggle. It took her, at moments like this, that human beings are ridiculous. Our desire for control leaves us ridiculous. Her own inappropriate high voice shocked her.

No more than thirty soldiers faced the crowd directly, holding weapons in front of their chests. Where the others stood she didn't know. Constance looked for Ignacio. She wanted him to see her standing here. She wanted him to know that mothers do not always forgive their sons. Love them, yes, but not forgive them. If there were shooting. Would he order her killed? Or let it happen and pretend it was an accident? He couldn't hold love for her as she did toward him. Because we only love those we have taught.

Her left hand was swallowed into Harry's. She wanted to look at him but it wasn't possible right now. She looked straight ahead, into weapons, into faces of unsmiling armed boys. Any one of them might have been a student of hers. All uniformed, pants tucked into their boots. Well, thank god. If they were here only to kill, like the paramilitary, they would dress in civilian clothes and arrive in darkness.

Her search found Ignacio. He wore his uniform, his insignia. Of course. Other platoons stationed on the next rise blocked the minimum roadway. Nobody moved. In the distance dust floated. More military equipment and troops might be moving up to circle the town. She didn't ask herself why.

Anyway, like crippled toothless ancient beggars, or runny-nosed child beggars, the soldados deserved eye contact. Therefore, at the face facing her, Constance smiled. The soldier returned her smile. The smile lacked teeth in the upper right quadrant. Behind the boy she saw Ignacio, who did not make eye contact with Constance.

When the three gringos approached to within five meters nobody seemed to know what to do. The two lines stood, each with partisans banked behind them. The colonel, off to one side, suddenly whirled. He was confronting yet another person. A figure on a motorcycle emerged like a genie from a bottle of dust.

A man draped in a long mud-stained white wool poncho kicked down the kickstand and stepped off the moto. His boots were splattered with mud, and standing in the road he bent and picked up a twig from next to Ignacio's feet. He began to scrape his boots. Ignacio's face was invisible but the hunch in his shoulders pulled tight his uniform shirt. With the forefinger of one hand he gesticulated fiercely, jabbing back down the road. The rider spoke too softly to be heard clearly by the three Americans. The word drifted to them. Paz. Along the line of campesinos in the road the word floated like incense. Martin was smiling. A madman, Harry hissed. The man's gone round the bend.

The long white poncho like the robe worn by gurus was lifted to reveal jeans beneath, and then Martin's pale hand reached into the pocket on his skinny hip, and brought forth a document. A letter. Not his passport, this folded white paper. Martin began to read, and as he read, he paused every few sentences and translated into Spanish. Constance could finally hear Ignacio as he bellowed, "Pendejo gringo, I understand English!"

Martin was reading HM's Declaration of Peace and Love. "Within a few months, Holy Master will establish the first of four permanent groups of 10,000 Pandits for Peace. Between their effects on world coherence through doing their Sidhi meditation program together twice a day, and their special yagyas for peace and progress for the whole of society, more dramatic changes will follow. One hundred fifty thousand trained Pandits have spread over Mexico in small groups. The next contingent will arrive soon in Chiapas.

'Keep hope alive.

'Do what you know to be right. Don't eat poison.' These are words of Holy Master."

Martin concluded the reading. He repeated the final words directly to the colonel. The veins on Ignacio's forehead bulged. "Don't eat poison," Martin told him.

Ignacio whirled around and waved to the platoon. In five minutes they had descended to their vehicles and vanished.

"I like the message. It's the poison that gets us," commented Constance, still rooted in the dirt. She let the tears flow now. "I got it. Nacho," she called after his vanished form very softly, so that only Harry and Emily heard, "Nacho, don't eat poison!"

Harry said nothing. The hillside shrubs and trees shielding armed Zapatistas quivered, but the shooters remained hidden. The women and children behind them vanished. Harry turned and trudged up the hill toward the doorway of the community meeting room. Constance trailed behind his soaked shirt back, with Emily and then Martin, pushing his red motorcycle.

The room was empty, as if no meeting were necessary now. Constance found a liter Fanta bottle and calmly began rationing orange soda into plastic cups. From inside the small shack, they saw curious faces of children inspecting them through holes in the boards. One child inserted a finger, waggled it in the hole like an antenna to sense what was going on inside. Emily extended her finger and touched the child's. A moment of communion, finger to finger in silence. Martin smiled.

They all wilted. Constance balanced her plastic cup of soda and sank onto the rough wooden bench. Martin assumed the lotus position on the floor against the wall. "They've been vanquished by love. It's the Holy Master effect. All that's necessary is to speak aloud the love of all mankind and benefit flows."

Constance felt oddly humiliated. Somehow she imagined that she would be saving Cuates. Discounting Martin's nonsense, Ignacio had stopped simply for the number—four foreigner witnesses. "I'm an old hand at simultaneously believing mutually contradictory ideas. So for the moment that's all I have to say about Mexico," she responded to Martin, while including the others. Harry remained silent.

Emily regained her finger and leaned against the wood boards. She knew better than to believe this was the end of the struggle in Cuates, or for José. She also remained silent.

Silent herself now, Constance passed around a refill of soda. Outside Harry could see men carrying boxes of their precious clamps. He straightened his back and went out.

48

Frank's Revenge

Frank rumbled his van off the road and waited in it, shielded by a clump of trees. He watched from within filtered sunlight while jeeps and armed vehicles drove by, on the same road Frank traveled only an hour before. From his vantage point he counted—three military trucks lined with soldiers. He had tracked them carefully, and guessed right—he arrived here ahead of them to watch them pass. And there was only one road up. And they would have to come down.

He waited until they moved out of sight. Then he turned on the ignition and slowly maneuvered higher, his back to the road, again crossing terrain, as he had been doing for several hours. He bumped and jolted a rough west from the Cuates community, toward another turn-off and higher elevation. He heard no reverberations of gunfire, but perhaps the troops went in only to snatch José. Surround the townspeople and grab him. They wore uniforms, so they weren't here for massacre; they arrived on an assignment. Accountable.

Finally he braked again and stepped out. He paused by the side of the van, and as if Tomás could hear him through distance, soil, and fabric wrapping his bones, he spoke to the old man. "Stay calm, Tomás," he whispered. "Don't worry. It's nothing. Only I'm gonna kill the sonuvabitch." He lifted his binoculars on their strap around his neck and gazed down from the rise where he halted. He could see army vehicles, so far away they were soundless as they churned dirt down the hillside. One troop vehicle traveled in front, one behind. The colonel in his open jeep rode shielded in front and behind.

He climbed onto the hood and then the van's roof. From his height his binoculars could make out the two jeeps and their occupants, spaced between trucks. Truck, jeep, truck, jeep. No José. The third truck. So that was something—José had escaped. If he were captive in a vehicle, there was no way to know if a shot would make one of the bastards simply turn with a pistol and shoot José through the head. Thank God he didn't need to make a decision.

He hefted the rifle. Frank guessed the troops would not see him, so far away and high on a hill where trees disguised the van as just another rosette in the rough embroidery of landscape.

He adjusted the telescopic lens. Despite boozing he still kept a sharpshooter's eye and the training came back to him in a surge, as if he'd never vowed to embrace peace, never gave up war, never renounced murder. Once and for all was a damned short time, it seemed. He sure as shit swelled with desire, to place a bullet, a single shot, into that ear, like a whisper, like a reminder. "A word in the ear of the colonel, Tomás. To remind him of you. Won't that be nice?"

Carefully he followed the slow motion of the jeeps, seeming scarcely to move in the distance. The closest they would pass to his perch wouldn't work, the line of sight could be obstructed if the slightest wind stirred leaves on the trees. He chose another spot, got down off the van and hiked carefully through loose dirt and rocks. He wanted to see a fragment of straight road—twenty exposed meters into which he could aim and fire, in which he could swing the scope only the tiniest fraction to place his shot.

"Well, Tomás, I believe I can do this."

And he worried briefly if the murder would bring reprisals down on the village, but hell, the village was too far away. Anyways, nobody in the indigenous population owned a piece like this. The weapon was class A American. Would they figure that out? Frank guessed the vehicles would try to put road behind them, not knowing if there were one shooter or a dozen, after the colonel was taken out. It would be a while before they arrived at barracks, and a while after before a doctor would figure out the weapon that blasted the colonel's skull. Frank grinned to himself. He'd be long gone by then, and this time he was heading for Belize, where nobody knew him and he could forget the Zapatistas. He could vanish as he vanished from Akron, from his family, his parents, his buddies. Frank the Fugitive, on the road again.

He chose a tree, and looked for a fork where he could prop the weapon. Few of these mountain trees offered sturdy branches; within reach they weren't much more than shrubs, flexible and thorn-covered. He gave it up and finally settled on a rock, in haste now as the convoy's dust told him time was getting close. He let his body down behind the outcrop. It was low but he had view and range. He swiveled the rifle, and satisfied himself that his target would be clear in the stretch he selected. And then he tightened his finger on the trigger and waited.

He spoke a few more words to Tomás before he killed the colonel. "The man responsible for your death," he explained, "I'm going to blast his fuckin' head off. Because I loved you, Tomás, and you're a good man." Not was, are. Inside your family's rectangle of earth, lying on top of the fleshless bones that preceded you, parents and uncles and aunts. Lying quietly healing the flesh as it vanishes from this tiny place on earth, where poor people grapple with grand ideas. "For you, Tomás. A good man in a good struggle." Fancy words, Frank's epitaph because he never went to the funeral, never cried with the children or embraced their mother, Alvira. Finally in the silence of a hillside swept with sun and blue sky he listened to his own thoughts. Yes, a good struggle.

The first vehicle rolled onto the piece of road Frank had chosen. And then the second in line, the jeep with the colonel in the front passenger seat, in Frank's scope so clearly Frank saw how the colonel's hand held the side frame near the window. He saw the deformed ear, evil, tiny and exposed, in the far sight of his gun. He felt the presence of Tomás. His fingers tightened.

Part Four: Beyond

49

Aida in San Fransisco, Summer 2000

She heaped the lot in plain sight on her desk beneath strands of sun-shine that occasionally drifted into her room. By the second week dust motes began to swarm in the air above the folders, and settle like wasps on sweet cakes.

Months slipped past. She went to see her adviser and assured the woman the thesis work was in progress.

Finally, one Sunday morning the following spring, Aida finished her coffee and sat down in front of her battered desk. She flipped though her four notebooks, the pencil and pen scribbling stained with rain or beer or coffee, whatever. Material from last year retained as background information for her thesis. Loose clippings and flyers lay tucked among the pages.

Clandestine indigenous revolutionary committee-general command of the Zapatista National Liberation Army of Mexico.
To the people of Mexico,

To the people and governments of the world.

Brothers.

Today, in the early morning hours of 22 of August of 1999, troops of the Federal Army, Public Security police and PRIistas cut the access road to the community of La Realidid.

The road is cut-off. Trenches have been dug, trees have been felled and huge stones deployed. The paramilitaries are guarding the blockade, stopping everyone.

We're waiting another attack any minute. The last bulletin we received from Subcomandante Insurgente Marcos this morning reported heavy land and air military.

The war goes on.

That's all.

Democracy, liberty and justice.

Comandantes Felipe, David, Moises and Daniel.

Awesome, that was only last year. Months of brainless work had transpired before she wrestled herself back into thinking academic. If she was back. No piece o' cake. Just opening the notebooks gave her a bellyache. Most of what she had scribbled was an omelet of events, not just women's issues. To formalize the role of women in the Zapatista struggle into a hypothesis, she'd need to clear out a lot of non-essentials—non-essentials to her thesis, that is.

Aida began to read. She paid several visits to the university library and took home whatever she could lay her hands on. She examined her journals; she searched the net. She needed to understand globalization, women joining the Zapatista army, women trapped in old customs in the pueblos. The men's councils, the women's councils. Not very American! She guessed that Marcos encouraged accepting women into the Zapatista army because of the shortage of fighters; egalitarian ideology followed after. Necessity impelled new attitudes.

Like always. Never imagine indigenous people hang onto old customs. They're the vanguard.

To get out from under the IMF, World Bank, the government's thumb, the threat of withholding money or interfering, the Zapatistas set up their own schools, hospitals, clinics. Was that a long-range solution? Those things take cash, and there's no income except foreign donations and some migrant workers sending home US pay checks. That was a lousy system, in her book. Where was the global solution? She turned over her notes:

Since 1994 social programs in Chiapas have been used to divide the indigenous and campesino populations. Not much effect on the Zapatista movement.

Gov trying with economic and military effort to hold them down, contain social discontent, isolate Zapatistas. Spending a lot but it doesn't help.

Keep in mind Mexico is country of mestizos and poor. Why sympathize with the rich?

Campesinos hanging tough for land reform. Gov buys and gives land to campesinos affiliated with PRI. Not a winning solution.

Military presence pervasive. Towns forced to take sides. Military raise hell with water pollution, rape women, steal/kill animals. Military creates Zapatista sympathizers.

Gov sharpens divisions inside communities. Gives out rifles to paramilitaries. Entire communities abandoned in face of internal conflict. Feds keep armed uprising from spreading outside Chps., but civil movement definitely growing.

Well, it was a bad year for sure. The most rational stuff she wrote in DF, before she went out into the countryside.

Gov supports paramilitaries, operating with impunity. Campesino leaders thrown in jail or killed.

After massacre at Mocotlán, no solution. Children suffer trauma. National solution only. Moral solution. Support the marginalized. Recognize different ethnic groups. Equity. Personal respect. Tolerance. Equal law. End to authoritarianism.

No thesis there, she could sell it in Sunday School.

70 NGOs demand army out and compliance with San Andrés Accords. Support movement in Mexico DF spread to rest of country. A caravan of 300 or 400 Zaps plan to travel to DF. Taking the long route.

She mulled it over. Amazing to have recorded anything, amid so much turmoil. She hadn't begun to tackle the women's new militancy, confronting face to face the troops, and together literally chasing them away. Run after them down the road, hollering! How many of the jillion foreigners, before they arrived in Chiapas, had a clue about what community means? Not me! Now, yes.

Night after night for nearly a year Aida gobbled Sara Paretsky mysteries and pop Tom Wolfe, flopped on her bed like a rag doll; she spaced out over re-runs of TV shows she would never have watched the first time around. Post traumatic syndrome, she diagnosed herself.

Now phase two. She moved. She walked walked walked through the spring and into the summer city. Thawing out. She sensed the juices trickling out through the colander.

It was more than sifting. The notebook material required reconstruction from a distance, plus the bag of computer disks which represented eyestrain hours in Alvaro's café in San Gregorio. During the past year she'd gone to see her mother twice a week, and eaten the indifferent cooking her mother claimed was Chinese food. Her mother looked at the new thinner Aida and didn't suggest she eat more. Instead she asked, "So? Was he good?"

Aida declined to reply. Her mother giggled and wagged her finger, without asking again. Her mother's view of life was simple: Sex! After that, food! Frank and she parted amicably, maybe sadly. Nothing to talk about. She got up every day and went to her agency work.

Now what? It wasn't so easy. She read in National Geographic a description of "peasant" life in southern Mexico. Appalled, she couldn't remember if she herself saw those exact scenes, or if she only recalled a prior National Geographic picture. They don't photograph outhouse flies, barren dirt-scrabble yards, dusty kids playing in discarded pots or cars or sofas or broken plastic tubs. The women appear smiling, colorful and clean; if they have no teeth, it doesn't show.

Nor does National Geographic, Aida had to admit, show Mexican cities with shopping malls. Even San Gregorio set up in an old building its interior set of shops called "a mall". On Saturday nights teenagers gathered to imitate American TV teenagers in vamp clothes. The dirty war was far away. They went for Women's Changing Roles as dictated by TV commercials. Girls wore lipstick so bright it looked plastic. McDonald's and Pizza Hut opened next to the cinema which showed Mexican spaghetti westerns Friday night, American James Bond on Saturday. The difference in San Gregorio only was security guards carried automatic weapons.

Her colleague Alfred declared, "This is their share of the good life, smoking allowed. The real point is not cuisine, it's corporate takeover. Burgers brought to you by the ruling class." Aida held no quarrel with Alfred's analysis. In her deeper fears loomed corporate takeover of the selva, of lands, of water. She found her hands oddly plucking at her sleeve or her buttons. She became self-conscious. She saw Alfred watching her, and began to watch herself. What this was all about she wasn't sure. She wasn't an indigenous Mexican. She was a moral person, however, living in an immoral world, where people killed for reasons that wouldn't hold up in kindergarten. She thought briefly of Maeda and Ricardo, and shut it down.

Another wave of fatigue hit her. At odd hours of the day she couldn't stay awake. At the office she drifted into the Ladies Room and fell asleep on the sagging couch. She fell asleep in her car in front of strange houses. At night she sprang awake at two A.M. and read.

Her case load went on hold, and Alfred took over the futile phone calls to mothers whose assistance had vanished. Aida read. The indigenous women in communities, with no aid whatsoever seemed better off—except for dying of diseases and malnutrition, of course.

She told her agency boss she was working on her thesis and needed a little more time.

She watched cable Mexican television, Mexican TV stations. In sports bars she saw only fútbol games, rarely news. Then it seemed the news was fake, Xed out: government issued sound bites.

The San Francisco summer proved lovely, with cool days and sweet fog off the bay. Some of what she'd loved in Chiapas came back to her—mist on the early mountains, greenness of wet vegetation, flame-colored flowers of the framboyan—"dear Lord or Lady," she said to God, "congratulations to You for a splendid job."

She was reawakening. Mornings saved her sanity, but everything hurt.

Not that she believed in God, no way a personal, thoughtful, watch-the-sparrow type of god. No Holy Marys for her. Not in Sub-comandante Marcos' stories about the Old Ones, either, although she dreamily read the tales published in his book, turning pages slowly and pausing at each picture to observe shapes and colors. Meanwhile her brain dashed ahead, simultaneously embracing ideas hitting her from all compass points. It was like closing one eye to look out of the other, and then switching eyes to watch the frame of vision jump right to left, left to right. Some objects actually disappeared from view when she did that.

Finally, seated again in an old stuffed chair, she began to thumb wrinkled pages in deliberate search of her thesis. The notes contained fragments of sights she witnessed with one eye or the other; fragments of ideas, of propaganda she copied, articles she cut and saved, hopes expressed by one woman or another.

She had no photographs of Zapatista women, it was dangerous. One of Constance and Harry Skelba, whom she still thought of as her friends. One of Maeda and Ricardo. Her fingers went to her lips. She swallowed hard. The picture was in case they needed to identify.

Carefully she lifted the two pictures and placed them in a separate pile. Frank? None of him. Frank was as paranoid as the rest of them.

Photos had not seemed necessary to what she was there for. She might have shot National Geographic scenes. Now she regretted not having done even that. She had diskettes and notes, some of them numbered; for some without datelines she had to deduce their time sequence from their physical sequence on her pages.

After fifteen minutes she took off her glasses and pulled on a sweater.

She strolled toward the embarcadero, toward the crowds. People streamed into the huge out-door Golden-Oldies concert.

Alone in a crowd of thousands she folded herself onto the grass to hear the Temptations sing Motown rock. The loudspeakers blasted to every corner of the open area, and after a while she got up again, dusting the seat of her jeans. She meandered around and accepted from outstretched hands free samples of Vanilla Bean Coolatta, fruit flavored yogurts, hummus and pita bread snack kits, apple juice, lemon-lime soda, chewing gum. Half an hour later she sat again, on a bench, to peer into her free AT&T Calling Card plastic bag, like a kid after a Halloween orgy.

"I don't even like this stuff," she mumbled. A woman next to her asked, "What? You don't want? I take!" and she accepted the bag from Aida's willing hand, smiling with two gold teeth.

In the darkness Aida hiked back across the park to her apartment, and without undressing fell asleep on the sofa. The next day she bought herself a laptop and internet service.

According to Mexican news, Federal pre-election activity consisted of police aggression and paramilitary attacks. The military was confined to barracks.

The situation for state rule was bitterly different in Chiapas. A fiefdom is not relinquished. Death threats, incursions into lands, violent and arbitrary detentions of campesinos, road blockades by armed paramilitaries. Finally she began to focus.

She signed up for e-mail service and sent off a dozen notices to friends. When a note shot back promptly from Constance Skelba Aida hunched before the screen with her mouth open, as if to ingest the news.

Autonomous municipalities of the north, and of the Lacondón Selva stay on permanent high alert, she read. A new network of satellite and radio-based communications connected PRI communities in the indigenous regions with the emergency 066 of Tuxtla Gutiérrez, controlled by the Federal Army. The rural telephone network was turned off, leaving indigenous areas incommunicado. Communal farmers faced attacks by Peace-and-Justice paramilitary who controlled the roads.

Aida was entirely alert. Her skin and hair felt alert, she leaned forward on the edge of her seat. The information flowed into her like a blood transfusion. On line she read La Jornada and Reforma. Some way to reconcile the input must be within her, behind her eyelids, inside her nostrils. Peering into her monitor like a crystal ball, she read everything she could find.

On July 2 the PRI did badly and dismantled two polling places. In the selva of Ocosingo eight other polling stations vanished, and in Chilón, three.

Then. The peaceful July overthrow of the PRI happened like the fall out of the sky of Icarus, unnoticed in San Francisco. Campesinos walked four hours each way to vote. The PRI lost Chiapas to independent Pablo Salazar with the eight-party Alianza coalition behind him.

On the national presidential miracle day of August 20, when the ruling party lost a reasonably clean election, Aida threw a sweater on over her slacks and shirt and rushed out into the evening to gaze up at the San Francisco sky. Nothing special again! No fireworks, no neon lights proclaiming viva chiapas! viva mexico! The next morning she dashed into her Social Services agency.

"The PRI lost! The PRI lost!" They thought she'd lost her mind. What was the PRI?

Her colleague Alfred saved the day. He got it. They bought a bottle of champagne and went to eat Chinese noodles and drink to Mexico. In a few months Alfred would scream and shout about the new President Fox's neoliberal policies, and collaboration between the two right-wing parties. But for the moment!

They watched a replay of President Zedillo preempting any fraud after the vote, jumping onto the TV even before Fox could claim his victory, or Labastida admit defeat. Zedillo announced the winner. Hooray! In front of the small screen, seeing only the thirty-second fragment of Mexican cable news, she hollered, "Yes! Yes!" and pumped the cushion with her fist. To Alfred she proclaimed, "Zedillo goes down in history, and right up to heaven, the Gorbachev of Mexico!"

Alfred, neither Mexican-American nor naive, replied, "It only happened because the country has nothing left to steal after Carlos Salinas."

In the following days Fox announced plans to invite increased foreign investment: more Coca-Cola corporations, more seduction for Mexico's petrochemical complex as well as for its culture.

Alfred whined; nevertheless Aida's joy held, as profound as witnessing the birth of a baby. Sure neoliberal policies would screw them over. She knew she was nuts to feel so good. But a crack in the iron rule! Some sanity might return to Chiapas.

For the first time in a year she remembered sex, how nice that was! About Frank, that he must be safe.

Future president Vicente Fox visited Canada. Vicente Fox visited Gore, Bush and Clinton. Vicente Fox broadcast new visions for USA-Mexico relations. Legalize workers across the border. Aim for two-way efforts for reducing drug demand. And a future economic union with open borders Canada to Mexico? Oh, Diós.

She wasn't stupid. Fat chance for any of this. But at least the PRI stranglehold was broken.

She went into the supervisor's dingy green office. "I'm pregnant," she declared, a flat-out lie, a strange truth. Holding her flat waist protectively, she arranged to take maternity leave without pay, knowing she would never return to that job. She told her mother she needed to follow-up her thesis material, the day was coming when women would be aware of their rights in the new Mexico. It was a reasonable idea.

Her mother, unflappable as always, wondered how would she live? and Aida answered, "Very simply!"

She didn't say a word to her mother about finding life in San Francisco boring and trivial; that would be sacrilege. She bought a ticket and packed.

50

Merwin Returns

PROMOTING WORLD HERITAGE
Another essential task is building awareness

EDUCATION PROGRAMMES
The UNESCO Special Project "Young People's Participation in World Heritage Preservation and Promotion" was launched in 1994 to encourage and enable tomorrow's decision-makers to participate in heritage conservation and to respond to the continuing threats facing our World Heritage. Through the development of new educational approaches, the Project aims to provide young people with the necessary knowledge, skills and commitment to become involved in the protection and promotion of heritage from local to global levels.

Merwin returned to San Gregorio. It was August, 2000. Once again he found a small apartment, two rooms plus a bathroom and kitchen. His anonymous neighbors didn't know him or Carmen. It was vendors in the market who remembered him when he went to make his small purchases of brown smoked fish or half a chicken. He ate rice and beans, tomatoes and chilies. He kept himself fed.

Only his thirst could not be satisfied. The chores of identifying the trash bell, water bell, gas horn, the shout of the man who sold oranges filled him with a sense of belonging yet not belonging. Daily rain cooled him and sun absorbed him. Who was he? Was he Mexican in his blood? Such an identity was fantasy; he knew biology. Not much to choose between, the blood of so-called peoples and so-called races. Culture determined everything. Blood comes only in four types. Bones are all the same.

The peaceful electoral revolution had happened. While he was reporting to the UNESCO committee on his research, and attending the World Heritage Convention in Switzerland, the PRI buckled. While he was in New York fretting over teaching programs and educational materials for use in schools and universities, the PRI crumbled. He didn't think about the continuation of the government's low-intensity war against communities in rebellion. He absolutely didn't think about Carmen. He would not think about Carmen, not her firm dark body next to him, nor her gentle mouth. To think of her was to immediately recall the small scars on her feet, and tears that flowed down her face when she told him she must remain in Chiapas. How she could feel an obligation was beyond him. Imagine a lovely woman with her nose running. He couldn't even do that. He couldn't.

Instead, he busied himself updating the internet page for World Heritage sites. An astonishing number in Mexico—nineteen. He traveled slowly and carefully to view rock paintings of the Sierra de San Francisco and newly excavated town of Uxmal. His role was official scholar, on official business. He cut off his ponytail, resumed wearing his hair at a respectable length. He never thought about Carmen. The

PRI had fallen. He thought of her almost never. The effort made him thin.

Many ordinary people in San Gregorio seemed to light up with enthusiasm bordering on glee when the election was mentioned. Others were frightened. They feared the paramilitary would eventually burst loose in the countryside.

In the small rundown city Merwin saw no changes. Merwin returned to the painted stucco and neglected church nearly against his will, if you didn't count letters, faxes and e-mails he sent steadily for a year to gain permission. The new 1999 sites required documentation, photographs and preparation of pedagogical material. That was his field, right?

The daily scene persisted: on Wednesday a mobile demonstration in front of the municipal building with several hundred men traveling from town to town in pick-up trucks to demand the usual health services, roads, education and potable water. They were not Zapatistas bent on self-rule; they were fishermen from the Pacific coast. They gathered in the park on benches and perched on fountain rims to eat their packed tortillas, drink water from plastic containers. The men waited quietly for the close of the bureaucratic day to collect their banners and depart on the next five-hour leg. Merwin sensed that as the previous style of repression cooled, towns like San Gregorio would percolate and boil, slowly shedding the PRI's weight.

Not looking for Carmen he re-acquaintanced with the city week after week, his sunglasses in his shirt pocket, his rain hat in his pants pocket. Along the streets he noted afresh the panorama of paint-peeling buildings, repaired buildings, earthquake damaged walls, some graffiti on new walls, some old adobe walls worse than before. Daily rain in the rainy season made him curious to see the flower-filled patio the Skelbas enjoyed. If Constance and Harry still lived there, it was high time to stop and say hello.

Carmen's patient efforts in the patio had produced hundreds of meters of flowering vines, draped across the roof and walls. Merwin arrived before sundown, a time he hoped was neither their comida nor their cena. He could use a drink, a beer, a shot of mescal. A between-times beverage. He opened the outer gate and went in. Nobody answered the doorbell. He stood quietly.

In the growing twilight Merwin saw bats fly, but maybe they were birds. He smelled the sweet aroma of pan dulce baking somewhere on the other side of the patio wall. He seated himself at the patio table, and lifted his head to watch the twilight move into darkness. A few stars appeared very high overhead. We are so close to the equator here, he thought.

For several weeks now Merwin considered living in Mexico. He could speak the language; he could easily fit in, looking "Mexican" as much as anybody, whatever that meant. All he needed was a mission. And one possibility was to make culture central to decision-making as development inevitably overtook the countryside. For the sake of all Mexicans, sure, for his own sake, not to lose what he had found. He could do local museums. He could help communities plan projects to protect themselves from being wrenched apart in the adjustment to new economic and technological realities as globalization invaded. There was no way the country could remain the same, and who the hell wanted it to. The culture vultures who liked quaint little pueblos with rutted dirt streets? No way.

He recognized the crickets' whir. They made a deep hum more than a scraping sound, and hereabouts they sing in October, and all year long.

Give them something to grab onto that will benefit and empower them. Globalization will come, but these people could hardly be made poorer. Tourists will come, the Zapatistas will get screwed. Not outright. Just little by little.

Merwin listened again to the throb of night falling. For all our sakes, we have to master the interaction. There'll be social, economic, environmental, and physical changes. Human groups can flourish without loss of their identity or betrayal of their heritage. That's what they want. To flourish. Nobody wants to stay impoverished. Nobody wants to feel a boot pressed on his back. His mind worked right along now, and he pulled out of his shirt pocket a ball-point pen. But it was too dark. Merwin smiled to himself.

Okay, here's what I want. The goal is to create conditions of respect, not only in economic but also in social and cultural terms. Culture is a tool. Museums have the responsibility and opportunity to bind communities, livable and sustainable. Keep 'em down on the farm despite global market takeovers, technology, and contrived temptation.

He ran his hand over his head. People don't need to migrate, not undocumented to the US and not into overcrowded Mexican cities. Not with economic self-sufficiency, civic vitality, environmental soundness. A sustainable community is what we want. Not one of these dead towns with no male adults. Plan for the future. Modern-day challenges as opportunities. Museums can't have the luxury of being passive warehouses of the world's indigenous cultures. Come on.

He rapped the table for attention from stars and flowers. These Indians are alive. They are the First Mexicans. They can run their own show and make it work for them.

He stood up again and walked back and forth, in the patio belonging to Constance and Harry who somehow weren't here to listen to his ideas flow. He could list without half trying a dozen towns where a museum could be a cultural and economic center. Teotihuacan. Palenque. Chichen-Itzá. El Tajín. Ixcatlán. Hell, Mexico was the seat of civilizations going back thousands of years, and the remains, as Carmen showed him, lay everywhere. The campesinos dug history out of the ground every time they plowed a field.

But somebody was here, no? He heard the gate open, a creak of metal, and then silence. He thought he was hidden by the darkness and might frighten the shit out of Constance if she spotted him in the patio like a burglar. He stepped forward, looking for a patch of light where he could identify himself.

Someone walked very slowly toward him. Suddenly light hit him full in the face. He waited, almost patient, almost prescient, as if he knew he mustn't himself be afraid, or frighten the other person. He waited and not knowing what else to do, looked up again toward the stars. The light went out.

"Did you see today's paper?" Carmen asked. "Is that why you came?" Merwin stood absolutely still. "Today's headline reports the "sorrow" expressed by the colonel in Georgia of the United States, for the army's role in Chiapas: 'We didn't want to be there but it was our Constitutional duty.' I like it that the colonel grieves. It makes him appear human."

Merwin finally moved forward. He put his arms around Carmen.

"It's okay," she whispered. "Está bien." He was trembling, and she pressed against him.

"Where are the Skelbas?"

"They flew north for two weeks to visit their grandchildren. I check their apartment. But I was ready to find you."

Merwin, regaining his presence of mind, still held her. He spoke into her ear. "Did you know I was in San Gregorio?"

"Yes, how not! Since many observers left, each foreigner is noticed." She smiled in the darkness. "Many believe you are a foreigner. Some believe you are one of us, come home from the United States with money in your pocket!"

"Yeah. That's me, come home." He kissed her gently on the side of her temple. "What about Ignacio?"

"I doubt he will return too soon. It's not so safe for him, right now!"

"Will he let you go?"

"I paid the debt, twenty years. He will do well enough with his new relationship, the USA. I think he does not need me any more as his wife." She exhaled gently. "You understand the word impunidad?"

In English, impunity. Ignacio was safe and would never be called to account. Ignacio would come back in due time, to a bigger better job. But never to rural Chiapas.

Merwin heard the soft breath, could not see the new smile against his shoulder. "Are you okay?"

"Sí, `okay', Carmen replied, "As we say, `We don't need permission to be free.'"

51

Billy and Frank Visit Polho, December 2000

"Soup is inherently good," says Frank, "and helicopters are inherently bad." This is the type of profound political conclusion to which Billy was treated right before he left Mexico. He looked over at Frank. "Man, that's profound."

Billy returned to the Peace Observers' San Gregorio house ten days before the presidential inauguration. About the same time Frank showed up, wheezing with a mean bronchial cold he shared with Billy. They observed the end of the PRI era and the Presidential Inauguration of Vicente Fox with fancy-footed hope and a lot of toilet tissue used instead of kleenex. Their hope flew in the face of Frank's denial of any possibility of a good government—but what the hell. Hope had done him that way before.

The players and games of this triumphal season were as clear as crumpled snot-covered toilet paper. No way could Billy sort it out. Not even Frank could guess what behind-the-scenes machinations the elite worked, power trade-offs to allow the PAN Party to almost govern, and maybe almost control the military. It was all like, take it one day at a time, Frank said.

In preparation for his return to academic life in the spring semester the post-child poster child Billy, locating the town's few obscure bookstores, read biographies and histories and newspaper accounts, and then figured: Pin a tail on the donkey. Four years in Mexico and his ignorance was bottomless. Even resident pundits wouldn't guess as to what would happen.

Billy hung around Alvaro's when he recovered some energy. The air was electric and scattered, like fireflies jumping every which way. Even Frank went along, his jeans washed and his perpetual t-shirt ratty. He sat at a small table drinking espresso, his arms down by his sides to hide underarm rips that exposed his brown hair through the open seams. A sober world-change came over him, quiet but not down at the mouth. Expectations flew high among some, bitter among others. The corner TV flashed. Speeches and posturing. "Fox's good, or they're co-opted? What do you think?"

Frank never said anything dubious about anyone who wasn't actually shooting at him. But for sure anyone who worked for a national government did not make his Top Ten. "Keep in mind, Bill," Frank offered, "some see Fox as shit, another US tool who'll lay more poverty on the masses while rich guys buy the place up." He blew his nose. It remained pale, unlike Billy's, which shone red from toilet tissue abrasion, and peeled along his nostrils. "In this camp you have Subcomandante Marcos, who rakes over Zedillo every chance he gets. Chavo, we're talking here six years of el ex-presidente's low intensity warfare and fuckin' paramilitary crimes. Now comes along Fox who also is a neoliberal, offending the hell out of indigenous people. He gets on screen and offers television and western goods. And oh, yes, give up control over your land. Like offering Nintendo to monks. Misses the point completely. Of local autonomy."

"But if constitutional changes for indigenous rights pass in Congress, that will be good?" Back in their house, Billy sprawled on the stained old sofa, watching news replays for the third time, with his head twisted. Frank couldn't guess why Billy was still here in San Gregorio after telling everyone he was on his way back north. Billy, looking out from the side of his head, was having difficulty getting his mind ready for a mature re-entry.

Frank snorted. It was one of his less pleasant traits. Having a bad cold made it worse, sort of like a horse with nose drool. Billy tried not to be offended. He was facing up to how ignorant he was, years enough out of school to qualify him as a drop-out, and no manners neither. The re-entry to university life scared him shitless, but here, he was played out. Time to get gone.

When the inauguration hour arrived, Billy was out in the town. He stepped into a convenience store and watched a tiny black and white TV in the rear. He leaned against the moldy cement wall, next to the potato chips, trying not to breathe spores, captured by the moment of history in the ceremony.

Fox swore. In the dim light Billy witnessed the witnessing on screen, by the Latin-American presidents including Castro, other foreign dignitaries, and even Madeleine Albright. A few kids drifted in and bought cokes. Another man watching next to him asked, "Who is Fox?"

The storekeeper pointed. The one with the green, white and red banner across his chest, but on black and white there was no way to tell. Billy left quietly.

After his inauguration Fox withdrew the military to barracks. The Zapatistas broke their silence and accepted his gesture of good intention, although 60,000 troops remained in Chiapas. Marcos and the Zapatista commanders announced plans to travel to Mexico City in February to address the legislature, for consideration of the San

Andrés Accords. Billy knew the Accords included an agreement to let autonomous communities control their own resources.

No way.

A guy in Alvaro's told Billy if the army left, the Zapatistas would work it out with their indigenous PRI neighbors, because the supply of money and arms would dry up.

Pablo Salazar suggested the paramilitary be given sheep in exchange for their guns, like a rural buy-back.

"Is that weird or what?" Billy asked Frank rhetorically. "How can massacres be forgiven—I doubt they can be. Not by me, anyway."

"Don't put anything past the Zapatistas," Frank advised. He didn't offer any explanations based on his own choice. To kill or not to kill, that wasn't strategy, it was orientation.

Finally cured of la gripa, they drove to the village of Polhó in Frank's beat-up and dusty van, with the usual supplies, including some antibiotics they were still scarfing down themselves. Billy felt bad using stuff people needed but Frank said Go ahead. They would provide foreign witness, so no further bad things would happen in this place of bad things, during tense days when nobody knew what Fox and Salazar might do to resolve the standoff. Privately Frank guessed the standoff between the PRI and the Zapatistas would never resolve, but he didn't say so. Give it another fifty years, he figured—but he would be dead by then.

They traveled in daylight. Their passports were recorded and their photos taken as usual; no hassle, immigration guards let them pass. Frank didn't try to pretend anything so Billy didn't either.

Frank, behind the wheel, glanced over at Billy's profile as the van pulled away from the checkpoint. "They can't pull any shit right now, but we'll be in Polhó just in case."

When they arrived it was unreal. The old men stood like posed extras, on a cement pavilion. Women sat and rested in the shade. The women smiled. Like a movie set.

Showing their letter of credential from the medical team of Estación Norte in San Gregorio, they drove through the wire and wood gate. The guards never had weapons, had none now. The van lurched down the dirt road into the ravine where Polhó sits. Behind the front lot on the movie set.

The Authority who let them in gave permission for them to sleep at night on the cement floor of one of the schoolrooms. The small wood shack used by regular observers was occupied. They brought bread and peanut butter, water and canned tuna, tangerines and bananas to feed themselves. "The 950 original campesinos can't feed 9500," Frank informed Billy unnecessarily. "Supplies are brought when they have pesos. Money donated, mostly by foreigners."

Polhó squeezed between the road, the military encampment, and neighboring PRI and paramilitary communities. The terrain sloped. Green and beautiful, it lodged in the mountains like a raisin in a pudding. Clouds on top of mountains looked like frosting after you stuck your finger in. Within the beauty lurked possible attack.

The two Americans were greeted formally in a shack built on stilts over space, by the compact wiry man who was the EZLN contact in Polhó. He sat on a rough wood bench beside the civil Authority who spoke no Spanish. His face when he smiled became lively and intelligent, his expression good, like welcome and alive and nice to see you. He was handsome, really, if Billy could say that. At least his skin, creamy brown, wasn't white with spots. When he stopped speaking, his face became the saddest ever seen, with a bruise of sorrow punched around his eyes.

The announcement that EZLN leaders would travel to Mexico to address Congress crossed Billy's mind as he hunched on the handmade wooden chair and listened to the man, who hadn't ventured outside the community he guarded for four years. They claim Marcos, except for brief incursions into San Cristóbal, hasn't left the jungle of Chiapas for fifteen years. Billy was as good as on his way home.

Maybe Marcos has a family still alive. Who thinks of a hero, a legend, with a mother? Like mine. Mine wants to see me, but maybe Marcos' mother is pissed off at his politics? Looking at the man greeting them in a shack in Polhó, Bill knew if this guy had a mother, a wife, children, they were all dead. That kind of face. I haven't been in touch with my mother that much, but she knows what country I'm in. Get your ass back here to the university, she writes to me on e-mail. Will you be a bum all your life? Grennich takes care of her. But still. He needed a life, an American life.

"You have a mother still living?" Billy asked Frank when the interview ended.

"Sure. She's in Akron. Thinks the US government is the source of all wisdom. Can't understand how anybody could mount a rebellion after 1776." He laughed lightly. "Can't get it why the Zapatistas struggle. No connection in her brain between government policies and poverty."

"Ah," Billy replied. What more could he say? Frank's mother sounded like his own. Well-meaning, nice and nowhere. They walked down the road to unload their gear into the schoolroom. A young guy, one of the promotores, came in with a worried expression. "Class begins at 8:00 A.M." he said.

"It's okay, we'll leave your space by then." The cement floor, broken window panes, and chalkboard weren't all that enchanting. We ain't gonna sleep in. One light bulb, the usual moldy peeling paint. Splintery wooden desk-and-bench combinations. A few mildewed books on a corner shelf. The teacher was younger than Billy, eighteen or twenty years old, small and thin, like most of the men. He showed Billy on the chalkboard his lesson for Spanish-Tzotzil synonyms. No government employees here. Billy printed the English translation.

"Just goofin around," he assured the teacher.

Beyond the cement schoolroom, shacks of wood boards and tin roofs built along the ridges hung over ravines on wood or cement stilts. It looked like a nasty wind would take it all down, but it stood. Mud in the two dirt roads dried into ridges and lumps under the hot sun. Tiny stores—the same wood shacks—lined the mud trail, to supply sodas, embroidery thread, a few cans of chipotle or tuna.

"There's no competition," Frank explained. He popped the top off a coke. "Equal opportunity non-profits. There's sheds with shelves supplied by the one store original to Polhó," he waved upward at a cement box fronting the high road. Military vehicles passed by on routine harassment.

Some recommendation, passed through Billy's mind.

The original Polhó residents donated their land to take in the refugees. All over the world, refugees. These grow and sell coffee for cash so they can buy supplies. In a manner of speaking. Coffee prices were like playing the lottery. And this was what they struggled for. This, and dignity.

They hiked around the community land, away from the dirt roads which Frank had hiked before, but he did it again for Bill. It was pretty steep. They sweated the trails up and down. In some plots women dried coffee beans spread on plastic sheeting on the ground. The visitors accepted cuts of sugar cane to chew. Several women called out "Buenos días".

"That's all the Spanish they know."

"It's hard to believe the community absorbed an extra 9,000 people. Talk about overcrowding. In the States if this was a school or prison they'd shut it down. They must be living eight or ten people to a shack."

"Correct. They grow a few small gardens, bananas, a corn field

—not enough." Frank, unlike Billy, seemed elated. But Frank had turned believer: community was the foundation for survival. A future without reliance on distant government. For Frank, government meant not just small dirty wars but big dirty wars. Fuck that shit. Fuck all that shit. Poverty is no goal, but it's sometimes better than other options, especially if in the end they were gonna screw you anyhow.

They made their way back onto the main dirt road. A few elders with baked brown skin in gleaming contrast to white tunics and knee pants, saluted them. The women wore traditional embroidered blouses, amazingly white and dazzlingly colored. Some wore traditional wool wrap-around skirts. The children wore rags. Nobody had underwear, a luxury item. Billy couldn't help seeing when one of the women got up from the ground where she sat. The dark between her legs flashed briefly, and Billy was neither shamed nor aroused. He was used to seeing breasts exposed, and naked unshaved legs and naked callused feet, not even plastic shoes or rubber boots. Only a few young men wore leather boots, probably for climbing back country as look-outs. Naked feet shocked him more than naked crotches.

The men cropped their hair. The stiff black bristles formed a natural and enviable brush atop their skulls. The women's long braids hung down without those bright colored ribbons women in San Gregorio braided into their hair like butterflies perched on their heads. Not in this place.

"Well, man, what do they have?"

"Fertile land, not enough to feed so many. They're clearing the hillside below the outer road, an act of faith, I'd call it. They have a plan for coffee shaded by oranges and mangos."

High up where Frank pointed, men wielded machetes, chopping in a line along the slope to clear out the parcel. They bent into the hill to go up. They jogged getting down.

Some kids raced by, playing and laughing. Some ran away when they saw Billy's white face and orange hair. One boy approached and looked up. He wanted to touch Billy's eyelashes. Billy bent over, his eyelids hiding the blue. The small brown fingers touched briefly and fled. Billy opened his eyes.

Inside the community kitchen kids hung in the window frames to look at the foreigners. They waited for an inch of banana, a gift sliced by the long-term foreign observer. The observer told them about the cement clinic, plus a trailer labeled Cruz Roja Mexicana, with a European insignia. Except for some embroidered blouses and purses sold in the market of San Cristóbal, foreign donations were the only source of cash. After the shared meal Billy bought a purse for his mother at the tiny shop.

With no Tzotzil, there was no way to learn but observe. Frank disappeared into the clinic. Billy sat on the cement wall next to the basketball court, and when his butt began to hurt, on grass further away. He let his thoughts churn. It was globalization and progress all over again. He needed to have a point of view, didn't he? Like the university students in DF. Or did he? Or had he already, just by being here, at this time in this place? He hoped you could hold a position without articulating an ism. Isms turned him off, because in thirty years if it didn't work out, you were trapped. That guy Paco in DF made him cringe. He liked Frank's practical approach better, oppose bad and do good. Pretty simplistic, not something you could get away with in the millennium world of a US university. But he knew at least what to think about, like local control and direct democracy. Billy heaved a sigh. The sun was falling, and pink stained clouds spread like a blush over the mountains.

At night they pushed aside some classroom benches and placed their sleeping bags on the cement floor. The community loudspeakers blared scratched dance music from a few tapes. This racket informed outsiders the community was alert and awake against attack all night. At least Billy was awake. It's damned cold in the mountains and the bathroom area stood to hell and gone down the hill. He scrunched inside his bag until 5:00 when dawn arrived, and the music stopped, and then thrust his bare feet into his untied sneakers and stepped out. Clear as crystal, with a light frost. He took a piss behind the building.

Around eight the broadcast system played again, this time through a speaker lifted overhead by one guy, while another held a microphone. The message was in Tzotzil. Little kids arrived for their classes. Billy and Frank shoved their gear out of the way and went down toward the bathrooms and basketball court to watch teachers lead the five year olds onto the empty cement court. They marched in line, like he remembered from St. Agnes. Only no nuns. The words were shouted out in Spanish and Tzotzil: "Let's go", "Stop", "Hands up!" (all hands go up like the teacher's) "Hands down!" Down went the little hands. "A circle" (some little guys had to be captured) "Sit"! Tap with sticks: "one two three," they counted. Cute. Bilingual education was essential. The Zapatistas didn't intend to be backward.

"You know the slogan," Frank said, "We don't want a handout, we just want you to get off our backs." Frank's ratty t-shirt had been exchanged for a local pull-over shirt woven of flimsy cotton. Billy nodded. He pulled on his baseball cap and yanked the brim down to shield his eyes from the morning sun. Out on the cement two little boys galloped around escaping class. Billy smiled, but basketball was also the chief recreation and outlet for older boys who couldn't go anywhere. Like animals in cages, back and forth is all.

"Electricity but no phone service. A few television sets in the shops receive one station, wavy as hell, on a black and white. Some teenagers still don't know Spanish, maybe they learned it and forgot. Their mothers probably only use Tzotzil. The fathers maybe speak Spanish."

"Yeah, the Authority relied on the EZLN leader to translate for him."

"That's how it is," Frank assented. He spoke calmly. Billy wanted out after just the second day in self-enforced captivity. He'd bet his ass that local boys yearned for some freedom.

They bumped back to San Gregorio. "Maybe the shooting is over," Billy hoped out loud.

Frank grunted. "What, you don't want to go out into the countryside any more?"

"My plan is to pass my sleeping bag along to a son, for Boy Scout camp. Like, peace."

"Don't hold your breath, Bill."

In San Gregorio Frank bought chicken entrails and vegetables. Boiled into soup it made a kind of post-travel insurance. After three days of being none too well nourished, he gnawed bones and admitted his body craved the change.

No shit. Billy gifted his half-jar of peanut butter to Polhó. It was all he had for the poorest community he'd ever in his life seen.

52

Constance Writes a Letter

January 25, 2001
Dear Sally,

I'm late, but happy New Year. The fiestas concluded, and now the big news is, the Zapatistas are coming to town. Not like they're not here all the time anyway! But this is the formal show. They leave San Cristóbal on February 25 in a caravan, a mix of foreign observers and Chiapanecos, on their way to Mexico DF to address the Mexican Congress. San Gregorio is included on their route. Local people are deeply excited, including me and Harry. This is probably close to the highlight of our stay here so far—seeing the EZLN emerge, and go on the road.

First: the national sibling quarrels; who will do what with whom, and where. My God, what shall we wear? This is no simple business like tumbling out of bed in your PJs and running downstairs to open your Christmas gifts. Fox says no ski masks for the Zapatistas, but of course Marcos won't go without.

Fox claims he is dismantling military posts, but Marcos points out he's not taking troops out of Chiapas, only moving them to different barracks. Some complain Marcos is ungrateful. Marcos complains that Fox is putting spin on events, mostly untrue. It is definitely true that troops quartered adjacent to Zapatista towns, four of seven posts, withdrew as of January 19, to other bases inside Chiapas. It's true that Fox says he won't and then he will, pushing against forces in Mexico who Just Say No to the Zapatista caravan entering DF. It's debatable anyway that Fox can't pull all troops out of Chiapas because of Chiapas' border with Guatemala: drugs, guns and undocumented workers heading north. The latest group of Guatemalans crossed with a professional pollero who disguised them as Zapatistas. They got caught in San Gregorio. Someone shouted out the window of their rickety bus "Viva Zapata, ustedes vos!" which I took to mean Long live Zapata, you all. Oops!

The daily papers print articles about the Zapatistas, how to contact them, how to donate supplies, where and when the National Indigenous Congress will take place. The media war portrays the Zapatistas as dangerous and intransigent, so who's controlling the media?

Meanwhile, here in San Gregorio, to fill the dreadful dull void between Day of the Kings and the caravan, the locals imported a festival from Guatemala. So there went yet another torch procession, fireworks like artillery, bands thumping, the whole thing. The morning after, I met my neighbor at the garbage truck (an inevitable meeting place after a big fiesta) and we chatted a little about the situation. Her family descend from the Spanish colonizers, but nothing remains of their grand fincas. Consuelo has a soft spot in her heart for the poor, although the original Zapatistas of 1930 killed her grandfather. She remembers her grandmother speaking of how their finca cared for the people who worked there—benevolent paternalism. But I'm fond of Consuelo, whose heart is good and whose body is round and soft.

"It's complicated," she says. "Only one cousin of nine brothers still has a finca, the land is now lying unused while people go hungry," she tells me. "Who knows what's really going on in the jungle". During this monologue, we drank deep Chiapas coffee in my patio.

Consuelo earns some money by sewing quinceañera dresses for nubile adolescents, and wedding gowns with seed pearls, and now she has a second job selling a lactobacilli drink guaranteed to clean the intestines. I declined, although my intestines are inflamed. (The doctor here says, Number one disease is skin, second is intestines. A hygiene problem, you might say).

Meanwhile, Fox claims to have dismantled 53 road blockades; suspended over-flights by helicopters; presented the COCOPA initiative on behalf of the indigenous to Congress; opened a special visa for foreigners to enter Chiapas and accompany the Zapatistas. "No one who wants to go will have any trouble," Fox tells us. "How good it will be for everyone to see what we're doing!" and "Masks don't matter," Fox says now, "it's the dialogue. We're calm; we have patience, We'll continue doing what we're doing."

Please admire my ability to translate! As a language instructor I feel like a doctor visiting a proctologist. I'm finally learning, you might say. I doubt Fox's rhetoric, but I know what it says.

The newspapers receive communiqués from Marcos, and publish daily bulletins on the caravan route, where to make your contacts, the order of states to be traveled, etc. Harry wants to be in San Cristóbal February 25 and set out with the Mexico Solidarity group to accompany the Zapatista caravan through its tour. So he'd double back through San Gregorio. Sort of like Rudolph the red-nosed engineer. For my part, no bus agony. I want to see our hero (Marcos, not Harry) in San Gregorio, and then fly to Mexico DF to witness the entry there. It's a great opportunity for foreign observers, or I might say tourists to the rebellion, dressed up in backpacks, with our romantic revolutionaries' gear.

I know you told me not to put myself down, or scoff at our contribution. But more and more I see we don't really contribute much, or maybe that's me, because Harry is doing good with the water systems. But I learn, and maybe not everyone our age manages to do that.

Anyway, the good news is, the government no longer confronts foreigners who seek to aid the cause, since Marcos has undeniable support globally among non-governmental organizations who could damage Mexico's image. God forbid any investors get queasy and pull out! It's going to be very interesting with thousands here again, like at the beginning, participating in the French Revolution or something. Nowadays in Chiapas hundreds of foreigners do social work, and often it's difficult to distinguish when this is converted into political action. I simply never try – don't ask, don't tell. Foreigners give classes in religion. Proseletyzing for Jesus. In what moment do they leave spiritual material for political? I don't think our guru Martin whom I told you about is so neatly categorized anymore. Before, most people ran scared regardless, because you never knew if expulsion would end up as murder. Now it feels safer.

The upshot is, it's a huge change in the environment. The sense of repression has lifted, not for the indigenous, but for everyone else, especially the press, the NGOs, and towns trying to get PRI officials off their backs. So Harry and I benefit, although I doubt the people who started it all and have suffered so long benefit much. When I look into my crystal ball, I'm not so happy. I don't see corporate development backing off; the poor will get displaced. Maybe the other side in Mexico is that if autonomous communities can hold on, they'll do for themselves what vanishing social programs did in other countries. And, maybe, the idea of bottom-up organizing will float out onto the atmosphere. Community's very appealing to those of us who've lived with individualism so long.

So along those lines, Harry wonders if he should accept any other jobs—I think Cuates, although a great triumph, almost did us in (and I include myself in the near fatality!) We've been away so long, except for two weeks last August, I feel like I've lost touch with Ann Arbor, and we don't know the grandchildren, and also, I've changed. Gotten older, I suppose. The future of course will be something else again—first, we let ourselves celebrate. And then, we decide if we should stay.

If we stay much longer I may have to ask you to shop for me—my jeans are growing beards around the ankle line. Are you ever going to get e-mail? Join the world, my dear!

Love,
Constance

53

Aida Returns

January 26, 2001

Dear Judith,
Daddy and I want to invite you and Curtis and the kids to visit us in here Mexico during spring break, for Semana Santa which is Easter week. The kids will get to see the ruins, and maybe the national eco-reserve. Anyway the weather will be wonderful, although now it's a bit chilly, at night especially.

Another moron letter. She couldn't seem to say anything meaningful to Judith any more, as if they lived on different planets. Which in a way she guessed they did. Anyway she couldn't invite Judith and the family to look at the Zapatista rebellion. It wasn't something so visible, although she saw it, and it wasn't something you could read about, although she read unceasingly about events in the news. Constance discounted whatever she did or learned in the last few years as being too difficult to convey, although last August they'd talked about nothing else. And it wasn't just her, it was everyone not here and now. Something was happening and nobody knew how to frame it—what? The experience? The philosophy? The culture shift? She couldn't put her finger on even how to name what she'd seen. People standing together. Autonomy. Despairing at her say-nothing letter she pulled her disk and looked for a table to have coffee.

"Hey!" Aida called.

Constance beamed and hugged her and drew back and then hugged her again. Aida!

"Are you here for the Zapatista caravan?"

Really, Aida wanted to say, I'm here to have sex. She hadn't found Frank yet but figured she would.

"I need to follow-up with women I interviewed. Better late than never. Finally working on the thesis. And yuh, I think I'll jump on here in San Gregorio and travel the rest of the way. Will you go?"

"Couldn't do it," Constance replied. "Arthritis, old age, et cetera. It's bound to be brutal. You know the Zapatistas will set their own pace; and the NGO's never get organized, they forget people need to eat and pee. I'll fly into DF and meet up with Harry there." She beamed at Aida. "I'm so happy to see you!"

Aida had regained her sturdy appearance and her equanimity. Her dark hair showed threads of gray; her skin was flawless. She looked ready to ride.

"How's Harry doing?"

"Pretty good! He pulled off a never-before-seen-in-Chiapas-system, with fairly simple materials and he's pleased as punch with himself. He received a couple more offers to think about."

Constance smiled again. It was on her mind a lot, and one of these days Harry would have to make a decision.

"So if Harry wants to work here, is that cool?" Aida asked.

"Not really. Somebody has to sign and say he's necessary and no other person could fill the post. I suppose a municipality could do that. But the real question is…" Constance drifted off, turning her spoon in the cup and making the coffee swirl in a circle.

"Is like, do you want to live the rest of your life in Mexico?"

"Yes, that's the question." Connie looked across the table. "It doesn't need to be decided, in quite those terms, you know. We went back to visit for two weeks last summer, and I know we could live in both places." She paused. "I'm not sure we'd achieve a sense of community in both places." She meant, not in Ann Arbor.

"You can take it as it comes, without ever deciding."

"How about you? Could you do that?" She tilted her head and waited for Aida to answer.

"I could write my thesis here. I can use the UNAM library, and there's other resources." Aida frowned. "In DF, I mean. God knows I couldn't do much here in San Greg." This was a strange conversation, for sure. What were they talking about, after all? She sighed. Maybe she was talking about her chances of re-connecting with Frank, who kinda had a hold on her sentiments, but god knows plenty of other men were available. No, honestly, she'd come down here like a bullet shot from a cannon, so why not admit it. She needed to be here. So why not admit that, too?

"Constance," she began, slowly. "Have you ever thought you need to be here? I mean, like it's become important, to be in at the beginning?"

"Beginning of what?" Connie looked definitely interested by the line of conversation. And since she'd had the same thought, she waited with anticipation for Aida's response.

"Oh, well. That's like, the question, isn't it. But something."

"Dear Aida, I could be that articulate all by myself!" She was zipping her chaleco. "I can analyze the question—is local autonomy and/or communality, a new phenomenon politically, socially or economically? Historically?" She laughed ruefully. "Are we witnessing for real the birth of an alternative to corporate globalization, or maybe a new world? Or are we just pumping ourselves up like we wished we were part of something important?" The letter to Judith was dead on her disk, and here she was, doing better than she thought she could, to articulate ideas. Aida was an inspiration, clearly.

Aida buttoned the top button on her shirt against the chill. She couldn't narrow it down so easily. She knew grass-roots activism was hardly new, and this wasn't quite that, anyway. Too old or too new! They paid their bill and got up. Out on the sidewalk Aida turned and threw her arms around Constance. Connie felt the solid warmth of her body, and hugged her back. They began to walk.

"I guess it's all of the above," Aida replied. "It must be more than my private gut feeling, else why are foreigners still here? Why are we here?" She looked at Constance. "Ah, we don't know. If we knew we'd know."

"Yes. And thanks for your insight, sweetie! Do you have a place to stay?"

"Yeah, no problem. I found a room for a few days in a house. There's space nowadays. A lot of people cleared out. The rebellion phase is over, I suppose." She sighed. She still believed the rebellion would continue forever, because she didn't see the Fox government giving in to indigenous demands. Not with the US breathing down Mexico's neck for all the goodies in the selva. And whatever new thing they witnessed, it was going to keep hope alive as long as the indigenous communities were alive, and then some, because by now the genie was out of the bottle and flying around the globe.

"Well, you be sure to call me before you go off. And I'll ask Harry to keep an eye on you, in the caravan!"

"You mean," Aida asked, "you want me to keep an eye on Harry, in the caravan? Will do! Don't worry!"

They embraced again, and Aida sped off. She wasn't headed to her room, but toward the Peace Witness house. By now Frank might be back in town. She hadn't come to Mexico for sex, but sex was always a nice thing to do.

54

Anticipation

Emily, her short hair shaped and brushed up in the latest style, prowled the streets of San Cristóbal with her camera. The coffee shops were crowded with young people wearing floppy hats, toting bedrolls secured with ropes and backpacks adorned with cords. The local papers estimated three thousand people would accompany the Zapatistas on their drive to Mexico DF, including indigenous people, members of national civil organizations, and foreigners.

The more important foreigners lodged at hotels, preparing Human Rights statements, and zipping off video sound bites for TV broadcast. Emily, not important at all, got back on the horse, as she phrased it to herself. She was over José. That dream had not burst, it dissipated, slowly, without fanfare, like morning fog off the mountains. Months went by in which she wove José into her self-image, herself as survivor. Her therapist told her that nightmares of Mocotlán might linger for years, but her best antidote was to complement herself for behaving well, doing what she was able to do, giving attention and care not only to José but to the women and children. Remind yourself every day that you are a good person, the therapist advised her.

She tried to. Her mother chatted on, completely unable to understand. If Emily changed her politics, if she was now a Socialist, or worse, an Anarchist. Emily had not changed her politics because she didn't have any to begin with, she told her mother. But you always vote! Her mother exclaimed. "And you went to a rebellion!"

Emily used to resemble her mother. Now she was a little older, a little wiser. But maybe not much further along. She understood the communitarian ideal of the indigenous people, but to submit all your choices and options to a council of Authorities was not her style. If she wanted to belong, she could have belonged to David. When it came down to private property, her ability to earn her living, her apartment where she could lock the door, her freedom to unlock the door and leave, to speak for herself, to feed no one but herself, to nurture no one but herself—ah, she voted for that.

Perhaps in the future it might change. But not yet.

In San Cris she took a small room in the hotel where she first stayed, four years ago. She looked around carefully, at the window and walls, to see if she occupied the same room. The same colorless painted cement—gray? Cream? Beige? It was beyond recall. She inspected the stairway, leaned over the balcony, peered down into the courtyard. The flowers didn't change.

She packed for the caravan. First order: toilet tissue. She was carrying several plastic bottles of liquid wash, packaged paper washcloths, small manageable bottles of water, tubes of sunscreen and skin lotion. Birth control pills, tampons. Forget shampoo—if there was a hotel there was a town, and if there was a town she'd buy shampoo. No point in worrying about clothes if they slept on stadium floors or fields or god knows where. The organizers held out hopes for hotels with hot water. Emily didn't bother to hope. She planned to throw away dirty tee-shirts and replace them when they arrived at the next town. Panties could be rinsed almost anyplace, if she didn't mind wearing them damp. Socks under her sneakers, throw away. Mexico specialized in cheap socks. Her new digital camera, backup batteries and a spare disk. She could e-mail photos as she went. Laptop. Was she better off carrying a notebook and pen? Maybe so. Less to carry, less to lose. One of the first caravan stops would be San Gregorio.

In San Gregorio Merwin occupied an efficient two room apartment Constance visited once. Frank appeared and disappeared. She lunched with Aida twice. They talked about hopes for the Zapatistas in Mexico after the public surge of admiration subsided. Slight.

She saw Martin in town on his motorcycle, risking the lives of everyone nearby. Once in a while he tipped and fell off. If he had momentum he hovered with his arms spread wide, Constance saw, his spirit still striving for peace. He came down hard. The moto toppled, roaring, dented and bruised. It gasped with pain as its wheels stopped. She hoped he wasn't in town to join the caravan, God forbid he planned to roll alongside.

At night she lay sleepless in bed and imagined a vacation bus in which Judith and Connie's grandsons traveled in the USA. It fell off a mountain before it reached the beach. She imagined their plane crashing into the Atlantic. She pictured herself in Ann Arbor in some future time hearing unmistakeable Mexican indigenous music and weeping, as she did when she heard strains of "We Shall Overcome." She cried a little in sympathy for her future self.

Constance suffered a bad case of diffuse anxiety. Even her hair looked anxious, escaping from its combs and straggling alongside her face. The front of her blouses turned gray from clutching her chest.

Harry waited in San Cristóbal, ready for the caravan to set out.

Constance, in San Gregorio, worried. Carmen cautioned her about the caravan, "Dangerous. It's going to be dangerous." She knew Harry was accompanying it. Carmen somehow could afford to speak of danger. Her face, with its clear skin luminous, had acquired an inner happiness. Clearly she admonished herself as well.

For the past year and a half Ignacio had not visited their patio. Constance was reluctant to ask if he and Carmen formally separated, although she saw a little newspaper bit indicating he was in the United States for his long delayed training. Interviewed like a big shot for his role in controlling the rebellion. The fucker. After Cuates, she referred to him only as the fucker, and didn't want to think about him. Her humiliation overwhelmed her. Her silly insignificance. She tried to gauge the color of Carmen's skin, to correlate it to release from Ignacio's cruelty. Or to Merwin's presence. More than ever, Constance believed other people's lives were secret and mysterious. Their comings and goings remained unknowable. Unless of course one asked. She was afraid to ask. She preferred ignorance. She preferred mystery. Anyway, people lied.

In the zócalo where the usual banners and slogans hung for unending causes, the EZLN agenda and itinerary attracted dozens of people. They planted themselves in front of the TV attached to the church's electric cables. Like babies wired to an umbilicus. From early morning long into the night, the television continued to breathe, to inhale the breath of watchers who leaned forward as if to blow events into its mouth. It exhaled colors and gaudy incomprehensible commercials. By radio, the government broadcast that a police guard would protect the caravan. God forbid the popular heroes of Zapatismo be attacked.

Connie's unease stirred afresh when she passed the TV screen. The newscaster on Televisión Azteca sported a bright green ribbon on his lapel. The Public Service announcements showed an indigenous

unisex figure releasing a white dove into the sky. A huge "peace concert" was planned for March 3. Rock groups would sing about peace
before the Zapatistas entered Mexico DF in quest of an interview
with legislators who, in turn, would or would not agree to ratify the
San Andrés Peace Accords, would or would not amend the Mexican
Constitution to include civil rights for autonomous peoples, human
rights for everyone.

"Listen to this quote, from the writer Juan Bañuelos: `We live in the
totalitarianism of global usury. These television consortiums confirm
what many studies show, a videogracia to manage poverty.'" Merwin,
carrying his coffee out to the patio, read the papers. Constance wondered if Carmen would show up.

Merwin translated as he read: "`In an interview, the National
Poetry Prize winner agreed that the concert carries an undertone: To
distract public opinion. Owners of the TV stations want to be good
guys for peace, and the Zapatistas never respond, they go on being
Indians. On one hand it's manipulating consciences, and on the other
it gives by remote control a legitimacy to all the groups of caciques in
Chiapas, to paramilitaries who murdered so many people... We are
living at an excruciating crossroads.'" Merwin tossed the paper onto
the table. Strands of dark hair escaped from his renewed pony-tail. He
wore a white cotton indigenous shirt over his jeans. A costumed doll.
That was how Constance described him to herself. But he—he looked
toward the gate as if to pull Carmen into his presence by willpower.
"The more Fox trumpets Peace the uneasier I get. If peace doesn't
happen, the implication will be it's the fault of the Zapatistas. He's
priming the classic 'Blame the victim' scenario."

"The caravan goes anyway."

"And you're worried?"

"Yes," Constance acknowledged. "Here it is, the fantastic climax of a six year struggle, and I'm wild with anxiety."

"Don't worry. Fox will be careful not to let anything go wrong. You'll see—motorcycle escorts every inch of the way. Furthermore, Harry will be there!"

"Civil Society. Yes." She wasn't prepared to think of Harry as Savior. Even at Cuates, they'd been saved by another, or by chance, or by the stroke of some nonexistent God.

Merwin stood up, disengaging. The newspaper looked damp where his hand had gripped it. No Carmen. Briefly Constance wondered how his passion for Carmen could be so intense when they saw one another every day. Merwin wondered the same thing.

Around town in San Gregorio a certain number of foreigners and church people collected money for the caravaners. Food and water, places to sleep overnight for as many indigenous delegates as possible. The Zapaturistas from around the world going along as witnesses (three thousand?) like Harry, must manage on their own.

TV personalities with lapel ribbons continued to proclaim. Constance, hunched on the closest bench, stared at the small green bows while the screen showed today's popular ballot question: "Do you think the Zapatistas are refusing peace?" Hello? 80% of the responding public agreed, the Zapatistas refuse peace! This while low-intensity war in Chiapas smoldered barely out of sight, while political prisoners rotted in prison, and military occupied the state! The war of disinformation continued.

"Marcos wants to be famous. He doesn't really represent the Indians," she heard. Well, ok. Ordinary people like this couple on a park bench will repeat what they hear on TV. But a minute or so into the conversation the couple reversed field.

The wife showed Constance a piece of paper handed out at the teller window of Banamex, unsolicited. It showed the official-looking Mexican eagle, the Banamex logo, and in tiny print, "Fundación México Unido".

Several banks and businesses joined in sponsoring the "vote" méxico unido por la paz, and the peace concert. You signed your name on the ruled "ballot", and these thousands (17 million, it turned out) of votes then appeared at the concert stage to be publicly "counted". The woman agreed, We are all for peace. She frowned. Her skin was a smooth brown, like that of her husband. The furrow between her eyebrows darkened to chocolate.

"If the government really wanted peace they could give the Indians here in Chiapas what they need. A little clean running water so they can at least wash!" She made a washing gesture with her hands. "A little food! A few hectares without struggle and torment!" The woman turned toward Constance to see how she received the words. Constance nodded. The husband nodded. "The Zapatista caravan is a good sign."

Beyond that, no more to say. Nobody with power could tolerate the Zapatista dream coming true. Those without power remained quiet in the sun, while children scuttled about selling chiclets and bracelets. Abruptly the man turned toward Constance, leaned across his wife and placed his brown hand on Constance's jean-covered knee.

"We need to defend natural resources as sustenance for Mesoamerican cultures! The people must struggle against bio-piracy in Chiapas! The communities must defend forests of the region of Los Chimalapas! Refuse the new industrial corridor! Denounce expansion of eucalyptus plantations, and transgenic cultivation!"

His dark eyes met hers with burning intensity. The white lady, la gringa. Constance sat with her mouth agape. The couple stood up and left.

The caravan arrived in San Gregorio in late afternoon. The crowd jammed the zócalo, filling to oveflow space in front of the cathedral. Small boys climbed trees, little masked kids stood on their fathers' shoulders. People lined the road halfway down the mountain.

Harry appeared at their apartment, tired, smelly, and elated. Crowds along the roads had shouted and waved. They arrived late to San Gregorio. The bus blew a tire. Constance embraced him. Harry ate a bowl of soup, showered and changed his shirt. Then he left. She booked her bus to the airport and her plane ticket.

Connie's anxieties focused by remote, on shoddy, worn, collapsing vehicles, busses with bad clutches and bad brakes. Sure enough, an accident happened two days later. Brakes failed on a bus, killing one of the Federal Preventative Police motorcycle escort, and injuring another.

A troop of Italians and indigenous men guarded Subcommandante Marcos. The FPP guarded the caravan from shooters along the route. Nobody guarded clutches and brakes.

On Saturday Harry phoned. Yes, it was his bus that careened brakeless downhill, while the driver shouted "Get down! Get down!" to the hapless passengers. Aida yelled aloud "Are they shooting at us?" The bus banged to a halt against the car carrying the Zapatista information service, against flesh and motorcycles.

"Good thing Aida joined our bus, she's a trouper!" Harry told her. Aida hollered a seat check to see if anyone was hurt. Shaken but okay, the riders left their gear and got off the bus to form a human cordon with the Italians. Elbow to elbow they surrounded the bus carrying Marcos and other delegates. Ambulances arrived to carry away the injured motorcycle cop. Nobody knew if sabotage might be a factor. Standing in their boots and sneakers they speculated, went to piss, purchased bottled water from vendors who magically appeared at the scene. Finally the driver summoned them to board.

But here they were at the day of Peace! Constance sat alone in the apartment. Carmen knocked, and when she saw Constance watching the screen, perched beside her. Carmen had become opaque. Work on the apartment trickled to a halt.

Constance had lost weight. She twisted her rings while she worried. She hadn't fretted when Harry went on the water project, vanishing into the mountains for a week at a time. She experienced no advance anxiety when they rode up to Cuates to fend off the whole army coming to arrest José. This felt different. As if she staked a great deal on public acceptance of the Zapatistas. An internal choice, to side with some but not with others, moral choices, self-positioning? She confused herself. But a majority of Mexicans embraced the Zapatistas. Upperclass ruling elites, no. She sided with the right team, anyway.

Both women leaned forward on the sofa. The local channel showed a subtitled replay of Lost Horizons. Constance remembered Ronald Coleman. The movie explored Shangri-La, the Eden of Tibet, where the best of Western Civilization was preserved along with beautiful girls who never aged until they crossed to the world outside.

Constance clicked to watch the concert.

"Absurd," Carmen muttered. A father and son Indian team performed a sacred ceremony burning sage in a bowl. During holy prayers the crowd screamed for their rock stars. The scene with clouds and lights was over-staged, under-musicianed. The stadium bulged with exuberant teens who waved green lights in time to the music. Gyrating pelvises everywhere. Well, Constance was not a Puritan.

Beside her on the sofa Carmen drifted a million miles away. She fingered her red bag with the tassels. One by one she braided and unbraided them until they twisted at odd angles. The two national TV anchormen together in one booth wore green ribbons. Interspersed with blasting music flashed videos of lively fair-skinned children dressed in white and singing about peace, and happy indigenous people dancing around their villages. Waiting for somebody to turn on the TV, she supposed.

Harry was somewhere en route to Mexico DF. Constance was long packed for the flight to meet him, to cheer as the caravan entered. She knew she would cheer. Her heart was more intimately involved than at a ballet recital with six year-old Judith in a pink tutu. These were and were not her people. The complexity of relationships in which she swam vanquished her. She always had been so good at one on one.

Carmen stood to leave. The concert bored her, and she had asked Constance none of the questions on her mind. She knew Merwin was not really a Mexican. He loved her, that she knew. She loved him. But in her life love was not so clearly a determining factor. Decisions must be made. Merwin must declare to stay or go. He could not wait for the UNESCO to make a grant. He must declare.

At the door she turned.

"Lots of foreigners passed here. You saw many old friends, no?"

"I saw Aida Elizondo, she went on the bus. Did Merwin go?" A preemptive strike!

"Yes. Or I would not be here watching with you." Carmen stated it quietly as a fact. She could not betray Merwin by voicing her doubts. Anyway, Constance was not one to ask, truly, Carmen often regarded her as no more than a sweet aging child. She pulled the door shut behind her.

55

Zapatista Roundup in Mexico DF, March 13, 2001

It was the eve of Zapatista entry into the capital of their nation. They passed through a dozen cities, where people thrilled and cheered. It was as miraculous as traveling loaves and fishes, as wonderful as resurrection, as ramshackle as twine and twigs.

For participants the trip was grueling, as Connie foresaw when she wisely opted out. Harry endured long kidney-banging hours on a rickety-rackety bus. No bathroom stops until the women raised a fuss. No food except what you bought handed through bus windows along the crowded route. Nevertheless a weary Harry felt crowds lift the caravan's spirit and impel it onward. He rejoiced in participation of Zapaturistas—above and beyond! This was not a duty but a deeply private impulse to support—he wasn't sure what—indigenous peoples for sure, and movement toward self-rule. His own beat-up body put on the line.

Constance bussed on a more comfortable vehicle to Tuxtla, and flew to Mexico to meet him. She booked a decent hotel room near the Zócalo. Hot water in the bathroom. Priorities for her, and, Harry had to admit after the caravan ordeal, a priority for him. Age and heroics don't jibe.

Emily journeyed with the Zapatistas without ever running into Harry. She thought once when the bus accident occurred that she spotted him in the circle guarding Marcos, his mop of grey hair amidst black heads. But she was too busy interviewing medics who bent over the smashed motorcycle cop to hike over. She had accepted a series of free-lance assignments from the Boston Sunday Magazine, during her year home in the United States. Now they wanted a story on Zapaturistas.

She was eager to see Marcos and the EZLN delegates enter the city. They'd become world famous for promoting community, and Emily didn't doubt that in the teeth of enforced globalization, other communities gathered in Latin America. Incidentally and quietly, she hoped to see José, who she supposed traveled with the EZLN delegation. She heard rumors of him, his steady presence in several villages. No word on his private life. For the moment, filthy and stinking to high heaven, she kept her distance.

Although Emily took the trouble to stay in touch with the Skelbas by occasional e-mails, she never inquired about José, and neither Constance nor Harry volunteered. The Skelbas were her link. They knew she was—had been, she corrected herself—deeply attached to José; silence might indicate a new woman. Or an eternal vow of celibacy. Or whatever Zapatistas did. Something pure, she knew.

You bitch, she scolded herself. Yes, but. She had chased him high and low, literally. He never suggested she stay in Chiapas with him. So she left. She was not Mexican after all. She had no real reason to stay. No work reason.

Her new life in Boston, she admitted, felt trivial. Sometimes she woke from a nightmare; since the therapy, more often she slept and woke in the morning with aware, manageable levels of grief. Her life included no men. Now. A dry period, as she expressed it. A time in her life when she functioned well beyond David and his crap, and in firm control of her hormones. She earned money for the first time, and that drained away some of the terrible yearning. If pain overwhelmed her, she could buy new suede shoes, right?

At the hotel desk in the center of Mexico DF Emily ran into the Skelbas. None of them expressed surprise. The hundreds of foreigners who rode with the caravan mostly were youngsters who enjoyed the all-night noise and discomfort of cheap youth hostels. Aida vanished into the Women's Studies group. Big shots lodged in better hotels. So that left a few modest places for modest people—herself, for example, another journalist or two, and older enthusiasts like the Skelbas. Harry found José when the caravan busses emptied. They made plans to meet later. Would Emily? Yes, she would.

Constance and Emily set out together on foot. The streets were thronged, not surprising in the hemisphere's biggest city. Mostly youngsters: Mexican demographics. So Connie was curious when Emily stopped with a shout, "Don Fernando!" in front of a dignified and gorgeous older man.

"Where are you headed?"

"To the bar on Calle Cinco de Mayo called La Opera. We're meeting friends."

"And so am I. We'll go together."

"This bar is famous," Emily told Constance, "for live strolling musicians in western suit jackets, and a bullet hole in the ceiling fired by the original Zapata, or maybe by Pancho Villa. I don't remember which," she admitted. "but they preserved the bullet hole, they put a brass washer around it."

"That's why we meet there, we Zapatistas!" Don Fernando inclined toward Connie so that she admired his white moustache and thick head of hair. He continued without pause, "The Zapatista commanders will ride into the Mexico City Zócalo on horseback! What a sight that will be!"

Connie's eyes widened and a huge smile lit up her face, turning the wrinkles around her mouth to dimples. "Ah," she breathed. The annunciation of an angel descending could not have affected her more.

"On horseback? What a great story!" Emily cried. She carried her camera, her notebook.

Constance had thoughts about Emily. The trip of course exhausted her, as it had Harry; both lost weight. But Harry bounced back, and Emily, to the contrary, showed purple shadows beneath her blue eyes. Lovely, nonetheless. Constance supposed the young woman was breaking her own heart.

"Let be," Harry instructed her firmly. "She'll have a chance to see José tonight, and it's their business. Not yours," he added sternly.

Constance knew that José said nothing, made no attempt to keep Emily in Chiapas. He had nothing to offer an American woman, after all. His life was simple and dignified, like his face and body. In quiet conversations he asked Harry about life in the USA, Harry reported to Constance. What a woman earns. The life she leads. The freedom from family obligations, freedom from patriotic obligations, freedom from cultural obligations.

Harry reported to Connie, "It couldn't work, and José is smart enough to know it."

Constance agreed.

"Very symbolic," said Don Fernando, referring to the horseback entry. Constance, who by now put nothing beyond the magic of Mexico, believed him.

Increasingly, old and young, fair and brown, strollers who came with the caravan or for it, crowded onto the sidewalks. The three cheerfully detoured around those who stopped to greet friends or acquaintances. Truly, the entire world was present.

Inside the bar they gazed around and finally spotted Harry's familiar silver curls at a corner table. The wood-paneled room throbbed with music and people. At the table with Harry sat another American reporter, and José. The three men stood. José waved to Don Fernando. The waiter pulled out chairs and they crowded in, Constance next to Harry and Emily beside the reporter whose name was Jim. Jim smoked, and Emily looked at his yellow fingers and silently groaned. Clearly a headache night. Don Fernando took his seat, and instantly became head of the table. José on the other hand faded into the group, a dark discreet shadow.

Emily turned and deliberately met his eyes. She reached across the table. He grasped her hand, and released it. They all ordered beer.

For a moment Constance worried. Maybe the idea that it wouldn't work was false, and one or both of them would feel cheated. Certainly, without discussion, she and Harry settled into San Gregorio. It wasn't their culture, either. But when you're old maybe it's simpler, reversion to a prior life. Mexico was not so different from the world Constance experienced fifty years ago. Emily, twenty-five years her junior, never knew life like this.

Constance sighed. Maybe Emily was more political than Constance gave her credit for. Maybe her thoughts went beyond daily sunshine, fashions and a circle of friends, and she could be lured by love into the bowels of Mexican life where corruption and struggle never ended.

Constance noted Emily's perfectly manicured fingernails when they raised their glasses to toast the Zapatistas. I don't think so.

They drank, and now José became the important visible presence. Not the beautiful Don Fernando, at whom Constance gazed awestruck. He looked like a movie star. Made for display, not real. José was real.

On Sunday, March 11, Constance put on jeans and sneakers. She wore her canvas hat against the blazing sun, and Harry donned his baseball cap. They left the hotel without seeing Emily, who the night before made an arrangement to meet Jim. Since they both were writing the same story. Maybe exchange info, in a non-competitive way. The Skelbas headed out.

Traffic was cordoned off. At 11:00 A.M. thousands milled through the Zócalo waiting to cheer the 2:00 P.M. entry; vendors of Zapatista souvenirs, straw hats and baseball caps, fruit, popsicles, bottles of juices and water, all jammed together; dark-eyed people strolled and jostled toward some astonishing vision. Youngsters kneeled on the sidewalk to paint WELCOME EZLN. Befeathered Indians danced to drumming. Mexican humanity teemed.

Constance held Harry's arm. In truth she felt a little frightened by the density of humans striving to earn their $3 per day, shouting "Batteries! Powder for cockroaches! Socks for fifty cents a pair!" striving for space on the adjacent sidewalks to set up plastic sheets or snow-cone wagons, crowding along unmarked corridors agreed to by some unspoken instinct for order or self-preservation. The shouting, humming, throbbing lived behind their own conversation, like the thrum of crickets. The Skelbas crossed streets helplessly, caught, moved with the wave of people.

They swept past indigenous people camped in the Zócalo in tents, and on the pavement under porticos. "Rights are not written, they are exercised." More men wearing cheap sandals than boots, clothing Constance recognized as being Mexican: shabby, cheap and badly made. "Santa Caterina Tapotzlán, we are here!" "Puebla with the EZLN!" "Fox's peace No, peace and dignity Yes!"

Lined up in the sliver of shadow provided by the high flagpole, more people waited in the sun-dazzled center of the Zócalo. The Mexican red white and green stirred and wilted with snatches of breeze. Costumed Indians burned sage, an odor that stuck in the hot air and in Connie's throat. A TV screen flashed: a nurse, a clinic, a classroom, impossibly bright and clean.

Led by the crowd they moved toward the intersection of Calle Izazaga José Marta and 20 de Noviembre, where the caravan would turn for its Zócalo entry.

Constance clutched Harry's hand. People clumped and dispersed, clogged the sidewalk to discuss the history of Mexico, all the movements, all the reasons. Constance eagerly awaited Marcos on horseback. Harry held onto her firmly, sensible to a crowd that could sweep away her slight form.

They pushed toward the intersection. A man passed carrying an infant in one dangling hand; Mexican style, the baby was bundled in blankets despite intense heat. An indigenous band passed, trumpets blaring. An older man held up a sign, "We are here for a better inheritance for our grandchild 3 months old."

They stationed themselves at the corner. The crowd held its breath, a moment of silent suspense. As the Zapatista open truck swung into view the watchers surged around the 20 de Noviembre corner as the comandantes loomed above them balanced on the moving flatbed. On street-level a yellow rope guarded them, a group of linked arms guarded them, Harry and Constance guarded them.

"Wait a minute!" She yelled over the din to Harry. "Where's the horses!"

Surely others believed too!—a massive rumor, not simply the charming invention of Don Fernando. So many imaginations grabbing for the same image, heroes galloping on horseback to fight bad guys! People shouted to the Zapatistas, "You are not alone! You are not alone!" She looked at the crowd of brown-skinned faces.

Marcos, distinguishable on the flatbed by his pipe and soft hat perched atop his pasamontañas, waved. Other delegates waved. Harry didn't wave, he ran, yanking Constance along and keeping her upright and moving so as not to fall trampled, until the crush diminished and they could maintain a normal pace.

"Ok?" he breathlessly gasped when they slowed.

"Yup. Ok.", she rubbed her upper arm where Harry held her upright. "Only Marcos didn't come on horseback! I was really looking forward to that!" They retraced their steps back toward the Zócalo, through lined streets.

On roofs and balconies surely it was "the intellectual elite" who viewed the scene, but also the elite who bought expensive reservations at the grand Monte Albán Hotel. The not-so-elite crowded every other space. Harry pointed to figures under the massive green bell in the cathedral tower, small humans up on roofs, two hundred thousand together in the Zócalo under the fierce sun.

The speeches began, surprisingly on time. From the crowd came shouts, "You are not alone, you are not alone!" Raised arms and V-signs. The national anthem. The chant E-Z-L-N, Ay-Zay-Ellai, En-nai! One after the other, people in the audience holding cardboard periscopes raised their mirrors. A man on stilts, dressed to resemble Marcos, bobbed through the crowd.

"Greetings" from the stage. The invisible delegates, introduced by an invisible voice. Even if she were taller, the crowd blocked her view. Constance balanced on aching legs behind a back with a braid of black hair falling across it. She examined strands of captured hair and tried to listen; fragments reached her: "never in the 500 years of retreat to the mountains…the earth, moon, sun and Indians…chose to sign accords or make war against the people...we are here only to say we are here...no more 'you' and 'us'...the color of all, not the color of money."

"You are not alone!" the crowd shouted. From the stage the Zapatista anthem pounded. A woman standing next to Constance burst into tears.

When it was over she realized she didn't know which hidden speaker was Marcos. In her hand she discovered a piece of printed paper:

Ya se mira el horizonte
combatiente zapatista
el camino macará
a los que vienen atrás.

Now you see the horizon
Zapatista warrior
you will mark the road
For those who follow after.

Vamos, vamos, vamos adelante
para que salgamos en la lucha avante
porque la patria grita y necesita
de todo el esfuerzo de los zapatistas.

We go, we go, we go forward
so we may move the struggle forward
because the country cries and needs
all the strength of the Zapatistas.

Hombres, niños y mujeres
el esfuerzo siempre haremos.
Campesinos, los obreros
siempre juntos, todo el pueblo.

Men, children and women
we will always be strong.
Campesinos, workers
always together, all the people.

Vamos, vamos, vamos adelante
para que salgamos en la lucha avante
porque la patria grita y necesita
de todo el esfuerzo de los zapatistas.

We go, we go, we go forward
so we may move the struggle forward
because the country cries and needs
all the strength of the Zapatistas.

Nuestro pueblo dice ya
acabar la explotación.
Nuestra historia dice ya
lucha de liberación.

Our people say enough!
It's the end of exploitation.
Our history says now
struggle for liberation.

Vamos, vamos, vamos adelante

para que salgamos en la lucha avante
porque la patria grita y necesita
de todo el esfuerzo de los zapatistas.

We go, we go, we go forward
so we may move the struggle forward
because the country cries and it needs
all the strength of the Zapatistas.

Ejemplares hay que ser
y seguir nuestra consigna
Que vivamos por la patria
O morir por la libertad.

Examples we must be
and follow our motto
let's live for the country
or die for liberty.

The crowd roared. Constance joined in.

The following morning Connie woke with a bruise on her arm, pain in her arthritic knee and a tired back. She carried a pill-case of ibuprofen down to breakfast. They ate slowly and drank coffee. Constance saw Harry was tired, too, but neither complained. How could they miss a moment of all this? They collected their hats and bottles of water, and set out again.

Lined up against the wall of the municipal palace, a hundred indigenous men and women stood holding red flags with black axes and hammers of their struggle, Frente de Lucha Popular. Signs hand-scrawled on cardboard with magic marker hung along the wall. The people came from Guerrero, Don Fernando's state, but they might as well hail from another solar system. Don Fernando not only resembled a movie star, but he knew José and by extension, the Zapatista leadership. Neither Constance nor Harry expressed surprise. Mexico was like that.

Here the signs read: primary school. electrification. clinic. secondary school. housing. potable water. a car for municipal services. day work. community store. fences for family parcels. musical instruments. roofs on houses. road repair. musical band. typewriters. sound equipment. ball field. teachers. medicine. street pavement. sewer system. interview with the secretary of development (sedesol). we demand.

Harry leaned in to speak to the leader. They walked eight days to get here, "not for the first time". They represented fifty-six communities, more than seven hundred people from San Luis Acatlán. Four indigenous groups in Guerrero; Nahñú from Hidalgo and Toluca from Queretaro. Most of them spoke no Spanish, and the leader apologized, "My Spanish is not very good."

"Mine neither," Harry replied. Both he and Constance preferred street information. TV news served to indicate what lies to discount.

Another Guerrero caravan group came with the Zapatistas, but these people lined up against the wall were long-term, camping in the capitol until their demands were heard. A brown-skinned woman less than five feet tall spoke up. "We have no choice. At home we starve. The price of coffee fell to one peso per kilo—ten cents! We have no money to call by phone, no money to return except on foot. We have nothing to eat!" Tears of rage and exhaustion stood in her dark eyes; she wiped them with her fingers.

Constance gazed around. They had created a center for yet another sidewalk group. Two men, one Mexican, one foreign, pulled out tape recorders. The small woman twisted her hands in the shirt over her jeans. They came with a truckload of sugar cane and pineapple but police grabbed them. The police told them to remove their blouses and pants. They stole their money. Then stole their food.

"They said 'Go Back', but where? There's nothing. Aid goes to the rich, and screw the poor. We are here twelve weeks." They had been told three people could enter the government office to negotiate. The deputy scheduled to arrive at 11:00 had not yet appeared. It was 12:00.

An old woman in their small crowd declared, "It's not the army that owns your land; it's yours!" She reached into her bosom. She handed the small woman a fifty peso bill. "Buy food!"

Constance shifted her position. Everyone stood close and bodies touched. She spotted Emily and Jim pushing into the circle. Jim held a video recorder. "What these people want is exactly what the Zapatistas want for everyone: the army out and political prisoners freed. But unlike the Zapatistas they also plead for government assistance. Their people teeter on the brink of starvation." His voice resonated, clear and professional..

He turned the video onto Emily, and began filming her while she interviewed the Guerrero people. He caught her summary full face as she stood slightly to one side of the group:

"Let me list the Zapatista demands of the past five years: home rule, or autonomía; human rights, and specifically rights for indigenous people; inclusion in the political processes of the indigenous voice." That was Emily, in a creased pair of slacks and crisp shirt. Her blond hair was combed smooth and gelled.

"The fundamental rights of indigenous people world-wide include the right to land or territory; the right to be recognized as a people; the right to free determination; the right to their own culture; the right to their own system of justice." That was Jim.

"Take two," Harry whispered into Connie's ear.

"Of these five, only the first strikes against the wall built by Fox and global corporatism." Jim directed the camera with Emily holding it, filming himself. Emily's face was hidden as she braced her arm against the side of her head. José disappeared last night with Don Fernando. Those two surely were with Marcos, in high level discussions inside Zapatista quarters on the university campus.

"Territory means indigenous land can't be opened to exploitation for oil, minerals, gas and biological uses without the consent and participation of its occupants."

"Fat chance," Harry whispered again. "Everything beneath the soil belongs to the government. Step aside, please!"

"I saw the Jornada headline: 'National sovereignty is obsolete, says the USA'."

Harry shook his head. Beneath the baseball cap small curls stuck out on both sides of his head, like a clown's. But he was serious. "The demands of townships that receive no services can be met. That's a question of caciques or outright thieves. It'll be in Fox's interest to claim, See we gave 'em electricity and musical instruments and we gave 'em food and sewer systems and computers. No problem. we gave them, that's the message."

He watched the two reporters who continued to film themselves. "And that will be the fact."

"They can't all get money to buy engineers and pipe on their own, Harry," Constance sighed. "Nor attract first class people like you."

Again Harry shook his head. That was exactly what he wanted for them now, the ability to lie low and fend for themselves. Some way to achieve awareness of dark-skinned people's strength. Screw big government handouts. He glanced at his watch. "We need to check out of the hotel, and think about our flight back."

They separated from the crowd while Emily and Jim were still wrapping up their interview. Behind her Constance heard the smooth American voice intone, "With lands occupied by indigenous in Chiapas and other states, how will Fox wrest territory for his vaunted Plan Panama-Puebla? How will he comply with the San Andrés Accords and still get the goods?"

"The preliminaries are over," Harry spoke flatly into her ear. "Now comes the real shit." He took her hand as they crossed the traffic circle. Uniformed police whistled and waved. The green Mexico City taxi bugs whizzed by. The odor of cooking hot dogs hovered in the air, over the same endless buzz of human voices. "We still have a few minutes to look at the ruins. Ok?"

"Yeah, ok."

56

Harry Philosophizes

Harry understood motive when a contractor tried to screw him. He understood when a worker goofed around too long at coffee or cigarette break, or smoked marijuana in the morning to get through his day. People like that were not so complicated. He understood Constance, more or less, after forty-some years of living with and around her. He understood how she fell in love with every student, of any age or sex. That was nature. In order for the human species to survive the old must love the young, knowers to love learners. Harry didn't think much of Freudian theories. The Oedipus complex wasn't a useful paradigm. Maybe among bison or antelope the young male had to replace the old to provide a sturdier breed, but among humans it wasn't useful. The young needed teachers.

All this went through Harry's mind while he watched Constance recover from the blow. Ignacio was a sadist. Ignacio was a murderer. Ignacio was power hungry, too ambitious. In fact, Ignacio had departed, to his USA military spy and torture training.

Constance reeled off her laments. In the long run, what it all boiled down to was two griefs: she taught the wrong learner, and Carmen suffered. The love that flowed from Constance the teacher lodged in a dead end, the mind of Nacho, and so went wasted. And Carmen had suffered, for years.

There was no excuse for that. They had known, in an unspoken way, of course they had. Those endless days and evenings of working on the apartment, repetitive tapping like a restless ghost at the window. And then this business with Merwin! Harry's ability to understand motive didn't stretch to romance, but he understood testosterone well enough. Merwin fell for Carmen. Now, why was that? She was pretty, and probably a year or two older than Merwin, which might be sexually interesting. But Carmen, pretty in her Cho'l way, didn't strike Harry as seductive. It emerged from Merwin's side, that need. Constance informed him that Merwin was in love, but she couldn't say why or what would come of it when Ignacio returned. Neither could Harry. He was glad that Carmen looked happy and work on the roof had stopped. Peace at last!

In the serenity of the zócalo cafe Harry took another swallow of his Dos Equis and looked across the sun-struck table at the youngster. This was one he hardly knew, latched onto an American here in San Gregorio because both went with the caravan. Billy also was drinking a beer, and stuffed tortilla into his mouth. They sat in silence, companionable enough. Harry figured sooner or later Billy would get around to asking. Whatever it was he wanted to know. And Harry learned from Constance, it's better to wait.

As for motives, Harry could not in any words explain why he himself traveled with the Zapatista caravan to Mexico DF. He wondered if the boy, who flew down from Texas to participate in the great ride, taking precious days off from his semester, knew why he went. Probably for adventure. Harry likewise. Probably to be able to tell about it later, tell his friends, grandchildren, a raconteur. Harry? I doubt it, said Harry to Harry. I think I'll keep this to myself. For one thing, besides kids like this one, who went themselves, there's nobody for me to tell around here. And here I am. And, I'm no radical—even if I should be.

"So you guys," Billy began. He meant the Skelbas. "So you guys seem to be staying here?" It was a question.

"So it seems," assented Harry. "Don't ask me why! Great climate." That brought a frown to Billy's face. "Did you want some big revolutionary reason? We're here to save the isthmus from Plan Puebla-Panama? Something political?" God knows some hope to do just that.

"Yeah. Maybe."

"You can return again, you know." Harry watched Billy's face. The pale skin looked peeled, as if the young fellow burned and new skin grew back tighter. Or maybe it was that in his twenties he stayed too thin, too fair. Late in beefing up to man-size.

"Yeah." Billy sighed a sigh of grief that came up from his belt. "I gotta go back home now, though. I mean, I can't stay here like you folks, retired. I'm in the middle of classes, and since I took a loan I better pass my exams. Besides, I have no money and no job and no passport. Well, I have a passport," he amended hastily to Harry's alarmed face.

Harry nodded. "It's always a good idea to get an education. Training, I mean. To do something useful. This country could sure use people who know how to do practical things."

"Like, for free, you mean. There's no jobs."

"Things change," Harry ventured. But of course it was true. Good Mexican engineers with degrees from MIT and Cal Tech got jobs in the States and never returned. Here you might as well forget it. That sad remark Constance made. All the towns couldn't afford him—hell, almost none could. "There might be a very different future." He took a lime to squeeze into his beer. "Technology, the internet, anyway. Springing up in every corner café. Look what the Zapatistas accomplished, will you."

But Billy looked away, his blue eyes slipping Harry's words. He was taking Political Science, and beside, something else worried his mind. Harry waited again. The jacaranda had come into bloom. Great smeared trees dropped purple flowers on the ground beneath.

"A lot of people left right away. Right after the election. They acted like it was all over, like now there'll be peace and democracy in Mexico." He made a snickering noise, an involuntary unpretty sound.

Harry nodded. "A long way to go," he agreed.

"So don't you think if we started—I mean enrolled kind of—us foreigners. We owe it to them to stay? See them through?"

"Nope." Harry wanted to reach out and touch Billy's hand, but that was something only Constance could do. He settled for a smile. "You owe it to them to go. Get out of their way, take your American culture away with you, as best you can. At least try to. Let them work it out. Their own way."

"You think they will?"

"Sure!" Harry exclaimed. "Do you think they're all stupid? Or do you think Americans have superior knowledge and ability?"

Billy blushed. "Shit. No. I never meant that. But you know, someone should speak up against the heavy hand." He meant the USA and corporate capitalism. "I know it's everywhere, with the IMF and World Bank, not just Mexico." His eyes shifted again. "Yeah, guys I know, they go to demonstrate at the summits, like in Seattle. You mean, the local people, they can speak for themselves."

Harry waited again. Constance must be a saint, he decided.

"Well, see, it's really about me."

"Ah."

"Like I shouldn't abandon what I started."

"What did you start, then? Not the Zapatista uprising, I don't think."

Billy laughed. "No." He laughed again, and this time he sounded happy, like he'd been let out of a dilemma. He stood up, and reached into his jeans pocket. "No," he repeated. He put a twenty peso note on the table. Harry picked it up and handed it back to him. Billy stuffed it back into his jeans. He grinned.

"I'll use it getting on the bus. Like, I started to grow up, for if you wanna know. Getting a grip. Adult. Whatever. Lucky to start right here, wasn't I. So I guess I can finish up north, where I belong?"

"A final word of fatherly advice," Harry remarked. "You belong everywhere. It's all one world. Lots of injustice, lots of problems." He felt proud of himself for thinking and articulating that. Billy nodded, and after a quick handshake bounded across the street.

57

Moon-landing in Congress, March 19, 2001

The Zapatistas went to Mexico DF to ask for confirmation of the San Andrés Accords and indigenous rights; hard-liners in Congress voted: No way. Fox complied with two other Zapatista demands: pull back the military to barracks, and free prisoners. Fox invited Marcos over for a beer. Marcos went to see his mother. His sister, a PRI congress-woman, in a TV interview said, He has his career and I have mine. The Zapatistas announced they would leave DF on Friday, tired of hanging around for a Congressional hearing.

All the jerking around, tactics for getting seven-second sound bites and your mug on TV—a daily World Cup game. Neighbors on the zócalo benches showed off for foreigners and Chiapanecos alike, sharing bottomless misinformation. Frank shook his head.

The jacaranda blossoms fell, the same deep violet waves as last year and the years before. Children celebrated the first day of spring in bumblebee costumes, flower suits, tutus and gauze wings—the same as last year. The national holiday celebrating the birth of Benito

Juarez, Indian president of Mexico, arrived. People celebrated last year, too.

On Wednesday March 28 Zapatista commanders finally were received by Congress. Fox didn't appear. Marcos didn't appear. Half the deputies, to judge by the camera pan of the chamber, didn't appear. It was an historic day.

Too bad history doesn't always come neatly packaged, like a moon landing or a Zapatista landing. Frank, despite the negatives, felt like he'd witnessed goal in a winning Superbowl game. Gratifying, his guys up there addressing Congress for the first time ever, although he wasn't dumb enough to believe it meant change. The government would claim any oil or gas reserves, and too damn bad if people lived on that exact land. This wasn't New York, you could expel Indians without even handing them bead money.

After the televised speeches Frank called Aida, who like the Skelbas hadn't hung around in DF but returned to San Gregorio. He was tickled, although he didn't think his luck would last. She had her thesis to write. But he yearned for a little contact comfort, the cushion of her sturdy hips.

They went out to celebrate with a seafood dinner, and played a game: what questions will TV Azteca and Televisa ask tonight for their phone-in polls? The questions posed a challenge to Frank's capacity to think idiot, the way TV stations put out crap for polls, and any answer meant a vote. Aida had a certain facility, but he wasn't sure if it was a complement to say so, so he didn't.

For Azteca, Aida nominated, "Should Marcos have attended the congressional session?" and for Televisa, Frank chose "Should Mexico DF build a new airport on communal land?"

"Ooh, that's sharp! I want another chance! 'How tall do you think

Comandante Esther is?'" Aida laughed in delight at her own jest. The women leaders, first tiny Ramona and now Esther, led her women's Top Ten list, and if she could believe woman talk around her, women lurked in every corner of Mexico waiting the chance to jump out and shout boo. She was doing well on filling in her thesis: Women as Exemplars of Cultural Change.

That Marcos didn't attend the congressional session was wonderful. As Esther said, as a subcomandante he led the indigenous people to congress, and then they did their thing, speaking clearly on their own behalf.

Fox didn't attend because he wasn't invited. His PAN party is a bunch of chickenshits, and most of them didn't attend either, a gesture of spiteful disdain Aida hoped would cost dearly in the future.

And then somehow they began to live together, enjoying the weather, the chores of lifting and opening large containers of water, lugging home from market chopped nopal and strips of beef to cook for dinner. Aida introduced into Frank's life a little lost domesticity. Since he came out of the army and left home at twenty-two he'd managed, but a little recovered mothering went a long way. He accepted it. A bemused softness overtook him. He melted into his surroundings, like cream into coffee. Next door another internet cafe opened, with the newest equipment; Frank could observe his somewhat puzzled square face on video camera, and if you cared to join him in a chat room, you could literally speak face to face. Ask him what goes on in his thick skull.

Frank wondered. After six years at the rebellion, there were no American friends who didn't list him "missing in action." He'd dropped out, and then some—down the mineshaft, down the hole you dig in the sand to get to China. He was gone. How Aida found him again, how she reached him again, made a miracle beyond explanation.

The contradictions are mighty. He lived internal and external lives simultaneously, maybe a trick most guys who had wives, families and children, goals and dreams, always did, but new for him. He'd been all on exterior alert.

Their conversation stayed exterior. "Zapatistas don't want to live in a neglected state; they want computers and schools and decent medical care."

Aida cheered. Then soberly she remarked, "It's only words, Frank. Words on both sides." In front of the sound-byte news she gazed along the sofa length to see how he reacted. "Fox said Plan Puebla-Panama will bring 'progress'. We know what that means: goodies for rich investors."

"Marcos said, in more or less these words, and I quote, not if it disrupts the Indian homeland."

"You think that can be prevented?"

"No. Probably not. Here, read this." He flung a newspaper at her, folded open. She began reading it aloud in Spanish, translating as she went.

Thursday, March 15, 2001 (La Jornada)
THE SOUTH THAT'S COMING   Armando Bartra
translation by N. Davies

"Solid lines radiate from there in all directions across the tropics...Lines which indicate their influence... The promoters of the companies usually are given to great imagination... They act here like engineers; Indian workers are brought up... The thing had arrived, finally, and anyone could now see clearly the consequences it would bring... "That is what they call development...and it splits us like a lightening bolt!"
Joseph Conrad. Victory

If the March to the South is not a malicious call for the people of Guerrero and Oaxaca to be thrown into the sea and the Chiapanecos and Tabasco people be sent to Guatemala, at least the Fox effort from the viewpoint of the north intends to make the Plan Puebla-Panama a new colonial conquest, and the southeast reconstruction an exploit led by men of reason—and money— who come from the north. By chance, presidential shouts of joy have been overwhelmed by an historic Zapatista caravan that sent Plan Puebla-Panama to the back pages of the press and newscasts. And it's true that the important march, the one that really counts, comes from the south.

23 commanders and a subcomandante, representing the more than ten million Indians, symbolize the presence of Mexico profundo in the capital. But this is not the only march to the north. Every day thousands of southerners take to the roads and highways in an invisible and silent exodus. They also are the color of the earth, but theirs is not the march of dignity but the march of necessity, as the small ruined farmers said in Tapachula last week.

The two great emigrations from south to north, from the country to the city, from the coasts to the center, form part of a same and recurring historic movement...Because before Zapatista Indians took the great city to beating drums, it had already been taken soundlessly by the migrant families; all the other Sundays they invade the Alameda to meet their sweethearts, the many-colored indigenous immigrants of the capital. Here they are. What happens is that they're not seen.

"Migrations are pretty much part of human history. But the important ones include women, right? No use without women! I'm writing that."

I am optimistic, I believe that the rights of the Indian people, agreed to in San Andrés and formulated by Cocopa, will be incorporated into the Constitution. Because they are just and necessary, because the Indians are fighting for them as never before since the Revolution has anyone fought for a law, and because the rest of the Mexicans and many foreigners are helping them; but also because in them Fox sees all his mediating capital, which is his political capital.

I am confident that the men and women whom the communities sent out to defend their political rights will not return with empty hands.

"Ai, Frank, he's confident. Are you? I'm sure as hell not."

But will the economic emissaries also have a generous return? Seven years of circling consciences and the symbolic taking of the center of power will achieve, I hope, the recognition of decisive political and cultural rights...

But what about economic and social rights? Possibly the law of Cocopa will pass. Will it also promulgate, and without impoverishing amendments, the tortuously negotiated law of Rural Development? Isn't it the case that Plan Puebla-Panama is the economic negation of the towns whose political know-how negotiated in San Andrés? I hope the hundreds of thousands displaced who left their communities to cheer the caravan, and the millions who put their hearts into the meeting in Nurio, one day soon can sleep as acknowledged and dignified Indians, but without doubt they will wake up, as always, poor and ruined campesinos.

"Now he's got it."

Perhaps the future of those who identify themselves with the ideas and practices of the EZLN will be formally constituted in a grand and renewed national political current.

"Aaah."

> But the destiny of the Chiapanecos at the grass-roots bases of aid, of the rural Zapatista-sympathetic organizations of the whole country, and in general the indigenous and campesino people moved by the struggle, is structuring an extensive social insurgence, a net of multiple nodes tied to the community, the region, the ethnicity, the type or productive sector. ..

"Humm, humm, humm... This is the significant part, Frank, those nodes across the communities."

> One could think that the concentration of land at the cost of the ejidos and communities, in dizzying plantations specialized and technologized like those of Porfirio Diaz, destroys what remains of the campesino economy created by the Revolution and won't generate much employment. But our technocrats care little about that, since the growth it promises has nothing to do with the wellbeing of the people: the strategy to push development of Chiapas and the southeast in general—writes Levy—should separate the objectives of combating poverty from that of regional development... That is to say, capitalism saves with hot pincers and, above all, that the political economy isn't contaminated by social objectives.

"Oh, man. This is pretty raw. Frank are you awake?"

> Joseph Conrad wrote: That is what they call development... and it splits us like a bolt of lightening!
>
> Their political and cultural rights conquered, the Indians and the other poor of the country will have to employ the strength recently acquired to stop the Plan Puebla-Panama and others like it.

They will have to tie up neoliberalism and in another sense the historical clock, inventing in rural Mexico for the first time, inclusion and justice.

It will be the next battle. Marcos already announced it during the caravan… there won't be any Plan Puebla-Panama nor a Trans-isthmus Project nor anything else that signifies the destruction of the Indian home. Nor will they be alone in this imminent battle, since in the dispute for the future—that some call debate over the model of development—for everyone, not only for the Indians, our life goes.

Frank indeed was asleep on the sofa, his breath wheezing in gentle sounds. She gazed at him. What the hell is "the long haul", anyway? How long is long? A lifetime, she thought, sadly. But better not think about it today. For the moment. She turned on her side and stretched out next to Frank.

Not everyone watched the televised Zapatista appearance in Congress. Hector told Frank he couldn't, he was in classes; his brother wouldn't, because the brother thinks it's all a fiasco; and his mother didn't, because she has absolutely no interest. Hector, although indigenous in both physical appearance and heritage is not an Indian, by choice. Indians are despised, so why should he choose that, and besides, he lived in San Gregorio and attended university classes.

The old woman who lived next door sold home-made tamales from her blue painted doorway on the street, dressed in her vendor's apron. Frequently at night when her door was open she dozed at her table, and when she stood, she measured only four and a half feet tall. She didn't watch because she was cooking. But she was enthralled by the discussion; she supported the Zapatistas.

Juan who was young, watched, and Raul who was old, watched. They were Euro-Mexican, well educated. They both supported

Zapatista demands.

Aida and Frank compared poll notes. Then it was wait and see. The Zapatistas returning by their bus to Chiapas attracted Hector who finally saw Marcos and a crowd, but not the sizable numbers who turned out for the northward journey. Everyone shared the wait-and-see style.

Frank was waiting sadly for Aida to speak up, and Aida waited hopefully for Frank to do the same. Frank thought if she broached the romance subject he could easily break off their affair at that time. Thanks to the restraining advice Tomás from the grave sent across hills or down from the sky—whichever—he was not an overt murderer, but his bursts of sudden rage didn't mesh well with long-term commitment. He experienced only two modes of being—hard, and soft. In this soft moment he lived with Aida, but who knew what would come? The day when he swallowed another outrage, and chased it down with mescal? He felt not so good most of the time.

Aida did the shopping, and he tried to make meals out of what she carted back to their tiny kitchen. Sometimes they had pasta with olive oil, and sometimes they ate a mix of stir-fried vegetables. Frank was eclectic. Some nights it was peanut-butter sandwiches. He ate to live, and she ate to be eating with Frank, a domestic communion.

The TV Azteca poll question on the Wednesday night news was, "Should Marcos have appeared?" If they'd been asked, Aida and Frank both would have voted No.

Frank considered, maybe it was time to get off his horse of resentment and guilt, riding him madly back and forth across the landscape. A decade had passed since his adventure in the employ of the US government as a Desert Storm gunner. Time to stop licking his wounds and say to Aida, "That was then, this is now." But he didn't. While murder and mayhem took place around him in Chiapas, he stayed a good guy. Every day, living on his tiny disability pension and

NGO allotment, he played the good guy. He could travel boldly now, with aspirin and penicillin, driving any supplies available from community to community. He feared rage would reappear the moment he moved off his repetitive path.

In the silence growing between them, Aida bussed back up to Mexico DF to spend a week in the library.

No Frank, no deep and permanent love. In her heart Aida was still a social worker. Do good to people, for people, because life doesn't deal everyone out equal. Not by a long shot. Aida decided to give him one more chance. Back to San Gregorio she charged on the rickety metal steed.

"Okay, Frank, this is it. This is your last chance! You wanna be my guy or not?"

"Guess not."

"Yeah, well answer me! You wanna be my guy or not?"

"Guess not!"

"Okay, well, dammit Frank, answer me! You wanna or not?" He shook his head, no.

In exasperation, Aida hurled a rolled newspaper and shouted "Well you fuckin idiot ass-hole, you wanna be my guy or not! I'm not kidding, this is your last chance!"

Aida pushed him down on the bed and straddled him. "This is your last chance! You wanna be my guy? Answer me, dickhead! Answer me!" She flopped down onto his chest. He could feel her ample breasts press the air out of him, and her ample thighs pinned him to the bed.

"Answer me, Frank!" She wept helplessly.

Eventually Frank turned his mouth into her ear and replied, "I'd have to start clean, honey. I don't think I can. I don't think I can make that promise." He stroked her hair and turned her thick braid in his hand. He licked the tears that fell off her chin onto his mouth.

"This is no conversation about going to medical school! This is about me and you," she bawled. They could live together in peace without saying so. The saying made the risk. So he wouldn't say. Frank stroked her hair and then her butt, hoping she'd forget it. After a while she moved off him. She sat up, and swung her sturdy right leg over to the side. She turned her back to him and placed both feet on the cool tile floor. He was free, or maybe you could say, discarded. A torn shirt, left for the cleaning staff. She was gone.

58

Report From Chiapas

They scanned newspapers for daily hoopla about Fox; not much different than regime change in the USA. President Ernesto Zedillo delivered his farewell address on the evening of September 1, to the Mexican Chamber of Deputies.

Zedillo hailed Mexico's economic improvements, reform of the Constitution, overcoming the huge debt left from the thievery of his predecessor Salinas, improvements in roads, health, education, the magnificent peaceful election. As one clever commentator said afterwards, he explained everything his administration did except why they lost the election.

Constance heard Zedillo trumpet his successes, but also credited him: whatever he may have done or not done the past six years, the grand finale was a turn away from autocracy—how else could these commentators be commenting?

Fox traveled pillar to post explaining how he'd make the new democracy real, quickly solve the problem in Chiapas, and be all-inclusive in his administration. Pablo Salazar mentioned that total troop withdrawal was not expected, but a return to pre-1994 strength.

"Ho ho," Frank commented in scorn. He was visiting in the patio. Constance received an e-mail from Aida in Mexico DF, preparing to return to San Francisco. She wrote that her investigation was over, but if she could set it up with her thesis director, she might return in the future to DF to do some of the writing. The Skelbas should come up to DF to visit her then.

Constance shared the message with Frank. That was all she could do. His expression didn't change. Poor stalwart Frank!

Their next-door neighbor was one of the gleeful electorate. "Have there been changes in your business?" Constance asked guilelessly. He reported, None. And yet! And yet! Forty percent of adult men migrate to work in the United States. Many rural towns become ghost towns with only elderly, women, and children hanging on. And yet! Harry told him three men die daily crossing into the US. And yet! Their neighbor smiled and smiled. Frank sat unsmiling. It was a stand-off. But all of them, Frank included, understood the man's pleasure. It was as deep as any beam in a dark tunnel could be.

The city draped itself in flags for September, Independence month. Constance ran into the basket vendor Antonio and shook his callused hand while he waited for the tourists who must surely return. To her patio sign for English Translation came a film-maker, documenting undocumented Mexicans working on a horse farm in Kentucky. She accepted the translation task. Everybody celebrating in their own way!

True to Mexico magic, on an evening stroll they met on the street a Chiapas couple they knew, whose business provided flags and balloons for festivities. The couple invited them to dinner, to celebrate the new Mexico.

More exhilarated faces, they and other friends. VIVA MEXICO

stenciled on the balloons. They chewed barbecued meat while the guests' four little girls scampered around pretending to be dogs and barking high sharp little girl barks. That's how it was.

Harry planned to accompany their host to visit prisoners in the most deplorable jail. Connie planned to talk more with their hostess about her study of Hindu meditation technique. The hostess, a diminutive lady with dark eyes, on a visit to her mother in Juchitán had met up with a lay guru on a red motorcycle, who explained the marvelous new ideas. Excitedly, while looking at Constance from the corner of her eye to see if Connie thought she was crazy, she explained that every person has the ability to release joy into the world.

Constance agreed. Privately she was happy because the world still turned, as it properly should, balanced on its axis through the stretching cosmos. And although she still didn't know anything or understand anyone, she nevertheless intuited that more rebellions would rise, and after death and changes, finally subside. For Harry and serious thinkers alike, balloons and smiles don't suffice. But then, she asked herself, why not smile anyway, or if you were Martin, radiate joy, or if you were Frank, bring an aspirin? She tossed one of the escaped balloons back to the four-legged barking child. On any day at any moment life was as good as it's going to get. Así es. That's how it is.

59

Martin Travels On

State police. Federal police. Military. Immigration officers. Food and crop inspectors. Truck inspectors. Martin passed everywhere smiling, but it wasn't easy. The newly imported soldiers in Chiapas looked and acted professional. Maybe eighteen or nineteen years old, spit and polish, working their jobs for the Mexican government. In darkness, they flashed their flashlights, sent for the sergeant, the lieutenant, the comandante, the chief. By daylight, they requested bribes or food; Martin's Spanish often left him uncertain.

He smiled and turned on his peace light. It was ignored, although Martin himself sensed warmth ignited in the center of his chest. It emanated from him like a ray of gold. He let it linger on the air, so that if a soldier unknowingly walked where Martin had passed, the ray wrapped about him like a mantle. Long after Martin left the danger zone on his motorcycle the connection endured. After a while Martin's threads of gold wove a fabric of peace.

He felt so close to Enlightenment. After twenty years, definitely he was close. Each time a roadblock stopped him, he radiated. He addressed each soldier individually, according him dignity and respect. Many came from indigenous families. Many were mestizo, hallmark Mexicans. They deserved joy.

Finally one inspecting soldier as Martin journeyed toward San Gregorio returned his smile. Sweetly, Martin asked, using the Spanish tú form, "What do you seek?"

The boy replied quietly, "Drugs. Plants. Guatemalans."

Martin circled through Chiapas. His own continuous peace tour, he called it. The nature of circles. In each town he rested a few days, using his bank card when he could, to withdraw pesos to buy food, and gas for the frequently repaired moto. He preferred sleeping in a hotel, but he accepted campesino hospitality when required. His bowels finally adjusted. Now, as the result of prolonged road jouncing, his kidneys ached. In a campesino's house he waded through weeds to find the outhouse, or pissed in the bushes.

If no other recourse offered, he slept in a field.

He placed a phone call once a month.

Months, then. Somehow he lost track. Holy Master whispered in his ear over thousands of miles separating them, Don't be surprised. You are beyond time now, you dwell on another level, in touch with the Absolute. Martin thought if that were true he should be able to hear HM without the phone. The phone connections remained inadequate, they cut him off or added strange croaks and gasps to Holy Master's voice. Often a town had no phone line, nor electricity. Martin tried to produce light from within himself, a one-man generator, but with little success.

He lived mostly on rice, beans and fruit. The seasons changed from dry to rainy and again to dry. In the mountains it rained in all months. It was cold. Martin imagined so much warmth broadcast from his interior resources that, left depleted, he might die of that cold. He bought another poncho to wear beneath his white one, and then in a small town he bought a cotton long-sleeved Guatemalan shirt with red stripes, and then he bought a cheap cotton undershirt and then another wool vest. He rode layered with clothing on the motorcycle, but wind penetrated anyway. On the phone Martin lamented needing to purchase so much clothing but Holy Master whispered, At the time you are truly enlightened, my son, you will thrive impervious to weathers.

Martin hoped it would be soon. He imagined it might be very soon.

He stopped again near the Pacific coast in Juchitán, a small city with a large market area under one roof, spilling into adjacent streets. Horse-drawn carts bumped through the narrow alley behind his hotel. Food stalls lined one block. He sampled tacos, joining the astonished local population on wooden benches. The women bulked around him, dressed in long gathered skirts. Smaller men straddled the planks. Martin showed nothing but bones beneath his clothing, but clearly American. They spoke to him.

Juchitán is no tourist destination. Nor a place for religious weirdoes, which he certainly was. Juchitanecos liked their Catholicism. On the zócalo flowers, and huge seed-pods piled up for sale. Boat-shaped bark-covered pods looked ready to sail into heavenly waters with crews of seeds: long yellow stems with flowerets grouped along each side. Flowers adorned the churches. Martin bought bunches to decorate his hotel room, and the battered red moto parked below his hotel room. He took to carrying a huge bouquet on his arm like a bride. Personal salvation, personal enlightenment—they were okay with either, not so different.

He rested on a bench in the zócalo and struck up conversation. Both men and women asked where he came from, a foreigner. Then if the conversation continued, he could explain how joy and peace spread. The people looked at him but they didn't flinch. He smiled and radiated brotherly love at every moment. Furthermore, he spent money. Juchitán would soon be a site for major development, according to President Fox's Plan Puebla-Panama. Maybe this American was the forerunner of good money to come.

His bench-mates anticipated the construction of a "dry canal" to traverse the isthmus north to south, for rail and road passage. To transport petroleum, mainly, and other products from the northern Gulf ports of Ciudad del Carmen and Villahermosa, south to the Pacific. Or in the other direction, crude oil headed north, along with fish and mangoes. To create an industrial parkway, little factories would spring up.

Ordinary people, waiters and shopkeepers who lived in the city murmured, Progress, Tourists, Money. Others were not so sure. For one thing, the isthmus held rich farmland. Such a "canal" would displace thousands of people, mostly indigenous, of course.

Martin was out of touch. He didn't know if Fox was good or evil. He didn't know if this plan would vanish the way all previous plans for Mexico vanished. It depended totally on foreign investment. Maybe foreigners saw future opportunities. Foreign money arrived with demands. Maybe local people would mount a campaign to prevent losing their land.

As he banged along the roads he imagined vast tree-less kilometers, strewn with cactus and snakes, depopulated, given over to the government's commercial traffic north or south. Are we talking narcotics here? Helicopters and staging areas would appear to fight drugs, or smuggle them, as they did for the shooting war. He fretted. How could he forestall that kind of militarization? Martin was only one person. Holy Master hadn't sent the promised thousands after all.

Did that mean he, Martin, must perform the work of thousands?

Or that Mexico was worth one-thousandth of India, to where aspiring gurus were dispatched instead? Or that Holy Master cared more for his home country? That was a nasty thought, and Martin regretted it as unworthy. He hoped Holy Master hadn't tuned in at the precise moment when it crossed his mind.

The struggle for Zapatista autonomy dwindled into skirmishes and quiet assassinations. Perhaps Martin could accept some credit for his accomplishment. Peace, for foreign eyes. But it wasn't settled right. He must do the work of thousands! Each time he saw the mustached face of President Fox on television he wondered afresh. How long, Holy Master, how long?

His mind wandered faster than his motorcycle. To be perfectly fair, he wouldn't reject decent roads with more than one lane in each direction. To be perfectly fair, the Mexican government contemplated for decades some replacement for railroads left to rot. To be perfectly realistic, if the USA wanted a corridor, a corridor would be built. Was corporate America likely to take a hand now? But how could Martin foresee what corporate America might want.

From Juchitán he rumbled west along the Pacific coast. Beautiful bays and lagoons lined with white sand lured him. He gazed across blue lagoons to mountains on the far side. In the foreground, cebú grazed, fawn-colored beasts, with huge molded heads and shoulders, oblivious as beasts in medieval paintings. Sea-birds fed along the shore, and wheeled overhead. A place of repose, far from the dirty war. Martin imagined tourist hotels and beach umbrellas, turquoise swimming pools, neat rows of cabañas.

He retraced his route, headed north.

Heavy rains flooded the roads. Martin tried to be indoors when it poured, but since a deluge usually lasted only ten minutes, and since, despite his incipient enlightenment, he couldn't guess when skies would open, he often got caught on the road. Rarely did he have enough warning to stop and pull from his side-pouch the blue plastic waterproof poncho. Mud-holes lurked wherever.

Martin drove. He dodged and detoured at the very last moment, like a boxer on a bike. Sometimes he tumbled into the mud or wet ditches along the road. His skin dampened beneath layers of fabric.

Run-off from the mountains filled the many rivers, which in turn spilled over into fields. In some towns families lived in water, afraid to abandon their homes to possible theft. Four feet of water in cement homes. Two feet in thatch chosas. Cement held better.

Adults mottled with skin diseases. The odor of baby shit predominated in many unpaved streets. Walking near the river he smiled and spoke to one young girl who guarded a drowned garden.

Martin sucked in his already flat stomach. He tilted back his head and closed his eyes. He began to radiate. He wondered if he could muster enough warmth to dry the earth.

Probably it would be better all around if the sun came out. Stretches of trees stood in water, cattle grazed in sodden grass. In tropical areas it rains ten months of the year, people told him. This will happen again, no one doubts. No one prepares. No money to move to higher ground.

Martin practiced spreading joy in all these intricate weathers, doggedly pushing his wheels through the mud. His head felt naked without his helmet, sun and breeze fell equally hard on his skull. He couldn't hide under the helmet without terrorizing children wherever he went. When a child pointed at his long robe and purple plastic skull and screeched, the mother snatched it up and fled. It wouldn't do, no, better let his bald scalp suffer.

Somehow he missed the turnoff to San Gregorio, and found himself in Villahermosa. The zócalo thronged with strolling teens, girls with slender thighs. The moist air weighed. Noise pollution overwhelmed Martin with blasting loudspeakers. He felt weak as he tried to walk. His feet buzzed like bees. He began to yearn for comfortable rooms and hot showers. Soon back to San Gregorio, soon the right road. He yearned to speak English, to eat the solid home cooking of a woman like Constance Skelba. He hoped she and Harry were waiting, would accept him into the paradise of their patio.

After all, Martin was an old hand at preparing himself for Absolute Peace. All he need do was close his eyes and look inward. He avoided doing so on the moving moto, where he needed all his focus to avoid potholes, but when he stopped to piss he took his Moment, without fail, without guilt over his lost brother and two dead French witnesses. He let slide irresolvable questions. Certain themes outdistanced his energy and scope: greed, power, the decimation of people's lives, destruction of the natural world, gutting and spending by corporate elites, conflicts of prejudice, the waste of hegemony. Only his own life flowed free of contradictions!

He recognized himself expanded and diffused into several selves, living several realities with several personalities, performing several tasks with several faces and even several languages. Every time he entered a new pueblo, people were singing.

He liked the idea that the human race is one race. He knew that we all are potential Holy Masters, that every woman hides within her Infinity, waiting. To those who would listen he explained the benefits of meditation. He closed his eyes in demonstration, with one hand securing his zippered stomach pouch. Within each person live many possibilities, many contradictory roles and precepts.

Once more he reversed direction, rolling toward San Gregorio, stopping at military checkpoints with his frayed passport as he did so many times before. While the soldiers handled his papers Martin always repeated, "Ultimate joy and peace come to everyone who follows Holy Master."

About the Author

Nancy Davies has resided in Oaxaca since 1999. She's the author of personal commentaries dealing with the Oaxaca uprising of 2006. They were published on www.narconews.com and partially collected in book form as *The People Decide*. Other commentaries by Nancy Davies appeared on http://upsidedownworld.org, from 2008 until 2010.

In her past life Davies' poetry appeared in small and literary magazines. Her previously unpublished works, including poems, novels, essays, and vignettes will be progressively available on http://www.nmsdavies.com/, her "writer's selfie."